From the
its back-u
ment syst
on U.S. sa ,
aircraft and ship made after 1985, to even simple memory chips inside children's teddy bears—every electronic fuse, resistor, or connector that was "Made in China" becomes dormant… forever.

At one minute past midnight on January 1st, every modern television broadcast of the U.S. New Year's Eve festivities on the East Coast black-out. Millions of motor vehicles with an engine management system or engine-computerized system suddenly die, causing loss of control and thousands of accidents only seconds into the New Year. Traffic lights, directional beacons, communication stations, and all aircraft landing systems black out a couple of minutes later, as their modern back-ups start failing. Children's Christmas presents, nearly forgotten, stop buzzing, moving, and blinking and go silent. Radios, computers, and all forms of electronic communication devices—even the latest 132 million electronic Christmas presents given only a week earlier (iPhone 5Gs, iPod Nano 4s, iMac Notepads and iPad 3s) go silent, never to blink on again. Ninety seconds after midnight, the entire electrical grid of North America deactivates itself and goes into close-down mode.

The shutdown of the United States of America, and 97% of the entire world, is accomplished by 12:30 am U.S. Eastern time on the first day of the New Year.

It takes only 30 minutes to completely dismantle the whole of modern Western civilization as we know it.

INVASION USA I

THE END OF MODERN CIVILIZATION

T. I. WADE

Published in the United States of America.

Please visit our website http://www.TIWADE.com to become a friend of the INVASION USA Series and get updates on new releases.

Library of Congress Catalogue-in-Publication Data
Wade, T I INVASION USA I / T I Wade.—1st ed.
TXu 1-734-502; 01-03-2011

Editor – Second Edition – Brad Theado, May 2012.

Cover design by Jack Hillman, Hillman Design Group, Sedona, AZ

Print edition layout by eBooks by Barb for booknook.biz

BOOKS BY THE AUTHOR

The Book of Tolan Series (Adult Reading):

Banking, Beer & Robert the Bruce
Hardcover and eNovel.

Easy Come Easy Go
Hardcover and eNovel.

It Could Happen
eNovel.

INVASION Series (General Reading):

INVASION USA I: The End of Modern Civilization
eNovel – July 2011,
Trade Paperback Edition – August 2012.

INVASION USA II: The Battle for New York
eNovel – March 2012,
Trade Paperback Edition – August 2012.

INVASION USA III: The Battle for Survival
eNovel – June 2012,
Trade Paperback Edition – August 2012.

INVASION USA IV: The Battle for Houston ... The Aftermath
eNovel – August 2012,
Trade Paperback Edition – August 2012.

INVASION EUROPE: The Battle for Western Europe
eNovel – April 2013.

INVASION ASIA: The Battle for China
eNovel – June 2013.

INVASION USA: The New America
eNovel – August 2013.
(Final Novel in this seven novel series)

Acknowledgements

Thank you to all the people who have helped me over the last two years in bringing this story to fruition.

First, I'd like to thank the two "Jacks" for helping me send this novel to your eReader.

To Jack Beatty for enjoying my writing enough to aid me in finalizing this long story from manuscript to finished product. Only people in the publishing industry know how much it costs and the hundreds of hours of time and experience by several professional people it takes to turn free-writing into a readable book.

To Jack Hillman who has set up the website www.TIWADE.com and helps me with the book cover designs.

To my wife Cathy and daughter Tischan Anne who gave me space and peace and quiet when I needed to write.

And to my son, Alexander who was the first to read it and enjoyed it enough at the age of 11 to give me my first and best review to date!

Thank you all.

Dedication:

INVASION USA I – The End of Civilization:

Is dedicated to the Men and Women of the United States Air Force.

Thank you for all you do to protect the United States of America, its people and many others around the world.

Note from the Author

This novel is only a story—a very long story of fiction, which could or might come true sometime in the future.

The people in this story are all fictitious, but since the story takes place in our present day, some of the people mentioned could be real people.

No names have been given to these people and there were no thoughts to treat these people as good or bad people. Just people who are living at the time the story is written.

Are you ready to survive a life-changing moment that could turn your life upside-down sometime in the near future?

Think about it. You are the only person in the world who can answer that question.

Are your human survival skills honed like a sharp hunter's knife or a fancy butter knife sitting in soft butter?

Which knife are you?

Read on and find out!

TABLE OF CONTENTS

CHAPTER 1

Preston Strong and Martie Roebels

IT WAS NEARLY DARK OUTSIDE as the small yellow-colored crop duster aimed its nose for a final approach into the dark, asphalt-covered airfield now stretching out in front of it.

Ten homemade perimeter lights, 40 feet apart on each side of the runway, blinked on as Preston Strong double-clicked the "talk" button on his joystick and the gray outline of the runway came into view. The tarred runway was 920 yards, or 2,760 feet long—short for such a high-grade paved runway, but double the length needed for him to take off under a full weight of spray liquids, and enough room for any errors on dark, stormy-night landings when the sun had beaten him down to the ground. The runway lights, made out of large old truck lights, were aimed on high beam, a foot above the ground and facing inwards, lighting up the landing site enough for an experienced bush pilot to get in. Two green and one red light shone from either end of the long expanse of flat tarmac. A large D-8 caterpillar battery, always under-charge, gave the 26 lights enough power for ten minutes.

The wheels touched and Preston aimed the propeller at the open mouth of the hangar she resided in, away from the hot North Carolina sun during the summers and the odd snowfall in winter. He pressed a simple residential garage door opener button he had modified to operate the 30-foot roller door, which kept out the weather when he needed to work in the large hangar. Preston had another three aircraft under draped tarpaulins in the hangar, as well as a separate set of rooms—a lounge area, study, bed and a bathroom—where he dabbled in everything electric. His Golden Labrador, Oliver, spent more time at the house than Preston did, although normally in the shade of the white wrap-around porch.

Preston Strong lived electronics. It was a drug he was totally addicted to. Anything that moved or had a wire coming out of it, turned on or off, or smelled of making something else work fascinated him, especially the older, less technical stuff. It had taken him a year to get a 40-year old French two-cylinder car engine so well-balanced and so virtually quiet that it ran on a gallon of regular gasoline every 24 hours and powered everything in the hangar, as well as the runway charger to the D-8 battery. He had a slightly larger German 3-cylinder BMW engine from the 1950s, which powered up other 36-volt deep-cycle marine batteries in the house for the odd occasion he used it, and he could get by on a gallon and a half a day on needed usage. He hadn't used the electrical grid for several years now.

His masters in electrical engineering at UNC had been a blast. He had sailed through and his tinkering hadn't stopped since he had finished his studies. Some of his professors still popped by the hangar from time to time to see what he was up to. He lived a mile or so north of Jordan Lake, just outside Apex, North Carolina on about 40 acres of farmland his father had bequeathed to him many years before in his will.

The lights came on in the house, and Oliver barked a friendly welcome to a well-known visitor.

"Must be Martie," Preston said out loud as he switched off the inner hangar lights and pressed the outside door button to roll-close the large door. He looked back and watched as the real love of his life—a just completed twin-engine World War II P-38L Lightning—disappeared into the recesses of the darkening hangar.

"The four Brownings are now clean and ready," he thought to himself as he walked the 50 yards toward the house. "I'm sure that if I search the Internet I could find an old Hispano cannon, the only gun I'm now missing up front. I wonder where I can get some live ammo for her new machine guns. I'm sure I could also find some cannon rounds if I could find a cannon. They should go together, but maybe I should ask Carlos' friend at Hill Air Force Base in Salt Lake City, or even Martie's dad might know of a base where I could ask. I'm sure they could at least point me in the right direction. They could even point to some bombs or even some old rockets in storage somewhere... or maybe they won't..."

"I got a store-cooked chicken, a pint of vanilla ice cream, and a six-pack of Yuenglings on my way over," shouted a female voice from the direction of the house.

"I can smell the bird from here," replied Preston, as he mounted the rear stairs to the kitchen door. Oliver was suddenly as eager as he.

"I saw your landing lights come on and knew you were incoming when I turned off 64," she replied, turning to face him as he entered through the rusty screen door. Martie Roebels was nine years younger than him, a very lovely 29-year-old blonde from German stock and as clever as he was, both in the spoken word and engineering.

Martie was a real engineer, not a dabbler like him. She practiced what she had learned at MIT by working for a software company at the Research Triangle Park, or RTP, just outside Durham. A lover of flying as much as he was, Martie owned her own Mustang—a P-51D given to her by her grandfather who had restored it to perfect condition a decade earlier. Preston stored it for her in the hangar next to his own older model, a P-51C in the far corner. He only allowed Martie and his best friend Carlos Rodriquez to see the aircraft inside the airport's only hangar, since the antique aircraft were of extreme value.

Preston's dream was to fly his P-51 beside her P-51, and have his best friend Carlos, who lived in Salt Lake City, fly his P-51C on his other wing. Boy, it sure would be a sight to see that formation, but that day was still a few months away.

His trusty crop duster was his paying job and he knew every inch of the large farms in Orange and Chatham counties and further beyond where he was paid to spray the acres of new farm crops whenever he was needed.

"Get anything done today?" asked Martie, giving him a man-sized bear hug as he tried to get his flying shoes off by the back door. At six feet tall, she could hug like a grizzly and did not believe in soft men or being soft with men. Her six-foot, six-inch grandfather had been in the German air force during the war. He had been captured and became an American prisoner of war. In 1946, he had been released and had decided to stay in his new country. Wolfgang Von Roebels had become an American citizen ten years later. In 1950, his first son Michael, Martie's father, had been born to him and his new German-American wife in Redmond, Oregon.

"I sprayed organic fertilizer on the Holman farm in Chatham County this morning and the old Smith farm in Orange County this afternoon. A thousand acres in a day isn't bad," Preston replied, opening the fridge for his favorite beer. "Do you think I could write a letter to Hill Air Force Base in Utah... you know, to that guy Carlos introduced us to last year to see if I can get some .50-caliber ammo for our 51s? I want to see if all our Browning machine guns and now the four .50-caliber guns I've been replacing on the P-38 are still all working perfectly."

"Why? Are we going to war?" joked Martie. "I could always ask Grandpa if he knows anybody." She returned carrying two steaming plates of food to the kitchen dining table she had already set. She didn't live here, but she spent most her free time at the farm. Martie had a townhouse in Chapel Hill, left over from a semester at UNC after MIT, and just hadn't sold it yet. "We could search for ammo in California at the same time," Martie suggested, cutting into her chicken leg and stuffing a portion into her mouth.

"I suppose .50-caliber ammo would be easy to find on the Internet. You can find anything on the Internet these days," Preston answered. "But I hate the permits and questions the authorities might ask before they'll allow civilians to have large amounts of live ammo in their possession." Preston grabbed two more beers from the refrigerator and screwed the tops off. He handed one to her. "Doesn't your grandfather still have that Air Force buddy in Washington, or somewhere, where we could get some advice? I could also ask Buck in New York to see if he knows somebody. He said a few months ago that his Air Force contact—the one who has a share in *Lady Dandy*—was back in Washington with his DC-3 from somewhere overseas."

"I'm going to visit Grandpa and Dad over the weekend. I will ask them," she replied.

Her father, Michael Roebels was as big and strong as his father before him. At 20, he had attended UCLA and completed his first Ph.D. in engineering and modern electronics—the new form of communication excitement hitting the country in the early 1970s. He had been embarrassed about the "Von" in his name, thought it too brash, and had dropped it in everyday practice. It still showed on his official passport though.

After completing his second Ph.D. in electronics in 1975, also at MIT, Michael Roebels formed a new company with his father in San Diego right next to the main San Diego airport runway, and started designing navigation devices for fighter aircraft.

By 1983 and the birth of his daughter Martie, the two men had their first military order for low-level flight navigators. Michael purchased a new house in the growing suburb of La

Jolla, north of San Diego. The successful company was bought out by Raytheon in 1987, and after ten years of hard work, both men retired very comfortably for the rest of their lives.

Martie fell in love with flying at the age of four. Her father and grandfather had both purchased a couple of old biplanes and moved to a large slice of 100 acres of farmland in a new and popular wine area called Napa. The family invested their new fortune into wine country and decided to manufacture "German Liebfraumilch"—a type of semi-sweet white wine Wolfgang was partial to—and formed the unofficial Napa Luftwaffe Airport on their land at the same time.

Martie still remembered her first solo flight in her father's self-built small taildragger, an aircraft with a small rear wheel, at the age of 15. She was in heaven, flying over land and sea, and had to land the craft, with a coughing engine, totally out of fuel three long hours later, much to her father's dismay. She was then hooked for life, and her most recent flight, in an old Cessna 172 as a flying instructor, was in Hillsborough. Afterwards, both she and Preston had celebrated her 2,000th flying hour with champagne and shrimp at a local restaurant. It had been a fun and great day to remember—October 12th.

* * *

Preston Strong was from American stock, with his great, great grandfather from Ireland and great, great grandmother of Puritan English descendants. His grandfather and grandmother had been born to farming families in Georgia, got married, and after the war in 1949 had moved further north and purchased the 200 acres of prime North Carolina farmland where Preston currently lived.

Times were tough in the 50s and 60s for the Strong family. His grandmother had passed away in 1954, when his father Michael was ten. Most people believed that she took her own life, but his father told Preston long afterwards that his grandmother had lost two children—the daughters she had always dreamed about—to miscarriages before Michael had been born, and she had never gotten over it.

Farming was not a well-paying profession in the 1960s, especially on a small farm of 210 acres, and Grandfather Strong was forced to sell 150 acres of it to cover growing farm debts and pay the mortgage off. This allowed the remaining 60 acres to become free and clear of debt. His grandfather gave up trying to make a living wage on the land, and learned to drive a truck in 1960 as a profession. He signed the best 40 acres with the house over to his son Michael, the only heir, and sold the other 20 acres to buy his first rig.

Four years later, Grandfather Strong was killed in a multiple-truck crash while crossing the Rockies in mid-winter and his son received a small insurance policy payout and a bigger lawsuit payout from the national company whose rig driver was at fault. This had paid all other debts and allowed Mike, as he was now known to his friends, to learn to fly, to get a commercial pilot's license, and to be hired on to an airline ten years later in 1974.

Mike Strong was a new pilot with Pan Am when he met Mary Strong, née Parkins, who was a flight attendant instructor at Pan Am in Miami, and immediately fell in love. They were married within six weeks and Preston was born the same year. Mike was a good pilot, and was often away during Preston's young life. His mother had been forced to give up her position with Pan Am and had become a doting housewife.

Preston always remembered his father's advice when he saw him. *"If you don't do well in school, son, you won't get into college."* Those words were relayed to him every time his father returned home from flying. Sometimes he was only home once or twice a month, but when he was home, he constantly drilled Preston on what was important; *"Electronics, engineering and mechanics are the professions of the future, son."*

They often discussed Preston's future, but it was cemented when he turned 12. In those days, air travel security was far more lax. As a belated birthday present, Michael took Preston with him on one of his short work flights. He was shown how all the gadgets in the cockpit worked. Preston was glued to every instrument and was even allowed to ride in the cockpit jump seat behind his father on the short leg to Atlanta and back. He never forgot that night. It was December 21st, 1986 in the airport restaurant when Preston told his father that he didn't need to lecture anymore—he was hooked on electronics, any type of electronics.

Mike and Mary Strong were killed exactly two years later to the day. They were traveling on vacation in Italy over Christmas. Mike Strong was the number two pilot to Captain Macquarrie on Pan Am Flight 103 when it blew up over Lockerbie, Scotland. Mary was sleeping in First Class and, Preston assumed, never awoke. Preston's life was never the same. At 14, and on a farm, nobody really knew the Strongs or lived close or missed them after the accident. Living away from everybody on the 40-acre farm, he missed school for a few weeks, then forged a note in his late mother's handwriting that his father had been killed, and then carried on his life living alone, keeping his head down to avoid any questions and catching the yellow school bus every school day as if nothing had happened.

The young man never had to worry about money again. He received a very large payout from the Libyan government a year and a half later. He had already received a $100,000 insurance check addressed to his mother, which he had deposited into her account. He asked the manager to allow him signing power on the account, took home and "signed" the necessary paperwork to allow him temporary access to the account with his mother's signature, and lived off the account—taking enough once a month to pay any bills, farm upkeep, and food.

This existence was not without stress. At one point, a letter from the bank arrived addressed to "Mrs. Mary Strong." She was needed at the bank to sign the acceptance letter for a large sum of money. Preston went in, stated that his mother was still very ill in bed, and took the paperwork home for "her" to sign. "She" also signed a new note that told the bank to allow Preston access to the account, and that she would be in once she was better.

"Your mother must be very ill," the bank manger observed when Preston returned with the signed paperwork. "I guess I should go out and see her myself."

"Her doctor suggested that she stay at home and not have visitors for a couple more months," stated Preston innocently. "She still hasn't got over my father's death and I have to look after her all the time. She's been bedridden for months now."

"I see," continued the manager, looking over the signed documents. "All right, you have the authority to make withdrawals on her behalf and that will suffice until she is well enough to come in and see me. It is a very large amount, and we will look after it for her until she tells me otherwise. Please tell her that this is a temporary arrangement and I need to see her when she feels well enough to come in. I will allow you to withdraw funds once a month and take the money home for your mother to pay her accounts. She has signed for a monthly withdrawal allowance of $500.00 a month and that's fine for now."

Luckily for Preston, the bank manager was promoted to another area a few months later and the branch forgot about the temporary arrangement and Preston diligently went in and took home the monthly funds to live on until his 18th birthday.

When he turned 18, he took in a new letter, again "signed" by his mother, allowing Preston to take over full control of her accounts. He had grown up that year, looked adult and mature and the bank allowed him to take over full control of the accounts even though no one had seen his mother for several years. He told the bank personnel that she was still at home on the farm, and still doing very poorly. The branch manager was not keen on asking very many questions. Preston opened a savings account and the majority of the large six-digit account was transferred into a new account with a small annual interest accrual.

He never forgot his father's words about college, and for the rest of his school days he worked hard to achieve his father's wishes. On his graduation night, he cried long and bitterly for his father and mother, and knew that his father would have been so proud of him on that very important day in his life.

A week later and toward the end of October, Martie and Preston were at the same dining table with Oliver, who was looking for any donations. This time, Preston had cooked a casserole and Martie had supplied a bottle of her grandfather's semi-sweet wine.

"Guess what?" Preston volunteered with his mouth half full. He didn't give her time to respond. "I spoke to Carlos in Utah on Saturday about the ammo, and he said that I shouldn't worry about illegal possession of .50 or even 20mm ammo for the Hispano cannon if I can find it. He emailed me a few hours ago saying that we could buy ammo on the Internet and that it is legal to own all caliber rounds in North Carolina. He suggested that I take the four old Brownings out of the P-38 and replace them with a set of four larger American Browning AN M2 .50-caliber machine guns—the same guns as the six on your P-51D and our two P-51Cs." Preston stopped for another bite of casserole. "Nobody would really know the difference. It's a pretty simple operation of changing the four major connection bolts by a few millimeters per gun. He knows a place where there are a set of four in working order, and I could keep the old ones for spares. They are $12,000 each and are in perfect condition, from a disassembled Mustang in Reno, Nevada. AND, we can legally buy as much already belted ammo as we want on several Internet sites."

"It will be fun to shoot your slower 51Cs down," Martie

replied in a very strong German animated accent, and Preston nearly coughed out his food, his face going rather pale. "I'm only joking!" Martie laughed. "Can't you ever take a joke? Besides, you are far too handsome to shoot down—I would have to go look for a new man!"

"Remember the end of the Red Baron in World War I," laughed Preston, regaining his composure. "You Germans are far too full of yourselves sometimes. By the way, your Mustang is only seven miles an hour faster than mine. I have already paid for the guns and they are being delivered by a special delivery service. Carlos said that he is going to fly in on Friday afternoon in his Mustang and help me set up and drill the new bolt holes. He is as excited as I am about a weekend playing with real live machine guns. I know it's a little early, but I went ahead and purchased 12,000 belted rounds for you and 8,000 belted rounds for me. It will cost me a year's work with the sprayer. But remember, with your guns spurting out 400 rounds per minute each, your supply will last you five minutes and you will owe me $36,000 for that five minutes of pleasure—if I'm not dead by then and there is a tree left standing in North Carolina! Carlos has already purchased as much ammo as he could find."

Preston had not touched much of the money left over from his parents' estate. After he turned 21, he closed all the old bank accounts and invested most of the money into electronic stocks. He had invested heavily into Qualcomm in the late 1990s and had turned a $3 million investment into four times as much. He had then sold and transferred the profits into Microsoft and a startup company called Google, and replaced the original $3 million he had borrowed from the payout from his parents into CDs. Preston did not want to spend his parents' money. To him it didn't feel right—it still didn't feel like his money.

He didn't need it anyway. For the first couple of years, with the two new and ever-rising stocks, he had paid over $10 million to the taxman in income tax and had lost any interest in learning, or needing, to invest further. He always withdrew the annual net profit from all of his investments, deposited the amounts into long-term CDs and letting the initial investment grow again for the next year. Stock exchange "farming," he called it.

Martie's grandfather was now in his nineties, and her father was still living with him—both playing wine farmers in California and spending much of their time flying. Grandpa Von Roebels was far too old to control an aircraft, but that did not mean that he couldn't be a happy passenger. He had also parachuted as a hobby until he was 85.

Preston and Martie were stacking the dishwasher when the old ham radio in the lounge gave its familiar beeping sound. Preston loved communications enough to have two sets of the best antique 1960s radio equipment any ham radio enthusiast could wish for. One set was in the house and the other in the hangar. Both were left on continuously and were the most powerful sets ever made. His massive radio antenna was spread high above the hangar.

"I think that must be young Ben," grinned Preston. "He said something last week about his latest report card coming home this week."

"Perfect!" replied Martie. "I can say hi to Maggie. She might be pregnant again."

"Ben Smart, Los Angeles, to Preston Strong, Raleigh, North Carolina, come in, Preston," stated a young voice over the speakers. *"Come in, Preston Strong, Raleigh, North Carolina."*

"I'm here, Ben Smart. How are you, my friend?" answered Preston, getting to the microphone.

"10/4, everything is good over here on the west coast, Preston," replied Ben, a young eleven-year-old ham radio enthusiast and son of Martie's old MIT roommate, Maggie.

"Ben, this is Martie, is your mother home?" asked Martie into the microphone on the table in front of the large radio.

"Hi, Aunty Martie. How are you doing? Mum is at choir

practice with my sister, and she told me to relay to you that she 'isn't,' whatever that means," he replied.

"Thanks, Ben. Tell her I said to look after herself and that I'm still coming to visit in January. I have to visit Grandpa and Dad at the farm, and I will be spending a few days with you guys in L.A. on the way."

Ben Smart was only 11, but loved being a ham radio operator, much due to his mother completing her final paper for her Ph.D. in electrical engineering at UCLA the previous year.

Martie had lived with two roommates for a single semester at MIT—Maggie Bridges, now married to Will Smart, a police detective with the LAPD; and Sally Powers, who was based in Yuma with the Air Force and about to complete her flight training on F-16s. Sally, jealous that Martie had her own Mustang, couldn't afford such a luxury antique aircraft, but had put in an offer for a much cheaper aircraft she could afford—an old 1981 Swiss Air Force Pilatus PC-7 training turboprop aircraft that had just arrived in the U.S. from Switzerland. A private American buyer had purchased the aircraft, but then had purchased a newer 1985 version for sale in Bolivia and just wanted as much of his initial purchase price back as possible. It was a great deal and nearly affordable for Sally. The PC-7 was a single engine trainer that was set up to carry wing bombs, but did not have any guns. She had trained for several hours in one while in Europe as a U.S. Air Force exchange pilot with the Swiss Air Force and had fallen in love with its flying abilities.

There were going to be a couple of big celebrations on the West coast shortly, with Maggie finally getting her Ph.D. and Sally hopefully getting her flying wish, and Martie was looking forward to spending a lot of time in her Mustang. With Preston alongside, flying across the vastness of the United States was going to be fun.

Preston spent most nights on his radio communicating to his friends across the United States. He often dialed into Raleigh-

Durham (RDU) International Airport's ground frequency and listened to aircraft traffic, or listened to other radio communications from around the world. There was no privacy with any ham radio communications.

Ben and Preston continued chatting for awhile and Ben told Preston that he had gotten all A's for the semester, even in music, which even he still couldn't believe. It wasn't long, however, before another friend hailed Preston on the same frequency. It was his New York buddy and fellow radio enthusiast, Buck McKinnon. He and Buck had found each other over the radio one night several years back and they had become good friends. Buck was also a pilot and owned a Huey helicopter and a share of an old 1950s-era Super DC-3—a twin engine transport aircraft he was looking forward to flying down to North Carolina to spend his first New Year's Eve at Preston's New Year's Eve Fly-In.

Preston had organized his first New Year's Eve Fly-In three years earlier and always had one or two of his friends fly in to share the festivities from December 28th to January 2nd. Carlos had flown in all three years, and Michael had flown in Grandpa Von Roebels last year in their Beechcraft Baron. This year would be the first time for both Sally, if she got her new aircraft, and Buck. It was looking to be a really busy hangar party with the best collection of old aircraft in the United States of America.

A year or so earlier, Buck had introduced Preston to another of his radio buddies who wanted to sell a recently semi-refurbished P-38 Lightning, and it quickly became Preston's newest purchase. It had taken six months to ship the entire not-yet-flyable aircraft (the wings broken down into two long crates) from Reno, Nevada to North Carolina, and another year and a half to get it back together again. The refurbishment was completed with Preston's buddy Carlos helping on weekends.

Martie sat next to Preston, reading a magazine and listening in on the conversations.

"How's the P-38 coming?" asked Buck.

"I have her all together," replied Preston. "I completed rebuilding and cleaning her Browning last week and my friend in Salt Lake City found us four .50-caliber Browning guns from a downed Mustang in Reno. I want to replace her old guns with P-51s. That will give us all the same ammo for the new Air Wing we are building over here. A friend of mine also has a Mustang, and with Martie's Mustang we can now all purchase the same ammo in bulk."

"It sounds like you're starting an Air Force up there. You better be careful! The real Air Force might get worried about your firepower," laughed Buck. *"On a more serious note, Martie, Preston, have you had any glitches with electronics down there? Manhattan had a complete power failure last night for over ten seconds. Funny thing was that it took three relays from other areas to get the power back up. That means that there was more than one area grid with problems at the same time. Then today, all the traffic lights on the Avenue of Americas went dead for over an hour. There was total gridlock. On the news, they said that several small computers had malfunctioned and that's all they would say."*

"No, nothing major," replied Preston. "Although, I was listening to the traffic pattern earlier this morning and there seemed to be a problem with Raleigh-Durham air traffic control. They asked all aircraft to fly in a pattern for well over ten minutes because they had a problem with something they wouldn't elaborate on. All they would say is that there was a control problem with aircraft traffic on the ground. Why do you ask?"

"Well, over the last few weeks, there has been a large increase in electrical component malfunctions across the country," replied Buck. *"Three nuclear power stations—one in Nevada, one here in New York State, and one in Pennsylvania —had minor electrical malfunctions and all had to go into safe*

mode for a short period of time. All three happened at different times last week. After the problems in Japan in 2011, we had better be on our toes with these nuclear power plants. I don't trust them."

"I heard about the New York one on the news," injected Preston.

"That's not all. CNN reported that a cruise ship went totally dead in the water," continued Buck. *"An engine-management malfunction, they said. Then, the World Space Station went two degrees off course for over an hour and a new directional transformer had to be installed by the crew. An Abrams tank in New Mexico went crazy and overturned itself before its electrical control system went dead, and an F-16 lost its fuel control system and went down in San Diego. It wasn't Sally, thank God. All this in less than two weeks, I think something very weird is going on."*

"I can ask my friend Carlos at the Utah Observatory if we've had any sun flares or radiation pulses lately," replied Preston. "It could be due to increased radiation activity from the sun."

"You mean the Carlos Rodriquez out of D.C., currently at the observatory above Salt Lake City?" asked Buck.

"You know Carlos?"

"We worked together briefly in the global communications department in the Pentagon," replied Buck. *"We wrote a military computer scenario on Possible Communication Satellite Aging and worked on the probability of potential electrical component malfunctions. We flew together a few times, too. He has a small share in my* Baby Huey *and the DC-3. Yeah, let's see if he's at work and can get on the line tonight. I'm really curious about all this activity."*

"I haven't heard anything on the news, except for that New York power grid glitch and the military aircraft crash in San Diego," Martie whispered to Preston as they waited for Buck to contact Carlos via radio. "The media seems to be downplaying these glitches, as if they are minor and just everyday events. It's as if they haven't learned anything from those 2011 meltdowns and what it did to the Japanese people."

"I don't think the powers-that-be really want the public to know much about any problems these days," added Preston. "I think they don't want to spook the American people while over 80% of the U.S. armed forces are out of the country fighting wars here and there."

"We still have the National Guard," returned Martie.

"I've heard that a large number of the National Guard has also been deployed to Iraq..."

"You called, Buck McKinnon?" came a familiar voice over the radio.

"Hi, Carlos," Preston and Martie heard Buck reply. *"I knew you would be working at this hour; it's dark outside. Listen, Carlos. I have a mutual friend of ours listening in—Preston Strong from North Carolina."*

"You guys know each other?" Carlos' radio voice sounded surprised.

"Know each other!" interrupted Preston. "It was Buck's friend who sold me the P-38 we've been working on for the last year or two. Thanks to Buck I have a war bird that will beat you around the sky in speed."

"In your dreams," laughed Carlos. *"If Preston is there, then my future wife Martie Roebels is hanging around that miserable excuse for a North Carolina wanna-be fighter pilot."*

"In YOUR dreams, Carlos!" interjected Martie with a smile on her face. Carlos had fallen for Martie the first time they had met, but had little chance of winning the prize. Martie was Preston's girl and she was the first to say it to anybody, but naturally, she enjoyed the interest good-looking Carlos paid to her. Preston just smiled. It was Carlos' way of trying to rile his best friend. He also knew that best friends could become the most dangerous in a girl situation, however, and didn't let him get out of hand.

"No good-looking girls in Salt Lake?" asked Preston playfully. "Didn't you know that Utah's girls are some of the best lookers in the USA?" he added. "A lot of good-looking blondes, I hear, but you won't see them on top of a mountain and not looking through a billion-dollar telescope either!"

Buck laughed as the friendship between his buddies became easily visible. *"Hey, guys,"* added Buck to the verbal argument. *"I quite fancy fabulous Martie too, and I bet she can out-fly both of you! Oh! Martie, Preston, a little news... Sally Powers had her Pilatus offer accepted and she's coming over to New Jersey to pick it up. You better contact her, as she is ecstatic and babbled to me last night for over an hour about it. I'm sure she will be on the blower to you pretty soon to tell you, too."*

"Wow!" exclaimed Preston. "Carlos, Sally Powers is a ham radio friend of ours and an ex-roommate of Martie's. She is about to finish her flight training on F-16s at Yuma and also wants to join our private air force. Oops, sorry, Carlos. I forgot you have met Sally... Hey, wait a minute! I must be the odd one out here, guys! You guys know everyone, but I don't. I must be out of the loop somewhere. At least it sounds like we will have met everyone by New Year's Day. Martie and I know that Sally can't afford a Mustang. That older '81 Swiss Air Force Pilatus PC-7 is a gem of a deal. I believe her version can carry either two 1,000 pounders under the wings, or up to four 500-pound bombs of all sorts, plus two missiles. The P-38 has the same type of bomb holders and I'm going to try and find some dummy 500 pounders that we both can fit and play with. Sally and the P-38 can be our bomber command and can be troop transport command with the DC-3. You know what I just remembered? All three Mustangs can carry 500-pound bombs as well."

"Preston, tell me something I don't know for a change,"

laughed Carlos. *"You can't fly two airplanes at once and both you and I are the only two who can fly the twin P-38."*

"I believe both Sally and I could with an hour's instruction," interrupted Martie.

"Girls flying a P-38?" joked Carlos. *"Not in my lifetime!"*

"Go fly a kite, Carlos! You can't fly much else!" was the response from Preston.

"Shit, guys!" exclaimed Buck in New York.

"Buck McKinnon! Mind your manners, there's a lady present," interrupted Martie. An apology was mumbled over the airwaves.

"Living in New York is your problem, Buck," continued Carlos. *"Owning a share here and there is great, but that means you can't fly it when you want, and getting out of that concrete monster to fly every now and again is a problem by itself."*

"And where do I get the money to buy a complete aircraft, like your P-51, Carlos?" asked a quieter Buck. *"It cost me an arm and a leg to get my shares of* Baby Huey *and* Lady Dandy, *after the initial investment of my private pilot's license and my first 200 hours of boring flight time in a ruddy Cessna 150."*

"Mind your mouth for the second time," injected Martie. "First there's a flying instructor present. You mind your manners about 150s. Secondly, most of my last 500 hours have been on ruddy Cessnas, as you call them, and as far as I'm concerned, a Cessna 150 is still better than being on the ground." The men all laughed.

"Buck, I'm not interested in your flying situation at the moment," laughed Carlos. *"You called me in the middle of work and I do have a job to do. We can yakkity-yak when we all get together and talk flying over New Year's Eve at the fly-in. I'm the only person here tonight and I need to get back to studying the new black hole we've found. It is quite close to our solar system, only a couple of hundred light years away."*

"Sorry, Carlos," replied Buck, *"but we actually contacted*

you for a reason. We have had some weird occurrences here on Earth in the last few days and need to know from our space commander whether there was an external reason for all these upsets in the electrical systems down here on Mother Earth, mountain boy."

"Nothing that I've seen in the last 30 days here on my hill," returned Carlos. *"The sun has been quiet, and apart from me dropping coffee all over myself last night, the universe is peaceful with no big bangs. The electrical and x-ray pulses coming out of this black hole have been doing so for about 20 years, so no problem there. It must be a loose connection down there in electrical Earth land."*

They chatted for another minute or two before Carlos had to get back to work, the electrical problems on earth quickly forgotten. It was yesterday's news anyway.

Carlos told Preston that he would not be able to fly to North Carolina in the near future, due to a heavy workload, but he was definitely going to fly in over Christmas and New Year's. Buck also mentioned that he thought a very single Sally Powers might also be in attendance over the festive season. He was sure that if she had her new toy, that she would need no small excuse to fly in, and that Preston and Martie should expect her.

Sally Powers called them ten minutes later and sounded very excited. *"I got it, I got it, Martie!"* she shouted as soon as Martie answered the call.

"We heard, from Buck, a few minutes ago," replied Martie, the excitement of the transmission growing on both sides. "I'm dying to see it. Where is it? When do you pick it up? Can I go with you?" Martie asked as girlfriends do, by asking several questions at once.

"Trenton, New Jersey and yes fly up next weekend and meet me. We could fly it down to Tucson together until our fly-in. I was hoping to keep it in Preston's hangar in Raleigh next year, if he doesn't mind looking after it for me, until I find her a

home, I mean hangar, here in Arizona," the still excited Sally continued.

"Of course we can give her a good home for a while," answered Preston. "I should have enough space in the hangar if we rearrange planes and you are coming to our fly-in, which is only just over two months away, anyway."

Preston and Martie sat down on the couch after the radio conversations were over, each with a single malt, and talked a little and relaxed. Martie was thinking exciting thoughts about her friends and Preston, especially with the New Year's Eve party only two and a half months away. The BBC news came in over the radio and Preston dialed it in to grab the best coverage.

"It is three o'clock in London, and here is the early morning news," stated the announcer over the radio. *"The President stated in Washington yesterday that another 150,000 American troops are to be deployed into northern Pakistan to fight the Taliban. Amid growing concerns about U.S. home defense in the United States, the American administration continues to move troops into foreign war zones to fight terrorism around the world. During a press conference, he admitted that the number of troops in foreign countries far overstretched the troops remaining on bases at home, but he was confident that no attack on the United States was imminent and that the Pentagon would start bringing troops home by the middle of next year."* The voice of the President of the United States came over the radio.

"We need to end these foreign wars in Pakistan, North Korea, and Iran," he stated. *"We cannot do that without a major increase in force. Nobody can or will or is thinking of attacking us here at home. With our new Defense Satellite Monitoring System above us, we can monitor any troop movement anywhere in the world, and the latest word from Homeland Security is that we are safe from anybody trying to attack the people inside the borders of the United States."*

The President then took a few questions and argued with the reporters about the deployment of nearly 90% of the U.S. armed forces abroad.

"People must understand. The next war is not a war of people fighting people, but a war of technology. We are ready here at home and have the best technology in our modern war machines that everyone else in the world would love to have. We have the best aircraft, guns, and ships. We have the best scientific and latest engineered weapons. We have the best satellites and world communication systems. Nobody is even close to the fire power we have at our disposal. And to you skeptics out there, many of our troops are only eight to ten hours away from American soil. With 90% of our fleet of Air Force troop carriers ready and waiting on foreign soil, we could have a quarter of a million troops back on U.S. soil and ready to fight before any attack could be launched. We are the United States of America."

"Pompous ass!" replied Preston, turning the radio to Receive mode, grabbing Martie's hand, and pulling her up to head for the bedroom.

CHAPTER 2

Buck McKinnon

BUCK MCKINNON WAS BORN in 1969 into a middle-class family that had lived in New York for several decades. He was the only child of Joe and Mary McKinnon. Joe was a welder and as far as Buck could remember, always worked in the shipyards. His mother, Mary, was a secretary and worked for a small firm in central Manhattan.

His younger years were typical of an American family in the mid-1970s. Television was a growing fad, and his favorite show was "Leave it to Beaver." He grew up in the small-town life of school and soda fountains where the youngsters would meet after school. School was simple for Buck. He loved anything to do with science and dreamed of being an astronaut one day. He had studied the space race and especially the Sky Lab development of the 1970s with fascination as it developed into a fully-fledged space station under NASA's management.

He excelled in science and math and ended up being invited to study with a scholarship at MIT in Boston in 1988. He was quickly absorbed into electronic development in CSAIL and completed a Master's in electrical engineering and then his Ph.D. in electronic communications a couple of years later.

His interest in flying started in high school. To be an astronaut, he knew he would have to join the Air Force and fly. The McKinnon family lived a few miles away from a local airfield and Buck would often ride his bicycle over to watch the goings on. He became known to many of the private pilots there, often mowing the grass runway and, for his work, was taken up in all sorts of aircraft for pleasure flights. He helped put the gliders away and managed to get several hours of flying in the club's two-seater trainer—an old aluminum Blanik—with an instructor.

During his time at MIT, he did as many jobs as possible so he could afford to fly, achieved his private pilot's license, and flew as many hours as he could at a local airfield that was not much different than the one close to his home. He managed at least an hour every other week or so, and by the time he left Boston to return to New York he had added 173 hours to his log book.

For the next ten years he flew little, working for a national communications company in New York City. It was only in the late 1990s that he was transferred to the newly formed Future Design department of the company in Cambridge, just outside Boston. He was also invited to lecture at CSAIL at MIT and went back to his favorite airport to catch up on his flying. His financial worth had grown considerably since the last time he had visited the airfield, and he purchased a share of a Cessna 172 to continue flying.

In 2001, he was offered a share in a more technical aircraft—an old 1967 Cessna 402—in which he completed his twin-engine rating. After selling his Cessna 172 share and his newer Cessna 402 share in 2003, Buck borrowed $100,000 and purchased a quarter-share in a 1985 Beechcraft King Air B90. For the pricey sum of $200,000, this was flying at its best for Buck—twin turboprops, luxury seating for eight, and an arm and a leg in costs to use his allotted time. He managed to get his turboprop license and complete 100 hours before it became too costly. In 2005, Buck sold his share and deposited $130,000 into his bank account after paying off the loan.

By this time, there was a promotion offered and a grand pay raise if he would return to New York, so grudgingly he returned to downtown Manhattan.

Luckily, a month after his move back to the "Big Apple," he met a new friend in one of his local Friday night bars—a very pretty young lady who flew helicopters for one of the sightseeing companies operating in Manhattan. She was fun and took him with her on flights when there was a free seat. Buck got interested in helicopter flight and completed his helicopter license in December 2006.

After lengthy searches, Buck found what he was looking for—his latest machine. In late 2007, he purchased his very own Bell Huey UH-1D from a desperate seller in Tel Aviv. Being a later 1969 model, the Huey had been in the Air Force in Israel as well as the later years of the Rhodesian war further south. She had many hours under her belt, but was in perfect condition. For a desperate "must sell it now" sum of $290,000, she was a bargain, and after a few dealings became affordable for Buck. He immediately sold two small shares to a couple of ex-Vietnam War Huey pilots—ham radio buddies of his in New Jersey who wanted to fly—for $65,000 each.

With over 80 hours in the Huey, and enjoying every minute of his new baby, he decided to visit the Experimental Aircraft Association's annual fly-in in Oshkosh in 2009 for the first time in his life and show off his helicopter. He had been invited by one of the EAA board members who had heard of his Huey still in perfect condition and offered him a prime place in the viewing area.

Buck was excited. From his home airport of Bayport Aerodrome, or MacArthur Airport as it was known, three miles west of Islip on Long Island where he had found hangar space for his Huey two years earlier, the adventure was 798 miles and he needed to refuel twice. The flight was one of the longest overland trips he had ever flown in his life.

It was only a week before his trip, out of the blue, when his old girlfriend Chloe—the one who had introduced him to helicopters two years earlier—looked him up again. She had lived with him for a couple of months until she had received a better flying job offer in Dallas. They had spent their last weekend together before she left for Texas, with Chloe promising to look him up as soon as she was able. That last weekend they shared together was only a week before he found the Huey for sale on the Internet. Chloe and Buck had not wanted a long-distance relationship and parted ways as good friends.

This time, however, both were ecstatic to see each other again. Buck was a hard worker and had little time or interest in the opposite sex unless it fell into his lap, so to speak. Chloe was not happy in Dallas and had returned to her old job in New York. She was even more excited when Buck invited her to be co-pilot on his long trip—really excited to experience her old boyfriend's new toy and have a chance to fly a real Huey.

Buck could not believe how passionate a Huey could make a girl. She made love to him and snuggled close to him all that night and the next, after he had taken her for a spin around Long Island, letting her fly most of the time. She was a good and experienced chopper pilot and easily adapted to the heavy Huey. They first flew up to Rochester, refueled, and stayed overnight in a hotel close to the regional airport. Then they flew on to Lansing, Michigan to refuel again. The Huey cruised at 130 miles an hour at a happy altitude of 11,000 feet due to its very light cargo load.

The cargo aboard consisted of a new porta-potty, two luxury military-style camp beds, a tent, a DC refrigerator, a television, ten days of food, beer, and wine, and water and clothing, which was less than 300 pounds of a maximum 3,500 pound payload. She flew fast and easy. Her normal range was 340 miles and her flight manual reckoned on an extra 40 miles with less than 500 lbs. of cargo, including the pilot and co-pilot's weight, with full fuel. Each leg was blessed with beautiful weather and took three hours of cruise time.

From Lansing, it was a shorter 200-mile leg, first across Lake Michigan and then over the much smaller Lake Winnebago. Buck headed out of Lansing in a northwest direction on a blue and cloudless morning. They headed over Grand Rapids at 11,000 feet and headed for the lake. They crossed the eastern shore of Lake Michigan ten miles south of Muskegon, and 30 minutes later crossed the western shore just north of Milwaukee. They then turned north and followed I-43 and then Route 32 up to the small town of Kiel. From here they flew due west and 15 minutes later moved into the already busy flight pattern for Oshkosh.

It was on the ground several minutes later that Buck saw the most beautiful DC-3 he had ever seen, parked less than 100 feet away in a line of fixed-wing aircraft on display. It was the day before opening ceremonies, and there were small aircraft taxiing everywhere, slowly filling up their allotted spaces.

Oshkosh was fun. Buck was proud of his Huey, and dozens of older pilots came up to him and told him their war stories about Vietnam. They slept overnight in the Huey, which served as a museum by day and home by night, and they got friendly with many of the pilots around them. An old friend, Sally Powers, came over to say hello. She did not own a private aircraft, but had piloted a C-130 in for the Air Force show stand from Tucson. His good buddy Carlos Rodriquez, who was currently on the move to his new assignment in Salt Lake City, flew directly there after the show. Carlos' always perfect Mustang P-51C would be one of the most popular aircraft there.

The last night after the show had closed was the most fun. Buck, Chloe, Carlos, Sally and the two owners of the DC-3 Buck had admired throughout the show had a party around the Huey. Also in attendance were a dozen or so of the older ex-Huey pilots, and these guys were fun enough for Buck to throw a party on their behalf. Carlos found and secured an old 44-gallon rusted drum that had been cut in half and used as a BBQ grill at a few earlier EAA meets. Sally and Chloe bummed a ride into town with the board member who invited them, and returned with charcoal, three dozen T-bone steaks, a dozen large pork chops, several raw whole chickens, sandwich rolls, several cases of beer, a box of wine, and a case of Wild Turkey whiskey. Buck and Carlos shared the $800.00 tab and the party was a blast.

They found chairs, and the board member, who couldn't stay, offered them a cooler of ice, a large fire bin, and half a cord of wood. Turns were taken cooking and opening drinks. Music from the radio on board the Huey was good enough to dance to.

"Reminds me of 'Nam," shared one of the older pilots. "Often when there was a ceasefire, or we had a break in the fighting, we used to sit around the Hueys and have a party. It didn't take much over there to start a party. We had parties to respect any guys who didn't come back too. We just didn't have any girls over there."

It was a warm cloudless summer night and the party raged until the early hours of the morning. The BBQ coals died down at about midnight and the rest of the wood was placed in the fire bin. Many of the show aircraft had already left and there were spaces everywhere. But the ones that stayed overnight were eerie in the growing shadows cast by the glowing fire and many of the older boys fell asleep in their chairs.

"Bob, how do you keep the DC-3 in such perfect condition?" asked Buck. Bob Martin was the majority owner of the DC-3 and had eight other shareholders who clocked flying hours in her every year.

"It's very difficult," Bob replied, staring into the dying embers of the fire. "I've owned her for going on 20 years now and every year she takes more and more money to keep pristine. I'll be looking for another shareholder pretty shortly. She needs both engines overhauled when we get back, and that should set us back $50,000 to $75,000. The price depends on where we take her, but the best guy to service her turboprops is in Tucson, Arizona and he is expensive. The turboprop engines were replaced on the DC-3s in the early 1950s; Pratt & Whitney Canada PT6A-50s. They are rated at 972 shaft horse power, drink like fishes, but give a 181 mile per hour economical cruise compared to the usual drop dead slow 150, and at only 60% power. She is fitted with the drop tanks under each wing and these have increased her range from 1,200 nautical miles to nearly 2,000 with a 45-minute reserve. Also, with her double freight doors, she can pack in big stuff and carry her full payload of 9,000 lb., and get off the ground in 2,800 feet and land in 2,500 feet with no reverse trust."

"She could get into a friend of mine's airfield in North Carolina with a little expertise," interjected Carlos, who was listening in on the conversation with a blanket around him and a glass of whiskey in his hand. The girls had gone to sleep in the Huey an hour or so earlier.

"I could screw her down into anything bigger than 2,300 feet," laughed Bob. "I live in Denver and she has as much runway as I want. We keep her in our hangar at Denver International."

"I might be interested," Buck stated quietly. "Bayport Aerodrome, where I keep *Baby Huey* on Long Island, is 2,740 feet long, mostly turf, and has several 30-foot trees about 400-500 feet from the most-used end—Runway 18. The other end, Runway 36, has trees a lot closer... how much would you like for a tenth share?"

"$150,000," replied Bob Martin seriously.

"A little out of my league at the moment, I'm afraid," muttered Buck, the wind taken out of his sails.

"How much do you need?" Carlos asked his buddy a few seconds later.

"I'm about $75,000 short," replied Buck. "*Baby Huey* here takes a lot to keep going."

"I have always wanted to learn to fly a helicopter," replied Carlos. "Give me 50 hours of lessons and a small share in the Huey, let me co-pilot with you in the DC-3 now and again, and I will give you the $75,000 you need. Hell, we might as well enjoy our flying!"

Buck knew Carlos was a lot wealthier than he was, and comfortably off with family money. A deal was struck just before dawn between Bob and Buck, and a gentleman's handshake was orchestrated between Buck and Carlos with Bob as an unofficial notary.

Nobody from the party could fly out the next day due to the heavy drinking the previous night, except for Bob, who had to get back. His co-pilot and one of the shareholders that had flown in with another aircraft flew him out just after lunch and a six-hour nap.

Buck's first flight hour in *Lady Dandy*, as the DC-3 was named, was two months later. He had paid his money and was offered the right seat for the flight from Denver International down to Tucson for her engine overhauls. It was a clear day, and Buck enjoyed the stability *Lady Dandy* had in flight compared to the smaller aircraft he owned. She flew like a rock in the sky. Carlos joined them on the flight, flying in from Salt Lake for the occasion.

Tucson had a long runway like Denver, and as they touched down the engines were feathered. *Lady Dandy* slowed and exited the long runway towards the commercial hangars opposite the airport's main terminal. The crew stayed overnight at a hotel and had a few drinks with Karl, the engine specialist who had a hangar at the city airport.

The contracts for a pricey sum per engine had been signed earlier and the work would take four to five months.

"I want everything kept original, Karl," Bob directed over

dinner. "I don't want any new fancy management systems or computers. I know they would help with fuel monitoring, but I want these engines as original as they came out of Pratt and Whitney in 1952.

"You could save up to 5% on fuel usage with the new gadgets they have come out with," replied Karl. "But *Lady Dandy* is as clean as I saw her last... When was it, in 1998 or 99?"

"1997," replied Bob.

"You're right. A lady of her upbringing should be kept as original as possible. Her value can only go up if she is original," answered Karl. "I might even have an interested buyer for her."

"Not interested!" replied Bob and Buck at the same time.

In 2008, Buck completed 38 hours flying the left-hand seat in *Lady Dandy*, and received his license to fly her. Carlos had flown in twice that year and also completed 10 hours of flight time. He only needed another 10 hours to get a competency license to fly her solo.

Buck was again promoted within his company and posted to a new satellite communications operation in Aurora, Colorado. He and Chloe flew *Baby Huey* out to a nearby airport. One of his shareholders had passed away a few months earlier and the other had been bought out by Carlos, who wanted a larger share in her now that he was licensed to fly Huey helicopters. Carlos was especially happy that Buck was coming his way and would be closer to Salt Lake City. His P-51 could easily gobble up the 300-mile distance in an hour.

Chloe had been offered a new position with a flying service in the Bahamas in the New Year and was currently between jobs.

Buck's move was intended to be temporary and he planned to be in Colorado for nine to eleven months. His intention was to fly as much as he could before going back to New York. And what New York pilot would not enjoy flying the Rockies?

As was normal, radio contact was maintained between the ham radio friends. Buck, who had not yet met Preston, chatted on a weekly basis. Sally Powers also chatted weekly and flew up to visit whenever she could, and it was funny that Carlos was always able to fly in when Sally was there. Sally did not own an aircraft, but was moving from Tucson to the Marine Air Force base in Yuma. She had just completed her final flights on C-130s and now was being promoted to jets. She had picked the F-16 Falcon and was excited to get into the world's best fighter.

Time sped by in Colorado for Buck. Buck and Chloe flew often in *Baby Huey* or *Lady Dandy* when they could afford the cost of flying, and saw every inch of the Rockies, often staying overnight with Carlos in Salt Lake. Buck even flew *Lady Dandy* as far as the West coast one time when he was asked to deliver a large and heavy cargo shipment to Martie Roebels' friends just outside Edwards Air Force Base. It was a fun flight with two beautiful women, Chloe and Martie, aboard. They flew into Fox Field in Lancaster and spent a day off-loading an old engine that Martie's boyfriend Preston had rebuilt, as well as a 200-gallon fuel tank and its tripod legs that had been disassembled to fit into the cargo door of the DC-3. Luckily, there was a forklift there and Will Smart and family were waiting with an old, rusty Ford truck to pick up the equipment. Preston had not had time to come along, even though he had wanted to. He was busy on a project and had a friend helping him with it.

Chloe's time came to leave and they had a tearful parting at Denver International on the last day of January 2009. The airport had been snowed in for a couple of days and neither of them had clocked any flying time since Christmas. Chloe promised to keep in touch daily and return as soon as she had some spare time, and then disappeared down the ramp to the waiting aircraft. Buck realized that they had grown very close over the last year, and wondered whether or not he should move to be with her in the warm climate of the Bahamas.

Slowly, the winter days warmed into spring and Buck spent all the time he had flying over snowed-covered peaks in either aircraft, but mostly the DC-3. In April, two of *Lady Dandy*'s shareholders were killed in a car crash in Denver, their deaths automatically releasing their shares to the remaining pilots. As if on cue, a third shareholder died a week later, leaving only six share holders and Bob, who had to front the ongoing monthly costs for the DC-3. Both Buck and Carlos invested a larger share and an equal number of shares as Bob. By the end of 2009, another three of the original shareholders had opted out for different reasons, leaving only Carlos, Buck and Bob with the responsibility of caring for *Lady Dandy*.

Also the daily phone calls or radio call from Chloe had slowed to weekly calls, and Buck found himself starting to look forward to returning to New York rather than moving to the Bahamas. In March of 2010, he did just that and became the boss of the entire Future Development division of his organization. With the hefty pay hike that came with it, he could now keep both aircraft.

In June of 2010, Buck heard from a fellow radio friend in Miami that Chloe had been killed in an air crash in heavy winds trying to move a helicopter to a safe haven in bad weather. She and a second pilot had been in drenching rain and had gone down in a sparsely populated area, crashing into an unoccupied vacation home. Their calls had become few and far between, and they had drifted away from regular communication as life and time often forces. He had never met her family and did not attend her funeral, since he had heard the news after her burial. Buck had heard about a helicopter crash a couple of weeks earlier, but the announcer had stated Bermuda instead of the Bahamas and the news had disappeared from his thoughts.

That summer, Buck felt empty inside. He had enjoyed Chloe's friendship and she had been the closest person to his heart, more than any of the rare girls he had ever dated. He was not the dating type and work and flying always took the majority of his time. After Chloe's death, he buried himself in his work and didn't fly much for the rest of 2010. His driving interest for the rest of that year was getting Lady Dandy down to Martie's boyfriend's farm in North Carolina for the New Year's Eve Fly-In and finally meeting his ham radio buddy. He looked forward to landing her on the 2,700 foot runway at Preston's farm. It was going to be a tight fit for the DC-3 and it would take all of his ability in her to get her in. Bob Martin had personally promised him a couple hours of flight training on landing before he left.

A major dilemma for Buck was that he had planned for Chloe to return to New York over the festive season and join him on the flight to North Carolina flying Baby Huey down to show Preston and Martie and completing the fly-in with every aircraft available.

Buck met Barbara one day later that Fall when she walked up to inspect him and the machinery while he was doing a pre-flight inspection of *Baby Huey*. Barbara had just piloted in a new-looking Cessna Citation jet, wore four stripes on her shirt lapels showing her Captain's rank, and was a six-foot-tall, leggy red-head. Buck felt scared for the first time in his life. He already knew by looking at her for a split second that she was an inch taller than him, could outrun him, out-fly him, out-drink him, out-party him and most probably could eat him alive any time she wanted. And he wouldn't mind! His past feelings for Chloe slowly became a distant memory.

CHAPTER 3

Jiangsu Province, China

REFORM—DUBBED CHINA'S "Second Revolution"—was one of the most common terms in China's political vocabulary in the early 1980s. Reform of the Chinese Communist Party and its political activities, reform of government organization, reform of the economy, military reforms, cultural and artistic reforms—indeed, China's post-Mao Zedong leaders called for reform in every part of Chinese society.

The leaders of the People's Republic of China saw reform as a way to realize the broad goals of the Four Modernizations; the modernization of industry, agriculture, science and technology, and national defense, and to bring China into the community of advanced industrial nations by the beginning of the new millennium.

Thus, the reform movement of the 1980s, which was attributed largely to the insights and determination of Wang Chunqiao, one of the most important figures in the post-Mao Zedong leadership, took its place in the broad spectrum of Chinese history.

It took time for Reform to change life in the rural areas of China.

In Beijing and Shanghai, reform could be seen quickly. In

Jiangsu Province and its largest city, Nanjing—one of the four ancient capitals of China—immediate changes could be seen in the new buildings on the Yangtze River. The Yangtze River Bridge had gone up 20 years earlier in the 1960s, and had been the largest project in the area until a new building several blocks south of the bridge was noticed in early 1979. It went up at a fast pace compared to normal construction work, and by December of 1979, the 30-story modern glass building was complete and its name appeared outside the main entrance—Zedong Electronics.

For the average Chinese population, all security was normal, but passers-by at the new Zedong Electronics building noticed extremely high security around the clock. Armed guards were always at every entrance, and anyone entering the building was frisked, and briefcases opened and thoroughly checked. The building had a basement car entrance a few yards away from the main entrance, and often rare black limousines for that era could be seen going down the ramp and through the heavy security once the garage doors were open.

The boardroom on the 30th floor was not be seen by many people once it was lavishly completed in 1980. Around the 16-seat table, each comfortable leather chair was taken by a man in an expensive suit. The oldest looked about 30 to 40 years old. Marble was everywhere. There were works of art, mostly ancient Chinese, but a few paintings that looked Western as well.

Very large windows for that period covered the outer wall and were reflective so that one could see out but nobody could see in. At the head of the table, a much older man used a wooden pointer and moved it over the display on the wall behind him. The display showed what looked to the average person to be small electrical fuses, switches, and electronic gadgets common in the West in the early 1980s. Apart from the abnormal wealth and luxury in the board room, it looked like a normal business meeting.

Chairman Wang Chunqiao, the man holding the pointer, was

dressed immaculately in a dark suit, red tie, and red handkerchief in his upper pocket. All the men seated at the table were Chinese, well-dressed, and affluent. Discussions of metals, glass, electricity, electrical engineering, and the uncommon word Strontium were heard around the room. For any person listening in, these men were experts in electronics, engineering, and modern day China—masters of their knowledge. Unfortunately, nobody could listen in. The room had been cleaned and checked for Russian, American, or even any Chinese "bugs" days before this meeting. Nobody other than the 16 men was allowed in the room and no notes were taken. There was not a piece of paper in the room.

Comrade Hu Lee, one of the slightly older men, gave a 20-minute lecture on Western computers. Then the younger Comrade Zhi Yun gave a lecture on modern Western satellite communications and the new American spy satellite project. Comrade Ri Yun, another member of the table, gave a lecture on the growing Japanese auto industry, and many of the men spat on the floor when the word "Japanese" was mentioned. Very few at the table had not lost fathers, mothers, and older family members during the Japanese invasion of China just before the Second World War. This part of China had been one of the worst hit areas, with more than 300,000 Chinese fatalities at the hands of the Japanese army in Nanjing alone.

Lunch was served by young girls in traditional dress carrying in dozens of delicacies from the Nanjing area. A large table was brought in and placed along one of the windowed walls and filled with delights most average people in this part of the world only dream about. Within five minutes, the mass of servers were gone and the men got up to help themselves. It was a working lunch after all. Tea and drinks had been placed at one end, and one-by-one they gathered their favorites and sat down with chopsticks in hand to eat.

For the rest of the afternoon, one man after the other stood and lectured on a different subject. All speeches were made with the same end in sight—to produce the best electronics possible for the developing Western world hundreds and thousands of miles away. Microsoft came up often, as did Apple. So did telephones, electrical grids, fuses, and aircraft directional equipment made in America, Germany, and France. Vehicle-management systems and control units were under development in Germany, and Japan had already started negotiating for them to be in every future vehicle made in Japan.

Pricing and opposition company prices were discussed the next day, and the day after that. Production of well over a hundred different components took three days of discussion. They talked about the dozens of new factories that would need to be built within the next 12 months to manufacture these new components. They would be of only the best quality, made with the best computers and workforce, and work better than any competitor's product. The pride of China's productivity would be at stake, and everything would be made in Nanjing.

Many of the discussions involved new gadgets the West had not yet heard of, but well-placed Chinese in every corner of every industry worldwide were already giving feedback to Zedong Electronics on every new electronic invention about to come on the market in the next four or five years.

Chairman Wang Chunqiao had been working on this project for over a decade now. Under the old regime many thousands of Chinese had been placed overseas and, at one time, were all under his control. With the changes in China's government and new people rising to power, the older communist party people were being ejected and replaced by new blood. Wang Chunqiao was no longer a part of the government elite, but he was still one of the most powerful, wealthy, and prominent members of the largest population in the world. Some Chinese reckoned that he was nearly as powerful in China as the whole new government.

After two weeks of daily meetings, the board room on the

30th floor became silent and empty. Nobody knew that a scenario for the destruction of the Western world had just been planned down to the day, minute, and second.

Nanjing became a hive of activity. In more than a dozen different areas around the city, large production buildings and warehouses started springing up. Young workers were hired from the city and surrounding areas by the thousands. Hundreds of prominent Chinese scientists and engineers began showing up in local restaurants. Most city folk did not notice the larger manufacturing plants being built further out from the cities, some as far as 20 miles away. Little towns grew overnight from a few hundred houses to big 10-story, or more apartment blocks and their populations doubled from month to month.

By the end of 1980, many of these new buildings were up and running—designing and producing electronic prototypes copied from the stolen plans of every company in Silicon Valley. These secret plans came from Microsoft, Apple, Boeing, Lockheed Martin, Volkswagen, Siemens, Honda, Toyota and even Grandpa Roebels and Michael's electronic business in San Diego. Neither of the Roebels knew that the old Chinese man they hired to clean their work spaces at night had a Ph.D. in engineering from Beijing University. He was never allowed into the design area and their top secret laboratory, but he had enough knowledge and training to break any code and get through any security device anywhere in their factory at the San Diego airport when nobody was around. He had been intensively trained in Nanjing.

The Roebels would have been even more surprised if they had visited the main Raytheon production plant after the company was purchased from them and found that the same old Chinese face was still cleaning floors and still totally invisible to the hundreds who worked there every day. Nobody knew if he was even on the payroll!

Nanjing had over four million people living within city walls built well over 500 years ago. Within 100 miles of the city lived another 300,000 rural people in 1979, and by 1981, this number had tripled. Zedong Electronics had become the largest employer in the area in less than two years, employing over 10 percent of the population of Nanjing, as well as another 600,000 people who had been moved in from all over China. Nobody apart from the Board of Directors could see the whole picture, since there were over 38 separate manufacturing buildings, all with bogus company names, all producing different electrical components. And these massive installations were well-placed and hidden over 500 square miles.

U.S. space satellites noticed this rapid growth, but China was starting to grow everywhere, and photos of all of Zedong Electronics' new manufacturing plants disappeared into different files and nobody thought to look at this massive growth area any closer.

Wang Chunqiao had designed his master plan well. Even the Chinese powers-that-be were too interested in foreign affairs to notice what was going on in areas other than Beijing. "Buy Quality, Buy Cheap!" was the motto started in December of 1982 as electronics from over 52 manufacturing companies in and around Nanjing hit the Western world with a vengeance. "Best Chinese Quality, Low Chinese Prices" was the second motto started in early 1983.

The electronic world was at first weary of these cheap parts. Nothing of real value had ever come out of China, but with the lowered prices, fewer and fewer international companies could resist. If their competition was buying these new components, then based on price comparison there would be no resulting competition.

Companies by the thousands learned in the early 1980s that these new parts worked as well as any parts manufactured in the rest of the world and were produced at half the price. Nanjing became a busy city, nearly as rapidly as Shanghai, where Zedong Electronics had another 50 large undercover manufacturing plants, again all under different names and all producing different small electronic products.

Within a couple of years, the whole world had entered a new era—the era of all machines running with electronically controlled parts. Gone were the old-fashioned carburetors in cars, trucks, buses, aircraft, ship engines, or military vehicles on land, sea, and air. Millions of old carburetor engines were redesigned and replaced with computerized electronic-control systems. Even some of the smallest car engines could only maintain forward motion with one of these fancy computers added to them that controlled every part of the working engine thousands of times per second. The only remaining engines that stuck to carburetors were small lawn mower engines and low-power generators.

Naturally, outside the immediate area of China, nobody knew of Zedong Electronics. In the west, the use of Chinese electronic products grew and grew. Nothing was said about where they came from. All the buyer could read was "Made in China," in English as large as the product's size would allow.

By 1985, children's toys were hitting the shelves with "Made in China" labels on them. Many Americans were still fearful about communism and anything from a "red" country was not to be purchased. As great as any country is, however, the price was always the winner in the end with shoppers. It took a couple of years, but Zedong Electronics and its many "subsidiaries" grabbed more and more market share. Microsoft, Dell, Apple, and other large American companies started looking at getting complete products "Made in China."

In 1987, Phase II of Chairman Wang Chunqiao's operation was launched into the world market. The board room on the 30th floor was again busy, with the same suits in the room. None looked any older, but there was a pervading sense of exhaustion like that shown by workers who are enslaved by their jobs. Paper was not present the room. All the men talked from memory. This time, the screen behind the Chairman's head was filled with photos of larger gadgets. More modern and smaller cell phones, circuit boards, and even mother boards passed across the screen on the first day. Then came tinier single parts, once again very small in size and something only an electrical engineer could name. Strontium was seen in every diagram and seemed to be a very important part of the overall discussions. Much of the discussion was about the half life of this grey, silvery metal.

For two weeks the men worked, and each day an exotic lunch was served. Alcohol was never seen in the room—only exotic food and drink served buffet style by the same young girls every day. As with the first two-week session six years earlier, each man played a part in the lectures and discussions. It seemed that each man was an equal to the others. The Chairman was the boss; the other 15 men treated him with respect but were not scared to argue a point if there was one to argue.

The last lecture was a long one. This time, Comrades Zhi Yun and Hu Lee both stood in front of the large screen and pointed to the different objects as they appeared on the screen. Anybody in the Pentagon would have loved to have been a fly on the wall. First, the blueprints of U.S. communication satellites were discussed for over an hour. All the small, intricate parts in the satellites made by Zedong Electronics were shown in red. There must have been at least 30 parts in the entire satellite breakdown. The sizes of each unit ranged from a pinhead to the size of a two-inch pencil. Then, the design of a modern nuclear reactor was shown on the screen.

This small reactor looked like it could have been from a submarine or ship. Over the course of two days, these two men went over many types of computer-controlled weapons, tanks, aircraft, civilian and military vehicle engine-control systems, and ships above and below the waterline. Even underground railway systems were included, and the first was from Washington D.C. They also showed a complete map of the electrical grid of several countries in North America and Europe, many gas lamps sold worldwide, what looked like several types of electrical back-up systems, and dozens of possible top secret information and designs (civilian and military) from different countries. After two weeks of daily work, the room became empty again and the world of electronics moved on as before.

The people of Nanjing who worked for the dozens of plants around the area were paid a basic wage, just enough not to complain, but not enough to live a better quality life than their countrymen. Complaining was not allowed in modern China anyway, and to most people the daily routine was long and boring, doing the same thing over and over again.

Several workers, however, started getting horrible sores all over their bodies. These special employees, over 12,000 of them, were paid a better wage and worked in special white suits in sealed laboratories. It seemed that something toxic might be getting through their protection. It wasn't long before these poor folk were separated from their loved ones and never seen again. So many people died every day all over China that these few became just numbers to the world around them, and family members were compensated well enough that they too said very little.

CHAPTER 4

Sally Powers

IN A SMALL TOWN just outside Savannah, Georgia, Sally Michele Powers was born to Peter and Marci Powers on June 12, 1988. Peter was an insurance salesman, and Marci was a nurse at the St. Joseph's Hospital in Savannah.

Marci worked in the ICU, and giving birth to her first child there was a plus. She was given 24/7 attention by her colleagues. Peter had access any time he wanted, and Sally came into the world in the birthing room of the hospital to a happy family with lots of smiling faces peering down at her.

By the age of three, Sally already showed a love of motor vehicles. Any ride with her father in the family car was a thrill to her. The wind was an added bonus when she was allowed to have the window closest to her car seat rolled down slightly. It rustled her hair and she would put her young chin forward, close her eyes, and let the wind caress her face.

Life became even better when, on her fourth Christmas, Peter bought a used Mustang convertible for Marci. When Marci put the top down, the wind gave Sally the full force of its power as she sat directly behind the driver's seat. Screams of ecstasy were often heard by passers-by as they cruised along coastal roads during their days off together, and a lunch at some little restaurant or diner along the coast somewhere was always included at the halfway point of the pleasure.

On her tenth birthday, her father took her out to Hodges Park Airpark in Georgetown for the first time. His insurance company had offered several small year-end prizes for new business in 1997 and Peter had won a couple of them, including an hour-long flight in a private airplane from Hodges Park. One of his managers owned the aircraft and had offered the prize to his team members. There was no way Marci would be caught in a little airplane, but she was still happy to go along for the ride on that sunny summer's day. Sally could hardly sleep the night before, and it took forever for the sun to slowly rise on the day little Sally would fly for the first time.

As usual the short trip in the Mustang was her special pleasure, but the feeling of leaving the ground in the back seat of the Cessna 182R was heavenly for the small girl. Peter thought that even Marci could hear their daughter's excited screams as the aircraft swept past and several feet above the shiny mustang sitting a little way off the asphalt runway. There was a clunk as the retractable undercarriage came up, and for the next hour over land and sea, the little girl was in heaven. At one point, Peter thought she might put her face through the rear window as hard as she was pressing her face against it.

After the enjoyable flight, both Peter and Sally reluctantly climbed out of the plane, and Sally thanked its owner profusely and apologized for her behavior during takeoff. The smiling man replied that they weren't the first passengers he had taken up, or the first screams of excitement he had heard. He rather expected some reaction from first timers.

Sally could not stop talking about the flight all the way home, or the rest of the week. It was the best birthday present she had ever had. Could she have another flight for her birthday next year, she asked? An only child, Sally normally got her way. Both parents enjoyed their jobs and life was easy. She got her second flight at eleven and her third flight on her twelfth birthday, this time in Peter's manager's newer aircraft, a Cessna 210 Turbo.

The 210 Turbo was a six-seat, single-engine aircraft, and much faster. This time, she sat in the co-pilots seat on the right and Peter sat in the second row of seats. She was even allowed to hold the joystick. Once the pilot had her in level flight at 5,000 feet and her feet on the rudders, the pilot gently let her fly the aircraft in a straight line. Sally did well, listening to his every instruction, and she completed her first turn to the right and then a gentle bank to the left, slowly putting pressure on the rudder pedals as she turned the joystick in the direction she wanted the aircraft to go.

On the ground, her father's manager stated that she had flown well and that she should look into flying in a few years' time. He explained that she was a natural at controlling a three-dimensional machine in the air. Sally had actually flown the plane for over ten minutes, unbeknownst to her. Once he had realized that she was rather good at what she was doing, he had let go of the controls several minutes earlier than he had actually told her that she was in control. Even Peter had watched when the pilot indicated with a tilt of his head that his hands and feet were actually off the controls and that the little girl, sitting as straight as a ramrod and peering through the front window, was in total control of their destinies.

Marci was pretty upset when she heard that her daughter had actually flown the 210, but eased off on her husband when she saw Sally's excited demeanor. She had never seen her little girl as happy and content as she saw her that evening over dinner. Sally smiled a dreamy smile and had a happy glow on her face throughout the meal, most probably lost in her own little world of flying.

It took the 12-year old at least a week to come back down to earth and get on with the everyday things in life. The feel of the aircraft stayed with her longer, and her nights were full of dreams of flying all over the sky and taking long trips all over the world.

A few months before her thirteenth birthday, Peter's manager was posted to a higher position back at the head office and Sally's father was promoted to the manager's position. Feeling a little more comfortable with a larger monthly income under his belt, he paid for an hour's lesson for his daughter's birthday at the flying school at the same airport. Sally was thrilled. The school's Cessna was an old 172, but that didn't matter. Within the hour, she had flown half of the time and had completed one take-off and nearly completed a landing. She had come in a little steep and needed the instructor to correct and level the plane for final touchdown, but it was bliss and the worst part of the lesson for Sally was that it came to an end.

"But I nearly landed it, Daddy," she exclaimed in the car on their way home. "I'm sure that if I could get another hour, I could fly it all by myself."

"I understand, Sal," as her Dad always called her. "You can't fly solo until you are 16 and that is three years away. You can get your private pilot's license at 17 and you can go even higher after that. It doesn't seem too good an idea to fly too much now since you must wait a few more years before the training will become worthwhile. I suggest that you start some sort of business at school and see if you can make enough money to do a couple of hours a year until you're a little older." Her father's words sunk in.

For days, Sally studied typical business ideas for young girls, from lemonade stands to washing cars. Most of them didn't sound too exciting or promising, and the many negatives stood out for nearly all of them. One, however, did bear fruit and it came from her mother's hospital.

A few weeks after her last flight, she visited Marci at work after school on a late Friday afternoon. Her mother normally organized hospital ward and office inventory on Fridays, and

Sally often went in to help her. This particular Friday, they were chatting over a cup of tea when a few nurses gathered around a lady who had come in the front door. The lady was elderly and Sally had seen her once or twice before.

"I have your dress scarves," the older lady told the nurses, walking in with the aid of a walking stick. She walked up to a chair in the hallway, leaned her stick against it, put her handbag on the chair and started fiddling around in a large plastic bag she had bought with her. "Mandy, here is your short pink one. Beth, I have the double-length blue thick wool one you wanted, and Sister Marci, I have the promised striped one for your daughter. Oh, there's young Sally Powers in person. Hi, Sally. Oh dear! I hope your mother's present to you is not a birthday surprise or something important!"

"Don't fret, Mrs. Masterson," replied Sally's mother. "It was just an idea for her for winter, for school. She needs one and winter will be on its way in a couple of months." Marci accepted the scarf and wrapped the thick, long yellow and green striped scarf around her daughter's neck. "Now I will be able to see you when you fly over us in any old open aircraft you might get your hands on, just like Snoopy used to wear in Charlie Brown," laughed Marci.

"Wow, Mom. It's beautiful." Sally modeled the scarf to the smiling ladies now looking at her. "Mrs. Masterson, you sure make pretty scarves."

"It suits you, Sally," complimented one of the nurses. "It brings out your red hair."

"Thank you," replied the old lady. "These are the last I will be making, and the only reason I took up knitting again was to thank you girls for making my long stay here bearable. Three months is a long time, you know, and it would have been even longer without your friendship."

Thank yous were exchanged by all the girls, each giving the

smiling old lady a hug before leaving. Marci was paged over the intercom and she made excuses to leave.

"Sally, why don't you chat with Mrs. Masterson for a while? I'll see what this is all about and be back shortly. Why don't you two have a cup of tea in the cafeteria?" Sally and the older woman moved over to the cafeteria and ordered two teas and two slices of the tasty looking cake sitting on the counter. The lady behind the counter knew Sally and knew to put any orders on her mother's tab.

For half an hour, Sally told the older lady all about flying and the thrills it sent up and down her spine. The old lady was happy for the young girl's company and listened intently.

"So, Mrs. Masterson," continued Sally. "Daddy said that I must find a way to make an income to pay for a couple of hours of flying a year before I can get my license. He'll pay for my birthday present flights every year, but I must make any more money if I want to add any more flying hours."

"Aren't you a little young to fly?" asked Mrs. Masterson.

"Well, if I practice, I can get my private pilot's license when I'm 17, but I can go solo when I'm 16," Sally replied.

"How old are you now, Sally?" asked Mrs. Masterson, sipping a little of the hot tea.

"I will be 14 on my next birthday," Sally replied. "And I will need at least 40 training hours before I can go solo and if I do hours now, I will have to do fewer hours when I'm older, if I practice and practice. Mrs. Masterson, honestly, I can't wait until I'm older!" The old lady laughed at the young girl's motivation and thought for a moment.

"You know Sally," the older woman paused to put the last piece of cake in her mouth. "I used to make good money knitting scarves.

How much money do you need for an hour's flying practice?"

"Eighty-five dollars," replied the eager girl.

"So much!" declared the older lady. "Well, if that's what you need, you had better get some lessons from me and I'll show you a few scarves that are fast and easy and you can make at least five dollars on each one you make."

Over the next couple of weeks, Sally spent several hours with Mrs. Masterson learning the art of needlework, and by the time she rented a space at her first craft market several streets from her house, she had a dozen scarves finished and for sale at $10.00 each. These were very short neck scarves made with colorful stretchy yarn that looked like a dog's collar on her when she tried them on for the first time. Once Mrs. Masterson showed her how to make different colors to suit people's clothes, they looked even better. The work took Sally an hour of fast knitting for the smallest length of 16 inches. The material cost just under $4.00 per scarf and her first sale was nearly as big a thrill as her first flying experience years earlier.

The first Saturday morning craft fair was a success. Marci helped her set up and paid the $5.00 table fee for the day. Sally sold eight of her 12 scarves, had an order for a longer double-wrap one for $15.00 in royal blue, and was advanced the money to make it. Delivery was set for the next market in two weeks.

Peter helped her with her accounting for the first day. Sally had spent $40.00 on different colored material and still had enough to make three scarves. Her income was $95.00 for the day, and because her mother had paid for the table, Peter made Sally include it as a normal cost.

"So, Sal," he concluded. "You used about $35.00 in material, plus you paid $5.00 for your table. You have to buy the royal blue material for Mrs. Swift. How much is a ball or two of that material?" he asked.

"$12.50 including tax for two balls," replied Sally.

"Okay. Now how much will you have left over to make more short scarves with that investment?" he continued.

"Three," was the reply.

"Right! Then let's say that Mrs. Swift's scarf will cost you

$7.50. That means your profit will also be $7.50. That amount plus your net profit of $40.00 for the day means that you made $47.50 towards your first flight hour. I think Mom will forget the gas money since it was only several blocks and the amount is unimportant. All you have left is your own labor costs."

"My labor costs are my flight costs," suggested an excited Sally.

On her second market day, she invited Mrs. Masterson to be her sales assistant and to come enjoy the day. It was a gorgeous day and Mrs. Swift happily accepted her completed purchase. She also brought two friends along who ordered the same scarf, but in different colors, and chatted for awhile with Mrs. Masterson. Sally's second day made enough for her first self-paid flight hour. She invited Mrs. Masterson to join her in the aircraft as a passenger. The older lady politely refused, but offered to go along and watch from terra firma—a much better deal for a lady her age.

This time, Sally flew a complete circuit with the instructor, again sitting in the right co-pilot's seat. She was still a little short for the windshield and had remembered to take a cushion along to improve seat height. She also took the new scarf her mother had bought her, even thought the weather was still far too hot to wear it.

"A good luck memento from Mom," she explained to Mrs. Masterson and her father on the car ride to Hodges Park.

Sally managed three to four hours a year for the next three years, plus the hour a year her father had promised her for each birthday. By the age of 15, her scarf business was in full swing. She had two older ladies who knitted them for her at $2.00 a piece. She had raised the price slightly to $12.00, and used slightly more expensive materials, which made the scarves look very chic. She sold them at the markets and managed good sales of 20-30 per event. The market had grown over the last couple of years and in addition to the market, she had three boutiques in

Savannah selling them for over $15.00 each. Her net profit per unit had decreased by 40% and her sales had increased by 400%, but it was her school work that was becoming more important and had made her search for help so that she could study.

Sally flew the necessary hours of training during those years, including her father's annual present, and she could put the Cessna down on a quarter placed on the runway if she wanted to. Her flying was already natural and effortless.

Just before her 16th birthday, she asked the instructor to give her something more demanding to practice on, and she completed two hours of training on a Cessna 210 that had far more complicated flying controls than the usual 172. This was like going from a bicycle to a motorbike for Sally. The constant-pitch propeller changed to a variable-pitch propeller, a fixed undercarriage changed to retractable undercarriage, and the pre-flight inspection made this aircraft far more exciting just to be near. It took all of her concentration to remember all the flight checks before take-off, but the instructor coached her. Once she was ready, she was asked to gently increase revs to maximum instead of just pushing the throttle control with the right hand to maximum as fast as possible like in the 172.

Sally felt the added power throb through her as she slowly pushed the hand throttle to full power and, as with most aircraft, the heavier the aircraft was, the more stable it felt throughout the flight. She was up and off the runway far quicker than usual and she pushed the undercarriage control button when ordered to. The aircraft climbed rapidly, and before she knew it she was climbing to 5,000 feet and the sky came down to meet her. At that moment, Sally knew that she would fly for the rest of her life.

At 16, it took her just ten hours of added practice to go solo, and at 17 she passed her private pilots exam with flying colors. She was now a pilot. The instructor was impressed and he said so once they left the 172 for the last time and walked across the apron to the flight school. It was also the last time she would fly a Cessna 172.

Now that she had achieved her dream, it was time for serious school. Her parents were doing well in their jobs and Sally graduated high school with honors and went straight to college. For Sally, science (especially physics) and math were her two best subjects, and she was offered a three-year scholarship to the School of Aeronautics and Astronautics at Purdue University in West Lafayette, Indiana. Her parents were thrilled, as was her flying instructor. An ex-graduate of the school had opened a door for her due to her ability to learn quickly. He had told her about the school and after her first flight in his own private Cessna 210, she had begged him to help her get into the school of her dreams. What had really excited Sally, once she had done her homework on this division within Purdue University, was that 21 engineering graduates from around the country had become astronauts, and 14 of them had been from the school she was about to attend. She couldn't wait!

Amid the tears of the usual farewells, Peter and Marci left her in her dorm room after touring the Neil Armstrong Hall of Engineering with her and seeing where their daughter was going to be spending much of her time over the next few years. It was costing them a good deal for her to attend Purdue, but being an only child nothing was too good for their daughter. It was also the first time Sally was away from home, but that did not deter her from her mission to be an astronaut one day.

The opportunities to fly were many, and during her time at Purdue Sally completed another 100 hours of flight time a year by bussing tables and selling her scarves to the thousands of students around her, especially during the cold winter months. Her nickname was "The Scarf Lady," since most could not get away from her without having to buy a scarf or two. With her 290 hours of flight time and much help from her father, she achieved her twin-engine flight rating and her twin-engine Instrument Flight Rating (IFR). She had just progressed to turboprop flight training when she received some great news—her father's company offered her an all-expenses-paid semester at MIT if she stayed another year and got her masters at Purdue. She couldn't resist that opportunity and worked her butt off; even giving up flying for most of the last year just like her parents knew she would.

She matured, grew into a beautiful woman, and left Purdue with a master's degree in electrical aviation engineering the following year. She was a competent pilot with nearly 500 hours to her name, and it was finally time for MIT.

CHAPTER 5

Jiangsu Province, China – 1980s

1983 WAS A NORMAL YEAR in Nanjing. The economy was getting better, due to Zedong Electronics employing most of the labor force. The population in and around Nanjing, and most of the population as far as the boundaries of the city of Shanghai were employed, content, and prospering as much as was possible in China at the time.

Apartment houses were still going up in all areas, and the influx of people from other areas of China was at its zenith. People came one year, rented an apartment, and disappeared a few years later. Many whole families came and went, but the majority of these apartments had single people in them—not very usual for China. Many apartments had a change in renters every two or three years, but that was normal in a city and once again the comings and goings of these people were a part of everyday life and they were quickly forgotten. Nobody asked questions.

On the island of Chongming, just north of Shanghai, a small new town was erected in 1983. The new town was across the river from the headquarters of Zedong Electronics in Shanghai, and was built on this sparsely populated island that had been nothing more than a few sandbanks several centuries ago.

Chongming Island was well suited for what Zedong Electronics wanted there.

At the small ferry harbor quay on this island, many of the people who had once worked for sister plants in Nanjing arrived. The people arrived alone or in family units, often like most Chinese do, carrying their life's possessions on their backs or shoulders. Many were older men and women well over 50, who often arrived on their own and needed help with one or two bags. By the time they arrived in this new town of five square miles, they had already been forgotten in their old job and apartment, which already had new tenants.

Zedong Electronics had powerful fingers in powerful circles. The company had purchased the entire island and made it off limits to all who used to live here or wanted to visit. Any inhabitants were swiftly ejected from the island by 1982, and a large workforce arrived shortly after that, tore down any shanty buildings, and started building the new town as if it was a backdrop on a Hollywood movie set. The only way in was the once-a-day private ferry service from Shanghai over the Yangtze River, which was more than a 15-mile trip and took well over 90 minutes. Zedong Electronics wanted this island to be cut off from the rest of the world.

By 1984, there were over a hundred new buildings, and hundreds of apartments within these buildings with every type of service a town needed. What was really different about this town was that if someone looked closely at its makeup, they would find over a hundred schools in session, seven days a week. With a population of over 10,000 people staying for about a year, and then most of them being replaced by new people, the town was busy.

One street had the exact replica of an American drug store, gas station, general store and several American-looking shops, from a typical flower shop to an American-Chinese laundry found in every city in the United States. Next to the gas station was a modern office complex and parking garage such as those found in all American cities. If anybody looked closely at the three cars in the 70-unit, always empty parking lot, they would have discovered that they were made out of cardboard.

On another street was a "petrol" station like those found in most English towns. Again, the whole street looked like an English village with several types of shops found in any English setting. Somewhere on each street was a three- to four-story office complex—modern, up-to-date, and with every electronic gadget available in the 1980s. There were fax machines, computers, the latest modern Western telephones and security devices found in high-security buildings like bio-labs or even the American FBI and other government buildings. Next to the petrol station was an English pub and betting office. The betting office was always busy, with television screens showing current horse races at every race track in England, and the language coming from the television was English. The Chinese loved to bet. Only English was spoken on this street, and the shorter than usual English policemen on the beat, called "bobbies," were in authentic English police uniforms and hit people with their truncheons if Mandarin was ever heard.

Another street had a German scene and another one looked like it was directly out of Paris and Moscow. Over 20 streets had a theme specific to other countries and Hollywood would have loved to own the whole town as a movie set.

The daily newspapers, in 20 languages, were only two days old and every person living in that street above the shops in the three- or four-story apartments had to read a paper a day.

The American district in the town was named "Washington, China" and it was the biggest area, covering eight whole blocks with each at over 200 yards in length. In 1,000 apartments lived several thousand single people and married couples. Even the spouses and children of the employees had to live in their new country and go to the American general store, go to the only

Winn Dixie supermarket to do their daily shopping, and attend an American-style school six days out of seven. The products for sale were often Chinese but had American wrapping. The school taught only in English and anyone was severely reprimanded if any conversation was heard in their native tongue. They dressed American, lived American, and learned to act American for one year—enough to be able to get a menial job when they arrived in the United States. They could blend in as Chinese-Americans from a second or third generation, and be confident enough to act like an American citizen and understand everything going on around them.

The most secretive part of the whole town was that all the employed members of each family had a minimum of a three-year degree in one form of electronics or engineering from either one of the 930 Chinese universities offering such degrees, or from one of the seven large universities owned and erected in 1980 by Zedong Electronics in Nanjing. Some had higher masters and Ph.D. degrees and were offered larger sums of money to attend classes in this new town with the opportunity for international travel once they had completed their training.

Underground and below-the-office complexes that stated "Underground Parking" on the wall were a different type of world. At the bottom of the stairs, the world became a police station where the American police, always seen above ground, had their headquarters and their school. Every town attendee spent several hours down here listening to lectures on what would happen to them if they disobeyed the system in America and if they were sent back to China, or if they disobeyed Zedong Electronics in America and what would happen to them and their families. Usually, this last form of education was meted out toward the end of their stay in town and just before their move to the country where they would be going.

Lee Wang was a married man, age 34, with a pretty wife and a two-year old baby girl. He had attended the University of

Shanghai and had achieved a master's degree in astronomy and one in electrical engineering when he was approached to join a new crowd of people who were being given the opportunity to work outside China. To most intellectuals, an opportunity to work outside the country was a blessing, and an education not often allowed or offered in communist China. He loved astronomy, but needed to complete a second degree in satellite electrical engineering to get a decent job. Lin, his wife of six years, had worked hard in a large hotel laundry to keep them fed and in school, and with a little help from both parents they had managed to survive the cost of Lee being in school.

He had been approached a few days after his daughter's second birthday by a man at his new and first real job in a small space laboratory in Shanghai. Lee had applied for the job with several other men, but for some reason the interviewer had liked his good manners and his two degrees, and he was hired at a small but livable salary. He had been there only a month when he was approached.

Lee had never seen the man who approached him before. Lee had left the lab to visit the men's room and was on his way back when he heard his name being called. He turned around to see that the man hailing him in the badly lit hallway had a mop in his hand and was obviously on floor-cleaning duty.

"Lee Wang," the man said with a remarkably educated accent for a floor cleaner. "I believe you would do very well in America if given the chance."

"Why would I think of America?" asked Lee, stopping and looking at the good-looking man in front of him who looked at least 40 years old. "I am happy where I am. I have a wonderful job, I have a wonderful family, and I do not think about anything else."

"You love Elvis Presley," the man replied, staring straight into his eyes, and Lee looked back at him in shock.

"Yes... well, yes... I mean I do... so that's allowed. How do you know that?" he demanded.

"There is much I know about you, Lee Wang. I spent a few weeks working with your wife in the laundry, and several days cleaning floors in your child's day care," stated the older man with little emotion. "We do our background work well on potential employees who we think might be beneficial for our company. If you are interested, I can offer you a move to a different department within this company with an increase in pay, better working conditions, an opportunity for foreign travel, and who knows... you could even visit Elvis Presley's house in America."

"But why do you offer me a job looking like an old floor cleaner and not like an owner of the company?" asked Lee, still trying to understand how this man knew more about himself than he cared to think about. "Why have you spied on my wife and child? Why not just ask me like any normal Chinese employer would do?"

"I am in training just like you will be if you join our company," the older man replied. "We are taught many jobs so that we can always survive in a capitalistic country like America. Lee Wang, I ask you to speak to nobody about our friendly conversation. It was simply two Chinese men talking about horse-race betting. If you do, I will hear about it and you will be fired from this company immediately. Do you understand?" the janitor continued smiling at the younger man. "Meet me back here tomorrow at 5 o'clock with an answer to my offer. I clean this hallway at the same time every day." With that, he turned his back and continued to mop the already gleaming floor.

Lee Wang was speechless and continued back to the lab as if he had just been part of a dream. Of course he wanted to live in America! They had bigger space telescopes over there, and people said that you could shake Elvis Presley's hand the Western way if you ever met him on the street. Lee Wang was so deep in thought that he bumped into one of his colleagues as they came out of the laboratory. He apologized, bowed, and walked back to his station.

For the rest of his shift that night, he could not stop thinking about what this floor cleaner, of all people, had told him. Naturally, he was scared that maybe the secret police had been spying on him and his family, but he had done nothing wrong except that he loved Elvis Presley songs. That wasn't against the law. He even had three old 45 rpm gramophone records he had purchased in a market several years earlier that he often played on his old gramophone. Even his wife enjoyed them, and his little girl's face always lit up when Elvis sang "All Shook Up."

His wife got back from work later than he, so his job was to pick up his daughter from day care on his bicycle and have some dinner boiling on the stove before Lin got home. He was still puzzled about his chance meeting at work, and even though he drank rarely, he could not stop from opening an old bottle of *shaojiu* and pouring half the bottle in a warmer on the already lit stove. He was about to pour himself a bit of the warming brew into a small glass when he heard his wife's key in the front door of the apartment.

Lin kissed him on the cheek, immediately smelled the *shaojiu* on the stove, and gave him a funny look. She then went over to their small lounge and picked up their little girl laying upright on a pillow on the two-seater couch, and gave Ling a big hug.

Ling's face lit up when she saw her mother, and baby gurgles escaped from her mouth. Then, with baby Ling in the crook of her arm, Lin returned to her husband who was still by the stove waiting to pour a stiff drink for himself. He took a second glass out of the cupboard, poured his and hers to the brim, looked at her again and drank the glass in one gulp. It didn't take Lin long to follow suit. She knew that this drinking was very unusual for him, and she patiently waited until after dinner to hear what he had to say to her.

Once the little girl was fast asleep and the dishes were done, they sat together, had another stiff drink and Lee told Lin what had happened at work earlier that afternoon.

"And he was the floor cleaner?" she asked Lee, deep in thought. "And he said he went to Ling's school also?" Lee nodded. "I remember an old man ironing shirts—an older man about 40 or 45. I saw him around once or twice and felt that he was watching me. In a laundry, the boss is always watching everyone and this man was ironing shirts, not cleaning the floor. He didn't stay long. He seemed kindly so I smiled at him a few times."

"It must be the same man," suggested Lee. "Was he a good-looking man?"

Lin nodded. "He is offering you a better job? A floor cleaner?" she asked, still trying to understand the logic of this person ironing shirts one week and cleaning floors the next. By this time the *shaojiu* had loosened her up and she cracked a joke. "Maybe he was the floor boss!"

Lee laughed but then got serious again. "Maybe he is secret police or something. Maybe they have made Elvis Presley illegal and I didn't hear about the new law. Maybe I should hide my records."

"Maybe you should hear him out and see what job they are offering you," Lin responded. "It must be a good, well-paying job if they even have to spy on little Ling to see if you are a good child bearer!" She laughed at her own joke and decided that a third drink was in order.

They went to bed that night and both somehow knew that a new destiny had entered their lives. In China that didn't happen to too many people very often. They made passionate love, the hot and lusty alcohol in their veins helping them along, and fell asleep in each other's arms.

At five o'clock the next afternoon, Lee excused himself from his computer to head to the men's room and passed the floor sweeper on the way.

"My wife says that you iron shirts very well but she noticed that you hadn't ironed shirts for too many years," Lee stated as he stopped in front of the man who had his mop in hand.

"Tell your wife that she is correct. And if you notice, I am not a very experienced floor sweeper, either. I talk far too much to strangers walking by," he smiled back.

"We discussed your offer and my wife and I have a few questions we would like answered before I give my answer," Lee continued.

"Well, let's go and have a tea in the cafeteria, and I will be glad to answer them. I know you are fond of green tea," suggested the floor sweeper. He placed the mop back into the bucket, moved it closer to the wall where nobody would fall over it, took off the floor sweeper's long grey jacket, and placed it neatly folded on top of the bucket. Underneath the jacket that had covered his clothing he wore a well-made bluish-colored suit and a beautiful Western-looking gold tie that had small green dragons with small blue stones as eyes. Lee had never seen such beautiful coloring. "Do you know that you passed me for three days in a row and you never saw me?"

"I don't believe a floor sweeper is supposed to be seen by other workers all the time. I'm sure that normal floor sweepers will not see me when I pass them by. They would only have interest in their clean floors, no?"

"Well said, young man," was the response. "People only see what they want to see."

They entered the cafeteria and several managerial-looking officials bowed to the floor sweeper, and their bows were long and deep.

"See the illusion," he explained to Lee, acknowledging the

bows. "That grey jacket would have made me totally invisible to them if I had walked in with it on."

For two hours, the man who never introduced himself told Lee what he wanted to hear. The family would stay united. Yes, they would always travel together. No, his pay raise would not cover his wife becoming a full-time mother, but she could work part-time and it would give her more time with her daughter. Yes, they would move out of their apartment and into a bigger and newer one on the other side of the river only 20 miles away on Chongming Island. Here, his wife Lin could work part-time in a laundry so that she didn't lose the gift of her experience. Yes, Lee would be expected to travel abroad with his family to a new country. The details would be decided later. Yes, he could continue his hobby of astronomy and yes, he could keep his Elvis Presley records.

Then the man needed some questions answered. First, how good was Lee in English? He could read it well and could say several sentences, but he knew all the words from Elvis Presley songs and knew most of the universe and space names in both languages. Lin could only speak a little English, but was a fast learner. How was Lee's knowledge of other countries? Quite good in geography and history, but bad in current affairs, was the answer. This made the older man laugh because this was normal in China; foreign news was a no-no for most Chinese citizens. How up-to-date was he with satellite electronics and modern Western guidance systems? As up-to-date as most scientists and engineers were allowed to be in China, he answered.

"I need to pick up my daughter," stated Lee, suddenly looking at the cafeteria clock and remembering the time. "My wife works late and I must pick her up from daycare every day."

"That has already been done," returned the older man. "Your wife was given time off this afternoon and was asked to pick up your daughter because you would be later than usual. Her boss is a friend of mine."

Suddenly, Lee got worried. "Am I going to be a spy or something?" he asked carefully. "You promised that we would not be in any danger if I took this position."

The older man smiled. "No, you will not be doing anything dangerous," he replied. "You will be in a totally safe environment as long as you do your job in the way you are taught in your training on Chongming Island."

"And who will I be working for?" was Lee's final question.

"Zedong Electronics," was the answer.

* * *

A month later, Lee sat with his wife in their Americanized apartment and opened a small bottle of Jack Daniel's.

"A friend of mine I occasionally have a drink with in the bar, Bo Lee Tang, bought me a glass the other day. He loves the stuff and even showed me a tattoo of a bottle of this whiskey he has on his shoulder. Remember, Lin, he is the boxer I won that money on a few weeks ago?" Lee Wang explained to his wife. "I bought a small bottle for us to try together."

They both smelled the evil-smelling brown liquid for the first time and each drank a small amount. It was vile and horrible stuff! Then Lee opened a new bottle of *shaojiu*, warmed it on the stove, and relaxed with the familiar taste of home. They talked about what might be in their new life. The Wang family had been in their new apartment for two weeks.

The company had sent a truck and gave Lee and his wife a couple of hours to pack their things and leave their old habitat. They were then driven to the ferry, and for the first time for both of them, they watched from the departing ship as the skyline of Shanghai disappeared into the afternoon haze behind them. An hour later, Chongming Island appeared out of the haze off the ferry's bow.

The island was natural and quiet after the city noises, and the same truck drove them over dirt roads for a couple of miles before entering a town they could not believe ever existed—it was like driving into an American magazine. The streets were exactly as they had seen in the occasional American movie or television show. Lee and Lin did not own a television, but with this street scene they didn't need to. Three American-looking streets, with the first traffic lights they had ever seen. The truck stopped in front of what seemed like a courtyard with large double doors and hooted. Once the wooden doors were opened, the truck entered an apartment courtyard. What hit them first was that with five stories of apartments looking down at them, there was not one piece of washing hanging anywhere on the building. Chinese apartment blocks were always draped with drying clothes during the day.

"What did you learn today?" asked Lin, sipping her little warm glass of *shaojiu.*

"The usual schedule of studies," replied Lee. "First was an hour of American English, then an hour of American geography, and then we had 15 minutes for tea. After that, another hour of English and then we were divided into different groups and marched off to laboratories. I was with five other graduates who had studied the same subjects as I did at university; mostly aviation and space electronics. Remember my paper on electrical parts that can be designed to withstand heavy vehicle vibrations, hot engine temperatures, and all climate weather conditions?" Lin nodded. "We were given instructions to take apart a new form of engine-control system for a motor car. It had Japanese on it and the only word I could recognize was "Toyota." It seems to be a new and secret type of engine-management system, controlled by a new form of computer microchip and the electronics controlled the complete workings of every part of the engine every millisecond. It was really fascinating to see the new electronics actually controlling the engine. We didn't study much of this at university, but we did do a crash study on the workings of a combustion engine for Western motor vehicles."

"What do motor car engines have to do with space travel?" Lin asked.

"Nothing," Lee stated. "But it wasn't the workings of the engine control system we were supposed to learn about. We were asked to totally dissect the computer and write down a list of small electrical parts that we could manufacture here in China. In other words, we were told to find the small, important working parts of the electrical brain and write them down so that I think somebody can copy them and make them here at Zedong Electronics."

Lin said nothing.

"That took up the rest of the day and we had the complete gadget broken down in six hours. It is very well-made and I don't know much about car engines but I did learn a lot about how to manage a system using computerized pulses and how a small part of the whole machine—a part the size of the top of a pin—could terminate the workings of the whole unit and make it dormant until that little piece is replaced. I found three simple parts and I wrote them down. Enough about my day, how did your day go?" he asked.

"This laundry system is so modern compared to what I was used to," Lin began. "Everything, as you said, seems to run with some sort of engine. The clothes are washed, pressed, and then hung on a long washing line made of steel. It drives around the shop like a never-ending train. It also has a computer of some sort, and I had my first chance to control it today. There is a computer screen with all the letters and numbers of each piece of clothing, as well as the name of the owner and a code. When the pressed items are put on hangars and placed on the line, the information is entered into the computer on the work side. On the counter service side, another person can enter the person's name and code on the invoice, and the line will automatically move to bring that person's order to the counter where the counter person can pack it into plastic bags. It is so modern compared to what we used at the laundry in Shanghai."

"I think America must be a world of computers and motor engines, and the horse and bicycle must be totally obsolete," added Lee. "I think we made the right decision in coming here." Lee paused for a moment to reflect. "I have not seen the old man since we moved here, but the others say that they were all approached in the same way by different men and women. I also heard that we will be learning the old man's ways of being invisible some day before we leave here."

For the next three months, Lee Wang dissected hundreds of different parts of electronics from all over the world. Many he could not read much about, because they were stamped in languages he didn't understand, but chips, wires, fuses, lights and pulses were part of his language and he didn't need to know where it came from.

One day, however, he got a shock. There on the table in the lab was the same Toyota engine-control system he had seen months earlier. Again he was ordered to take every little piece apart and give a report on what he found. It was the exact same system, and it wasn't difficult to complete his task. The shock he got was that three of the most important electrical-micro control fuses he had listed on the piece of paper months earlier now had "Made in China" stamped on them. The parts were well-made and just as good, or even of a better quality of workmanship, than the original parts. The report then ordered him to open a small bag in the box and replace the parts with extras that he found in there. It surprised him that each extra part had been carefully recorded on a sheet inside the bag, except that somebody had made a slight mistake. There were three small replacement fuses and only two were recorded. His engineering curiosity got the better of him and he slipped the extra fuse into his trouser pocket underneath his white coat. All the tests were done on the control system, and the Chinese parts worked as well as the original Japanese parts had.

At the end of the day, as usual, security police came around and checked each part against the recorded parts, and checked to see that the computer systems were working and complete before they were collected and only then were the employees allowed to leave for the day.

Lee had noticed on his first day that they were being closely watched by a security camera placed in each laboratory, and he had hidden the fuse carefully, away from the only camera in the room. A week went by before he had free time in one of the labs, when the parts had not yet arrived and they were asked to study a new computer chip from a company called 'Intel.' He had studied this chip before and there was nothing more he could add to the information already given to the controllers. He searched carefully in the lining of his white coat and found the fuse he had placed there. Everyone else was busy sitting and bending over working, so he didn't look out of place. With a microscope viewer on his right eye, much like a jeweler looking at a valuable stone, he slowly tried to open the micro-fuse to see what was inside.

It took him a few minutes, but slowly the microscopic inner workings of the simple fuse opened up on the glass slide in front of him. The whole fuse was about the width of a piece of lead found in a pencil, and nobody close to him could have seen what he was doing. Everything was there as he had known it would be, except a small, black carbon-looking dot the size of a pin head. It was stuck to the most vulnerable part of the fuse, and what was weird was that it had a minute antenna sticking out of one side. He turned his microscope up to maximum and looked at the black dot on his slide.

"Whatever this is, it is not supposed to be there," he thought to himself. “It seems to be some sort of fuse control device, and it looks like the device can be activated from external sources—maybe from a radio frequency.” The security guards entered with their daily work—electronic parts to dissect—and he had no choice but to quickly sweep the table with the arm of his coat and onto the floor around him. “I hope the floor sweeper doesn’t have good eyes,” Lee thought to himself, and got on with his work.

* * *

Ten months later, Lee, Lin and Ling found themselves in the largest aircraft Lee had ever seen. The last three months had been eye-opening for Lee. His daily tasks of dissecting gadgets were long gone. Instead, his days were comprised of learning American English and deciphering codes for security doors, computer codes, and everything a spy would need to do. He learned how to take a photo of himself with any form of camera and then take someone else’s photo ID card and replace their photo with his. They practiced on each other’s IDs in the class, and then tried to use the changed ID in dozens of doors, security panels, and card sliders. On computers, he was given new CDs with code decipher programs on them so they could try to unlock their college workstations. He spent a couple of days with his wife learning to press shirts and trousers, and mopped floors with an old grey coat on. He was taught how to look older by graying his hair, and smaller by hunching his back and letting his shoulders droop down as he mopped. He was taught how to flip meat patties and add cheese, lettuce, tomatoes and pickles to a vile-smelling hamburger and operate a milkshake machine. And lastly, he was taught how to bus tables in a restaurant and satisfy snotty American customers to the point that they didn’t even notice him take their plates.

To Lin, it was funny to see her husband and a few others

arrive at her place of work and try to control the computerized clothing hangers as well as she could. She taught them how to press and wash and disappear in a laundry by doing things without being asked.

"I hear you can sweep floors as good as I can," stated the woman, as Lee passed a floor cleaner in the hallway one day. Lee was not going to be fooled again, as he now carefully studied any floor cleaner before he passed them. He had seen this woman for the whole week, and today was Friday and time to collect his weekly paycheck. This floor sweeper, he thought, was a little shorter than the one he was checking for, but this floor sweeper was a woman and that fact had put him off his guard from the second day. She looked about 65-70 years old and had long, straight black hair. They had practiced hunch-backing in their training, but this floor sweeper was a woman, had a thick waist, long grey hair, and did not look like she was trying to fool anyone.

Lee stopped in shock and did not want to turn around. "Is that you?" he asked.

"A woman can always get away with more than a man can," was the reply from the familiar voice he had been checking for the whole year.

Lee turned around and was shocked at the disguise.

"Hide more skin and it takes less work," continued the man. "A wig, a blanket around my waist, a fixed ID badge, a grey coat, a mop and bucket and a closed mouth can get me anywhere I want to go. Remember, your Chinese eyes are your advantage in America, Lee Wang. Show them and cover your lower face with a shawl and very few will ask questions in a low-security building. As you have been taught, high security is much harder, but the only real difference is time. If people are used to you, they will become blind to you. Now let's go and get a cup of tea. Your time here is over."

Lee watched the man take off the wig, the grey coat, and the small wrapped blanket around his waist; put the bucket, mop, wig and clothing neatly on the bucket; stand up; and pull a comb out of his blue suit pocket to comb his black hair. As usual, there were the familiar bows when he entered the American-style cafeteria on the ground floor.

"You are to live in America starting next week," stated the older man. "You have been trained to seek out new electrical inventions or products about to come onto the market in all forms of electronics. We want to break these new consumer goods or military goods down and start making parts for them. Your jobs for us are reasonably safe. Always remember that the Americans believe that they are the biggest world power and nobody can infiltrate their security and systems. They are careful about other companies trying to steal their secrets, but a foreign man who doesn't speak their language and who can always disappear will never be seen as a threat."

The older man paused for a moment to give Lee a minute to digest the information before continuing. "You will be given papers to start your legal arrival process into the United States. If you follow the guidelines, you will become a citizen within five to seven years. You will be given $2,000 in American currency to help you get settled in the United States. You will arrive in San Francisco and then travel by bus to the home of American software engineering called Silicon Valley. The closest city is San Jose. Someone will meet you at the airport by the taxi pool. He will guide you to transportation to San Jose where there is an area called Cupertino Village. Book into a cheap hotel room and search out a small apartment you can afford near Cupertino Village. From there you are on your own, so just disappear for a few weeks. Don't worry, you will be surrounded by other Chinese nationals and everything you need can be found in Cupertino, or in San Francisco's Chinatown. Both of you will have work visas and you, Lee, must find a job in any electronics company as soon as you can. Your wife will find something to suit her."

"But my main job is to spy?" interrupted Lee.

"No, of course not," replied the older man. "Your job is to seek out new electronics. Once you think you have found something like... remember the engine-control system from Toyota?"

Lee nodded.

"If you find something like that, we want a copy. You phone the person you met at the airport and tell him what you've found, where it is, what security there is in the building, how he can get in, and any problems he might come up against. He will do the rest of the work. That gives you the opportunity to carry on safely and seek out your next object. Do you understand?"

Again Lee nodded.

The man continued. "For every good piece of equipment you find for us, $1,000 will be deposited into a bank account for your daughter Ling's university education in America."

"A person must pay for university in America?" Lee questioned in awe.

For another hour, Lee was grilled on what was expected of him. Silently, he worked out in his mind that based on the information the older man had just given him, he needed to find at least 50 new inventions or gadgets for Zedong Electronics over about 15 years to pay for Ling's university education in the United States.

Now, Lee was ready to go to America.

CHAPTER 6

The Smart Family

WILL SMART WAS A career detective with the L.A.P.D. and the Hollywood Police Department, and it was his last day, and the last day of July, in the surroundings in which he had spent the last ten years working. A few months earlier, he had filed a request to be transferred to the Lancaster Police Department north of Los Angeles. The Smart family had recently moved out of downtown L.A. and purchased a house in growing Antelope Acres—a more rural community north of Los Angeles, south of the city of Lancaster, and not far from Edwards Air Force base.

The Smarts were tired of the day-to-day crime in the city, even though they lived slightly north in San Fernando. Will had worked long and hard since he had been promoted to the detective branch in 2007. It had been fine for a while, living in the never-ending grind of L.A. His wife, Maggie, was doing her final year at UCLA and studying for her Ph.D. The kids went to a reasonably good and safe public school in San Fernando, and life was average for this Californian family.

It had not been difficult to get a transfer out of the city since the LAPD were also contracted to run the Lancaster Police Department. All he was asking for was a transfer within the same system, but just to another area.

A farewell party was in full swing and he thanked many of his colleagues who had gone through the same promotions and grinds of the daily and often dangerous workload with him. Even his Chief was there and who, within the ranks, was not known to be a friendly guy. Will and Chief Bennett lived in the same community in San Fernando, and were part of only a small minority of African-Americans in the area. San Fernando had an African-American population of less than 2%. Over time, they had commuted together into work and had developed a form of friendship. Will actually thought the Chief was going to miss him.

In November 2008, Will's father had passed away. He had been diagnosed with a cancer he did not often talk about, and lived alone in Burbank after the passing of Will's mother ten years earlier. Will was an only child, and naturally inherited the family's net wealth of over a million dollars. His father and mother had worked in Hollywood on movie sets for decades—he as a carpenter and she as a seamstress—and both had met, married, and done well for themselves.

Will had actually been introduced to several film stars, and his favorite had been John Wayne, whom he had met a couple of times. The famous star had even come over for dinner once when he was young and had made a large impact on young Will's life. Of course, after that dinner, the young boy's favorite movie was "Brannigan."

A young Will had grown up in Hollywood, survived school, gotten his diploma, and entered the police force as soon as he was able. All his life he had loved to solve puzzles and problems, and with his totally analytical brain, he was quickly nicknamed "Smart Dude" on the police force. In 2005, all police officers had completed a "DUDE" program. "DUDE" had stood for Diligence, Undercover, Detective work, and Education, and was meant to help the average policeman on the beat look at a new crime scene and memorize all surrounding information before the scene was entered by other official personnel. Small bits of evidence were often lost between the discovery of the crime and the arrival of the teams who sifted for information. Will had excelled in this, and his photographic memory always remembered the necessary "DUDE" tasks, like possible tire marks, cigarette butts, people's faces in the surrounding crowd, odors, and anything that looked amiss. Even the police chief called him "Smart Dude" because several homicides had been solved by the clicking memory of Will Smart.

Maggie was and always would be a "computer whiz." That's what her father called her at the age of 15, growing up just outside Dana Point on the West coast an hour south of Los Angeles. Her father Pete and mother Joanne Bridges were business owners, and ran a gas station close to the highway between L.A. and San Diego.

In 1986, new home computers were the "in" thing. BASIC was a new language, and it hadn't taken young Maggie long to learn the new language and become able to write new code to make programs run faster or just fix them when they broke. The television-like screens played simple computer games; her favorite was Tetris.

Both parents worked hard and Maggie and her baby sister Joanna were usually at home after the yellow school bus dropped them off. Pete and Joanne got home at about six, once their night crew of two employees arrived. Joanne worked on dinner while Pete spent valuable time checking his daughters' homework and getting them ready for the next day's school bus.

It was a very happy house. They lived in a decent rural neighborhood on a large lot with only three other houses on a dirt road they called a street, and only heard the continuous highway noise when the wind blew in the right direction. Both girls were at the top of their classes at school and Joanne always told visiting friends that they both had their parents' brains in the right amounts. The gas station had been in the family for 40 years and Pete's father had originally built the wooden structure in the mid-1950s. He had retired early and wanted Pete to run it, so he sold it to his elder son for $50 and retired to St. Croix in the U.S. Virgin Islands, where he had grown up as a child.

The young family never had time to visit the islands after the purchase, but Pete's father and mother often came to visit and to check up on them and the gas station every couple of years. The old-fashioned gas station had a country store on one side, a porch on the front, and only two gas pumps. It was painted in rich, bright colors, and by the 1980s it was a landmark famous for its originality in the surrounding area of modern developments.

A bell always sounded when someone drove in, just like the old days, and now with everything going electronic, even that had lost a little of its old charm. The country store made the most income, selling old-fashioned bottles and jars of produce made by local people—salsas, sauces, cakes, cookies, beer from microbreweries just starting up in the area and everything else a modern farmers' market would sell. Pete and Joanne made a very comfortable living from the business. Pete's mother made sure that they never ran out of homemade products from St. Croix, and the clothing, trinkets and hot sauces were always big sellers.

Maggie easily obtained her high school diploma, and with the aid of a three-year scholarship she had won in a computer software competition in 1990, she entered UCLA as a freshman majoring in electrical engineering. She found dorm life at the university to be rather close and noisy after growing up in the country. She looked down at people who thought drugs and alcohol were important and was called the class snob for keeping her nose in the air most of the time.

In her third year, she won a second one-semester scholarship in a Pepsi competition and was able to spend a fully paid-for term at MIT across the country in Boston during her senior year.

At MIT, life was more old-fashioned compared to the "plastic" Los Angeles life, as she called it. The school was so much older, and the students much more conservative. She was pleased to be in a room with three beds, a bathroom, and a small lounge/ kitchen with two other girls—both from completely different backgrounds.

Roommate Sally Powers always seemed on high alert, always in strike mode, and in much like "a cat looking for a rat" mode. Maggie's other roommate, Martie Roebels, was a very tall, long-legged blonde who was easy to befriend. All three girls liked each other immediately and a long-lasting friendship sprang up in the four months they lived together. Boys were out, as were binge drinking, parties, and unnecessary time off from studying. Study they did and they enjoyed every minute of it.

All three were fascinated with their studies, all three attended the same classes, and all three visited the local airfield for the first time a week or two after the beginning of the semester when both Sally and Martie felt a need to touch a joystick. Maggie was dumbfounded about "joysticks," and had a totally wrong idea about "joysticks" until the other two arrived at the airport. Laughing, they explained to their young African-American friend that she had the wrong joystick in mind and that yes, they were at an airport, and that yes, they were going flying. It was a fun joke at Maggie's expense, and she thumped both girls on the arm when she realized the trick they had played on her.

The look on Maggie's face in the rear seat as Martie taxied the Cessna 172 out onto the runway with Sally as co-pilot for their first flight was priceless. With both girls keeping an eye on the rear seat, they slowly watched as Maggie's reaction went slowly from shock and surprise to that look when a person realizes that life is a beautiful thing. It was over the town of Gloucester, north of Boston, when Maggie's face first turned serene while viewing the sea several hundred feet below them and sunbathers looking up at them from small beaches here and there. There wasn't much said during the first flight, each girl enjoying their own surroundings.

They landed and had lunch in the flight school's small cafeteria and all three again sat in silence, both pilots waiting for words to burst forth from the new flyer.

"I want to hold a joystick!" the still dreamy-looking Maggie finally exclaimed, and all three girls erupted into laughter.

That afternoon, on their second flight, Maggie and Martie swapped places while Sally flew in the left seat. Slowly, and much like her instructor had allowed her to fly the aircraft for the first time so many years ago, Sally taught Maggie and let her have control of the joystick between her legs. Once she had control of the joystick, her feet were allowed to control the two rudder pedals and Maggie's fate was doomed forever—she was totally hooked on flying—so much so that their only outside activity, other than studying, was driving out to the airfield and flying as much as possible. Martie was certainly not short on cash, nor were Sally and Maggie.

Maggie had 47 hours and a new private pilot's license by the end of their semester together. Martie had completed her twin-engine instrument flight-rating (IFR) and added another 40 hours to her logbook, and Sally had managed her first ten hours on a twin turboprop aircraft, a King Air. Sally was two years ahead of Martie, but who cared! Martie had often promised Sally that she would catch up with Sally's flight ratings, but she never could.

The semester came to an end and tears flowed as the three girls parted, all three with the best results achievable. They made a pact on their last night to always communicate and visit each other and the girls went their separate ways far stronger, far more mature, and far more open to life than when they had arrived at MIT four months earlier.

Maggie returned to UCLA, and it wasn't long before a police detective came knocking on the family's door one night. There had been a murder somewhere in Hollywood and Detective Smart wanted camera footage from the gas station. Since it was 9:00 pm at night, he was directed by the night staff to the owner's house to get permission. The police detective was young and extremely good-looking, Maggie noticed, and she watched his serious discussion with her father with a hint of amusement on her face.

"The tapes I would like to view, sir, are from Monday last week," continued the police detective. "Let's say from Monday midnight to Wednesday, also around midnight. That's 48 hours of tape. If the black SUV we are looking for ever stopped at your gas station for anything, it would have been within that 48-hour period. Can we zoom in and see license tags with your cameras?"

"Yes," replied Pete. "We installed the more powerful cameras because we thought it would be valuable if we ever got robbed. Our store and gas station has never been robbed in the 40 years it's been there," Maggie's father stated proudly.

"Some sort of record, sir," replied Detective Smart. "It's not often we find any location in L.A. that hasn't had a problem of some sort in the last several years. You must have a lot of guardian angels around here." Will Smart turned, noticing that he was being watched by the station owner's daughter. It took him only a split second to give her the professional once over and like what he saw. "Detective Will Smart, LAPD, ma'am," he said, nodding to her with a straight face.

"Ms. Maggie Bridges, student of electrical engineering at UCLA, sir," replied the girl, nodding back and copying the way Will had introduced himself to her. Will was suddenly at a loss as to what to do with this young lady looking straight into his official detective eyes without blinking once, chin forward, showing off her toughness. As is usual for men when they have suddenly met their match, he tried to backtrack and gather grace by changing the subject.

"If you don't mind, sir, I could get a black and white to stop by the gas station in the morning and pick up the tapes."

"No problem, Detective," replied Pete with a slight grin on his face, understanding that the poor policeman was having an internal problem with the straightforwardness of his elder daughter. "I'll have them ready to be picked up by 9:00 am tomorrow morning." The detective bowed slightly, thanked the family, and left through the front door.

It just so happened that Maggie had the next day free from school and was helping in the store when an unmarked car drew up outside at exactly 9:00 the next morning and none other than Detective Will Smart got out and entered the gas station. His face showed signs of pleasure when he noticed that what he had hoped and come all the way out again for was there. It had been a very short introduction the night before, but somehow he knew that he was going to see her again, and there she was.

That morning, without thinking anything about it, Maggie drove her mother to work. Her father always left at 7:00 am, but Joanne always fussed over Joanna in the mornings, even though she was in her last year of high school and sometimes missed riding in to work with Pete. Pete usually returned for Joanne later if Maggie didn't bring her mother to the gas station on the way to school.

"Detective Will Smart, LAPD. Good morning, ma'am," he stated a little sarcastically to Maggie as he entered the store.

"Still the same Maggie Bridges as last night, just having a free day from campus, sir," replied Maggie in the same sarcastic manner as he had.

"I'm here to pick up the tapes your father said would be ready at 9:00 am, ma'am," Will continued.

"They are all here in the box, Detective Will Smart, LAPD," was her still sarcastic reply. "Do you want to sign for them?"

"Of course... Would you... um... like to meet for a coffee some time downtown?" was his answer, looking her straight in the eyes like she had with him the previous evening.

"If you will stop calling me ma'am, I might consider it," was her reply, not blinking or averting her eyes from his gaze.

"Of course!" he said, for the second time in three seconds. "What do I call you, then?"

"Maggie is what you call me, and 454-4747 is where you call me, Detective Will Smart, LAPD. I will be back on campus tomorrow."

Still feeling uncomfortable, the detective signed for and picked up the box, nodded to Maggie's mother behind the counter, then to Maggie, and carefully backed out of the store.

"Shame on you, Maggie," laughed her mother. "You scared the bejeezus out of that young boy! He's surely not going to phone you after all that!"

"If he's got a big joystick and instrument panel, he'll call," Maggie replied to her mother, walking off to the rear of the store. Her mother's face went quite white upon hearing her daughter's reply.

"I don't know what you learned at that MIT University," admonished her mother, holding a hand up to her mouth. "But it sure wasn't decent English."

"I was learning about engineering, Mother, and how to fly airplanes."

It took Detective Smart a couple of days to pluck up the courage to call, and he was pleasantly surprised at how nice she was once they got over the initial few minutes in the coffee shop. They were married nearly a year later and she moved into his small rented apartment in San Fernando.

In February 2009, Will and Maggie had fallen in love with the drier, desert-type life in Antelope Hills north of L.A., and they paid cash for a decent-sized, newly-built ranch house on three acres a couple of months later. It hadn't been cheap, but compared to renting the small townhouse with a 10-foot by 10-

foot garden in San Fernando, this larger house and yard felt like a more independent way of life to them. It was also surrounded by noisy aircraft of all sorts flying overhead. Three airports were in the near vicinity, including Edwards Air Force Base. This satisfied Maggie, since she wanted to continue her flying hobby, something Will certainly did not like.

Maggie's MIT roommate Martie Roebels visited them for Christmas in 2009, flying into Fox Field—another commercial airport close by—in a beautiful old DC-3 with two friends: Buck, who owned the old bird and his current girlfriend, Chloe. They flew in a few days before Christmas with Christmas presents from the East Coast. Mother Christmas Martie had even dressed herself in a Santa's hat and coat for the landing and reunion with her old pal.

Martie had wanted to visit her old friend from MIT for a couple years now and had brought several gifts for the new "Smart Dude Ranch." Martie's boyfriend, Preston, was a specialist in engines and had rebuilt an old three-cylinder car engine as a power plant for their new ranch as a house-warming gift. Martie had asked him to do it and paid for the old engine that they found on a farm in South Carolina. It was from a 1936 delivery truck and was nearly the same-size engine that Preston had built for his own hangar a couple of years earlier. It used only a gallon and a half of gas per day to provide enough electricity for a small to medium-sized house. At nearly $3.00 a gallon for gas, it would halve the Ranch's average electric bill.

With the engine, Preston had set up a system of a dozen large marine batteries that would store and run the day-to-day needs of a house. The Smarts' new house had already come with several batteries, an inverter, and a small solar system on the roof like those sold with many houses in California, but Preston had done his homework to perfect their system and purchased several more solar panels and batteries from a friend. On paper, he had designed a complete package for the "Smart Dude Ranch" that could bring down the gas consumption to a gallon, or less, per day.

With the batteries, panels, and engine, the DC-3 had carried an old farm-style 200-gallon gas tank Preston had purchased from a local farmer who didn't need it, and had separated the legs to fit through the DC-3's double cargo door. It was a great Christmas present and the Smart family would save a lot of money and could even make a few dollars selling unused electricity to their local grid.

Maggie Smart was very interested in the old DC-3, and once the new system had been unloaded, she was invited to co-pilot the old machine to the coast—out to Catalina Island and back, over Santa Barbara, with all aboard. Maggie was the only one of her ex-MIT roommates who did not yet own an airplane, but with Will's inheritance still not all spent, she was working on her husband to get her something cheap, fun, and old to fly. Will, on the other hand, did not like flying at all, and could not understand his wife's passion for leaving terra firma.

Christmas of 2009 was a fun affair at the "Ranch." Martie spoke to Preston and Carlos in North Carolina with Ben Smart's ham radio. Will's son, Ben, was an avid enthusiast, and this had been the way the friends had communicated for a couple of years now. Ben Smart had received his used, yet powerful, radio for Christmas in 2007.

Due to incoming weather problems, the DC-3 left on the morning after Christmas for its return flight back to Denver where Buck kept her. They took off in heavy fog and broke into beautiful, warm sunshine at 1,000 feet. They flew into Denver, left *Lady Dandy* in her hangar and completed the rest of the trip back to North Carolina in the Huey.

Buck was fascinated with the quality of workmanship and electrical design on the old truck engine, and after thinking about it on the flight home, he ordered one of his own through

Martie. He lived in a small house on Long Island and liked the idea of nearly-free electricity.

"I think Preston has four or five really big Man diesel truck-engine generators he completed a few years back," Martie reflected, sitting in the right-hand pilot's seat of the Huey and accepting a steaming hot cup of thermos coffee from Chloe, behind her. "They each weigh a ton and are tuned to put out a tremendous amount of power. They could light up a couple of city blocks."

"I'm sure," said Buck. "Those old big truck diesels are very powerful, but I bet they use a couple of gallons of fuel per day at full output."

"About 20 gallons a day, actually, and with diesel at over $3.00 a gallon, they are pretty expensive to run," replied Martie. "He did them one by one. His neighbor Joe had several old trucks from his father's trucking days and offered them to Preston over the years. We don't need these massive generators, but Preston is Preston and when one is finished, he starts another one."

"I think they are a little big for my 1,000 square feet of house," laughed Buck. "But, I'll remember the information and maybe a larger building or company might be interested in them."

"I'm sure they'll just sit in our old barn forever and ever," sighed Martie. "But if you know anybody who might need them as a backup system, let us know. I hate to see them go to waste. I offered one of them to Carlos' observatory on top of the mountain in Salt Lake City last year, but he got a lackluster response from management. All I had asked for it was $15,000 to cover the initial cost and the time Preston spent on them."

It took Maggie Smart a couple hundred dollars and a few weeks of work with her husband, but by the end of January 2009, the "Smart Dude Ranch" had its own power and a full 200-gallon tank of gas standing on its tripod legs next to their small barn. Will was quite impressed with the whole set-up and was even more so when they received their first check for a couple of hundred dollars back from the power company a few weeks later.

Maggie still had to travel into LA to UCLA, but managed to cut her weekly commutes down to three days a week for lectures and worked online to finally complete her Ph.D. in electrical engineering in November of that year. Will also now had a much shorter commute into Lancaster and, with far less crime in the more rural area, managed to spend more time at home than he ever did in his old precinct.

Ben and his twin sister Oprah got on well at their new school and their grades improved to A's during their first year. Oprah Smart was much like her mother. She helped enthusiastically with anything related to electronics and was her mother's right-hand woman in putting the final touches on their new electrical system. Oprah loved playing with the hardware on computers and her Dad proudly stated to his colleagues down at the station every time they had a car stolen that he hoped it wasn't his daughter, because she could hotwire "anything from a lawn mower to an aircraft carrier."

With Ben and Oprah interested in much of the same things, they were a team to be reckoned with. They studied Preston Strong's workmanship on the engine rebuild and tried to copy it with a Briggs and Stratton lawn mower engine. Preston never used any electrical systems in his work, but used engine-balance to allow the engine to work with as little effort as possible and produce more energy with less consumption. They used their pocket money and purchased three old John Deere lawn mowers in a one-lot auction from the local county surplus agency, and their rebuilt units worked well after a couple of upgrades. All three engines had a lot less power than the three-cylinder, 33-horsepower truck engine, and all drank a little more fuel. Two of their close neighbors each purchased an engine, which included several solar panels, a newly purchased wind power generator, several new deep-cycle batteries, a grid inverter, and complete installation for $15,000. Both kids made $1,000 each for each sale and they used those funds to add two 1,500-watt wind generators to their own system, which cut down the need for their engine to only excessive winter and summer usage.

In October, Maggie finally persuaded her husband to buy her a small plane. With only a couple hundred thousand left from his inheritance, he gave her $70,000 to buy a Cessna 172. It was really a graduation gift for finishing her degree at UCLA and in celebration of her new job with a local electronics company in Simi Valley. Her salary starting in the New Year far outpaced his meager one with the police department.

Maggie's next wish was to visit her other MIT roommate, Sally Powers. Sally had been transferred to Yuma, Arizona, with the Air Force. She was transitioning from C-130s to an F-16 fighter jet—Sally's dream aircraft since childhood. It was a short trip of around 250 miles, but in a slow Cessna 172, any flight can quickly turn into a long one with severe headwinds. Maggie's old 172 had an average cruising speed of 105 mph, but she made it there and back and enjoyed the solo experience.

Sally stayed with the Smarts for the long July 4th weekend in 2010. She had already spent a month at the Marine Air Corps Base in Yuma when she managed to hitch a ride up to Nellis Air Force Base in Las Vegas and then to Edwards with her old colleges in one of her old section's C-130s.

"Okay, you are Air Force, but you are training at a Marine Corps air base?" Will asked at dinner on her first night with them.

"Asking questions as usual, Will Smart," laughed Sally. She knew the Smarts well and always waited for Maggie's husband's questions on everything out of the ordinary. "I knew you were going to ask me that," she continued. "The Air Force owned the base in 1956. It was named Vincent Air Force Base. It was deactivated in 1959 by the Air Force and handed over to the Navy, if I have the story right. Remember, I've only been there a month. The Navy changed its mind about owning the base and offered it to the Marine Corps, and they have been in command ever since. Last year, the Air Force wanted to use the massive air-to-ground weapon ranges outside Yuma for training. We are getting some sort of new electronically-guided missiles later this year and the Air Command wanted the training away from Nellis Air Force Base in Las Vegas, for some reason. I think there is a specific difference in ground terrain between what they have at Vincent and what they have at Nellis. I don't mind, though, 'cause Yuma is smaller, the Marines keep to themselves, and they've given us our own area with hangars. We hardly mix with them. I think it's only for a couple of years and it looks like I'll complete my flight training at Vincent."

"Will, sometimes you do not need to know," Maggie admonished her husband. "I'm sure Sally can't tell us too much without getting into trouble."

"It's not a secret that our F-16s are based at Vincent," laughed Sally. "It's just not very important. There is a fun bar in town and the local folk are very friendly. Also, flying over the area last winter in the slower C-130s, I was surprised at how many RVs there were around Yuma. I flew over a small town north of Yuma called Quartzite several times last winter, and the desert around that one-horse town was full of luxury motor homes. There must have been thousands there."

"Where's Quartzite?" asked Ben.

"Just over the California-Arizona border on the Arizona side and directly south of Lake Havasu," answered Sally. "I flew up yesterday to Nellis and we passed to the west of the town. It was beautifully clear and I couldn't see an RV anywhere. The heat in that desert must have been well over 105 degrees yesterday."

"I'm sure the RV snowbirds find the area warmer in the winter than up north," added Will.

Didn't you want to do your training at Nellis?" asked Maggie. "You said last time you visited... when was that... Christmas 2008... that you were expecting to be at Nellis?"

"The changes were pretty recent and I only knew that I would be stationed at Vincent a couple of months ago. I was expecting Nellis, yes."

"So tell me, pilot-girl, how is the F-16 to fly?" Maggie asked the question she had wanted to ask ever since Sally had arrived.

One word – "*WOW!*" was the reply. "Take off is a little difficult up to air-control speed, and the air movement is active around the aircraft, but once she is airborne, she turns into a rocket."

"A little faster than a C-130?" asked Oprah.

"Like a hare and a tortoise," laughed Sally. "I can see why the male pilots love flying these babies. It's like a drug fix. I don't think I could fly anything else for awhile."

After dinner, they all gathered around Ben's ham radio and spoke with friends across the country. Martie and Preston were happy to hear of Sally's visit to the "Smart Dude Ranch." It was about to get dark and already 9:00 pm on the east coast. Preston told them that he wanted to visit soon, but they all knew that he was busy with his own aircraft rebuild and probably would not make it for some time. Carlos came online, happy to hear Sally's voice. He was in Salt Lake City atop his mountain doing computer work and waiting for nightfall, which was still a couple of hours away, so that he could look at the stars.

Buck was on Long island and got on the radio a few minutes after everyone else. *"Sorry, guys,"* stated Buck. *"Traffic out of Manhattan was just as bad as usual, even though it's a long weekend. I suppose there was more traffic out to Long Island for the weekend."*

"Hey, Lee Wang?" Everybody heard Carlos shout to someone in the observatory. *"How come you're cleaning tonight? Shouldn't you be off for the long weekend?"* They heard a

response, but could not hear what the answer was. *"Sorry, guys,"* continued Carlos. *"I thought I would be alone up here this weekend, but our cleaning guy is working. Somebody must have forgotten to tell him not to come in. I don't mind, though. He seems to love astronomy and I think he works extra hours so I'll let him look through the telescope every now and then."*

"How's your rocketry?" Buck asked Sally.

"Jealousy will get you nowhere, Mr. McKinnon. You should have joined the Air Force and flown real airplanes," was the reply. There was laughter from all listening.

"Don't expect a free ride in Lady Dandy," returned Buck, knowing that he was actually jealous of Sally's new toy.

"Jets are jets," added Carlos who had a jet license himself. *"Just a fancy computer you take off in and put down again when the gas runs out."*

"What's wrong with you men!" interrupted Martie. *"Can't take it when a girl has a faster airplane than you guys?"*

"Well said, Martie!" added Maggie.

"You all are a bunch of flying nuts," added Will. "They shouldn't have invented flying. If God wanted men, or women in my wife's case, to fly, he would have given all of you wings."

"Now, now, Will," stated Martie again from North Carolina, joking. *"At least we have a hobby. It's safe, fun, and keeps us out of jail—just a few less for you cops to put up with."*

"Real men have wings, other men just have arms and flap around all day," added Buck.

"Harrow!" came a foreign voice over the radios, and the resulting silence was instantaneous.

"Who's that?" asked Will and Maggie together.

"Harrow, fellow Americans," said the strange voice again, and this time Carlo's laughter could be heard in the background.

"Hey, guys, this is my astronomy buddy, Lee Wang," said Carlos.

"Hi, Lee," everyone answered in broken unison.

"I had a buddy in L.A. called Lee Wang," added Will Smart. "He cleaned my desk everyday at the precinct."

"Lee Wang, common name in China," added Carlos' friend. *"I clean lavatory in observatory."* Everyone broke into laughter at the way Lee rhymed his words. *"I, friend of Carlos from South America. He lets me look at the stars when he has spare time."*

"He's a good man and loves his stargazing," added Carlos. *"He has an incredible knowledge of the planets for a cleaner. I always tell him that he should have studied in China before he arrived here. His daughter is currently attending university in San Francisco. She is in her third year of law. Guess what, guys? Lee used to work at 1 Infinite Loop in Cupertino."*

"Where's that?" asked Will.

"Apple Headquarters," was the choired reply.

"Just south of San Francisco," added Lee. *"Before that I cleaned at Microsoft headquarters for five years."*

"Bloody Mary!" exclaimed Preston. *"Now you're going to tell us you've met Bill Gates and Steve Jobs?"*

There was silence on the airwaves as everybody waited.

"Mr. Gates and Mr. Jobs don't speak to cleaners," was the reply. *"But they often passed me in the corridors. So now I must clean Honaarable Mr. Rodreeequiz's lavatory in this observatory if I want to see my stars tonight. Good method for telling me horserace winners for tomorrow. Bye, friends of friend."*

Laughter and goodbyes were echoed from all listening. Even Oprah and Ben laughed at Lee Wang's clever use of the English language.

All continued chatting for another half an hour until Maggie stated that dinner, west-coast time, was ready and that the communication was about to end. Goodbyes and Happy Fourth of July's were called out by all, with Preston asking Buck to stay on the radio. The others turned off their sets or left them on "low receive."

The old friends at the Smart Dude Ranch had a great

weekend chatting and catching up. Sally was impressed with the Smart's new house and said that she would fly up and visit every chance she had while stationed on the West Coast—especially since she never knew where she would be next, with most of the U.S. military already deployed in several parts of the world and nobody very happy about it.

CHAPTER 7

The Beginning of the Lead-up to Midnight

THE UNDERLYING PROBLEM for the United States was that the country's armed forces were not winning in the fight against terrorism. In addition to this, a knowledgeable President was about to leave the White House, and a new inexperienced one was about to take over.

The recession that had started in late 2008 had finally disappeared by late 2011, but the current President had been blamed for the bad times that had actually begun during the previous administration. Politics was never fair in the good old USA. In 2011, gas prices went up to over $5.00 a gallon for most of the summer and led many to use other sources of energy in motor vehicles, including even electricity.

Ben and Oprah Smart visited Preston Strong's farm for their summer vacation that year. Maggie spent all the time she had off from her company with them, flying them there and back in the recently upgraded Cessna 210 she had invested in. The flight had taken three days each way, with five refueling airports carefully preplanned, and Will had stayed at work grumbling about how the rich and famous (his family) had the freedom to just fly around the country anytime they saw fit. And there was no way he was getting into one of those metal birds—no way!

Preston and Martie were excited to have Maggie and the kids around, and Preston, Ben, and Oprah spent their 10 week visit fixing up all the old engines they could find and turning them into home-electrical power plants. The young Smarts had orders for another five complete units with neighbors living in Antelope Acres, and because electricity costs had also skyrocketed, a gallon or two of $5.00 gas per day to run one of their engines was still a decent savings on electricity for a medium- to large-size house. The neighbors were now eager for the "Smart Electricity Units" being built by 13-year old Ben and Oprah Smart.

Sally Powers was happy flying in Yuma. She was due to finish her flight training in F-16s in 2012 and had already been given her marching orders. Her wing was going to deploy out of the country in February 2013, and she was rather excited to be going on active duty. She had acquired her new aircraft and had done most of her flight training on it. She was also looking forward to flying her newly purchased Pilatus across country to Preston's farm to attend the friendly fly-in over Christmas and the New Year. She had a month's leave coming up at the end of November and wanted to spend time with her friend Maggie in California and then fly over to North Carolina after that. Maggie was trying to get some time off, and was working on persuading her husband to fly with her and the kids to North Carolina to attend the fly-in in her smaller 210, but she was not going to win.

Buck was living with Barbara Wright on Long Island. They had only met a month earlier, and she was already sleeping in his bed when she was in town, which was pretty often. She had put her house up for sale in Flagstaff and was trying to get end-of-year extra leave with the Arizona Aviation company she flew for to attend the fly-in with Buck.

Buck didn't know whether it was he or the Huey that the girls really went crazy over, but he didn't really care. Before meeting Barbara, he hadn't known how pleasurable it could be to be with the same woman in bed and this redhead kept him completely exhausted when she was in town. Apart from flying Buck, she also flew the Huey with the expertise a very experienced pilot could put into any flying aircraft. Even though she was still completing helicopter-flight training, she was a natural.

Martie was happy to hear that her father would be flying her aging grandfather over from the west coast for Christmas and the fly-in. She found out a month before Christmas and sent Preston into a tail spin. He was just finishing up installing the Hispano cannon he had purchased online several months earlier in his beloved P-38 Lightning, when Martie reminded him that they only had beds for three visitors and there could be as many as 10 if the whole Smart family made it.

The next day, Preston looked around the hangar, and apart from the aircraft that belonged there, he saw hundreds and hundreds of metal and wooden boxes of .50-caliber ammunition rounds for the 16 machine guns he and Martie owned in their two P-51 Mustangs and his P-38 Lightning. She often joked over dinner that they must be the richest machine-gun owners in the entire world. Carlos also had a Mustang, and he had shipped another 20,000 rounds of his ammo for storage at the Strong Farm.

Preston has purchased the World War II Hispano cannon for $30,000, which included another ton of cannon ammo in old wooden boxes. He suddenly realized "If somebody puts a couple of rounds into this hangar, there won't be much farm left. The whole place will go up like a military munitions dump! We'd better not tell anybody, or we'll be run out of town!"

Then he looked inside the large bedroom he often used when he and Oliver were alone and suddenly remembered. "I'm also getting a dozen dummy 500-pound bombs next week. That should scare the life out of anyone staying here, even though they are only wooden dummies. Where can I put those?"

It took Martie and Preston a day or so to figure it all out. Martie knew a friend at work who owned an old gas-operated forklift. She drove into work in the old 1980 Ford big block farm truck the next day and got the forklift loaded onto its bed. The farm had an old cattle loading ramp that was nothing more than an ancient heap of hardened rock, and she and Preston managed to off-load the forklift and move the ammo out of the hangar. There was an old red barn about 50 yards on the other side of the runway where Preston stored his Man engines and other bits and pieces. Preston usually only went in it when necessary, since it had begun to lean very slightly to one side over the last few years.

On closer inspection, however, the couple found it to be sound and pretty watertight. The wooden floor looked quite clean and without much water damage. Three of the four barn doors on each end still worked, and the fourth one was permanently sealed in a closed position. It was perfect to serve as the farm's new temporary munitions dump for the upcoming festivities. Moving the ammunition was pretty tiring work, as the boxes of rounds weighed over five tons, but when it was finished, the hangar looked more spacious and could fit one more aircraft in a squeeze.

"How much do these wooden dummy bombs weigh?" Martie asked as they took a break and opened two cold Yuenglings.

"I forgot to ask, but they are coming in on a large and closed 18-wheel delivery truck, so I think they must weigh 500 lbs. or more each," replied Preston, downing half his bottle of beer. "Their specially-made connectors have been designed to fit under all four of our aircraft since they all have the same bomb-connector systems."

"How is the Lightning's bombsite looking?" Martie asked.

"I've serviced it, but it hasn't been used for nearly four decades. It looks in perfect condition but like all of the Mustangs, the dummy bombs look like they are in perfect working order, but we won't know for sure until we drop one somewhere. And by the way, they can only be used once. The expectation is that they will be destroyed on impact."

"Didn't they cost over $500? It's a rather expensive hobby we have got ourselves into, isn't it?" added Martie, looking at Preston.

"I agree, but since my share profits have started to rise again. I reckon my income this year will cover all our war-game expenses. I'm still going to be short on the Lightning by a couple of hundred thousand from last year, but she was worth every penny since there are less than 30 still flyable worldwide, and her value should double to at least a million, or even more in a couple of years. Apart from the ammo and the bombs, everything we have purchased has been a good investment. Hell, even the world's most expensive motor car is still more expensive than the million and a half we have spent on our three aircraft."

"I'm so happy Grandpa and Dad are coming this year," Martie said, changing the subject. "My grandfather will have to have your whole guest room this year. He's getting so old I think he'll need nursing care pretty soon."

"Not with the way he still gets about," replied Preston.

Martie nodded. "Yes, but he is only active for very short periods of time these days, even though his brain is as sharp as a pin."

"Your father does a great job looking after him," continued Preston. "I think both of them will enjoy seeing all the old flying machines once everybody is here."

"Well, I'm sure my father will want to sleep close to Grandpa, so he will have to have the last room in the house," Martie thought out loud as she grabbed two more beers out of the cooler. They were sitting on the raised pallet of the silent forklift and looking into the roomier hangar. It was starting to get dark, but the night was still a reasonable temperature, with winter not yet sinking its cold teeth into the North Carolina landscape. "That means that everyone else will have to bunk in the hangar. Hey!

Why don't we do a number on the hangar and set up some rooms. I bet that if you got your 'I can do anything' neighbor and his boys in here for a couple of days, they could set up three or four bedrooms with a pilots lounge above it. There should be room above the current room to build a second floor, no?"

"I was thinking of that, actually," replied Preston with a grin. "Carlos will be coming. As far as I know he's coming without a bedmate. We know that he has his eyes on Sally, but that doesn't help our cause much on bedrooms."

"They would be a good match," mused Martie.

"Buck has this new girl, Barbara I think he said her name was, and she is a fancy-pants pilot. They will share a room, no doubt. Then there is Sally. That makes three bedrooms."

Martie nodded in agreement.

"My problem is," Preston continued. "What happens if Maggie can persuade the Detective to actually set foot in her flying machine? That will be another whole family of four, and there is not enough space for another bedroom if you want to build a party room upstairs. There is only one bathroom with a shower and that will not change between now and Christmas. I could squeeze in an upstairs toilet, but I have no room to put in a whole bathroom."

"If the Smarts come, then my father will have to bunk in Grandpa's room. We can put a cot in there. If that doesn't work then he'll have to sleep in the lounge on the couch. Maggie and Will will have to take the last room with a queen bed in the house since we have two full bathrooms and the extra toilet. The kids will be happy to sleep anywhere and can have the new hangar upstairs room or the couch in the lounge if my father doesn't use it. I'll get a pull-down double bed and purchase all the furniture if you get the building built?" Martie offered.

"Deal!" agreed Preston. "I'll radio Joe next door. I know he's a little short on work and this could give a good Christmas boost to him and his sons."

The next morning, Preston tuned his ham radio to Joe's private CB radio frequency, which was set up in case they ever needed each other in an emergency. They were neighbors after all, with no others around for a couple of miles. Joe's larger 50-acre property bordered Preston's and most of the flights out of Preston's airfield took off or came in to land over Joe's property since it was situated due west and north of the airfield. To the south of Preston's farm were mostly lake, natural forest, and the NC64 highway two miles away. To the southeast and east was a forest reserve and no farms or houses for three miles. It was a pretty private section of countryside and Joe and family were the only people in the vicinity who saw arrivals and departures of the aircraft out of Preston's field.

Joe was a radio buff, but more into CB radio as he had several trucks and was in several types of businesses. He was also a carpenter and general handyman by trade. Two of his vehicles were old reefer trucks, with which he carried local beef and other frozen products for farmers. He also had two old Man diesel tractors and a couple of long-haul trailers. These 16-wheelers carried goods around North and South Carolina, and with five sons, he kept all of his work within the family. This was where Preston had gotten most of the large truck engines to build his generators.

Joe was also a jeep fanatic. He collected old army jeeps and three of his jeeps he had rebuilt to copy "Rat Patrol"—Joe's favorite old television show filmed back in the 1960s. Each jeep was painted its original army colors from World War II and copied with the desert colors of "Rat Patrol," and had a forward and rear machine gun steel stand. Over the years, Joe had also collected the odd machine gun here and there to add to his jeeps. He arrived 30 minutes after getting off the radio with Preston.

"Hi, Joe," greeted Preston.

"Howdy, Preston, glad you called. I'm a little slow with work until the New Year, and all my boys are available if you want them."

"I have a surprise for you," nodded Preston. "I have replaced the four old .30-caliber machine guns on the P-38 with bigger .50-caliber ones that I got out of a downed Mustang in Reno. So for you, my good and friendly neighbor, I have a couple of .30-caliber machine guns for you to borrow without ammo. You can't purchase them, since I might need them back someday. I have only .50-caliber ammo, however, so you have to buy your own. You can mount them on your jeeps if you want, as long as I get them back in the same condition you get them in, in return for some work for pay I want done here in the hangar."

"Great!" replied Joe, very excited. "I actually have tons of .30-caliber ammunition. I purchased two old .30-caliber guns from a collector last year and they came with thousands of rounds—enough to have a little war," he smiled at Preston. "If you loan me the four, I can fix you up with some meat. I purchased five head of cattle from a farmer in Hillsborough and just had them processed.

"Four of the carcasses are hanging in one of my reefer trucks. I'll butcher them for you, package them up, and bring the reefer truck over so that the meat can stay here and you'll have enough space to store the meat. It's about 1,200 pounds of prime beef. Actually, I still have some frozen lamb in the other freezer truck. I'll throw in 30 or 40 pounds for you. I know you have a large crowd coming over for the festive season and since we'll all be here for New Year's Eve, we might as well contribute. Got any new war planes I can look at?"

"No," laughed Preston. "But wait until New Year's Day. It's going to look like the U.S. Air Force in World War II here at the airstrip. Martie and I have several new aircraft coming in for the fly-in this year. Why don't you bring over your army, hang out here whenever you want and I can introduce the Rat Patrol to the U.S. Air Force." Both men nodded and smiled at each other. They could already smell the beer.

"I hope old man Von Roebels is coming this year," said Joe. "I liked talking to him last year, he's a good man. And guess what, Preston old buddy? I have a new collector friend you are going to love. He lives in Raleigh and collects stuff like me. He wants to meet you. I went over there for dinner last week—he has several old radios from Vietnam and I want to get 'hammy over Miami' on the radios and become a ham radio-jock like you and Carlos."

"I'd love to meet him, Joe," Preston answered.

Joe continued on. "This guy has two working Army armored cars. He calls them Ferrets. He's Jewish and spent time as a collector in Israel where most of the stuff was easily purchased at military auctions if you knew the right people. Not only does he have these two working armored cars, he has what he calls a Saracen, or something like that. It's beautiful! It's a six-wheeled armored personnel carrier. He also has a real troop carrier—British, I think—and tons of other stuff. He contacted me because he wants some .30-caliber ammo and my brother in Virginia met him at a gun show and told him that I might have some. I was thinking if he and I brought all our stuff around over New Year's, this place would look worse than a Hollywood World War II movie set! We could sell tickets to the Preston and Joe Military Museum and make a fortune!"

Preston laughed and said that Joe should bring his friend around sometime.

Martie had left before Preston called Joe, and by the time she called him over her lunch break, Joe was already returning from the Apex Home Depot with thick blocks of 4 x 4 wooden beams, dozens of 2 x 8s, 16-inch floor beams, two truckloads of building materials, and his five sons.

Preston walked over the design he wanted with Joe, which included five bedrooms on the new second floor over his current hangar sleeping area, plus a small room with a sink and toilet. Joe had built the initial ground-floor structure for Preston over a decade earlier. In it there were three rooms—Preston's lounge, a full bathroom behind the lounge, and his tool and work room, all of which were strong enough to hold another floor above them.

Joe explained to Preston that it would be okay to use the current wooden frame he had built years earlier for the second floor over the first two rooms. The workshop, the single open-plan room, and the bathroom were a combined 50 feet long and 20 feet wide.

"Joe, I think we should leave my current lounge as the downstairs party room. I can always put it back the way I've always had it after the party. The only change is that you will need to build a staircase up to the second floor from it and a bar counter and rear shelves in the opposite corner from the bathroom. Then build a second floor and divide it into five bedrooms with a hallway running down the front. Put the toilet and sink over the current bathroom at the top of the stairs and the windows from the hallway can face out into the hangar area and give some light since there will be no windows in the middle rooms. You can put a large window in the end walls so the end rooms get hangar light, and build the inner walls with wood panel sides and noise insulation inside. I'm thinking hotel-style rooms—I reckon 10-feet wide by 16-feet long. The guests will just have to come downstairs to shower. Create the staircase as close to the bathroom door as you can and make it and the bedrooms feel like hotel rooms with electrical installations for a queen bed on one side-wall and a corner hanging space in each room. What do you think so far?"

Joe nodded his agreement and reminded Preston that the initial structure had been built to have a good-sized load on the roof, and that it would take the added weight with no problem.

"Put in a wall air conditioner/heater unit high up in the front hallway wall or somewhere where nobody can bang their head or feet on it. We can put a nice carpet in the five rooms and varnish the walls with a thick boat varnish instead of paint, paint the ceiling white with a middle light set, and that should be it. A nice hallway wooden floor will be a nice touch. With a white ceiling and some quality wood products, it's going to be a permanent addition.

It had taken an hour and a half, but Preston and Joe already had the complete design on a piece of paper and Martie's initial idea came to life, except that the party room was now downstairs and the sleeping rooms upstairs.

Joe planned on four days of construction work with his team of six guys, with the fifth day set aside for wood varnish (which Preston liked instead of paint), carpet laying, the HVAC installations, ceiling paint, light fixture installations, and final touch-ups. Preston gave him a credit card and told him to buy what he needed, and Joe rushed off to collect his sons and grab his other truck.

By Thursday, the woodwork was finished and it was looking good. Martie took measurements for a day of shopping. She had taken Friday off to shop, and that was what she was going to do.

That meant lots of new people in delivery trucks visiting the farm, and Preston never liked that. He made sure that all his valuable aircraft were fully covered with extra tarps and hidden from prying eyes so the visitors would think that they were just the usual aircraft found in hangers. The faithful crop sprayer that was never covered always looked natural in the hangar. The ammo was now safe and secure in the old barn across the airstrip, and nothing looked really different to an outsider, except perhaps the fancier than normal airstrip.

Over the last decade, Preston had built up his airstrip to look really professional. His last purchase, a complete airfield landing-light system and directional beacons was on his list for 2013. In 2000, he had lengthened the runway from 1,600 feet to 2,200 feet. The next year, after reading about the needs of most average small commercial and older war aircraft, Preston had lengthened the runway to nearly 2,700 feet. In 2002, he spent close to a quarter of a million dollars and structured the undercoat of the runway to accept heavier aircraft, and then tarred the entire 2,700 feet. He had also increased the width of the landing area from 18 feet to 30 feet. That much good thick asphalt had cost a lot of money. Joe had supervised most of the work and made good money from Preston that year, purchasing his First World War II jeep in mint condition.

In 2004, Preston had purchased five large underground fuel tanks from a bankrupt gas station auction. Each tank held 5,000 gallons of fuel. One was for diesel—he didn't really need it but it was part of the lot. Two were for regular 87-octane truck and car gas. He filled them up when prices were down and drew off them when prices went up. The fourth tank was modified for aviation fuel and the last one was modified even more to hold jet fuel, in case he ever purchased a jet. It had hardly been used and he had filled it for regular aviation fuel every now and again and when prices were down. It took him another large check to drop these big tanks into large holes in front of his hangar and then add the asphalt over them to give him a very large aircraft parking apron —far larger than the hangar it stood outside.

In 2005, he completed his fuel project by buying and building a refueling point for all five tanks to the side of the parking area so that all aircraft refueling was at least 50 feet from the hangar for safety.

On Friday evening, Joe was done by 8:00 and it was beer time. It looked warm and cozy, and the new upstairs looked more like the inside of ship with all the varnish instead of the inside of a farm hangar. He had even redone Preston's downstairs rooms, adding new paint, carpet, and varnish where needed. The whole structure looked like it had always been that way. He and his boys had done a good job. Preston paid him well and gave him a decent tip as a Christmas gift and Joe left a happy man with four beautiful machine guns to add to his jeeps. Joe and his boys were also off to cut up the meat for Preston, promising delivery in a couple of days.

Saturday was also a busy day, with the comings and goings of several delivery trucks. "Martie... that is a massive new refrigerator freezer! Why on Earth did you get that?" Preston asked as the men brought the large silver unit into the downstairs room.

"For all the beer, wine and champagne, my love," she responded. But Preston suddenly had a new problem. His little French generator was not going to survive this invasion of all these new electricity-sucking gadgets.

"I'm going to have to forklift over and power up one of the Man diesels and connect it into the system for both the house and the hangar to generate the power needed for the holidays," he mused. "That reminds me, I'd better get the tanks filled. I don't think I have much diesel."

"Why don't you just move it outside and let it stay behind the old barn where the ammunition is? I bet it is noisy but we shouldn't hear it so bad from back there," Martie suggested. "Remember, you put in the oversized pipe to feed electrical wires over there when you wanted to light up the old barn."

"Good thinking, my beautiful German Fräulein. It weighs over a ton," said Preston, thinking. "The forklift should lift it, or at least allow us to put some rollers under it so we can roll it outside and place it behind the barn. Good idea. They are pretty noisy."

For the rest of Saturday, everything came in fives—five queen-size beds, five small desks, five chairs for the desks, five single lounge chairs, and five standard lamps. Five headboards and five large pictures for the walls above the headboards soon followed. Then came items in tens—ten bedside tables, ten bedside lamps, and ten captain's chairs to fit around the five corner tables for each room. Several truckloads later, the upstairs looked like a Holiday Inn. Even the bedding was perfectly matched and looked good enough for a three- to four-star hotel chain. The colors blended well with the varnish and carpets. Martie had done a fantastic job.

"The 'Officers Mess' is ready for occupancy!" Preston laughed, once everything was in its new place. Even his old and well-used California King bed downstairs had the same color scheme as the beds upstairs.

"I've been meaning to buy you some new sheets and pillowcases for a while now," stated Martie. "I remembered your bed here and decided that we didn't need a pull-down. We can always put this one somewhere in the hangar out of the way if it's not needed. Now, if you look in the new freezer, you'll find a bottle of good French Champagne getting cold—a gift from me for your new hangar house-warming."

"And what is with the fancy new speakers and music system?" asked Preston.

"Oh, yeah!" replied Martie with excitement. "We'll be dancing in here and we need music." She walked over to demonstrate while Preston looked in the freezer, and a few seconds later the beautiful and rich sound of a good system filled the air.

"U2! I should have known that Bono would be first if you had anything to do with it," laughed Preston, as he opened a bottle of champagne. "What date is it today?

"Saturday, December 1st, and I've noticed that the smell of varnish is nearly gone," answered Martie, sniffing the air. "Come, sit with me on the bed and drink a toast to our new boarding house. Who knows, you handsome officer, you might get lucky tonight. I've been known to loosen up after a bottle of bubbly, and I like the new bar. We can naughty-party here more often."

* * *

The President had not had a good term since taking office in 2009. The worst recession since the Great Depression had hit the United States very hard, as well as the rest of the world. Unemployment had reached 13% in November 2011. Most of the media stations were quite adamant that the real statistics were been withheld and that realistically it was more like 18% since unemployment benefits were being cut and new applications were being delayed for weeks in the system before any payments were released.

House foreclosures soared through the beginning of 2012, and another two million homes in the United States stood empty between early 2011 and April 2012. China was trying to cash in on its loans to the United States, as were any countries that had loans to other countries—especially the United States. The banks were grabbing at every cent they could, and small businesses had been neglected since early 2010. America wasn't happy and with the government only interested in bailing out big business, the whole U.S. population was in a foul mood. Politicians from both sides were often pelted by mobs anytime they tried to make a public appearance. The health-care plan was dead by the end of 2011, and the President seemed to have lost control of the government. He disappeared from television screens and it seemed like the first family was in seclusion.

On the streets, there was growing crime, hunger, and people sleeping on the streets. The nightly news was only interested in the bad news happening abroad and the daily killing of American troops on foreign soil. The media, it seemed, had a blackout on the bad news inside the United States. In July 2012, there was a little growth in the stock market, and the President came on the news to explain that mortgage rates on any home purchases would be held to 2% by the government and that any banks not offering mortgages at this rate will incur hefty penalties. Companies were offered a cash bonus to hire new employees by the government and another stimulus package was planned to help individual taxpayers in the New Year.

Slowly, the financial infrastructure was waking itself up a little, and there seemed to be a little life in the economy. The real question on everybody's lips was, "why were so many American troops fighting wars in five foreign countries?" We were in Iraq and against Iran, then in Pakistan against the Taliban, Afghanistan, Syria and the new war in South Korea fighting the North Koreans.

The Pentagon chiefs who often appeared on the talk shows kept telling everybody that more and more troops were needed overseas. Many of the hosts asked the same question time and time again: "What happens when we are left with no troops on home soil?" and the reply was that "we still have the National Guard." Unfortunately, the same news media showed more and more National Guardsmen being deployed. Many had lost their jobs and had no choice but to go back into the Guard on a full-time basis. Naturally, they were being shipped out pretty quickly.

Now, more troops were being deployed than any time in American history except for the Second World War. In January, the President stated that with growing concerns in Pakistan and the chance of the Taliban getting their hands on nuclear weapons, he was sending in another 15,000 troops. In March, fighting escalated in the Koreas. South Korea begged the United States for more troops and weapons and another 10,000 troops, and most of the country's remaining Air Force jet fighters were deployed. Seoul was under fire daily.

In May, Iranians started bombarding U.S. and NATO troops re-stationed in Iraq. Another 10,000 troops, of which 4,000 were National Guard, were deployed to Baghdad. In June, another 25,000 troops got their marching orders and were deployed around the world for no apparent reason—the media only getting wind of the massive troop movements after they were on the move.

The President's rating went down to less than 20% and he went on the airwaves to remind America that we were still the strongest country in the world, that the Pentagon was under his direction, and the people need not be worried. "Nobody can or will attack the United States," he said. "We still have thousands of troops across the country and, with the National Guard, we are strong and a real force to be reckoned with."

He allowed a short question and answer session for the press and the first question was: *"Numbers show that in the most recent deployments of 150,000 troops this year, 30,000 were National Guard. The Pentagon stated in January that we still had 70,000 to 90,000 National Guardsmen ready to defend our shores. Mr. President, how many troops are left in the country?"* The President answered that there were enough troops and that more information on numbers would be forthcoming. He was meeting with his Chiefs of Staff later in the week.

That caused the media to panic and life for the President went downhill from there. Historians were brought onto every media channel and the troop numbers were ground down like teeth. Some said there were less than 100,000 left inside U.S. borders. Some said that based on their numbers, the Chief of Staff and one or two other generals might be the only troops still in the States. Pictures showed empty National Guard stations all over the country. Bases were starting to block news programs from taping any footage.

Military barracks were scanned by the local population and nobody seemed to find many troops anywhere. A real panic started setting in August, when the President stated that things were not going well for our sons and daughters in foreign lands and he was thinking of sending in more troops.

More than 100,000 angry protestors hit Washington when,

on the Sunday after a Presidential speech, the media reported 157 American military deaths the previous week. Somebody had leaked the information. The information leaked to one of the national networks also suggested troop numbers in the United States for September. The network stated there were only 40,000 troops and 15,000 National Guard left in the country. They also reported that approximately 90% of the Air Force was overseas, as well as 78% of the Navy. There were less than 2,000 Marines, apart from trainees, in the United States.

Washington was ablaze for a whole week. Buildings were on fire, motor vehicles were wrecked by the hundreds and all airports, bus depots, and railway stations in the area were on police lock-down and closed tight. It was time for something to happen and after 100 riot deaths that week in Washington alone—and another 150 reported by the excited media around the country—the government began to listen to its angry citizens.

The President appeared on all media channels and asked for peace. He explained that he had heard the voice of the people and that he was overriding the chains of command and would make policy starting that day to start bringing troops home starting the first week of January. Since there would be a change in Presidents after the New Year, he would work with the new President to help him bring 50% of all American troops back into the United States by January 31st. His promise to the American people was that at least 80% of U.S. military forces abroad would be home by Easter.

CHAPTER 8

Carlos Rodriquez

CARLOS MANUEL FIDEL SENTRA RODRÍQUEZ was born in Bogotá, Colombia in 1973. His father was a very successful coffee merchant and Carlos was his first and only child.

Carlos left Bogotá when he was a week old and for some reason his parents did not tell him that he was actually born in Colombia until many years later. They sold their ranch the week before his birth and then his father, mother, newborn Carlos, and his nurse, Sissie, flew out of Colombia for the United States two weeks later. Once the family became citizens of the United States, his name was shortened to Carlos Rodriquez, his mother to Sentra, and his father to Manuel Rodriquez.

The pictures he still had of his nurse, Sissie, who had looked after him until he was 12, he kept in a special chocolate box in his sock drawer. Although a Colombian by marriage, Sissie was not born in Colombia but originated from South Dakota, and this was where the Rodriquez family moved and purchased a nice-sized house in a nice neighborhood called Rapid Valley, a few miles to the east of Rapid City.

When Carlos looked back at his youth in Rapid Valley, he saw a family of three who lived well by South Dakota standards, worked hard, and succeeded in everything given to them. Carlos was the only Latino in his class. He was actually the only Latino in the whole school of over 300 children, and it was a sure bet that the Rodriquez family was the only Latino family in Rapid Valley. He only recalled fellow Latinos visiting from other parts of the United States and talking with his father in the corner store he had purchased and now ran with his wife Sentra.

In 1983, when Carlos was ten, he started helping in the store. It was the only general store in Rapid Valley at the time and the only other shopping opportunity for the locals was a Safeway in downtown Rapid City. By the age of ten, Carlos spoke like an American because his father had forbidden any family member to speak Spanish after they moved to South Dakota.

Sissie had started working with him on the English language by the age of four and arithmetic at the age of five. She washed the dishes, cleaned the house, and looked after Carlos while his parents were at work all day. Sunday was the only day the family was together. The neighbors were friendly and everybody was polite and waved back and forth, but nobody was ever invited into the large house as guests and his family kept pretty much to themselves.

Over the first couple of years, Manuel added onto the house. First an extra bedroom for Sissie, then an added veranda and outside party area, then a swimming pool, which was fun for a couple of months in the summer. With the pool came a high stone wall around the exterior of the garden. The house was full of good and expensive furniture and Carlos' first memories were of a happy big house full of comfort and color.

By the age of 12, he was excelling in school. Sissie had worked hard with him, and his grasp of school was well mastered by having an extra teacher at home. His English and math were perfect and he never came home with anything less than an A.

One day, Sissie vanished—just disappeared from his life. He arrived home from school as usual, and for the first time he could remember, his father was waiting in the study for him.

Carlos looked around for Sissie while his father asked him to sit down with him and began to tell him a story.

"Carlos, my boy," his father started. "I need to tell you about Sissie. Sissie has decided to return to what she wanted to do when I first met her in Colombia many years ago. Sissie is actually a relative of your mother's and had just had a nervous breakdown when we met her, and that was why we invited her to come with us and act as your nurse. Sissie had been beaten up by a gang of boys in Medellin, hurt very badly, and was in the hospital for several weeks. She had been pregnant and she lost her baby as a result of that horrible beating. Sissie lost the child a month before you came into this world. She was born here and spent her first 12 years in South Dakota before she moved to Colombia, and after she told us what it was like, we decided that South Dakota was a perfect place for us to move to."

"But why is she gone now, Papa?" Carlos asked, focused on his immediate problem.

"When I met Sissie in Colombia, she wanted to go into the Catholic Church and become a nun, but the church did not like that she had become pregnant without being married. They are very funny about that," continued his father. "I went to see the Catholic Church in New York a year or two ago and gave them her full story. After much time and deliberation, they agreed to allow her to study to become what she wants."

"Will she ever come back to visit us?" interrupted young Carlos with big eyes, trying to understand why his only real friend and support system in the world was not there for him anymore.

"Yes, one day, my boy. You see, to become a nun, she loses her freedom to come and go as she wishes. For many years she will not be in control of her life, she will not be allowed to visit you, but one day she will come back to see us. She told me to promise that to you."

"But why didn't she say goodbye to me?" asked Carlos, white-faced and questioning.

"I think because she loves you so much, Carlos. To her, you are as much a son as you are to your mother. Sentra has always understood the love between you and Sissie, and she was happy to have such a loving nurse for you. Sissie is family and nobody minded sharing you, but because Sissie lost the only child she will ever have, you took the place of her lost child and that was good for you—good for helping Sissie mend and good for us because we needed time to start a new life and become successful. Believe me, Sissie will be back one day. Your mother and I will always welcome her back with love and affection."

Silence fell in the study while Manuel allowed Carlos time to grasp the situation.

"So I will see her soon?" asked the young boy, picking at any possible straws.

"Yes, Carlos. You will see her soon. But she is not in control of when or where." Tears did their best to wind themselves out of Carlos' eyes, but to be strong in his father's eyes was also important to the 12-year old boy. So he got up, thanked his father for the information, and slowly walked down the hall to his bedroom to let his emotions erupt behind the closed door. Naturally, his father heard the sobs from the bedroom, but smiled to himself about how bravely his son had carried off his departure with his head held high. He was proud.

It took a long time for Carlos to get over Sissie not being in the house, but the education she had instilled in him from an early age was like concrete, and Carlos continued to mature in excellent form. At age 15, he won his first science award, and at 16 he received his first math award. At 17, he and the family moved to Washington D.C.—a whole new world for Carlos, because he did not speak one word of Spanish, and for the first time in his life he was in school with many other Hispanics and Latinos.

It was not an unexpected move, since his father had put the general store on the market a month earlier and it had quickly been bought by the Safeway chain of supermarkets. Times were good in Rapid Valley, and their pretty house was also snapped up, only a week later. There was a week left of the school year and then there were goodbyes to the neighbors they had never really met and to several of the teachers and a couple of school friends with whom he sat on the bus. Then the moving van arrived, they packed up the house in one day, and left South Dakota, never to return. Carlos' father didn't tell him why they were moving, or even why they had lived in South Dakota in the first place, but Carlos had up to now never asked.

His father had driven all the way to Indiana before Carlos asked the first question of his adult life.

"Papa, why are we going to Washington?"

"A good question, son, and it's about time you asked a few questions. I know your head is full of astronomy and science and math, and you are a dreamer and have never really been one to ask questions, but you have got to learn that asking questions is a way of learning, too. It is very important to ask questions and it is very important to get them answered correctly. So let me start at the beginning, and I will answer your question well. We have another six hours of driving today, so that gives me enough time to give you a good answer. Are you ready?" he asked looking across to his wife and getting a nod of agreement from her.

"It sounds like another story, Papa," replied the teenager. "You haven't told me a story since Sissie left five years ago."

"Maybe I'm not good at telling stories, son," his father replied. "In my old job, telling stories was not a good idea."

"Is that why we left Colombia?" asked Carlos.

"We left Colombia to stay alive. But let me start at the beginning. Many years before I met your mother my father was a farmer—a farmer of certain types of plants that they now call "drugs" in the United States. We lived outside the town of

Florencia in the mountains, a couple of hundred miles south of Bogotá. In those days, it was normal for a farmer to grow those plants and my father was a large landowner, worked very hard, managed over a hundred laborers and their families, and owned an extremely large farm given to him by his father, my Grandfather. My father did not believe that he was doing anything wrong, nor did anybody else. People did not use drugs in those days as they do today."

"Your grandfather was a very good man, Carlos, and much respected in Colombia," added my mother.

"My father was murdered in front of my eyes when I was 13 years old, Carlos. He never had a chance to defend himself. In those days, there was very little crime nor as many bad guys as there are today. A large, organized group of men wanted our land and our money. They arrived in two trucks and shot my father as he went out to greet them. My mother, my sister, and I were all watching from the house, since it was a large group of men and we did not get visitors very often. They did not even say a word to him. He went out and greeted them as any farmer would do, and a dozen of them just shot their pistols at him."

"What happened to you and your mother?" Carlos asked, breathlessly.

"The boss of the group walked up to my mother and told her that we had half an hour to pack up our belongings and leave in one of his trucks to Bogotá," Manuel continued. "He demanded the keys to my father's safe in the office and my father's bank account number at the local bank, and threatened to shoot me and my younger sister in front of her. She gave them to him. The safe had a roll of money in it and fake papers for the farm, my mother told me later. The man in charge shouted to the others to load us up and get us off his property. They only gave us ten minutes to pack and then we were dragged out of our rooms with a suitcase each and placed next to my mother on the back of the truck. My father was still lying in his own pool of blood where they had shot him, and we were taken down to the main road where our land ended. They threw us off the truck there and told us not to come back ever."

"What did you do?" asked Carlos.

"My father was a clever man," replied Manuel. "He must have heard about this happening to other farmers and been prepared for such an occasion. It was about three miles into the local town and it took us about an hour. Nobody passed us and we were on the only road to town, so we knew the bad men had not yet reached the bank. There was a little money in the only account my father had in his name, but a lot of money in my mother's account. She told the assistant manager what happened to my father and ordered him to give anybody who gave the right information all the money in his account and tell them that her husband had gambled the rest of his money away. I remember everything she said vividly. The assistant manager was my mother's nephew and knew us very well. My mother told him to wire all the money in her account to another account in Medellin, in my uncle's name and delete her account and make it look like it had never existed. My father had a large safe deposit box in the bank, and she went in and cleaned it out. She then ordered her nephew to gather as much information about the men as he could. She planned to return one day to kill every one of them. She gave me the heavy bag to carry and we caught the next bus to Cali, which was west of where we were. It didn't matter where the bus was going, but that we were safe. We weren't heading to Bogotá anyway, but to Medellin."

"Did your mother really go back and shoot every man?" asked Carlos in wonder.

"Yes, son, but I'll get to that shortly," was the reply. "We arrived in Medellin two days later and found a room in a large house with family for a few weeks. My mother looked around the area and finally paid cash for a small farm with a ranch house with the money from the safe deposit box. The farm was only a dozen acres or so and the house only a few years old. It was a nice farm with beautiful views about 20 miles south of Medellin and pretty close to her family. My mother waited and looked after us until I turned 18. I was pretty big and a mean SOB as she proudly called me. I must have gotten it from her because I later found out that she was just as mean an SOB as I was."

"Does SOB mean what I think it means, so she basically called herself one of those?" Carlos asked, shocked.

"Yes, son, she was that mean. I remember her treating the laborers very well when my father was alive, but none of them wanted to get on the wrong side of her. My father was always the nice guy and my mother the controller. When I turned 18, I entered the police force and spent my first year training in Medellin. My family had some connections in the police force and one day I was told that I was going on plain clothes duty and they asked if I wanted to join a new drug squad that was being formed. A cousin of mine would be in command and he wanted me in. I joined, and we spent another six months in Texas, training under American trainers. My English had been good throughout school and I started speaking it fluently. When we returned to Colombia, we were transferred to a new nongovernmental-looking building above a large fruit and vegetable market. We became a coffee export company and completed a month's course in the mountains learning about Colombian coffee to use as our cover. We acted like coffee buyers. We were 11 men and the commander. The biggest shock of my life up to that moment was when we were called to a meeting one day, a week or so after we had moved, and my mother walked into the room."

"My own mother! I couldn't believe my eyes. Here was my mother in our secret building. She was introduced to the men but no mention was made to the other men that she was my mother. The commander told us that she knew an area in the south where many atrocities had been committed against farmers over the last ten years, and for our first year of work, we were going to start cleaning up that area. She was to be our guide. What she told me later was that the assistant manager in the bank had kept her up-to-date on all the killings, all the land transfers, and changes in bank account ownership. He even went back to the beginning of the bad times and worked out that several different gangs had killed over a hundred farmers, taken over their farms, and emptied their accounts. It had started a couple of years before my father was killed and some of those gangs were now in control of thousands of acres and had upwards of 30 to 40 men. He also gave the names of the gang members in the area's police force, which included the local police chief himself."

"That must have been a problem," said Carlos.

"Not really, son. We drove into Florencia and four of us acted like a gang of our own for the first couple of days we were there. The commander and my mother were part of the four. We stayed in a small hotel. In the 1960s, Florencia had a population of about 30,000 people—a small town with many rural people living just outside of it. There were several multi-story buildings, but nothing like today. The town and area's police force consisted of only 25 men, of which at least a dozen were in the pay of the different gangs. We knew their names and we started to work. Within a day, the police chief came over to the hotel and asked us who we were. My mother recognized him but he did not recognize her. We asked him to meet us outside town because we had a deal for him worth a lot of money. We also named six of the bad cops and asked him to bring them with him. 'Hey! There are only four of us!' our commander added to prove that they wouldn't be in danger. We mentioned the names of the several gang leaders in the area and said that we were under orders to offer him an opportunity with some of the gangs wanting to band together. There were only four of us at the meeting—my mother, who acted like the wife of our commander, him, me, and another guy. We did not want to show all our faces, and we had been well-informed by the bank's assistant manager, so he easily fell for the fake opportunity."

"Everybody agreed to meet somewhere else so no one would have the chance to tape our conversations. It was simple. They walked into our ambush and tried to fight back when we showed our badges. We had to kill three of them, and the rest we transported back to Bogotá with the dead. We made sure the place where they were caught never looked like anybody had ever been there. We were backed up by people in high places, and it wasn't long before every one of the captives spilled their beans. They were pronounced guilty and placed in a newly-built and secret high-risk solitary confinement prison several miles outside Medellin on an Army base where nobody could contact them. Even the special guards had been carefully picked for their jobs. Then we went back."

"Of course, many people were asking questions about the disappearance of the police officers, but we put the word out that was probably gang-related and then the gangs themselves came into town to find out. Our commander took over as the new police chief and my mother still pretended to be his wife. They arrived in a new police car and had three new policemen, our guys, with them. It was all Bogotá could send right now. Within a month, we had done something similar with all the other bad cops, one at a time, and we now had six of our guys in new police uniforms. Then our guys started getting offers and threats. The first gang of 20 men came into town one day, all well-dressed and driving fancy new American cars. They took the new police chief out for drinks, made him pick up his wife at gunpoint, and warned him about what would happen to his wife if he didn't do what he was told. Of course he agreed, and was ordered to tell the gang who had gotten rid of the old policemen. The commander told them that he thought that the three single men who had transferred with him were special policemen. Two of them had been in the area beforehand and had worked undercover at the station for several weeks."

"He was ordered to get the three new men to a farmhouse several miles out of town, and he was to come with them. It was time to get rid of the new Federalis, the gang boss told them. The meeting was to take place two nights later and if it didn't go according to plan, he and his wife would be buried quicker than scheduled."

"Was it dangerous for your mother?" asked Carlos, noticing that they had driven across the whole state of Illinois while his father was telling the story.

"Of course, but she was one mean lady, remember, and she told me it was so exciting. Anyway, a special company of 100 troops had been especially prepared and trained in gang warfare to back us up. I was still one of the new policemen and several of the original, but we thought good policemen were still there and they had been questioned about seeing me in town. They did not know what was going on, and we had kept them out of the loop on purpose, in case there was a spy among them. Word still got back to the gang boss that a couple of us had been hanging around the police station and had talked to the old police chief, so we knew we had to be careful. It took just six hours to get 50 men into positions around the farmhouse and then we arrived at the old, open gate. The four of us had made sure that there was nobody living there, and we hung around in the police car until dusk. Then we saw lights approaching from behind the house. It was just after sunset, and the scene was just like out of a movie. Several cars came over the hill at once, mostly open jeeps and trucks with men and guns everywhere."

"We waited until they started shooting in our direction, about 50 yards away, before we swung the idling car around and headed back the way we came, bullets going everywhere. It didn't look like our 'police chief' was going to be spared in the attack and we had predicted it. An American Huey gunship came over the horizon, loaned to us from our friend in the U.S. Air Force, a Major Pete Allen, and the Huey and our ground troops blew the trucks and the whole gang to bits within 30 seconds. There was not one body left intact out of the 32 that we could count. A couple of our guys had also hidden in the police chief's house with my mother, and three of the gang silently crept in through an open window. With the help of a silencer, they were dead before they even suspected that it was a trap. My mother was mean, had wanted blood, and she shot two of the three before the back-up guys got the last one."

"She shot them? She was sleeping in bed with a gun?" asked Carlos.

"That's right, son, she left the bathroom window unlatched for them. For the next year, we did the same to six of the seven gangs, and also found two of the original policemen who were working for the gang leader who shot my father. This remaining gang leader was getting a little worried. He had been left alone and was still living in our old house with over 50 men and dozens of women. He had killed several of our laborers, and the rest had been forced to work the fields, with three dying from malnutrition. We knew he also had another 60 or so men living on several other farms he had commandeered after killing my father. Every year, he flew into the United States once or twice to do business, and we could never find out how he got there. While we were there, one of our men had been killed and another had been wounded, so we were down to only ten, including my mother. She was scared that the gang leader would recognize her, so she stayed away from our farm."

Manuel paused for a moment, as if reflecting on what had happened so long ago, and then pushed on with the story.

"It was now well-known that the new police chief in town was not going to become one of the bad guys. Too many gangs had disappeared over the last several months, and the gangs knew it had something to do with the new chief. Twice they tried to kill him, but his bulletproof vest saved him once and his 'wife' saved him another time when they were attacked during the night. He and I always slept in the lounge, always waiting for an attack, and again it came through the bedroom window."

"She was a crack shot and slept very lightly. We decided to interrogate one of the bad police officers before he was sent up to Medellin. They got him to spill that his gang leader was arranging drug pickups in the United States and he was planning to be gone in the very near future. Nobody knew where he went to fly out of Colombia, but the narc thought south, across the border to Ecuador. He always traveled with a dozen of his best men and was usually gone for a week or two. The men all left at different times and maybe the bank could shed more light on it. He was right. Our assistant manager did a survey of all the accounts the branch had, and within a week came up with a three-year schedule of when money moved in and out of certain accounts. Most of these accounts belonged to old ladies who he had actually met, real people, and all were pretty secure with family money. One account was of interest, however. A couple of large payments were deposited into the account once or twice a year, and then smaller amounts were transferred out of the account and into a couple of other accounts in the same branch that also were owned by a couple of old ladies."

"That money was taken out in cash by the old ladies themselves a few days later at different times and disappeared. Then the deposit remaining in the first account disappeared a day or two later."

"Maybe it was the gang members' mothers," suggested Carlos, with the miles now flying by.

"Very good," was his father's reply. "Maybe my mother wasn't the only mean mother in the world." Manuel laughed. "Well, it was ten days later when the same schedule started occurring. We monitored it and then attacked the other farms a day after the account went back to zero. This time we had our complete backup unit—three helicopters loaned to us by our American friend; Major Allen—and we had five farm-houses to deal with. We got all of the gang members and used silenced weapons in case the noise could be heard at our old farmhouse. We lost three soldiers, but killed over 70 male gang members and five females who picked up weapons to fire at us. As soon as the major attack was completed, we dropped our team, fresh from the fighting, around the entrance to our old farmhouse. It was quiet and there was no movement until just after dawn when a truck came down the road. This time, my mother was with us and she stood in the middle of the entrance with typical farmer's clothes on and waved it down. The truck stopped. Three men got out, swaggered over to my mother shouting awful things at her for being in their way. The driver was shot with a rifle that had a silencer, while he sat there waiting. The truck's engine was still running and the other three all tried to grab my mother and push her around without hearing the gunshot behind them."

"My mother recognized one of them from the day my father was shot, she told me afterwards. She pulled out her pistol, shot the other two, and then shot the man she recognized in both knees. My mother stood over him with her gun pointing at his head while he screamed. She forced him at gunpoint to tell her how many gang members were left at the farm, where the leader was, and when was he going to get back. He tried not to tell her, but my mother put a bullet within an inch of his now open legs and he quickly told her what she wanted. Finally, she asked him if he remembered who she was. He nodded and tried to smile at her. She put a bullet right through his forehead."

"WOW!" breathed Carlos, amazed. "She was one bad mama!"

"I told you," Manuel replied before continuing. "We quickly surrounded the farmhouse and took the four men captive that were sleeping. One of the helicopters landed, this time with an American CIA agent in it, and they took the bound men back to Medellin. We were all in radio contact for that operation. We found out later that the information the Americans got out of these men (two were colleagues of the leader who killed my father) shut down a large drug operation in Texas a few months later. Somehow, word about that got out.

"There were five of us waiting for the old leader to return to the farmhouse. We parked the truck out front and waited with our backup several hundred yards behind the house in three of the old barns. After three days of waiting, there came a rush of a dozen or so jeeps and trucks from three different directions in front of the house. It was just after breakfast, and the attack came from nowhere. We were well-prepared, however, and had trip wires with mines planted just in case. I saw three vehicles blow up before they got into the circular driveway in front of the house, but at least another 20-30 men attacked from the driveway. We fired like madmen, and many of them went down. Several got to the porch and started throwing grenades through the windows.

"The grenades killed a couple of our guys before our back-up could be heard behind the house. Our poor commander was one of them. Three of us overturned our thick wooden dining-room table and jumped behind it before the first grenade went off. When they made their final attack through the door, I killed a couple and my mother got one or two as she always did. Suddenly, my mother was hit and I saw her go down just as I got a bullet in my upper leg. We continued to shoot back until the men ceased to come through the door and we could hear our backup men shouting from outside. It hurt like crazy, but I hobbled over to my mother. She was hit in the stomach and sitting up with the table behind her, smiling at me for the first time in many years. She looked at me and said 'That was the most fun I've had in years!'

"I called for the soldiers outside to come in. My mother ordered them to pick her up and help us outside. There were bodies everywhere. A group of injured men lay by a jeep that looked like a pepper pot because of all the bullet holes in it. She asked the men to carry her over to each dead body, one at a time, and turn them over if they were lying on their stomachs. It took a couple of minutes to look each dead gang member in the face. Then she asked the men to carry her over to the three wounded gang members sitting by the calendar-looking jeep. A soldier was helping me follow her, and I counted at least seven of the faces that had been burned into my memory that day years earlier. There were another two I remembered well sitting up against the jeep. One was the now old white-haired man who had shot my father. My mother looked at him for a long time before he spoke to her. There was nothing but silence with dozens of soldiers looking on. Not a leaf moved. My mother still had her gun in her hand and, with help she found the strength to stand. I could see that she was losing strength and the gun barrel was pointing down at the ground.

"'You should never have come back,' the old gang leader quietly told her. 'I knew the woman involved in these attacks was you searching for me. I have already ordered my colleagues to search for you and your children, and you will soon all be dead.'

"My mother just stared at him in silence.

"'I have friends in the government... in Medellin. It won't take long to find you.'

"The man next to him coughed up blood and gave her a wicked grin and tried to give her the finger. I watched as the gun barrel lifted and one silenced shot went through the front of his head. The old gang leader next to the now dead body did not even flinch, but kept his eyes on her like an eagle. The man next to him just fell forwards and one of the soldiers pulled the corpse away from the jeep.

"'And now it's just me,' the old man smiled at my mother. 'Remember, you might kill a branch of the tree, but you cannot kill the whole tree, and the tree is going to come back and kill you and your young boy here. I remember him well. He and his sister are going to die young. Very soon, the tree is now angry.'

"'This is what I have promised my husband in my prayers and I now fulfill my promise to the only man I ever knew,' replied my mother. She was suddenly racked by coughing and she spewed blood.

"'I doubt either of us will make it to heaven, José Calderón, but I hope I'm going where you are going, because my anger will burn for eternity.' With that, she fired the last three bullets in her gun, first in each knee, waited for the pain to register and his smile to die, and then sending her final bullet between his eyes before keeling over to be caught by two men. She lay on the ground on her back and looked up into my eyes. 'Your girlfriend Sentra is waiting for you and she is pregnant. I know that, but you don't know that yet. Manuel, my boy, marry her quickly and allow my grandchild to be born in Colombia. Tell the authorities what Calderón said here today. Warn all my family.'

"She coughed several times and lay still for a few seconds. 'Your uncle Philippe Rodriquez will know what to do and will help you get out of Colombia. Sell our farm. Philippe has the real papers. Promise me, and kiss my crucifix, Manuel, to seal your promise to me. I take promises very seriously. It's in our family. I did as I was told.' She died right there, with that satisfied smile back on her face. I closed her eyes gently."

Carlos had tears in his eyes. He and his mother had been silent for a long time and it was getting dark outside.

"The rest of the story is pretty quick," his father continued, looking over at his wife. "Your mother told me about you when we got back. I spent time with my Uncle Philippe warning all our family. There were dozens of them, and my sister was the first to be killed a couple of weeks after the death of our mother. It was a simple car accident, but the detective branch, also run by a family member in Medellin, spent weeks on the accident, found evidence of brake lines being cut and one fingerprint they found to be a known criminal. That one finger print led to that criminal being interrogated and more names provided. One was a police officer in Medellin. The next was a government official in Bogotá. Then poor Sissie, the only daughter of Uncle Philippe, was attacked and would have been killed if a policeman hadn't seen the group of boys dragging her into an alleyway. The policeman recognized one of the attackers. The son of a prominent government official, he was found guilty and sent to prison. His father got him released him a few weeks later and the boy went out and killed the policeman. The police then went in and took the father and son into custody and they were both found dead the next morning in their jail cell. Both their throats had been cut."

"As I told you five years ago, after saving Sissie's life the hospital revealed that she was six months pregnant and hiding the fact from her father. He was not happy about it. When you were born, I asked her to become your nurse, but Uncle Philippe was a very strict man. My life—our life—was definitely in danger. We left for America with everything we had, even the money we got for my parents' farm. All together it was enough for us to live well in America for a number of years. Thanks to your grandfather, Carlos, your education was paid for a long time ago."

"Did any of our family die after we left?" asked Carlos as the sun set over the horizon. It was time to find a motel for the night and refuel the car.

"A few weeks after we left, the ranch house we had been living in was blown up. Then somebody made the mistake of trying to kill Uncle Philippe. He got really mad and started a massive government investigation, which made him very unpopular. He told me that they got the main part of the 'tree' that Calderón had hinted at. The 'tree' was a very powerful government minister, and not liked by many. He was about to flee the country when they caught him in Bogotá International Airport getting on a really fancy private Italian jet with about 20 heavily trained bodyguards. There was a big firefight and the Special Forces who went after him had no choice but to blow up the aircraft and everyone in it. Nobody from Italy ever questioned the missing jet, and Uncle Philippe told me years ago that he thought it was a Mafia-owned aircraft."

"Where is your Uncle Philippe now?" asked the young boy, ready for a rest from the car journey.

"In Washington at the Colombian Embassy," answered his father factually. "He is the new Colombian Ambassador to Washington, and I am to become his Chief Liaison Officer." Carlos looked at his father with his mouth open and said nothing.

* * *

Twelve years later, in 2002, and over a large whiskey in the comfortable lounge of the Colombian Embassy in Washington, Carlos sat with his father and his uncle, the now white-haired Ambassador. The two older men were congratulating him on his recent Ph.D. from MIT in electrical engineering. Carlos was explaining to the two older men that he was not ready to get a job but wanted to start studying for a second Ph.D.—this time in astronomy and global communications—and maybe get a job with NASA.

"It will only take a few more years, Papa," Carlos was explaining. "Hey! What job do you want me to do? Be a gas station attendant?" he asked the two older men with his hands outstretched. They laughed at the grown-up boy. No more quiet Carlos, always thinking and silent.

Carlos had really matured at MIT and now was a very confident pilot who flew hundreds of hours a year. He also stood tall at one inch over six feet. His father really enjoyed his son's company whenever he came to visit them in the Embassy, once or twice a year. Manuel had never seen anybody work as hard as his son did. Aging and now white-haired, Uncle Philippe was also proud and also looked forward to the visits. The guy was becoming quite a comedian. They were about to go out for dinner to a really good Colombian restaurant in Georgetown.

Carlos' mother had died a couple of years earlier from cancer, and it had taken him several months to get over it. Manuel thought that it would hurt his son's studies, but Carlos had just worked harder to soften the pain.

"Uncle Philippe has a nice surprise for you tonight. I believe it's his way of giving you a gift for your success," stated his father. "I also have a gift for you, but first we should leave for the restaurant."

The Ambassador signaled to the attendant to have the car brought up from the basement. They slowly finished the 18 year-old single malt and then got up and made their way to the front steps of the Embassy where a black diplomatic Mercedes was waiting for them. They fit easily into the rear of the car and each was lost in their own thoughts as they drove towards Georgetown. As usual, there were two men in the front seat and a glass partition in between the front and rear of the vehicle. They arrived and the two men got out, one walking into the restaurant to see if their private dining room was ready and inspecting the interior for possible problems, and the driver scanning the street and passing cars with his trained eyes. Both wore suits and had ear and mouthpieces, common in Washington society. When the coast was clear, the driver held open the rear door and guided the three men to where the second bodyguard was waiting by a closed door.

"All clear, one occupant Ambassador. Good evening, Manuel. Good to see you are looking after your health," the bodyguard stated, smiling a relaxed smile and then looking at Carlos. "Good evening young Carlos, you have grown up some since I saw you last."

"Thank you, Mannie," replied Carlos' father. "A perfect job as usual. It's also good to see that you have not forgotten Carlos. I nearly didn't recognize him myself when I saw him yesterday. He's nearly as tall as you!"

"I always remember faces, Manuel," the bodyguard replied. "It's my job."

As they walked into the room, Manuel told Carlos that Mannie had been with him through the Colombian gang wars and had saved his mother's life twice. Talk was forgotten as they all looked at the rectangular table in the posh dining room and saw a middle-aged lady sitting at one end of the table, waiting for them.

Carlos' mind suddenly went into overdrive. He stopped and looked at her, studying her every facial feature. His face went white and his mouth hung open. "It couldn't be. It's not possible," he said aloud. The lady got up and rushed to him, excited. "Sissie!" was the only word he got out before she gathered him up in her arms. He looked over to the smiling older men.

"That is my graduation present to you, Carlos," Uncle Philippe said, enjoying the reunion. Sissie and Carlos hugged each other for a long time, with tears flowing freely from both of them.

"You are so big," Sissie stated, wiping her eyes and trying to compose herself. "How I have dreamed of this time."

"Me too!" shared Carlos, still rather speechless. He looked in Uncle Philippe's direction, questioning.

"Sissie has been in Guatemala in a convent since she left New York ten years ago. She has done our family proud," said the Ambassador. "Sissie is now the Mother Superior of the small mountain mission there and was very scared to come, but I asked the church's permission to allow her to travel to meet family and they consented. It took her a little time to pluck up the courage, but here she is."

Sissie went to Manuel, who also had tears in his eyes, and gave him the same hug she had given Carlos. "Thank you, thank you, Manuel, for looking after our boy. I can see that everybody is proud of him."

"Thanks to your early teaching and love, he had a head start on all the other kids," replied Manuel, still hugging her.

"Sorry to hear about Sentra. I was only told by Uncle Philippe yesterday when I arrived."

"Yes, it was tragic, but she was a strong lady and she went with dignity," replied Manuel.

Uncle Philippe moved to the far end of the table and sat down at the head of the table facing the door. He asked his daughter to sit back down next to him, and Carlos to sit next to her. He asked Manuel to sit on the opposite side of the table. Carlos noticed that there were places for eight as he pulled out Sissie's chair to seat her before his own. There were only four of them. There was no restaurant staff in the dining room, just Mannie standing by the one of two doors leading into the room. The man who had driven them opened the other door, entered, and stood by the door. "The car is ready in the basement parking lot if we need it, and Manuela and Antonio are looking after it," he stated to Uncle Philippe, who nodded.

"It feels like you are expecting trouble," observed Carlos, not used to this level of protection.

"Drugs are drugs, and since they never go away, neither do the bad guys trying to make money from them," replied his father. "Uncle Philippe has had over a dozen attempts on his life in the last 30 years—mostly in Colombia—but since the Mexican drug dealers have become braver, so have the Colombian dealers and several over-the-border cartels are working together, which means that there is more danger, even from non-Colombian drug dealers."

"I've always stayed one foot ahead of trouble," added the white-haired man who must be well over 70, Carlos thought. "Ever since Sissie was attacked all those years ago, I have worked hard to stay alive, even sending Sissie and your family to the most unlikely place in the United States for so many years. It was only once I was promoted to Washington by a few reliable government colleagues and good friends that I could use your father's training and services again. The old and trusted team members who fought the start of the drug wars back home with your grandmother and father, are still here tonight—Mannie; his newly recruited sister Manuela who filled your grandmother's place after she was killed; Dani, our driver; and Antonio kept a low profile here in the United States until I was posted here. A woman in law enforcement, in South America, is unheard of and this is why we won our wars."

"Carlos, beware of Manuela," his father said to him and winked at Mannie smiling by the door. "She is more deadly than a rattlesnake and is as mean as my mother was, right, Mannie?" Mannie smiled back. "She is our secret weapon!"

"I was always the liaison officer between the Colombian military and the armed forces here in the United States," continued Uncle Philippe. "And I have worked hard with both governments to lower the drug crime between our two countries. It took a decade of opposition from within our government before I was finally posted here. It's crazy to think how many high-ranking government officials have been influenced by the drug cartels, and who even lead some of the cartels from Bogotá. Not many can be trusted any more, apart from the several of us who were in positions before all this stuff started in the 1960s. Now I will now shut up and enjoy our evening—your graduation party, the pleasure of having my daughter back with me after such a long time, and the company of some of my special friends for the first hour. First, we will have some *bocas* or snacks and drinks, Carlos, since your Spanish is the poorest I have ever seen for any Colombian—my fault not yours. Then at 8:00 we will be joined by four more men and have dinner with them. I want you to meet my friends."

For the next hour there was much talk around the table. The

restaurant's two smartly dressed wait staff attending to them were called in by Dani. It was weird to see Uncle Philippe get up and hug each man dressed in black and white restaurant gear as they came in. Carlos' father was next, and as they shook Carlos' hand, his father explained to him that these two had also been with the team for many years and now worked here at the restaurant. Carlos got the drift, as this was the best Colombian restaurant on the entire East Coast.

Drinks were plentiful and the *bocas* came in on several silver platters. It didn't take long before Uncle Philippe again asked for silence. He suggested that everyone take their seat. First, a young man entered the room dressed much like Carlos and Dani, and looked around. Then, two much older men entered, both wearing very well-tailored dark suits and the door was closed behind them. Uncle Philippe walked up to them, shook their hands and welcomed them. He introduced his family around the table, Sissie first, and then introduced the men.

"Family, may I introduce you to Jonathan Dover, head of the CIA, and Casimiro Sanchez, his Assistant Chief for South American Operations." Carlos was surprised to see a Latino in such a high position. "Cas Sanchez has been my best friend since high school in Medellin," Uncle Philippe continued. A few seconds later the main dining room door opened from outside this time by a lady. Carlos assumed was the deadly Manuela, as she looked at him and gave him a smile and a wink. Again, two older men walked in, both in the same type of dark suit as the last two men.

Uncle Philippe did the introductions. He went around the table and introduced each family member.

"Gentlemen, I believe you know Mr. Dover and Mr. Sanchez?" The two new men did and shook hands. "Family, this is General Pete Allen, United States Air Force and Vice Admiral Martin Rogers—my long-time best American friend and my naval brother-in-law." Everybody shook hands and sat down.

The table was now full. "Dani, we can now commence with dinner."

The table was quiet as the first course was delivered to the table by the two wait staff. "This is *'Potaje de Garbanzos'* or Spanish bean soup in Colombia, gentlemen—one of my favorites," said the man at the head of the table. "My old grandmother made for me when I was young, a couple of centuries ago." Every laughed and then silence was king as the attendees enjoyed their soup.

As the soup plates were cleared away, the wait staff checked and refilled the wine glasses. Only Sissie was drinking water. Uncle Philippe motioned to his two men still standing by the doors and the two bodyguards left the room and closed the doors behind them.

"We thoroughly checked this room before any of us came in and it was clean. We are not here on business, but as you all know, we must always be one step ahead of the rest," Philippe began. "Tonight I am excited to have two of my family back in town. It's the first time I've seen my daughter Sissie in 18 years and Carlos, Manuel's fine son, has just finished his Ph.D. at MIT and now it seems wants to do a second one. I believe its time he got a job like the rest of us, and maybe went back to study in a few years time!" The guests smiled at Carlos.

"So, tonight you have been invited to have dinner, a little Colombian finery. Please, eat, drink and enjoy yourselves. I'm certainly going to." With that, he took a large sip of wine and buttered a piece of roll on his side plate.

"What did you major in, Carlos?" asked Casimiro Sanchez with everyone listening in.

"Electrical engineering. My minor was computer engineering," replied Carlos.

"And your next field of study, Carlos?" asked General Allen.

"I would like to study global-communications engineering next," replied Carlos. "It would give me an opportunity to go into global, orbital and space communications, and my hope is to be invited into NASA one day."

"You will get into NASA much more easily if you are a member of the Air Force," replied General Allen. "I was told by your father that you are a pilot already?" the general asked, winking at Carlos' father.

"Even though my father thinks I'm a little weird to love flying so much, I believe that it is a necessary requisition for NASA, and I can't think of many other hobbies I would rather do," was Carlos' reply, smiling at his father who smiled back at his son proudly. Manuel put his hand into his coat pocket, pulled out a small black box, and placed it in front of Carlos.

"Your graduation present, my boy, well done, I'm proud of you."

Carlos couldn't believe his eyes when he opened the box. It wasn't the three new keys on the gold key chain that were in the box that caught his eye but the description on the soft leather key ring. It read: King Air C90SE-661972. Carlos was at a loss for words.

"She's brand new and just finished her delivery tests," said his father. "She's waiting for you at Andrews to pick her up, thanks to the General's kind permission."

"I completed a couple hundred hours on a B-90," the General explained to Carlos. "I flew President Lyndon Johnson around many years ago in the only B-90 designated as "Air Force One." I use to fly him from Bergstrom Air Force Base near Austin, Texas to his ranch in Johnson City, Texas. She was sweet to fly and the same aircraft is now on display at our Air Force Museum in Dayton, Ohio. I go and see her every now and again when I'm in the area. She brings back many memories of my chats with the President, a man I really admired. She's a great bird, Carlos; you're going to love flying your new C-90." Carlos was still speechless.

"Say something, Carlos," added Uncle Philippe. "If you can't,

I will give you your graduation gift from me." Philippe opened an envelope and read from the piece of paper inside. "Two weeks, all expenses paid for two people in Nassau. The hotel's best Presidential suite, and everything is included, but you have got to get there by yourself," he laughed.

"For two?" asked Carlos.

"I think it's time for Sissie to have a real modern vacation as well, and you two can catch up on your lives and have some relaxation away from the human rat race," replied Philippe, smiling at his daughter.

"Thank you, Papa. Thank you, Uncle Philippe," were the first words Carlos could manage.

"Here's a pass for both of you into Andrews," added the General. "Take the Embassy car and hand the pass to the gate. They will be expecting you. Manuel, what's so special about the C-90SE version?" the General asked. Manuel looked over at Carlos for the answer.

"Thank you, sir," replied Carlos, trying to get his mouth around the words. "The SE is a simplified version of the C-90B. She has three-blade propellers instead of four, a simple interior that I like, and all mechanical instruments instead of the usual Electronic Flight Instrument System, or EFIS, usually found in the C-90Bs. She is the old and real way to fly, except for the twin Garmin GPS systems, which I find an excellent backup for longer flights, as well as fuel efficiency in side winds, sir." The General nodded. "Papa, she is a two-million dollar aircraft. How could you afford a C-90?"

"Let's just say that your late grandfather helped out," replied Manuel. "When I was given the money from the sale of our old farm in Florencia, I did not want to spend the money. I put it away in U.S. government bonds and stock for many years, and it grew and grew. I believe that your grandfather would appreciate me using his money to give to you, his only grandson, on such an occasion." A clapping of hands around the table erupted in the room.

"I second that, as your father's older brother," added Uncle Philippe. "He was an honest man and would be proud of you today, Carlos. Sissie, enjoy your time with Carlos, catch up on your lives, and I will get you back to your mission when you are ready." There were tears in her eyes.

"Thank you, Papa," she said getting up and giving him a big hug. "There is nothing more that I want in the world than to spend time with my son. Manuel, you don't mind me saying that, do you?"

"Never!" replied Manuel. "Sentra would be more than happy for you if she was here with us tonight."

The group turned back to chatting. The CIA chief offered Carlos any help he might need in the future. The CIA was seriously in debt to the Ambassador for all the help he had given them in Central and South American drug-related information. The chief handed Carlos a card and told him to call him or Cas directly at any time. Slowly the courses came, and it was over dessert that the Vice Admiral was able to chat with Carlos.

"We are really moving forward with global communications at the moment," the Vice Admiral said. "I believe that we are in the forefront of very new communications. Scrambling messages between ships, submarines and their home bases has always been an especially tough nut to crack. It could be of interest for you to look at what we are doing, and you could study at the same time. And we do fly airplanes in the Navy, Carlos. There is nothing more exciting than putting a turboprop down on an aircraft carrier."

"Except putting a turboprop down in Nassau," laughed the General. "Carlos, how many flight hours do you have?"

"Seventeen hundred, with two hundred on turbo props and another hundred on jets," Carlos replied. "I'm already qualified on King Airs, did most of my turboprop time on C-90s, and now

I'm working on getting qualified on twin jet Citations. I don't like jets very much. They're too sterile for me. I love the old-time flying and I'm just as happy in a Cessna 172 or even a sailplane or glider. I have over a hundred hours on gliders and after my next jet certification I want to complete a helicopter license."

"What is the one aircraft you would like to fly?" asked the General, "apart from the one your father and grandfather have just given you?"

"In earth's lower atmosphere, an old P-51 Mustang. In earth's higher atmosphere, the space shuttle," Carlos replied with a smile. Everyone laughed at that one.

Carlos flew Sissie down to Miami late the next afternoon, since he had drunk more than usual the night before, and on to Nassau the next day. They had a very restful vacation, enjoyed each other's company, and talked for hours.

It took time, but he finally understood his second mother's (as he called her) dream to be in the Church. They reminisced about the days in South Dakota and all the ups and downs they had shared, and she told him a lot about his mother and father and what good people they were. She told him about her horrible ordeal with the gangsters trying to kill her and her father's reactions to her being pregnant and not being married. She explained how straight her father was and what he had been like when she was a young girl. They had often had to hide, and twice the family had been shot at by gangsters, long before her terrible ordeal.

They flew back refreshed—he, darkened by the sun, and Sissie, who was not happy about swimming or wearing a swimming costume, the same color as she arrived. She had enjoyed wandering around the streets of Nassau while he spent time swimming, scuba diving, and sunbathing. She had spent time on the dive boat, but was not interested in going in the water. Swimming or scuba diving was the opposite direction she wanted to go, she joked with Carlos.

* * *

Carlos was offered several jobs in the months after his graduation. He understood his father's idea about working for a while before going back to school and accepted a position with the Air Force as a civilian-paid employee at Andrews Air Force Base. The job offer was in research in a small and secret building on the base, but gave him unlimited flying opportunities in new and interesting aircraft, and somewhere where he could base and fly his new toy with ease.

He stayed at Andrews for three years before he started back at MIT on his new degree, paid for by the Air Force. That was also the same year that he asked his father's permission to trade-in the graduation gift for something more exciting. There was a beautiful P-51 Mustang that a friend of his, Preston Strong, had found when looking around Reno, Nevada for parts for his own P-51. Carlos had flown Preston's Mustang once or twice, and wanted the chance to exchange for one of his own. Manuel told him that it was his aircraft and that he could do what he wanted with it. The King Air, now with 300 hundreds hours total time on her dials, went for a $100,000 more than its purchase price, and since the Mustang was only a quarter of that, Carlos had a lot of money to put into the bank. With his friend's suggestions, he invested wisely into tech stocks and quickly tripled his money with Qualcomm in 2006, doubled it again with Microsoft in 2008, and then tripled that investment with Google stock by the end of 2009.

CHAPTER 9

Preparations for the New Year's Eve Fly-in

BY THE 2ND OF DECEMBER, Preston and Martie were ready for the annual fly-in. The first guests were not expected before the 24th and they had a lot of time to check to see if they had everything they needed.

With the forklift, Preston set up one of the large Man diesels on a secure wooden platform, screwed it down with large screws and bolts, and connected its wiring into both the hangar and the house systems. It took a couple of starts with the original key and a new starter motor, but on the fifth try, the old diesel engine started. It coughed out a lot of dark smoke from the exhaust, pointing skywards and was reasonably quiet through the new truck exhaust silencer. Slowly, Preston increased the rebuilt and modernized throttle, an old water-value wheel, and opened it slowly by screwing the wheel to the right, stopping at 1,000 rpm. He then pushed a switch to "On" to allow the generating power to feed through to his two large sets of deep-cycle marine storage batteries. He signaled across to a waiting Martie, and she ran around like crazy turning on the lights in both buildings, as well as all the new ones, and then pumped the new sound system to an ear-piercing blast. Preston listened to the noise of the diesel engine as she did this. It didn't even show any strain from beginning to end. Martie came panting over the runway to the rear of the old barn where the diesel was now warm and happily grumbling away, and Preston screwed the large screw back to 750 revs—its usual idle speed.

"Didn't even feel anything," Preston shouted to the still panting Martie. "I reckon about a gallon or so an hour and she could light up three or four times as much on idle. At her limit of 2,500 revs, she could light up the UNC campus in Chapel Hill, or at least most of it," he smiled.

They then went about checking the well where the farm got its water, cleaning the filters, and making sure everything was in good order. They then checked both the house septic tank and the second one behind the hangar, ordered a "honey" truck to come out and empty them, and then put some Redex into the systems to make them ready for the extra work they would be doing over the festive season.

Joe brought the meat over a few days later and set up the freezer trailer to run, which prompted Preston to fill up all the underground gas tanks, just in case.

"What the heck," he told Martie over steak and red wine that night, with the faithful Oliver waiting for bones or other tidbits to come his way. "Gas prices will be on the rise closer to Christmas, and word is that prices are going to soar next year, so I might as well fill everything up we have."

"At $4 a gallon, what do we have now and what do we need to fill them all up?" asked Martie.

"I need a full 5,000 gallons of diesel or close to it, since there are only a hundred gallons or so in that tank. I might as well fill up the 5,000 gallon jet-fuel tank as well, and I've never done that before. This year we have a few turbo-props coming in with the 5,000 gallon jet-fuel tank—*Lady Dandy* and Sally's Pilatus—so if prices are going up, I can always put in some fuel preservatives and keep it as an investment. To have everything filled to the brim, I reckon we need around 20,000 gallons. That will be nearly $90,000, including the jet fuel, plus Joe will want his tanks filled up—he has four smaller 200-gallon above-ground tanks, and it would save him a delivery fee."

A couple of days later, the last tanker from RDU airport arrived and pumped in the necessary jet fuel. Jet fuel was not freely available at the average gas station. Preston paid for everything and Joe came over to ask him what he owed. They discussed the matter over a beer, sitting on the semi-warm porch with a heater blowing warm air over them.

"Your share, Joe, for 720 gallons of regular at $4.05 cents wholesale a gallon is..."

"$2,916.00," interjected Martie, walking up and working on her iPhone. She had three fresh beers under one arm and handed them out.

"Thank you, Martie," smiled Preston. "I was working it out in my head."

"That was what was worrying me, Preston," laughed Joe, winking at Martie. "By the way, do you remember the only gas station on the 751? The one with the big blue sign? A lot of work trucks used to stop there at daybreak."

"I go past that way most days into Chapel Hill," replied Martie. "I know the one you mean."

"I think so," added Preston. "Does it have a road junction from the right as you're driving north?"

"Yes, that's the one," answered Joe. "The owner, Pete Wilson, is a friend of mine and he is retiring at the end of the year. He closed it down last Friday for good and asked me if I wanted some beer for Christmas. He has a lot of stock and owns all the stock himself. I'd say he got a couple hundred or more cases of beer and he did have some nice beers, like Bud and these Yuenglings you like," Joe showed them the bottle he was drinking from. "You know I'm a Busch Light guy myself, and as long as it's wet and got color I'll drink it. So, my idea is that I buy the whole lot, and since old Pete wants to turn everything into money, he will give me a little discount. I could keep the "crappy" beer, as you call it, and you could get the fancy stuff for your fly-in. What do you think?"

"As long as you don't take the bad stuff home and then come over and drain all our good stuff over the festive season," laughed Preston. "I've seen how you guys put them away."

Joe and Martie laughed at Preston. He was only pulling Joe's leg and it was always a bit of competition between these two neighbors, but they wouldn't survive very long without each other. Preston agreed with the idea and told him to buy whatever Pete was selling, including snacks and candy. If it wasn't used at the party, they could all eat it for the next decade.

Preston was in for a shock at what Joe returned with the next afternoon. He took off his cap and scratched his head as one of Joe's sixteen-wheel tractor trailers entered the driveway and it looked pretty heavy.

"Sorry, Preston," mumbled Joe, looking sheepish. "I offered him a lump sum and he told me to take everything."

"How much did you offer him?" Preston asked.

"Well I looked over what he had in the store, and in the back. It looked like about a hundred cases of beer and a ton of boxes of all different things. I thought $10,000 was about the right amount. He looked back at me as if I were stupid and said he wanted at least $20,000 for everything. I couldn't say no, Preston, he's a darn good friend. It didn't look like what I saw was worth what he wanted, but I said 'alright.' Then he drags me over to his old tractor trailer in the back of his house next door, and the thing was full of even more stuff—double what I had seen in the store! I think my mouth must have dropped open, 'cause he laughed at me and told me that I might as well get everything at one time and that I was getting a pretty good deal for the money."

"$20,000!" Preston stared at Joe, not believing a number of that magnitude.

"Yep!" replied Joe. "And this is your half." He pulled out a list and read it to Preston.

"Did I hear right… 840 cases of beer?" stated Preston. "It'll take us years to drink all that!"

"You think YOU have a problem," laughed Joe. "I have twelve hundred cases to drink. At around $10.00 a case, we paid about 50% of the wholesale price. Some of the cases are only a few months old," added Joe carefully. "Don't look too hard at the merchandise—these cans might not have a 'use-by' date on them!"

"They could be years old already?" cautioned Preston.

"As long as they are wet and the right shade of brown, who cares?" smirked Joe.

"Then you have peanuts, peanuts, and more peanuts, potato chips, potato chips, and more potato chips. Actually, you have 20 large cases of each, 100 boxes of chocolate bars, another 100 boxes of other types of candy, and then cases and cases of assorted food stuffs. I reckon we got about $40,000 to $50,000 worth of merchandise at less than half price." Joe slowly folded up the paper, put it into the top of his farmer's overalls he always wore, smiled at Preston and waited for the shock to wear off.

"Sometimes, Joe, I want to move and go somewhere where people are normal," stated Preston, still staring inside the truck.

"Mars or Alabama would be a good place to start," joked Joe. "My boys want to get the stuff off-loaded. It's going to be beer time by the time we finished and we have already emptied one truck at my house today."

One of Joe's sons drove around the truck to the hangar door, carefully backed-up into the area where Preston guided him, and started the off-loading.

It took an hour for all seven guys to off-load just the beer. Joe had forgotten that Preston had the use of a fork lift and had not loaded the stuff onto pallets, but he had some in the truck and they moved the fork lift up to the old truck interior and loaded the beers onto eight pallets, one case at a time. Then came the cases of soda Joe hadn't told Preston about, and then the hundreds of boxes and cases of so many different varieties of peanuts, chips, and candy. Preston had never seen so much in his whole life.

"Are you sure this is everything?" checked Preston sarcastically as he opened the new refrigerator in the hangar downstairs area and took out seven cold beers. "Only one more round after these!" Preston called out to the men around him.

"No problem, Buddy," stated Joe's eldest son. "We are nearly halfway and I think we have enough beer here if you run out. They were pretty cold when we picked them up."

By the time they were finished, the refrigerator was empty, as was one of the cases of beer an hour later. Preston couldn't believe what he had gotten himself into, nor did Martie when she arrived to see a rather drunk Preston sitting in the hangar staring at a mountain of food stuff that hadn't been there the day before.

"Preston Strong!" stated Martie, looking at his sweaty, drunk appearance and the new mountain of food that now took the place of a future aircraft that might want this section of hangar.

"What the hell have you been buying? We have maybe ten visitors over Christmas and New Year's and you have purchased enough for the U.S. Army in a dozen states. Are you intending to feed Fort Bragg or something?" Preston looked back at her, smiled sheepishly and hiccupped.

"Hi, Martie, grab a beer," he suggested, slurring slightly with his face showing signs of blushing. "We have a few left."

"A few! A FEW!" She looked in wonder at the eight packed pallets of beer, and shook her head slowly. "I bet Joe gave you everything from that gas station. I bet he could not pay you for the gas and gave us beer and peanuts instead!"

"No, Martie," Joe responded, looking at the food mountain

and still trying to fathom what he was going to do with all the stuff. "He paid me for the fuel and I paid him for this stuff."

"And I think I know who paid more," she replied sarcastically, going up to the nearest pallet and pulling out a six-pack of Yuengling bottles from a case. She walked over next to Preston, who was sitting on several brown cartons of corned beef.

"Preston, you don't even LIKE corned beef and you said I would be fired if I ever bought some. Now you're sitting on what looks like 72 cans of the stuff! Move over and let me see if there is something exciting about sitting on corned beef while you tell me what happened." She opened two bottles, took her position next to Preston and stared at the mountain of food while she waited for this sure-to be interesting saga on the Strong Farm. It took an hour and three beers before she understood the whole story. "What we don't need during our fly-in, we can give to a food bank or something next year," she suggested to a very drunk Preston as she helped him into the house. She put him on the couch and he was asleep before she started dinner. Martie went back to the hangar, picked up a case of 12 small cans of corned beef and took it back into the house. She loved corned beef.

An hour later, she sat down in the chair next to Preston and turned on the television, looking forward to the smelly corned beef and sauerkraut dinner she had made for herself. Preston did not like either, but since he was in the dog house, so to speak, she didn't really care, and Oliver was certainly paying her more attention than usual. "That beef sure smells good," was written all over his face.

The news was on and she decided to watch it. The country's problems had really escalated in recent months and with the riots in Washington and elsewhere, the American people were unhappy. Even the media had a hard time hiding the growing tension.

"The stock market hit the 10,000 mark today, for the third

time this year," said the pretty, local newscaster smiling out at the world she was facing. *"The market is finally rebounding and is looking promising for a renewed start next year, the President stated, giving a speech at the University of Kansas today. He will meet with State officials there about revamping Fort Riley as an army base. He was interviewed earlier after talking to the 1st Infantry Division about bringing back all American troops by December of next year. The President spoke to about 200 reserve troops who intently listened to what he had to say. The President stated that his most important task now was to keep his word and bring home the promised first 200,000 men and women by January 31st. He got a loud ovation from the crowd. In other world news, the Chinese Premier broke a bottle of champagne today on the commissioning of their first aircraft carrier. Her name is Shi Lang and she is currently moored in Dalian Harbor in northwestern China. Many might remember the oil spill from a gasoline explosion that closed down the port for four days in 2010. Much controversy has swirled around this ship since a Chinese conglomerate won this partially-built carrier from the Ukraine for $20 million in an auction a decade ago. The original plan was to turn her into a casino in Macau harbor, near Hong Kong. That never happened, and the last film footage showed her in October with a large 83 military ship-designation freshly painted on her bow. An ongoing report from Jane's Fighting Ships on the 'Varyag,' as she was called before her purchase, states that over the last several years she has undergone a massive refit in dry dock to complete her military makeover and now she is ready for sea trials. The report also states that the group of companies that originally purchased the carrier still has shares in the vessel."*

"There was another nuclear power station malfunction today, this time in Nevada. Again, the malfunction was a cooling issue and the reactor was put into emergency shutdown

mode in case the problem became serious. Eleven thousand houses in northern Nevada and Idaho were without power for several hours. The problem was quickly located and an electrical system within the cooling system was replaced. A spokesman for the plant stated that nobody was in any danger at any time, and there were three new backup systems for this type of problem. He stated that renewed tests on the cooling system would be completed by Christmas and they were implementing what the world had learned from the Japanese disaster a couple of years ago—new fail-safe back-up generator machinery."

Martie stretched and scratched Oliver's head as she took a break from her corned beef.

"North Korea is reported to have bombarded Seoul for the seventh day in a row. Five artillery shots were fired into the Samsung area of Seoul and at least 55 civilians are reported dead and hundreds more wounded. South Korea retaliated with over a hundred projectiles fired into several known North Korean military bases. A recent satellite image shows vast areas of North Korea blackened, or still on fire, with far more destruction than that on the South Korean side. A U.S. missile carrier in South Korean waters shot down five aircraft a couple of hours later. They were approaching from North Korean airspace and flew inside its 50-mile fly-zone. The United States has repeatedly told North Korea that action will be taken if unidentified aircraft enter any American warship's 50-mile no-fly zones in the area."

"New attacks hit American Forces today in Iraq and Syria. The Pentagon reports that a troop-carrying helicopter was shot down, and a second attack this week on the same road hit a fuel convoy heading to the Iranian border to resupply forward troops in the area. Over 50 trucks were destroyed, as well as a number of escort vehicles. This is the seventh attack this month on fuel convoys, and reporters are saying that a

lack of fuel is starting to hit the entire Iraq-Iran border area. Over 150,000 American troops are reported to be in the area."

"In Syria, a fuel convoy was also hit heading to the southern area where most of the fighting is taking place with the rebels in hard combat with pro-government forces. Again, reports in from the BBC reporters who are covering the area are that there are three large new American military bases in the intermediate area, one large, recently built airfield and approximately 100,000 American and 12,000 NATO troops."

"A U.S. Air Force F-16 was hit by a ground-to-air missile a few seconds after take-off from the airfield. A BBC reporter believes that the pilot ejected before the aircraft exploded in midair."

"One of the most advanced drone aircraft was hit and captured by the Taliban today in northern Pakistan. An American airbase in Afghanistan was attacked by ground missiles early this evening, killing a number of American Marines. Casualty numbers have not yet come out of the Pentagon... the weather looks cold and below normal for Christmas, and Chris, it looks like most of the country could have a white Christmas this year?"

Martie took a quick look as Chris, the weatherman came on smiling, and she watched the long-term weather forecast and then switched off the television.

"Enough good news for one night," she told Oliver as she got up to take her plate to the kitchen. She put the leftovers in his bowl and loaded the dishwasher. "Good news from the kitchen department, Oliver. I think you had better like corned beef. You could be getting a lot of it soon."

"Are you crazy?" Martie asked Joe as he drove in early the next morning in one of his Rat Patrol jeeps. She did not have time for any more words and her mouth hung open as a fully armored tank-type vehicle drove around the corner and into sight.

"Hi. Martie, my love," shouted Joe as he pulled up next to her. "Don't worry, that's my new buddy Israeli David in a Ferret coming to meet Preston. Is he around?" Martie quickly regained her composure and looked Joe straight in the eyes with her hands on her hips menacingly.

"Thanks to you Joe, he nearly died of alcohol poisoning last night. He's just gotten in the shower and now I'm late for work, also thanks to you."

"I suppose you had to give him mouth-to-mouth resuscitation to keep him alive," Joe laughed. "If you get tired of him, my farm is next door."

"Oh, shut up, you redneck!" Martie laughed back. "Preston will be out in a minute. Oh, my Grandpa said to tell you that he's looking forward to chatting with you again over Christmas. He wants a ride in one of your jeeps!" Martie smiled as she got into her car, started the engine, and drove around the armored car waving goodbye.

Nobody was allowed to look inside the hangar without Preston's permission, and the large door was closed anyway, so Joe and David sat in the jeep sipping coffee while they waited for Preston to emerge. Joe gave him ten minutes and then honked his honk as he always did when driving up to the house.

A hung-over Preston emerged from the house, cup of coffee in hand, with Oliver trotting briskly next to him and barking at the visitors.

"Place stinks of corned beef," moaned Preston to Joe as he walked up. "I can't stand the stuff! Martie must have cooked some for dinner last night."

"Hey, Preston, this is David—the guy from Israel I told you about." Preston focused further than Joe's face, looked at the second man in the front seat, and then his gaze saw the armored car.

"Nice to meet you, David!" he said, shaking hands. "I believe that's an Israeli version—.30-caliber machine gun turret, completely armored top and possible rocket launchers, no?" asked Preston. "How did you get it here? You can't just drive this thing down NC64 in the right-hand lane!"

"Shalom, Preston! I've heard a few things about you and your P-38 Lightning. I've been dying to get a look at her. My father flew one during and after the war. He died several years ago and I still have a photo of him standing next to his aircraft in Tel Aviv in 1951, I think."

David motioned to the armored car. "And yes, this is my favorite. Joe told you I have two of them in perfect working order. The rebuilds took me ten years and I have had them under wraps in a large barn in Raleigh for the last several years working on them. They are both British-made Mark 2 Ferret armored cars. I have a trailer and Joe came over yesterday with a tractor and brought them on the trailer over to his farm. I had tarps over them and nobody really gave us a second glance. I was not allowed to bring the rocket launchers into the United States," explained David.

"Joe said that you had lots of other stuff?" Preston asked.

"That's right. I've always been a collector of World War II machinery, as well as more recent stuff. I just finished a Saracen —a British-made armored troop carrier I purchased from an auction in Israel a couple of years ago. It, too, uses .30-caliber rounds and I started searching for ammo just recently to test it. I did not want to cause any ripples here locally, so I went up to a gun show just outside Richmond to find some. That's where I met Joe's brother and he guided me to Joe. I also collect army radios and have a dozen or so working units that were pretty modern stuff in Vietnam."

David looked around the airfield and spied Preston's radio tower. It was atop what Preston called his control tower—a 50-foot forest ranger tower he had purchased many years ago and rebuilt. He called it his air control tower, but it had little use apart from a large spider-looking antenna system that spanned another 30 feet above the tower. “State-wide reception with that aerial?” asked David.

“I have a second aerial on a 250-foot radio tower about 20 miles north of Chapel Hill,” replied Preston, beckoning them to follow him to the hangar. “I have a friend in the national communications business and got the OK to mount another one on the top of that. We have several friends around the country we can talk to and my friend got aerials placed on several cell phone towers across the United States, all powered by solar panels. We needed two to talk to New York and several more to get West Coast communications, and he managed to get permission.”

They toured the hangar for an hour and David impressed Preston. He had been in the Israeli armed forces for several years and knew his stuff.

“David and I have ordered more .30-caliber ammo,” mentioned Joe as they left the hangar. “I hope to store another 10,000 rounds when it arrives later this week.”

“Don’t you have any ammunition?” asked David. “You have 12 beautiful machine guns in there and all are .50-caliber.”

David whistled when Preston opened the door to the old barn on the other side of the runway and pulled one of the tarpaulins off the stored ammunition pallets. “You have the Hispano operational as well?” asked David.

“Between Joe, Martie and I, the U.S. government would have a nervous breakdown if they saw what we have,” nodded Preston. “And now it looks like you are involved, and we have to be a little careful.” Both Joe and David got serious for a few seconds and nodded their heads. “I certainly don’t want anybody else to know what we have here. There are lots of weirdoes out there—civilian, military and others. Even I’m getting a little worried.”

“You have my word,” pledged David.

“And mine,” added Joe.

Preston invited David to the fly-in and told him to bring whatever he wanted to transport. He could store them at Joe's house, or even better, bring everything over to show off when all the aircraft came in. It would be quite a show. Joe agreed and laughed, knowing what Martie's grandfather would say.

By the end of the first week in December, Preston and Martie had gone through their long lists of things to do, and the airfield was ready for the fly-in, which was only two weeks away.

* * *

The Smart family was certainly not prepared for Christmas. Maggie was not speaking to her husband because he refused to join the fly-in, and she had even offered to buy him a return ticket on Southwest for him and the kids, who looked pale when she asked them to fly commercial instead of with her. He was ruining their Christmas vacation plans, and the Smarts would be the only ones not there. Maggie was very close to leaving him at home and taking the kids to North Carolina without him. She was furious, but she loved him, knew about his fear of flying, and fought within herself to try and understand him.

The kids were just as unhappy, but the neighbors were planning to have a big New Year's Eve party and the whole community of six houses, now all under self-powered electrical systems thanks to the Smart children, was hoping the Smarts would stay and join in the festivities. Tons of food and drink had been purchased by the neighbors for the event and Will used this as justification for not going to North Carolina. The seven homes in this rural area covered 30 acres, and apart from a similar group of houses more than a mile away, there weren't many other occupants in Antelope Acres for several miles. The demise of the building industry in 2010 had stopped any new construction, and even though they were within a hundred miles of the L.A. beaches, it felt more desolate than in areas of Arizona. Everyone loved the peace and serenity at Antelope Acres.

* * *

Buck McKinnon was busy. In addition to his new love life and teaching Barbara how to fly *Baby Huey*, he was hard at work in downtown Manhattan, getting the year's work up-to-date before he left for North Carolina. Barbara was a natural at flying and was about to get her helicopter license. Buck had suggested she fly Baby Huey for the fly-in, and she had worked hard on her new skills.

As usual, the days were short at this time of year and already snow was on the ground. Buck had prepared Lady Dandy for the flight and her exterior and interior were clean and ready to show off. Baby Huey had been thoroughly inspected and her engine serviced and ready for the trip south.

Lady Dandy's original owner, Bob Martin, had had a stroke a few months ago and Buck had gone to see him in Denver. Bob had looked a little rough around the edges, but told him to enjoy the DC-3 while he was recuperating. He asked Buck to look after the DC-3 and keep it in Long Island if he wanted to. Buck could rent space for it for a couple of months keep her on Long Island, fly down to North Carolina for the fly-in, and then return her to Denver. The doctor had suggested to Bob that he not fly any airplanes for at least a year.

* * *

Carlos Rodríguez was also busy. He had his P-51 at Hill Air Force Base and wanted to service her and have her ready for the 1,800 mile flight to Preston's airfield. He had permanent extra tanks, called drop-tanks, fitted underneath the wings, but still could not make the entire flight nonstop. Carlos had done the trip several times and found that refueling in Denver was the best way to get across. The first short flight to Denver was just over an hour and he loved this part—flying over the Rockies. Then, in Denver, he would ask the fueling attendant to fill the tanks to the brim, which would give him enough to get into Preston's field around four hours and 25 minutes after taking off. It was a 1,450 mile flight at a normal cruise speed of 325 miles an hour at 20,000 feet, and he usually had a tail wind going east that could cut down his flight time to four hours dead. Of course, on the way back his longest flight back to Denver had been five hours and on that trip he was down to reserves on fuel.

He had much to do at the NASA observatory before his two-week vacation. There were only three other astronomers stationed at the classified Air Force and NASA observatory in the mountains 20 miles east of Salt Lake City, and it seemed like nobody was expecting to be around for the year end. He wasn't in charge at the observatory. He still worked for the United States Air Force in a civilian capacity.

He was about to finish his second Ph.D., and had worked hard throughout the year on his papers. He still didn't know which direction to take once he was done, and he could leave the Air Force at any moment he wished. General Pete Allen, his father's friend and now his, was Commander of all the Air Force bases and could be Air Force Chief very soon. The General had put Carlos with a team of scientists and they had looked at communication possibilities, always using the satellites in space as the main way to get communications anywhere instantaneously. His team had been working on lasers as a form of message delivery, as well as bouncing messages across the solar system. He had tried bouncing messages off the moon, the planets, and even the stars with no luck, but one thing had worked by mistake. He had found an old satellite that must have been demobilized a couple of decades ago high above the United States and bounced a laser signal off into space—not the way he had wanted to go, but for some reason he had received a response from the no-name space craft still in space. He must have hit something with his beam, because the simple DOS computer aboard seemed to buzz awake, giving its name, or its "pseudo random noise (PRN) number," to Carlos. "USAF Block 1 Navistar P" came up on his screen, and it asked if it should activate itself. He replied no and the satellite went back to sleep. It was weird, and he checked the logs but could not find any information on this satellite ever being there.

For a couple of days, he did some study on the Navistar satellites. Most knew them as the satellites people use with their GPS systems worldwide. The first 11, Block 1 they were called, all went up over a four-to-six year period, and all were still active and had few problems. The more recent ones, Block 2, were more widely used. Deactivating and sending the older ones deep into space or bringing them down to burn up in Earth's atmosphere had been discussed since early 2011.

Carlos asked General Allen about it, and the General came back a day later saying that it was still pretty classified, but they had lost contact with the prototype satellite in early 1990 and had given up on it as being destroyed. For Carlos, the satellite was not important—there were tons of debris up there, and he logged the information on his daily recording pad and forgot about it.

* * *

Sally Powers was flying. She was always flying these days because her F-16 flight training was in its last week. She was with five others of her wing practicing formation flying at altitude. The six F-16s were 50 miles out to sea, west of San Diego, and their radar controller was watching their formation flying. It had been a grueling week and this was her second-to-last training flight with two scheduled refueling appointments over Hawaii. Her wing of F-16 recruits had worked hard for the past seven months. They had started with 12 recruits but six had left for various reasons and they were down to six. This flight was a long one. They did not have drop tanks and the main training in this flight was mid-air refueling. It took organization to refuel six aircraft, one at a time—hooking-up, getting fed the fuel, and then dropping back into formation.

They had taken off from Yuma with little fuel, but heavy with dummy bombs and rockets, and needed refueling when they arrived over the coast ten minutes later. One-by-one, they hitched themselves up behind the Boeing 707 Air Force tanker. Sally was second in line and the hardest part of the refueling would be getting her exact speed to two miles per hour faster than the approaching boom 20 feet below the forward aircraft and then bonding her aircraft to the mother ship. It was the most exciting and demanding flying she had ever done.

This refueling schedule was completed more quickly than normal because the six aircraft only received enough jet fuel for two hours of cruise time at 50,000 feet.

The flight was just over 2,600 miles, and their aircraft would only need refueling once if they had drop tanks attached, but they didn't and 90 minutes later, cruising at a little under 700 miles an hour, they slowed as the radar blip of the second tanker out of Hawaii showed up a hundred miles in front of them. Again, refueling took less than 40 minutes for all six aircraft, and by the time they left the tanker far behind them, they only had another hour of flight time to the islands. They stayed overnight and did the exact same routine back to Vincent Air Force Base.

Sally got a shock when she climbed out of her F-16, wiped her brow, and noticed an Air Force car close by. Her flight commander walked up and asked her to get into the rear seat. She was being given a ride back to the OPS room. The commander took her helmet, something that was not normally done after a flight, and told her that her visitor was important enough to break protocol. She did as she was told and slid into the rear seat of the Ford.

"Good afternoon, Captain Powers," stated the four-star general from the rear seat next to her. "I'm General Pete Allen. I'm sorry to interrupt your training and I'll keep this short and sweet. I remember being pretty tired when I did refueling training back and forth to Hawaii. I did it in F-4s many years ago."

Sally was surprised to see who was in the vehicle with her, but she held her tongue as she waited to hear what he had to say.

"My job in the Air Force is to make sure all the bases run according to Air Force protocol, and I was coming today to do an inspection at Vincent," continued the general. "Yesterday, on my way here, I stayed in Salt Lake City. The Hill Air Force Base commander is a good friend of mine, Colonel Peter Wilkes. Colonel Wilkes and I go back as far as high school together. Another old friend of mine joined us—a friend of yours I found out—and he wanted me to give you a 'hello' when he found out I was coming down here today."

"It could only be Carlos Rodriquez, sir," answered Sally. "I knew he had family friends in high places, but I didn't realize it included four-star generals." General Allen laughed.

"His father is a good friend of mine and Carlos has done some extremely good work for the Air Force. He sort of hinted to me that he would really like it if you could transfer to Hill after your training. It wasn't too hard a mission to complete, since Hill does need a few new pilots, and I thought of suggesting the transfer myself. Captain, I am just the messenger. Carlos put me up to this, so don't shoot the messenger."

"May I assume, sir, that I have time to think it over?" Sally asked.

"The rest of your career," laughed the General. "But I looked at your flight record late last night, and we need you and your wing person, Captain Jennifer Watkins, for a flight mission over

Christmas sometime. You both transferred from C-130s and at Hill we have two old girls who need transfers. Both have just been repainted in their original colors with the 314th Troop Carrier Wing insignia. They are the two oldest C-130s the Air Force has and they go back all the way to the beginning in 1956. They are nicknamed *'Tom'* and *'Jerry.'* I trained on *Jerry* in the early 1960s. Both are being mothballed and put on display, one at Seymour Johnson Air Force Base in North Carolina, and the other at Pope Field, just down the road from Seymour at Fort Bragg. We are extremely short on pilots and I would like you two to complete the transfer for me. Carlos told me that you were heading that way anyway so I will get authorization for you to fly the girls—one pilot per aircraft instead of the mandatory two."

Sally looked a bit skeptical and General Allen hastened to reassure her.

"I've flown *Jerry* single-handed and so can you. I'll authorize you to pick them up once your training is finished and you can get them over to Seymour Johnson at your earliest convenience after the New Year. I'll issue you special leave papers. Carlos said that you were all heading out for a friendly fly-in over Christmas and you can show them off at the fly-in if you want as long as they don't get scratched. They have been decommissioned and don't have official log books anymore."

Somewhat over her shock at sitting next to a four-star general, Captain Powers acknowledged that she and Captain Watkins would be happy to complete the transfers. And she offered to drop in and introduce herself to Colonel Wilkes once she landed at Hill after their training was completed. General Allen nodded his approval, and told her that she could pick up her flight orders from the Colonel and that he personally would OK the free time over Christmas with their CO. With that, the car rolled up to a stop in front of the building where she needed to debrief from her training run. She got out, saluted, and the car drove off.

CHAPTER 10

Jiangsu Province, China – 2010

THE BOARDROOM ON THE 30th floor at Zedong Electronics was filled with people sitting at the boardroom table again for the first time in many years. The only real difference in the same men sitting around the large boardroom table was their ages. Two were missing—both had died—and two younger men, either their sons or those next-in-line from their departments, were in attendance.

A much older Wang Chunqiao, now 83, was still well-dressed in his usual western-style suit made in Savile Row in London and commanded the room on the first day, bringing the table up to date since their last major meeting in 1990.

"Our progress really ramped up to complete world dominance in 2004," he explained to the men from the front of the room, pointing to a large diagram of companies and numbers in U.S. dollars on the large wall behind him.

"It all really started with our friends, the car manufacturers in Japan, allowing us to build their complete management systems here in China starting in 1985, and later at our new Japanese factory built just outside Tokyo. The next big jump was our winning bid with the American, European, and Korean motor companies—to supply them with our cheap engine-management systems from 1987 forward. We also got the contract to refurbish all Japanese-built systems built after 1983 —not many, but it gave us the chance to repair and manage every system in the world, except in France which stayed away from our systems until 1989. They could not resist the price after that, and we offered Renault the first 250,000 systems for their 1990 models at cost."

"That, gentlemen, was our plan in this room 20 years ago, and I will now advance our timeline forward. That difficult discussion with the French car makers cost us a billion U.S. dollars, but after that signing of long-term contracts, we had 98% of the world's transportation market in our grasp. That was the year we also made a profit for the first time and got the Chinese government off our backs. For the first ten years—1980 to 1990—we invested $130 billion of the government's money against 10 billion of our own. The third big breakthrough for Zedong Electronics arrived a couple of years later from the United States—actually from both IBM and Hewlett Packard in the mid-1990s—when they accepted our bid to start building the internal workings for their new personal computers, first in 1993 with their domestic market and then in 1995 for their growing international markets. At the same time, we reached our project projections by building software programs as well as the hardware for the software programs. The following year, we got contracts from every computer manufacturer in the world, again except the French and Compaq, who tried to beat us for one year and had no choice but to lower their pricing by using our parts. By 1995, we had repaid 27% of our debt to the government, and our investors were receiving profits for the first time."

"Microsoft in America begged us to produce software for them, and our most profitable break came in the early 2000s when every company from Samsung and Nokia to Apple negotiated with our shadow companies to build their new and advanced cell phones. Over the last ten years, we have built 300 billion cell phones, PCs, laptops, tablets, and other communication devices here in China and abroad. In the commercial world, we are currently building 81.3% of all new electrical units for sale around the world. But more importantly, 99.87% of the world's new electronics have one or more of our parts inside the units. Our profits from these contracts are still extremely small—cents on every part or complete unit we sell—but to-date we have paid off 87% of our loans to the government and we expect to have all our debts fully paid off by September 2012. Since 2008, we have been able to increase our profits on Apple iPhones and Dell computer parts from 1.7% to 3.9%, and that massive profit increase has led us to complete solvency with our most current and most dangerous enemy, our forward-thinking Chinese government. That is the end of the Chairman's report on our commercial business. More information is in the fact sheets in front of you and you have the rest of the day to study them. As usual, no paper leaves this room."

He took a drink of water from a glass on the podium in front of him and studied his papers for a second.

"Comrades, are there any questions before I allow Comrade Hu Lee to take the podium and bring us up-to-date on the Military Contract Department's advancement of our products?"

"Have we completed our supply and refurbishment on American and European electronics built between 1982 and 1985, when we only started controlling the world's new spare parts, Comrade Chairman?" questioned one of the new men Lee Wang would have recognized as the floor cleaner he had met years before. Mo Wang was one of the two new men in attendance, due to the death of his boss.

"Good question, Mo Wang," replied the Chairman, looking at his papers. An associate ran up to the front of the table to the chairman, bowed, whispered in his ear and handed him a couple more sheets of paper. There were several associates in this meeting sitting in a row of chairs against the wall opposite the large windows. This was where Mo Wang had sat for the first day only at the previous meeting in 1990—his first official meeting as his boss's assistant. He was now in charge of recruitment and was second-in-line to give his department's report.

"Reports show that on the commercial operations side, we have refurbished an estimated 93% of the world's electronic output, of which 79% of the commercial gadgetry has been long outdated and lies in some landfill around the world somewhere. Only in America do people keep their old motor vehicles and I have two conclusions for you."

The Chairman paused for dramatic effect.

"Conclusion One: Of the motor vehicles built without engine-management systems, 8.2% of those vehicles are still running. We expect that worldwide number to decrease in 2011 to 7.6% and in 2012 to 6.9%. For some stupid reason, the Americans still have 12% of their pre-1980 vehicles in operation and 9% are owned by the British who still drive around in these old machines. The next highest numbers are from third-world countries that are not a threat to our program, and they have 8.9% of these vehicles still operating—mostly in South America, Asia, and Africa."

"Conclusion Two: Of the remainder of all vehicles built in the 1980s, 87% had engine-management systems. We built 47% of these and have refurbished parts in 98%. We believe that 71% of these machines have been ground up into new vehicles. Of the 23% we missed and were not built with engine-management systems—around six million vehicles—67% are scrapped and only around two million vehicles remain. Of these vehicles, 500,000 or more have been refurbished with one of more of our electronic parts. The balance is insignificant to our program."

Comrade Wang Chunqiao stopped with the statistics and thanked Comrade Wang for the question. "There are three final success stories, gentlemen, from the commercial side of our business. Footnote One and Two: 97% of all commercial aircraft flying today and 93% of commercial shipping larger than 50 feet have our electronic parts somewhere in their management systems. Footnote Three: We believe that 99% of all current operating space satellites include electronic parts from Zedong Electronics. There are a couple of outdated American Air Force satellites, one Russian military satellite, and one Chinese military satellite that do not have our parts, but we have heard from our sources in NASA and the U.S. Air Force, from our Russians sources, and from our own government spies, that these will be decommissioned within the next year or so. Those results will give us 100% success in space by the end of 2012—success even beyond my own dreams!" he exclaimed, smiling at the men listening to him.

He returned to his chair amid a standing ovation from all in the room. There was much chatter and conversation between the 16 men around the table. The others sitting by the wall sat upright and were silent. Again the room returned to silence as a bell sounded and a dozen girls entered to refill drinks.

Fifteen minutes later, Hu Lee walked up to the podium and silence reigned. "Chairman Chunqiao, comrades, I give you my report on military advancements since our last meeting in 1990. The world's military strength has grown 20-fold since the start of our operation to sell electronic parts to the world's armies. We are lucky compared to the commercial side, in that the world's major superpowers, including the old Soviet Union, are quick to either sell outdated equipment to countries with less power who are not a risk to our program, or destroy what remains. Military equipment is extremely expensive to run, and outdated equipment is destroyed at a far more rapid rate than commercial equipment in the private sector. Since 1985, when we got our first contracts to supply electronic parts to the United States and Russia after long and extremely secret meetings with their military personnel, we have electronic parts installed in 90.1% of all the world's military weapons that are fitted with some sort of electronic devise—whether it's an engine-management system in ground vehicles, rocket-guidance systems, aircraft-management systems in the air, virtually every electronic system at sea, 100% of all the mobile atomic military reactors, and 99% of the commercial atomic reactors worldwide. As Chairman Chunqiao correctly stated—and the Chairman and I have worked together on behalf of our Space Management and Atomic Reactor Departments—100% of the spacecraft in orbit will soon be fitted with several of our systems. We have only had two major breakdowns in our military department, in 1995 and 1999. In 1995, the Russians found that we had been delivering the same parts to the Americans and vice-versa."

"In 1999, NATO and the Americans found out that all our replacement parts were identical in their electronic equipment. By then, we had made sure that nobody had been making these minor parts in bulk for a decade, and their military departments had no choice but to continue with our programs. There was one very large and powerful company in Delhi, India that had been trying to make their way into the market for several years, but we had our friends in Pakistan terminate five of their seven board members in 1993. The owners sold the company to an American shadow company of ours in 1994. Several other minor companies tried to achieve entry into our market in South Africa in 1994, the United States in 1997, 1998, and 1999, Britain in 1994, and Germany in 1999. We ultimately purchased all of those companies through shadow corporations. The results, gentlemen are as good as we could ever anticipate. I go back to my figure of 91% of the world's current military weapons. The reason it is 91% is because 2% of those untouched numbers are our own company military here in China, and 7% are the growing Iranian, North Korean, and Pakistani military forces—all Zedong Electronics allies.

Hu Lee stopped for a moment, took a drink from the bottled

water on the podium at the head of the table, and resumed his report.

"Let's look next at the findings on Blue-Water International Strength. Blue-water power is a program we created to show each military's strength on world coverage and in an attack-mode only, not a defense-mode. China currently ranks second in power, but with our limited ability to reach every corner of the globe with our forces and attack the other countries, we only rank fourth. The strongest military in the world is America, with 57% of the world's blue-water strength, then Russia with 23%, and then NATO with 21%. We decided to include the separate armed forces of NATO together for the purpose of this report. Our own country is ranked fourth, with only the 4% I previously mentioned, and India is fifth with 2%. This shows that without the futuristic space weaponry we think America and Russia have in their most modern space satellites and the world's nuclear weapons, China only has only a 4% chance of winning in a world battle for supremacy. Gentlemen China is currently one of weakest in an attack, but the 16 of us at Zedong Electronics are going to change that equation very soon. Thank you."

Again his speech received a standing ovation and he stayed at the podium waiting for the clapping to die down. "Questions please?" he asked. "I see Comrade Zhi Yun."

"A great report, Comrade Lee, and I would like to be the first to congratulate you on your success," replied Zhi Yun, standing to ask the question. "My first question, however, is that your first percentage of all military equipment that has our electronics added was 90.1%, and then you skipped to 91%. What is the difference of 0.9%? Secondly, why has our government not kept up with blue-water power around the world?" He sat down.

"I was hoping that my intellectual comrades would notice my figures, and I knew you, Comrade Yun, would be the first one. As Chairman Chunqiao stated in his report, we must take into account any equipment still in operation before we started our program. Again the Americans and the Europeans collect old equipment. For some reason, the collection of old equipment seems to be a hobby for individuals in these countries. The difference, Comrade Yun, is that 0.5% of all 30-year or older military equipment worldwide is, or could still be, in operational condition. The 0.4% difference relates to known active military equipment, mostly ex-American, in third-world countries, or Russia, and our own weapons held by terrorists, or other forms of mercenary military establishments around the world. These are certainly not a threat to our program. If we take into account the 0.5% of equipment that is either in museums or still active in first-world countries, 20% of the threat—or 0.1% of the old military weapons—are atomic and either based in Russia or America, and the other 0.4% has no blue-water usage and is useable only for defense. It is impossible to gather information on this 0.1% atomic threat to our program, but in my department we believe that all atomic weapons older than 30 years, and especially their control mechanisms in both America and Russia, have been refurbished over time with our more modern electrical components."

"Is there any way we can be sure, Comrade Lee?" asked the Chairman.

"We have tried to get our personnel into these old control centers, but they have been sealed and are on complete lock down in both countries. Inspections are only done by very high security personnel, if at all. We have received information on nearly all of these older installations over the years and I believe all of them have been decommissioned under the nuclear arms pacts between the two countries. We know of every one of these old rocket installations, and have completed reports on every single one, except one in Kansas and one in Siberia. They are so old—some of the first ever made back in the 1950s—that I believe that the rocket silos are either empty or no longer exist, and the atomic rockets stationed in them have long since been destroyed. Most of those older rockets were terminated in the most recent arms treaty between the two countries and there is even talk of more reductions this year and in 2011."

Again, Hu Lee stopped for a moment to hydrate—a necessary task with such a long report.

"Now I will answer your second question, Comrade. This time, I express my own ideas and opinions. I believe each one of you have your own ideas on this subject. The main reason our government has not worried about blue-water domination as we have looked at it, is because nobody is ever going to attack China again. It has been many centuries since China was a large offensive power, and we have lost our need to create and model attack scenarios, and now only look at economics and defense."

"I believe that the idea of defense only is due to the new government's thoughts on economical strength versus military strength. As we will soon prove, economical strength can win a war versus a major power, but a direct invasion on its homeland is still an attack scenario, and that is what we have lost in our thinking. Attack is a difficult scenario, because if the country has fire power, we would end up being no stronger than the useless United Nations, who can only talk and hand out sanctions. Unfortunately, and with the changes in the thinking of our leaders, we have gone from a country who really wanted to be a superpower in military strength to a power whose economical strength is more important as a deterrent from attacks on our own soil. Money is now king, not the sword or gun, and a totally false sense of security exists around the world. Please excuse me, Chairman Chunqiao, for saying this, but I beg of you to understand what I'm saying."

Hu Lee moved from the podium to start pacing in the front of the room as he moved from the rehearsed speech to his own personal beliefs.

"Our old way of thinking, which we started with in this room 30 years ago—the old way of thinking that the sons of communist China grew up with, under our great comrade's leadership—has become obsolete, and our thoughts and actions are as old as the useless atomic weapons being destroyed, unless we succeed and lead our people into world dominance with our program and let it reach its conclusion."

There were sounds and words of shock from many of the men around the table. Comrade Lee returned to his seat and there was complete silence in the room. The Chairman got up from his chair and approached the podium.

"Interesting, Comrade Lee," mused the Chairman. The room was breathless with anticipation about what was going to happen to the man who just had called the Chairman obsolete. "I thank you for your report and ideas on current China. I also appreciate your frankness about our 30-year old program, and in many ways, I agree with you. One thing we did not predict was change, advancement, and the ideas modern society would instill in humanity. We as a planet have changed faster and faster over the last three decades. We at Zedong Electronics have noticed this through the rapid advancement of keeping control of the modern parts and electrical gadgetry given to us by our spies and workers around the world. Comrade Lee, I thank you for being honest and allowing your thoughts of our project into this meeting. I believe that reality is a necessary equation we must all deal with every day. Fortunately for us, our 30-year project is nearly complete and we must continue to fulfill our destiny. Comrade Lee, I believe like you that our attack scenario is going to be the making or breaking of our program, and I have been working with members of our armed forces and government for the last year. All I can say is that there is a scenario in place, and we will cover that at our next and final meeting before the start of Z-Day—a couple of years from now. I now call on Comrade Wang to give his report on our men in the field." Mo Wang got up and went forward.

"Comrade Chairman, fellow comrades. It is an honor to give my report to you today."

He started off a little more respectfully since he was a new and younger man in this week-long meeting. "All of our departments have succeeded in our program, including the one I am currently in charge of. It has been a big learning experience watching our citizens and comrades going off to every part of the world imaginable. Before the passing of my comrade boss, I was in charge of our biggest unit within the department—the exportation of our people into the United States of America and Canada. So I will first give you a full report in my new capacity as the Head of Department and the whole world, and then a short report on North America. The program got off the ground as soon as Zedong Electronics was formed in the early 1980s. We had our first operative in place within three weeks of the first meeting that I did not have the pleasure of attending in this board room."

"The complete "Global Village," as we called the project on the island north of Shanghai, was completed a year after the first man went over. The startup of the project cost US$50 million to build and then US$20 million a year to run. It is still in operation 25 years later, and has cost a total of US$560 million. In its lifetime, we have secured, taught, and sent 1,700,000 operatives into the world outside Asia and another 300,000 operatives within Asia. Our costs include the three universities we had built here at a cost of US$20 million per university, as well as bonuses and operational costs and needs once the operatives reached their destinations. The total also includes a loan of US$125 million to our country's airline in 1985 when it needed to lease new aircraft to grow its international travel. This loan and the lease of new aircraft from Boeing also gave us entrance into Boeing headquarters, and we have cleaned all their offices worldwide ever since."

The boardroom laughed at the interesting remark. "Of the

two million operatives, 83% have given us the information we needed to get where we are today. Of the rest, 14% could not stand living in the 'outside world,' and returned to work in our local offices in many important positions. Only 1% needed to be terminated. I believe that our numbers show our success in recruitment. The balance of 2% did not survive in the foreign country they were assigned and died or became unstable mentally within the first year of transfer. Of the 40,000 in this category, most were single men. The biggest problem was driving motor vehicles for the first time in their lives. We lost 30% of these people due to car accidents. Another 35% were in other forms of accidents—so many different types that I could spend the next few weeks explaining them. It is unbelievable what happens to people in the world. Thirty percent of this group, or 12,000 operatives, tried to become citizens of their new country, found a spouse, and forgot that we had introduced them to their new life. Of these people, 10,000 were terminated by our termination squads over 25 years, or about 450 per year. These operatives were in over 170 countries and no notice was taken of their 'natural' or 'accidental' deaths at all. We have a very refined termination program that does not cause attention with any authorities in any country. The remaining 2,000 where returned to China and either used in other positions if they had certain skills we needed, or terminated. Of the last 5%, or 8,000 operatives, we have 2,200 in extremely powerful positions around the world that are sleepers for when we might need them. Another 5,500 are in military service somewhere and ready to relay information once our program is put into operation.

"That leaves 300 operatives who just disappeared off the radar screens and have never been heard from since. My best estimates are that many of them were killed once somebody was not happy about them being around, or did not like our system and became outlaws to Zedong Electronics. Some might be in hiding and still on our side. They all have the technology and know-how to contact us, and maybe they will after the start of our program."

There were a few murmurs from different listeners. "Now, to get to the really exciting news! Of the 83% of our successful operatives, or 1,690,000 people we trained and sent out there, 90% of those have given us one to three important contacts or pieces of information and now live happy lives wherever they are. They completed their missions and cost us very little. Of the balance, 9% gave us information, or got us into high-risk establishments, both civilian and military, and gave us five to ten contacts. These are living happy lives with families, have been paid a retirement package, and are now retired. Almost 1% of the balance are still operatives and will give us anything new, even though we don't need any more information or contacts. They are just monitoring the systems we have in place, and at this time these very successful operatives have given us over 20 contacts during active service and are still being paid an income by us. The last and smallest group of people, the last 0.01% or 170 of our best people (and I'm proud to say that I found 70 of them over the last 25 years) have completed and found 70% of all the contacts and information we have needed so far—such a small group with so much success."

"Now let me complete my report with a look at North America. In my initial department of control—the United States of America and Canada—115 of these 170 most successful operatives worked in my area. A couple of operatives are still based in Canada and gave us Blackberry and several other important companies, but America was the most important part in the whole Operative Department. We sent the best to America and these people gave us everything from DOS to Apple iPhones, from Microsoft to Sun Microsystems, and from Chevrolet to NASA's space programs. For example, even though the current space shuttle project ends this year, we have over 12,000 electrical parts in each of their space shuttles, just in case they decide to lengthen the project. Europe and Australia were just as important, but because our attack will start in the United States, it is imperative to have our first success there, in the most powerful nation on earth. Thank you."

There was another standing ovation and Mo Wang waited for questions.

"A great accomplishment, Comrade Wang," stated Ri Yun who was to be the fourth and last speaker before lunch. All 16 members of the board would give their report, but there were only four scheduled per day, with the afternoon time set for discussion and arguments regarding the morning's reports.

Ri Yun continued, "I assume by your report that the majority of our operatives know very little about the big picture?"

"That is correct, Comrade Yun," was Mo Wang's reply.

"They are not a problem for Zedong electronics in the future and are forgotten?" Mo Wang nodded yes. "Then what is your department's protocol with the men who have done a great service for the program—the 170 super operatives and the other 0.99%, or by my figures another 1,600 operatives, who do know a lot about the information and contacts they have gathered for us and could be embarrassing in the near future and are past our program time?"

"An unfortunate question you ask, Comrade Yun," was Mo Wang's reply. "Of the 1,600 operatives, the Chairman feels the need to terminate all of them who know certain information that could be embarrassing, as you described. More than 100 termination squads will be deployed at the beginning of next year and these necessary terminations will be completed by the end of 2011. They are in six countries and there will be no problems making them and their families disappear. It is a shame, but necessary to do this to our brave and best-producing troops. There will be no pain and death will be fast and all under accidental circumstances. Of the best 170 operatives, 157 of them will be terminated closer to the last few months by the same squads in four countries, but mostly the United States and Canada. They are still in their positions giving us important information weekly. The remaining 13 of our extreme elite operatives are planned to be terminated in December. Any missed operatives are expected to be terminated shortly after the beginning of the New Year, or if they slip through our fingers, they are expected be terminated by the American people in the expected mass panic." There was silence as Mo Wang took his seat.

Mo was quite sad, as many of the people he had just described had become good friends of his over the years. He knew their wives and children, their successes, and he did not enjoy being their executioner. It was not within his authority to let them live. His mind turned to his nephew Lee Wang, his best operative of all—the man who had gotten them a dozen very large information packets that ended up being billion-dollar contracts with the larger American computer companies. Lee Wang had swept the floors as Bill Gates and Steve Jobs walked by him, had played chess with Warren Buffett, had been introduced to the boss at NASA as a Chinese professor and had solved a problem they had, and had even shaken the hands of the Clintons when Bill was President. Lee, his wife, and now-grown daughter were his family, and they were the last termination order in December in Salt Lake City. This thought made Mo Wang a sad man.

CHAPTER 11

Christmas in North Carolina

THE LONG-RANGE WEATHER FORECAST looked good for North Carolina over Christmas and the New Year. Preston was studying future weather conditions around the country for his fly-in and the temperatures looked a little above average for the season. A storm was expected in Seattle and Portland by the end of the week, due to hit the Rockies just before Christmas and then pass to the north over New York and Boston on New Year's Eve. It was a cold Saturday morning on December 15th, and Preston was drinking his first cup of coffee and looking at the computer screen in front of him. On the NOAA website and a few good pilot websites, several variations of the long-term weather forecast could be viewed all the way up to the last day of the year.

Winter was expected to be warmer and drier than normal in the Carolinas and across much of the central United States. There was not a freeze date shown, but temperatures were expected to drop into the upper 30s closer to New Year's Eve. Rain was in the forecast the last two days of the year, but coming from a southwesterly direction, and that meant warmer air bringing in moisture. The next storm on the West coast was projected to be a slow-moving one, and was not expected to hit Salt Lake City with snow until the weekend before Christmas.

Martie came into the lounge freshly showered with her hair wrapped in a towel, carrying a plate of toast with marmalade, and set it down beside the mouse Preston was using.

"Thanks. Weather is still looking good for Christmas," Preston said. "It wouldn't be much fun if we had a white Christmas and had to shovel the entire runway for takeoff."

"We've only had one white Christmas since the 40s," answered Martie, "and that was two years ago. I don't think there's much chance of a white-out."

"It's looking a little problematic for Carlos from Friday night onwards, though. There's a new storm expected in Seattle and I'm sure he's looking at the weather later today, too. I'll call him and see if we should expect him a day or two earlier." Preston clicked to another website as he was talking. "Buck might have to leave a day or two early as well. The snowy weather over Denver right now looks bad for New York starting early on Monday. New York is going to get at least an inch or more of snow the day before Christmas and then a really big storm over New Year's. He was going to leave early on the 24th and be down here for lunch. It's certainly going to be a white Christmas for the Northeast. This latest storm is moving slowly and is going to pack a punch with snowfall."

"Since we will experience a beautiful day this coming Monday, Mr. Weatherman, with no clouds, a slight breeze from the north, and temperatures in the upper 40s to mid-50s, why don't we take our P-51s out over the Outer Banks and then follow the coast down to Charleston, or even further, or until we need to return in a triangle back to base. We haven't had a decent day's flying for months now, and we could even ask your buddy Colonel Mondale for permission to fly into Seymour Johnson to visit. He might even offer us a cup of coffee," suggested Martie.

"Best idea I've heard all day," answered Preston, looking for his cell phone. Colonel Mondale had been a friend of Preston's for several years. They had met at a fly-in in Jacksonville, Florida and found out that they only lived 40 miles apart. It had been the first fly-in where Preston had displayed his new P-51, and the Colonel had flown down in an Apache attack helicopter to represent the U.S. Air Force.

They met again once or twice at other aircraft gatherings, and when he told the Colonel that he was about to take possession of an old P-38 Lightning, the Colonel offered Preston the option of flying into Seymour Johnson any time he wanted to show him the new plane. That had been a year ago, and Martie's suggestion to finally give the Colonel his viewing was an excellent one. Preston hinted to Martie that they might even be offered lunch if he flew the P-38 instead of the Mustang.

It took a couple of minutes and clicks on Monday morning as the call was connected through to the base. It was only 8:00 in the morning, and a few seconds later the Colonel's voice came on the line. After a few pleasantries, Preston explained their plans and Martie could hear the excitement on the line when the head of Seymour Johnson Air Force Base in Goldsboro responded positively to the visit of both a P-38 and a P-51.

Civilian aircraft flying in tight formation was not normally allowed, except with prior permission, and Preston asked the Colonel if he could grant permission for two aircraft to fly in formation from a southerly direction and then into Seymour air space. The Colonel responded that he could give permission in North Carolina only, but if they kept out to sea further down the coast, he thought that little interference would be made by traffic control if they stayed a couple hundred yards apart.

Both aircraft were already fueled up when Preston phoned Carlos to see what his plans were. Carlos was up, had seen the storm on the news, and told Preston that he would be leaving Friday by midday. They should expect him just before dark.

Preston wheeled out Martie's P-51 first with his small tractor, and then did the same with his own aircraft, parking them on the apron at such an angle that when they fired up, the air from aircraft's propellers wouldn't hit the hangar door. The two gleaming aircraft certainly looked beautiful waiting for them on the chilly, sparkling morning, and as usual, the blood pressure of both pilots rose as they looked at the aircraft waiting for them to fly. Life was certainly worth living!

The major difference, apart from the engines and frames of both aircraft was that Martie's P-51 had a rear wheel and Preston's much larger twin-engine P-38 had a front wheel. And Martie's aircraft was silver, while the P-38 was still painted in camouflage colors.

They climbed aboard their aircraft and hit the starter motors. Within seconds all three engines coughed out their usual belch of dark smoke and were warming up nicely. Because of the colder weather, they let the engines run for a few minutes longer than normal to warm up. Both pilots had dozens of pre-flight checks to do anyway. They took their time and talked to each other over their intercoms as they mentally ticked off each check.

As with all aircraft, pre-flight checks were necessary before they took off, but they had always been kept to a minimum in fighter aircraft due to the built-in urgency to get off the ground as quickly as possible. Most of the checks had to do with fuel flow, wing and propeller configurations, engine pressure and temperatures, and then their outside surroundings—other aircraft and weather conditions.

"Wind is about five miles an hour from due west, with slight gusts," Preston informed Martie over his radio. The runway ran from southeast to northwest in a 290/110 degree configuration, and he had built it in this direction because most of the wind in his area was either from the west or north in winter, and the south in summer.

"Martie, you taxi out and take off first, do a left turn out towards the lake and wait until we get permission from Raleigh Traffic Control before we climb above 5,000 feet."

They had both filed flight plans with the controlling air traffic control based at RDU over the computer earlier that morning. Anybody could fly without a flight plan up to a certain altitude. Preston always flew this way with the crop sprayer, due to not being involved with any commercial traffic under that level. Aircraft from, or going into, Raleigh-Durham International (RDU) were usually well above 10,000 feet over Preston's area. Military aircraft also tended to stay away from commercial flight lanes, and Preston did not often see military flights over the farm. Martie acknowledged him, increased the throttle, and taxied out to the south end of the runway while Preston went through his additional pre-flight checks for two engines.

It didn't take long before her screaming aircraft passed Preston, who was still waiting on the apron, and he watched as she took off, brought up her undercarriage, and then slowly turned the aircraft into a left turn. Preston gunned the P-38 down to the southern end at a faster rate, turned her around, felt that both throttles were locked together so that they would both work on the same revs, and opened them up. It wasn't more than 30 seconds and 1,000 feet of runway before he was also bringing up his undercarriage and trimming his flaps. He immediately decreased his engine revs down from maximum to after take-off power and then turned, gliding the heavy aircraft into the same left turn to follow Martie. He saw her glint in the sun a few miles ahead of him and aimed the P-38 in her direction. The P-38 was pretty light since it only had him and full tanks with no bombs or ammunition, and it moved fast through the air.

Preston got on his radio at 4,000 feet, leveled off, and asked permission to follow their flight plan. By now, they both were visual on all radar in the area and they were given permission to head west, but to keep below 7,000 feet. He blew Martie a kiss as he banked and passed by within a hundred yards of her, and she took up position a quarter of a mile behind him, pushed her sun glasses up her nose as the sun was now just off her starboard wing, and slowly gained altitude, following him up to 7,000 feet at a little over 300 miles an hour.

Several minutes later they were away from RDU commercial traffic, heading a little north of Smithfield, and had been given permission to climb up to 15,000 feet. Their current heading took them north and away from the military air space of Seymour Johnson AFB where they were expected for lunch in three hours.

Military air space was an area where no aircraft were allowed to enter without prior permission. Usually, the air space around a military installation was 20 to 50 miles around the base, depending on the base's size, and all commercial aircraft had to fly around the no-fly zones. In North Carolina, there were several of these zones, and Preston and Martie were used to them.

The two old war birds had planned for a flight level of 15,000 feet. At that level, they did not need to wear oxygen masks and it would be a scenic view flying out to the Outer Banks. They had throttled back their aircraft to 60% power and were cruising along at a fuel-saving 275 miles an hour. It was beautiful, and both pilots were as close to heaven as any pilot could get. The sky above them was a much brighter blue than normally seen from the ground, the traffic noise on the radios diminished slightly, and they were like two angels flying closer to God than anybody around them. They did this trip several times a year and loved it.

The sea came into view and they were 20 miles outside of Elizabeth City when Preston told Martie to get within 300 yards of his aircraft. They were still not in formation, or wing tip to wing tip, but pretty close. They decreased altitude once they were over the coast, and flew out another ten miles before Preston got onto the radio and called in their position. They were turning to head in a southerly direction along the coast and they were descending down to below 5,000 feet. He got the confirmation that traffic control had received his information and that he was to stay ten miles out from the coast and to watch for the military no-fly zones to their south.

Martie followed him down to 3,000 feet, and at this altitude they were much closer to the calm waters below them. The water was a rich royal blue on her port wing due to them flying close to the Gulf Stream with its warmer currents flowing northwards. It was beautiful and with the sun dancing on her left wing, she followed Preston slightly to his right and a couple of hundred feet below him so she would not get into his propeller wash. They throttled back a little more to enjoy the view, and began heading south at 240 miles an hour—a slow speed for these old war birds. Both aircraft could easily top 400 miles an hour at any time.

For an hour they flew south following the coast. Once they had passed the military no-fly zones around Cherry Point, the Marine Air Corp Station, the two aircraft headed closer to the coast toward Wilmington, and were only a couple of miles offshore when they passed into South Carolina.

Charleston came over the horizon 30 minutes later, and Preston asked Martie for a fuel report. They had under-the-wing drop tanks permanently installed on both aircraft, just like Carlos' and Preston's P-51s did, and they had only used a third of what they had aboard. Preston naturally had more fuel than Martie, with his slightly larger tanks, but he had two engines burning fuel instead of one. Their cockpit heaters were working well and both pilots were snug and warm under their bubble Perspex canopies.

They were over Savannah, Georgia when Preston turned gently to port, increased power to 60%, and headed out to sea. Once they had lost sight of land, the two aircraft turned again to port until they headed back to the U.S. coast in a northwest direction aimed directly for Seymour Johnson. The sun shone brightly and the air was as clear as could be as they slowly climbed past 10,000 and then leveled out at 16,000 feet.

In the world of flying, all aircraft flew at different altitudes in different directions—odd numbers of thousands of feet in easterly directions and even numbers in westerly directions. They were expected at Seymour in an hour, and Preston increased his throttles to 75% power. At the higher altitude, they flew back towards the coast. Preston called Martie over the radio to tell her of any changes he was going to make in headings, altitude, and throttle changes before he did it and all she had to do was to follow suit.

The happy couple were still over the ocean and had just reached 16,000 when she nudged her silver bird forward and came up to the right wing of the P-38 and blew him a kiss. Then she backed up and leveled off about 20 feet behind him on his starboard wing. They were now flying in formation and this took serious flying, but both pilots were extremely practiced.

Preston told Martie to tune her second radio, since both aircraft had two, over to the local military frequency used by all military bases in the area, and he called up Seymour Johnson. It took less than a second for the military air control to respond to Preston's radio call, because they had been routinely watching the pair's entire flight. Preston continued saying that they were two aircraft flying in formation, 324 miles out from Seymour, had clearance to fly into military airspace and would be coming in at their present angle, altitude, and speed with an estimated arrival time of 58 minutes. Seymour responded that they had them on radar and to stay their current course, speed, and altitude until they reached military airspace 50 miles out.

Forty minutes later it was time to go down, and both aircraft were given flight instructions to a long final approach into Seymour. Preston contacted Seymour Approach and was ordered to turn to 260 degrees for finals to Runway 26. He was told to decrease altitude to 4,000 feet, and Preston and Martie left their formation flying to become two separate flights again for radio purposes and started their landing checks 20 miles out. At 4,000 feet, they were told that winds were 295\12 and that Preston would be second to land and Martie third behind an incoming C-130.

From this information, Preston knew that the winds were nearly right down the runway at 12 knots and that he had to look out for a military aircraft that was somewhere close in front of them. He and Martie radioed back that they both had the C-130 visual and that the aircraft in front of them was turning into its final approach a couple of miles ahead of them. They could also tell where the military aircraft was by listening to its radio communication. They were then told to leave the runway at Exit B, because there were three F-16s coming in behind them, and they were a lot faster on their final approaches than the propeller-driven aircraft in front of them.

Preston and Martie landed and quickly exited the runway just as the first F-16 was about to touch down. Seymour Ground Control then told them where to go, and it wasn't long before they were ordered to shut down engines in front of a large hangar where an Air Force car was waiting for them.

Martie climbed out, ran over to Preston, and gave him a big hug. He always saw the excitement flying gave her in her bright blue eyes and he smiled at the pleasure they had both enjoyed from the fun flight.

"Been up for over three hours I noticed, Preston. And you must be the flying ace, Martie? Men's and ladies' bathrooms are in the hangar. Then I want my tour," said Colonel Mondale as he walked up and shook both pilots' hands. Preston formally introduced him to Martie.

"I notice she is a P-38 L, built in the Vultee Plant in Nashville," observed the Colonel as two relieved pilots returned.

"You certainly know your P-38s, Colonel," replied Preston.

"She did time in France with the D–Day attacks in Normandy, I was told. A few of these P-38L models were field-modified to become two-seat, TP-38L familiarization trainers, and I looked everywhere for one so that I could take Martie up, or even get a chance to give you a ride in it, but I could not find one anywhere."

"I see that she has 370th Fighter Group insignia on her sides. Is that original?" the Colonel asked.

"As far as I know it is, Colonel. She was based out of Britain and took part in several raids in Germany in 1944 before D-Day. I know she did take some damage during the war because two or three areas of her right wing have newer pieces that don't look like something she was originally put together with. They, I believe, are from a P-38 K model and are not recent repairs, as they have all the original time-line screws and fittings. Other than that, her guns are now operational, even the Hispano I found on the Internet a year or ago from a ground vehicle that had exactly the same gun mountings."

"The reason I know about the 370th is that my father belonged to the fighter wing that ended up being re-designated as the 140th Fighter Group and assigned to the Colorado Air National Guard on August 27th, 1946. I was born in Colorado in 1958."

"Then your father could have flown this aircraft?" asked Preston, and the Colonel nodded his head and smiled.

For another hour, the base commander walked around, asked questions, and sat in both aircraft before he guided them off to lunch at the mess. Several other pilots walked up and also inspected the rare birds and then Preston and Martie were given a hearty lunch. A reasonably sized group, including Colonel Mondale, watched them from the side of the runway as they took off and left for home a couple of hours later.

Once Preston and Martie were airborne, he asked the tower if they could do a fly-over, and Martie followed him as they banked and then went into a steep dive back down towards the beginning of the runway. This was dangerous flying, and Martie backed off slightly as they went into the dive and then caught up with him as they straightened out a mile out and together they screamed along the runway, towards the waving Colonel at over 400 miles an hour and 200 feet above the flat surface. Preston gave the order to go vertical to Martie over the intercom, and they pulled up once they reached the car and both went into a vertical climb under full power all the way up to 5,000 feet, where they carefully leveled off. Reducing their screaming engines back to normal, they waggled their wings and asked Seymour Tower for instructions out of the area.

"Enjoyed that," droned the controller in the tower. "Stay at 5,000 feet on your present course until you patch into RDU Approach. You will depart our air space in 90 seconds. Thanks for the visit. The boys enjoyed your show and I'm sure the boss did too. Out."

When they landed, they still showed a quarter of a tank left, so they refueled their aircraft and gave them a good wipe down once Preston towed them back into the hangar. There were still checks and preparation to be completed for storage, with chocks under the wheels and attaching the many protective sleeves over the guns as well as the several outside instrument recorders to protect them. That night they enjoyed a quiet meal with Oliver and reminisced about the day's flying, as all pilots do.

* * *

The storm looked menacing as Carlos took off from Hill Air Force Base just a couple of hours before lunch the following Friday. The dark clouds were grey and low and he needed to get over to Denver to refuel for the second, longer flight down to Preston's airfield. He had already wished the several people he worked with, including Lee Wang, a merry festive season an hour earlier. Lee had told Carlos that his daughter was coming to stay with them for the holidays and he and his wife were looking forward to her visit.

On the long and winding road down into the valley Salt Lake City and Hill Air Force Base were located Carlos turned on the radio and listened to the 10 o' clock news.

"Several large fires have gutted several houses in California in the last two days," stated the announcer while Carlos thought over his flight plan as he drove his four-wheel drive Range Rover down the steep and winding pass. The road was clear, with mountains of old snow already piled up on each side, but the road was dry with clear driving conditions. He half-listened to the news.

"Three deadly fires started just after midnight last night in different areas, totally gutted the houses, and two neighboring houses also caught fire. The worst fire was reported in a new Cupertino suburb, where Apple is headquartered, but not close enough to the headquarters to be a concern. The second and third fires were located in the Silicon Valley area. Three families perished in the blaze, all believed to be Chinese-Americans as reported by neighbors. This night of deadly fire follows much the same as the house fires last week, one in Seattle and one in Washington, where again two Chinese-American families perished. A report by the FBI now investigating the fires believes that these fires could be related to Chinese gang violence. The weather for Salt Lake City..."

"I haven't heard of Chinese gangs in the States!" thought Carlos and got back to driving down the pass.

Carlos reached Denver a couple of hours later without incident, and he prepared and refueled his aircraft for the longer stretch into North Carolina. The weather looked good, with strong winds from the incoming storm that would get him out of the Denver area quickly. "I might even beat my record of four hours dead," he thought to himself.

Carlos' voice came over Preston's radio just under four hours later, and just as the sun was about to set. He was five minutes out and descending to 5,000 feet. Preston radioed back that there was zero wind and that he should get straight onto final approach for Runway 11. Preston had the runway numerals on both ends of the runway for pilots to see. Carlos replied that he was already on a long final, 30 miles out.

Martie wasn't home from Chapel Hill yet, and Preston went out with binoculars and a hand-held radio to watch his friend come in. He noticed a split-second glint in the darkening sky and saw the minute spot that was Carlos' P-51. His friend came in fast and expertly, touching down only yards from the beginning of the asphalt, and swinging in the stop directly in front of Preston. Preston noticed that the aircraft still had that cold and frozen look about it from high-altitude flying.

"You came in at high altitude?" asked Preston as the propeller came to a complete stop and Carlos opened his Perspex canopy.

"The tailwind was better the higher up I went," replied Carlos, stretching and getting out. He didn't need help as he stepped onto the wing with a small backpack in his hand and walked down a small walk-able area to the rear and jumped off onto the ground. He refused Preston's hand as help.

"I'm not that old, Señor Strong," Carlos smiled before giving Preston a bear hug. "At one stage I was as high as 39,000 feet and even watched a Boeing 747-400 pass by close under my left wing. He was out of Chicago and still climbing through 33,000. He wasn't that much faster than me. I think I had a better tailwind and was doing well over 450 miles an hour ground speed at the time. I was cruising at 340 as usual and it looked like my tailwind was over 125 mph. The Garmin GPS I installed last year is extremely accurate, and what was the 747 doing, still in climb... around 500 miles an hour?"

"I'd say 500 is about right," replied Preston.

"Martie not home from work yet?" asked Carlos.

"No, she heard that you were coming in today and left for California," laughed Preston. "No, she won't be home for another 30 minutes or so. Go and use the bathroom in the hangar and I'll unpack the trunk of your rental and get it parked for you, sir," joked Preston, knowing what Carlos immediately needed.

"I have everything I need here in my pack and I hope you have washed and ironed my clothes," Carlos continued heading for the hangar with Preston walking off to get the tractor.

"Martie has hung your North Carolina wardrobe in the first bedroom on your right at the top of the stairs," Preston flung back over his shoulder. "Watch your step! We have a new wing, and stairs prepared by Neighbor Joe especially for your arrival," Preston added tartly, getting on the tractor and knowing that Carlos was in for an improvement shock.

Preston placed the third P-51 in the crop sprayer's usual spot in the hangar. The yellow devil, Preston called her, was the one of many aircraft that would have to stay outside for the fly-in. His hangar was not that big and had just enough room for the three P-51s and the P-38.

"Hey! I like the new digs," Carlos complimented, returning from his inspection. "I have the first bedroom you say and I think I also heard that Sally will be in the second bedroom, next to mine?"

"You wish, Carlos," laughed Preston. "Just to break your bubble of self-importance, Buck and his new girl Barbara will be staying next to you and I had to go and buy an extra set of single beds today for the third bedroom because Sally is arriving tomorrow morning out of Hill and is bringing a friend with her." Preston watched Carlos' smile fade from his face as he heard the news. "You can help me carry up the two new single beds and bring down the queen," chuckled Preston. "Think about it, you hot-headed American Latino! If it was a lover, I wouldn't have to change the beds! Her friend is a girlfriend of hers from Yuma;

they both just got their F-16 wings." Preston laughed as the smile and color quickly returned to Carlo's face.

"Then we can leave the bed and Sally can stay in my room," he suggested.

"I'm sure that is not the most important thing on Sally's mind right now," replied Preston, walking up the stairs and beckoning Carlos to follow him. "If you can get Sally into your room, I say 'well done.' You need a decent girlfriend. But I bet you $500 that you can't do it before you leave the farm in the New Year?"

"Bet on that, Señor Strong. I love a dangerous mission and I will be happy to take your money before next year!"

"Maybe she's gay!" laughed Preston. "I'll bet you hadn't thought of that angle." Preston walked into the third room and grabbed hold of one side of the queen mattress.

* * *

Martie arrived an hour later with food and a bottle of wine, hugged Carlos, and was happy to be told that the beds had been changed. The two men were sitting in the house lounge and were just opening two beers. "I have the booze for the party arriving tomorrow morning," she stated, hugging Preston and giving him a sweet, longer than usual, kiss on the lips just to piss off Carlos.

"You know I can't stand all that romance between you two, Martie," objected Carlos.

"Then you shouldn't look," was her response. "It's time you found your own woman."

"Oh!" He replied. "I intend to, and win money from your husband-to-be soon, too!"

"As long as the bet is not over my best friend, Sally?" remarked Martie, looking stern. The two men winked at each other. "I hear she's bringing protection for hot-headed men like you, Carlos," she laughed, going into the kitchen with her shopping. She came out with a glass of red wine and sat down with the two men in the lounge. "So when are all the pilots getting in?" she then asked Preston.

"Captain Powers and her friend Captain Watkins are expected in Sunday afternoon. She is currently at Hill AFB in Salt Lake and the storm Carlos got out in front of has delayed them a day. She was due in tomorrow afternoon."

"What is she doing in Salt Lake City?" asked Carlos. "And her Pilatus is from Switzerland and should already be primed for winter conditions, no?" Preston shrugged his shoulders.

"She told me that she wasn't coming in the Pilatus," interjected Martie, and the two men looked at her inquisitively.

"Then what are she and her friend coming in?" asked Preston.

"A surprise," replied Martie. "She wouldn't even tell me, but she wanted the exact length of the runway, as well as runoff area at each end. I told her 2,690 feet plus a 100-foot runoff on either end, and no trees over 30 feet in height for a second 100 feet."

"It's actually 2,670 feet of asphalt. If she uses the runoff area, there go my end lights. I was thinking of adding a few more feet so that Sally could visit us in her new government F-16-convertible," smiled Preston. "But I know that Sally's not coming in with her buddy and two F-16s to crash our party. I know she could get into the airfield using a drag chute to brake, and could get out with full afterburner and destroy my whole hangar, but I know that Uncle Sam does not loan out F-16s as Christmas rentals."

"She told me to expect her in something old and interesting," replied Martie.

"I bet it's her Pilatus and she's just pulling our strings," chuckled Carlos.

"My father and grandfather are arriving on Sunday morning," said Martie. "They're flying into Huntsville to visit some retired NASA friends of theirs on Saturday, flying south of the storm, staying overnight and then taking a couple of hours to get here. I was told to have lunch ready."

"Buck and Barbara are flying in solo with both *Baby Huey* and *Lady Dandy* tomorrow," added Preston. "They are coming in a day early to miss the storm. Barbara, Buck told me, just got her Huey rating and Buck is flying Lady Dandy."

"The Huey must be fun to fly compared to her Cessna work truck," said Carlos.

"What does Barbara usually fly?" asked Martie.

"A Cessna Citation V out of Phoenix, I think," replied Preston. "I wouldn't mind a few hours on her work truck," laughed Preston. "Nor would you, Carlos and you, Martie!" They both nodded their agreements. "Now, I have a surprise for you, Carlos. Tomorrow morning, our land army and airfield protection unit arrives to join us."

"You mean we are having a 'drive-in' as well?" asked Carlos.

"I suppose you could call it that," remarked Preston, going into the kitchen to refill Martie's wine and get two cold Yuenglings. "I was going to surprise everyone with ground troops in place before you all arrived, but your early arrival screwed that up a bit." Preston told Carlos about the two rat patrol jeeps Carlos had already seen once before, and the newly invited British armored cars and Saracen army personnel carrier. Carlos was impressed and asked the big question.

"Uh, where is everyone going to sleep?"

"Don't you worry, Carlos, you will not have a dozen men sleeping in your bed and cramping your style with the single women," laughed Martie. "I made sure that Joe's house will be full of men, including all his boys and David—the new guy who owns the new hardware. He's Jewish and got all of his antiques in Israel. If the single girls get bored with your antics, David is pretty good-looking for an older man."

They had a couple more drinks over dinner but like most

pilots who had been flying all day, Carlos was tired and turned in a little after nine.

Breakfast had just ended the next morning when the army paraded down the driveway. Joe and his eldest son drove the jeeps in convoy with the tractor trailer between them that had an armored car and the Saracen on it. They were quickly off-loaded and the convoy returned an hour later with the second armored car, a few minutes after the delivery truck Martie had expected with the booze supply for the party arrived from a local wine store. The wine shop owner had picked up Martie's liquor purchases at the ABC store on the way. He did look twice at the armored car and other armored vehicle standing alone next to the "Yellow Devil" on the apron, and said that they certainly weren't American. He was the last expected outside visitor, and from then on Preston's farm was off limits to anybody other than invited guests.

Once the convoy left, Preston gave Joe an automated gate controller to get in and out for the rest of the holiday season. All David's equipment was put on display around the apron where the incoming aircraft were expected to be on display, and next to the Yellow Devil, which was not officially part of the fly-in. Once everything was in place and the small mountain of cases of wine and alcohol had been put away, Martie went in to start lunch.

Three hours later, the unmistakable sound of a helicopter pierced the air and *Baby Huey* flew overhead from the north. Preston had been waiting for this, and was carrying around his hand radio so that he could talk Barbara down since she and Buck had never been here before.

He told her that there was a slight wind in from the north and that she should approach from the south and land just off the runway; on the apron and far away from the hangar in case she started a dust storm. The ground was dry.

Barbara came in as instructed and landed the helicopter just where Preston wanted it, on the outer area of the apron facing north. Then Buck came on the radio to say that he was still a few minutes out and that he had heard the weather report Preston had given Barbara and that he would also be coming in from the south. Preston recited the lay of the airfield to Buck and told him the tree distances and that Buck could put her down, if he wanted to, on the 50-odd feet of dirt directly between the runway lights and the start of the asphalt because the extra yards would give him more than enough room. Buck replied that he would work on the beginning of the asphalt as the DC-3 came into view a mile south, its wheels already down for landing.

Everybody heard the deep noise of the larger DC-3 engines, and the growing group of aircraft enthusiasts watched as Buck superbly put the much larger aircraft down, touching the asphalt only feet from the runway end, applying brakes, and then putting the engines into reverse thrust. He came to a squealing stop about a hundred feet from the northern end of the runway and turned *Lady Dandy* around to return to the apron. By this time, Barbara had already introduced herself to Martie, Preston, Carlos, Joe, and David, who immediately offered to help her gather her suitcase from the Huey.

The DC-3 approached, and Preston used signal batons, like those used at bigger airports, to guide Buck in. He made Buck continue on the runway, pass the apron, and then guided him around *Baby Huey*, onto the grass, and then back onto the apron between the hangar and his beloved helicopter. Preston lifted his batons to stop as Buck's tail wheel mounted the tar of the apron and he parked next to his other dream.

Once again, everybody was introduced by Martie. Even though Preston and Buck had been radio buddies for many years, they had never met, and it was a long handshake as they finally got to meet each other. A tour through the aircraft in the hangar was given for the two newcomers, and since all airport arrivals were done for the day, the first fly-in drinks and music got underway.

Early the next morning for the late risers and just after ten, Martie heard what she was waiting for. She ran outside the hangar just in time to see a Pilatus fly over the airfield from the southwest at a low altitude and then disappear behind the trees to reappear a minute later, coming in for final approach from the southeast over the lake.

"I thought Sally had a surprise for us!" shouted Preston to Martie. Carlos also looked puzzled.

"That's not Sally!" Martie shouted back, smiling as the single-engine turboprop came in fast on final approach, her wheels already down for landing. That's my father!"

The Pilatus, pretty quiet for a powerful turboprop, came in, touched down gracefully and took no more tarmac than either Preston or Martie normally used in the P-51s. It turned around slowly at the end of the runway, glided towards the waiting crowd, and onto the apron in front of the hangar.

Again, Preston guided the pilot with his fancy batons, but this time he parked the Pilatus next to the hangar and on the north side facing the helicopter and DC-3 on the south side of the apron. Everyone—including Joe, David, Buck, and Barbara—who had come out of the hangar door and was now watching, waited until the propeller came to a stop before going forward. The rear door opened a minute later and Michael Roebels's face appeared as the steps unfolded from inside the aircraft.

Martie rushed up, giving her father her usual bear hug, and then climbed in and disappeared to help her grandfather. She emerged a few minutes later helping a much older man with pure white hair down the short flight of stairs. The older man held onto both Martie and his son's arms as the three Roebels walked over to greet the group. There was much handshaking and introductions, but Preston and Carlos were still puzzled about why they had switched aircraft with Sally.

Joe was happy to see Grandpa Roebels again and vice-versa. The old man surveyed the vehicles placed around the apron with pleasure and Joe explained each one, telling him about his meeting with David, while the others looked on. Buck then offered him a tour of *Lady Dandy* and *Baby Huey* and the new arrivals were given the VIP tour treatment.

"Yesterday, we flew down to Yuma in the Beechcraft," explained Michael as he, his father, Martie, Preston, and Carlos slowly walked across the apron to the house and the others went back to the hangar to settle in. "Sally called us a few days ago, knowing that I had done some training on the Pilatus a couple of years ago in Europe. I had nearly purchased one but didn't like the price tag. Before I went over, I got flight-certified on the Pilatus down in San Diego, so that I could test-fly it, and I was excited about the potential of flying it from Ireland to Canada with a long-range fuel bladder in her. But, it wasn't to be, and when I heard Sally had purchased one, called her up and got the rundown on her new toy. Then she called me back a couple of weeks later and asked me if I was interested in flying it to the fly-in. She could not, had some other mission with the Air Force and she knew that it would be far shorter for Grand Pa-Pa in the faster Pilatus than our Beechcraft. It took three hours off our usual flight time and was non-stop into Huntsville, saving us an extra refueling stop in Austin."

"Well, that answers half our question," replied Preston, opening the front door of the house. "Martie will get you into your usual rooms and I'll go get your suitcases. But, do you know what the rest of her plan is?" he asked Michael.

"Nobody knows. I think it's meant to be a surprise for you, Preston," laughed Michael.

"A big surprise," added Grandpa Roebels, enjoying the reaction on Preston's and Carlos' faces as he followed his granddaughter into the guest room.

"I bet he knows," laughed Carlos, as they went outside to collect the suitcases from the Pilatus.

"It better not be bloody F-16s," replied Preston, now worried. "Their afterburners might burn up my hangar on take-off."

"I bet you $500 it's not F-16 Falcons," added Carlos as they got to the steps of the aircraft. Preston would not take the bet, but they did spend half an hour looking over Sally's new toy and it was as beautiful as she had described it to them. Preston then got the tractor started and attached it to the rear of the Pilatus and pulled her around at an angle so that she faced in a direction in which she could get out.

* * *

It was Sunday afternoon, December 23rd and Preston would not stop pacing. Carlos watched him from the cold porch, a blanket over him and an electric heater in front of his legs.

"She's coming when she's coming," stated Carlos, taking a sip from the glass of red wine in his right hand and smiling at his friend's anxiety—or was it inquisitiveness from not knowing was about to happen? He had never seen Preston like this. Being an engineer like the rest of them, he should be analytical and just accept what was going to land in the extremely capable hands of Sally Powers.

Carlos just knew that he would marry this captain of a girl—a girl he had been in love with since the second he laid eyes on her several years ago. Yes, he had had one or two other girlfriends since then, but unfortunately for the girls, they did not mean as much as his "little fly-girl" as he mentally called her, and now his "little F-16 Falcon fighter pilot."

When he had met her, he was a more competent pilot than she was, he flying more advanced aircraft like turboprops and jets. She was still beginning on turboprops and learning on C-130s, and suddenly he knew what she was coming in with. He heard the deep rumble of powerful C-130 engines far off in the distance, just above the faint rumble of the diesel generator behind the barn on the other side of the field. “Hey, Preston,” shouted Carlos jumping up, “I’ll help you move the lights. You have a C-130 coming in.”

“A C-130!?” replied Preston, his face going ash white as he now heard the grumbling engines getting closer. “Sally can’t land that here. The runway is several hundred feet too short,” he shouted out to Carlos, who was already running to the tractor to start it up. Carlos hadn’t driven down the runway 20 yards with Preston hanging on behind him before a C-130 aimed itself down the runway from the north directly towards them, less than half a mile away and only a couple of hundred feet above the trees. And that wasn’t all. There was a second C-130 in formation just off her starboard wing. The radio on Preston’s belt crackled and came to life.

“Hi there, Preston,” both men heard Sally say. *“Nice of you to meet me with your tractor in the middle of the runway. What sort of airfield are you running down there? Now be a good bunch of boys and go and move your lights from either end of your piece of blacktop, and give me a wind speed and ground temperature reading. I’ve got everything else I need and I’ll put this baby down for you. By the way, that’s my friend Jennifer in the 130 next to me. You are not seeing double. Oh, and hello, darling Carlos. I see Preston has upgraded your abilities to driving tractors now.”* Sally laughed as the first C-130 roared very low overhead.

Carlos turned around and saw Preston still looking worried behind him as they came to the end of the runway. It took a few seconds and the end lights were easily moved before they could be mowed down by some unforgiving aircraft. Preston picked up the whole unit plus the weights over the feet on the ground and moved them to the side out of the way. Then he and Carlos rushed off in the opposite direction to the other end of the airstrip and did the same. Carlos could see the two aircraft at about 1,000 feet over Jordan Lake, doing lazy circles a couple of miles away.

"Doesn't she need 3,000 feet minimum?" Preston asked Carlos as they were on their way back to get the information for Sally. Carlos shrugged as Martie came on the hangar radio.

"Hi, Sal darling. Wind is straight down the runway from the northwest at 6 knots, gusting to 10 maximum, temperature 49 degrees and chilly. The circus act will be off the runway in a second so turn onto finals and I'll give our fire truck team, Preston and Carlos, a bucket of water each and they can come and put your fire out if you can't stop on our little piece of tarmac. Out."

"Roger, old girl," replied an upbeat Sally. *"This baby is empty, I've landed 130s onto shorter runways than yours and I'll try not to leave any skid marks. Jennifer is just as good as me and I'll be ready for a glass of wine shortly. Turning into finals now. Jen, circle and wait till I'm down and clear of the runway. I think I'll park over in that clearing we saw on the north end and let you get in before we taxi back. There isn't much room down there for us big Air Force gals, but there are single men waiting for us."*

"Roger, partner," replied Jennifer, and she watched as the other aircraft turned into her final approach. Normally, in a more modern C-130, there would be an engineer and a co-pilot to help the pilot into small fields, but this time and with older and less complicated aircraft to fly, they were both on their own.

Sally went through her drills, brought the aircraft's speed and height down to the trained 1,000 feet, let her landing gear down, and then her flaps out slowly until they were extended to full flap, making them look like large barn doors to anybody on the ground. She needed to be at exactly 20% over stall speed for what C-130 pilots called a "maximum effort landing." Her glide slope had to be at 6%, which was twice as fast as any normal aircraft, and she came in steep and fast, a growing crowd watching on the ground. By this time, everybody was outside on the apron.

"I'm sure she touched the trees with her wheels," breathed Martie in wonderment. It was certainly a sight to behold. Once over the trees, she dropped faster and then flared the front of the aircraft up by pulling back on the stick and floated for what seemed like a second before her rear wheels touched down very hard, spewing up dirt as they hit the ground with a loud smack a few feet before the beginning of the asphalt. The front wheel dropped quickly and immediately. Sally put the four howling propellers into reverse-thrust and the ground shook slightly as she passed the onlookers and the apron still at speed. Preston could hear the squealing of the tires on his tarmac as she applied the brakes hard, but that was enough and she slowed and turned left off the end of the runway at a normal taxi speed. Preston noticed that he was sweating on his upper lip, as was Carlos. Carlos' serious face looked like he had helped little Sally down mentally all by himself.

"A piece of cake, Jennifer," they heard Sally encourage on her radio. *"Just routine, kiss the trees and you will be home and dry."*

Jennifer came in and everything seemed the same as before—the same height, speed, and glide slope. She kissed the top of the last trees with her undercarriage, flared out, and floated for a split second longer than Sally before her tires hit the asphalt and blue smoke erupted from the tires. Her nose came down quickly and like Sally, she hit the reverse-propeller thrust and brakes, passing the onlookers like an express train. She applied her brakes a little harder than Sally and Preston could see little blossoms of smoke coming off the tires, but she stopped with about 20 feet to spare and still on the runway.

Sally maneuvered her aircraft around the second C-130 that was still on the runway. She was on blowing up grass and dirt and the wing tips passed within ten feet of each other. Then she back-tracked the large Air Force transporter down the runway, with Jennifer's aircraft turning around to follow.

There was applause from the onlookers as the two massive aircraft drew up on the runway, then stopped as they came abreast of the apron. Sally asked Preston for parking suggestions.

"The best place is either side of the barn on the west side of the runway, Sally," he replied over his handheld radio, and they watched Sally go behind the barn and slowly work her way around it. There was just enough room for the C-130 to pass behind the barn and the tip of the outside wing slid over the first line of crepe myrtle bushes, just high enough to pass over, and the propellers missed the swaying crepe myrtles by just a couple of inches. Preston guided the aircraft with the batons one at a time, and within a few minutes both aircraft were parked, making the old barn look rather small in the middle as the eight giant turboprops slowly came to a halt. There was an eerie silence after the tremendous noise these two large aircraft had produced in such a small airfield.

"Bloody hell, Sally!" barked Preston as Sally came up and ran into his arms. "You scared me and all the wildlife for a hundred miles around!"

"What fly-in is a fly-in without an Air Force visit, darling Preston? And these were the smallest two we could find that would fit on your little runway."

The rest of the group walked over the runway and came up to greet them—Martie and Michael helping the older man across. "Hi friends, Romans and pilots," greeted Sally. "For those who don't know me, I'm Captain Sally Powers of the United States Air Force and this is my wing-woman, Captain Jennifer Watkins." The men watched as both girls removed their flight helmets and Sally's beautiful long red hair fell out while Jennifer's pitch black hair, a little shorter, did the same. Preston noticed that Jennifer was as beautiful to behold as Sally was—black hair and piercing green eyes—and he glanced over at Carlos to see his friend's reaction. Carlos was awestruck.

Martie came up and introduced her father and Grandfather before giving Sally her special bear hug for old friends. "What took you so long?" she asked.

"A little weather and these old birds don't fly as fast as my usual ride," replied Sally. "I did my toenails over three times before we even got into North Carolina."

Preston introduced the newest members of the fly-in and noticed that David held Jennifer's hand a little longer and she did not pull her hand away—just smiled as sweetly as a lioness in a corner would. Sally hugged everyone around, giving a boyish-looking Carlos a long hug, and Barbara was then introduced as Buck's co-pilot and Joe and David as the ground protection around the airport perimeter. Other than that, everyone had met each other before and were old friends.

"How did my new girl fly?" Sally asked Michael, as they all walked back to the hangar together, and Michael told her that it was time for him to trade in the Beechcraft and get a faster turboprop—it was so nice to fly.

Preston had turned on the large hangar warming fans on that morning for the first time, and the large hangar door was closed. It took a lot of power to warm the whole inside hangar, and he hadn't turned them on for a couple of years since they could not run on the smaller generator engine. This year, and since there were so many people and he had the large diesel engine running 24 hours a day, he had warmed the whole hangar to a crispy 78 degrees. Before they went inside, however, Sally and Jennifer were given a tour of the three aircraft standing outside.

Jennifer had not yet seen Sally's new purchase and was impressed. She also enjoyed the tour of the Huey and got Buck to promise to let her fly *Lady Dandy* soon. He agreed. What really made Jennifer drop her helmet was the display inside the hangar.

"If this doesn't look like I've gone back in time to World War II, then I must be dreaming," she said in awe, not even realizing that her helmet lay on the ground beside her. "Three P-51s and a Lightning all in one hangar! Dang it, Sally, why didn't you tell me about these!"

"We all are getting surprises today, Captain Watkins," replied Sally smiling at her friend. "I told you that coming with me would be worthwhile." One aircraft at a time, the girls climbed in and sat in the cockpits while their owners explained the details.

"Martie!" exclaimed Jennifer, sitting in Martie's P-51. "You must be the luckiest girl alive. I want to be your friend forever."

"OK, Sally, tell me about the Air Force allowing you to take two of its C-130s and being allowed to join our fly-in on a civilian airstrip," inquired Preston. "I know that's not the norm, and all C-130s are flown with two pilots and an engineer, not just a little girl who loves to fly. Are you going to jail when you get back?"

"Of course not, Preston," laughed Sally, sitting in the P-38 while Jennifer, sitting in the P-51D across the hangar, was busy chatting to Martie. She nodded to Carlos who was standing on the ground below Preston and listening. "These two are '*Tom*' and '*Jerry*'. My 130 was *Jerry*. Jennifer flew *Tom*. They are the oldest Air Force C-130s, built way back in their first year of production, 1956, and were recently rebuilt back to their original fittings with all the modern stuff taken out. We were asked by Carlos' buddy, General Allen, to fly them across to Pope Field. *Jerry* is going to be mothballed and put on display at Pope where the C-130 pilot school is. Remember, I spent six months at Pope. *Tom* is to be mothballed and put on display at Seymour Johnson."

"Martie and I had lunch last week with Colonel Mondale down at Seymour Johnson," shared Preston. "He wanted to see the P-38 and Martie flew in with her P-51."

"I'm supposed to hand *Tom* over to Colonel Mondale once we fly out of here on January 2nd. The General gave us special leave and allowed Jennifer and me to fly them single-seat. I'm just glad he didn't know where we were putting them down. After F-16 training, we could put these birds down on a quarter."

Preston was impressed and thanked her for making the fly-in so much more scary and enjoyable at the same time. "If you forgive me for putting black stripes on your runway," added Sally smiling her sweetest smile at him. "I'll let you right-seat with me and help me fly her over to Seymour. That is, if you forgive me?" Of course he did, and he gave her another hug as she stood up.

Once everyone had reassembled the large downstairs room, where the bed had been moved into the hangar and out of the way, several bottles of California bubbly were opened and Preston gave his welcome speech.

Martie loudly 'clinked' her glass a couple of times with a spoon and turned the music off to allow her man to speak. "First of all, after last year's fly-in, this one is going down in the record books!" Preston announced, raising his glass of bubbly to the 11 men and women standing in front of him. "We are now all together. Are we missing anybody, or do we have anybody else invited to fly-in, or anybody who could drive-in that we don't know about?" Carlos raised his hand.

"Yes, sorry to tell you only now, Preston and the group, but I invited a friend of mine who will be attending our New Year's Eve party."

"I didn't know you had a girlfriend, Carlos?" questioned Sally in a flirty manner with everyone smiling at her candor.

"You didn't?" exclaimed Carlos, getting back on her. "Well, to tell you the truth, Captain Powers, and I don't know why certain members of the United States Air Force should care whether I had a girlfriend or not, but no, my guest is not female," replied Carlos in a sarcastic tone. "It looks like Grandpa Von Roebels, Michael, Joe, David and I are the only available men here on base, so you single girls better make your choices on future husbands, or forever hold your yokes, I mean jokes."

The oldest man raised his glass to Carlos in salute for being remembered. He was 91 after all, and definitely single.

Carlos continued, "I just heard a few hours ago that an old friend of my father's would like to join us for our party for the New Year. He is a pilot and will be flying in on the last day of the year, weather permitting."

"Great, Carlos," applauded Preston sarcastically. "Joe, I knew we would fill up all five bedrooms before the end of the year."

"Preston, old buddy, you will enjoy his company. He is a great pilot," added Carlos, slapping his friend on the back.

"Uh hum!" interrupted Martie. "Preston, remember that Maggie Smart and the kids might make it, but we don't know for sure yet. Now, you were going to give us a speech and officially open the fly-in, not complain about the guest list."

"Ah ja... sorry, Fraulein Martie," joked Preston in his best German accent and winked at her grandfather. "Since we have now heard from friend Carlos here that more guests are arriving, we will officially welcome them when they land. Martie, keep a few bottles of bubbly hidden away from the troops for our new arrivals."

"Preston, we have two dozen cases of bubbly thanks to the several extra cases my father added to our collection. I don't think we will run dry," replied Martie, getting much laughter.

"Oh, get on with it, Preston!" shouted Sally. "We could get old standing here!"

"Captain Powers, I outrank you on this base so mind your military mouth," Preston replied. "I now declare this fly-in open!" There was a one-clap of hands. "Now for the rules and there are only two."

"Oh! The usual rules here on base—no fun and no naughty business!" stated Martie, smiling sweetly at Preston.

"Coming from the guru of the hit show 'Real Fun in the Bathtub,' Martie 'The Water's Getting Cold' Roebels herself!"

replied Preston, holding his hand out in her. There were shouts, laughter, catcalls and wolf whistles from the audience.

"Back to business, the two rules are: no drinking and flying, and no aircraft take-offs without first filing flight plans with the tower, which is me. Listen, friends, I am the tower and I will have no accidents at my airport... on my watch!" He mimicked an old line from President Bush and there was more laughter. "And don't wreck the bedrooms, or I'll have Joe's boys after you, and they are a mean lot. Thank you for listening." There was applause and Martie took his place.

"Food and drink is my concern," she began. "We have enough of everything to last us several months, even though we are here together for less than ten days. Thanks to Joe and Preston, nobody has to leave base for anything. We ladies will take turns with meals while the men will clean up and keep us oiled and gassed up with drinks while we cook. If you get hungry, help yourself. If you get thirsty..." She paused and everybody replied: "Help yourself!"

The party started in earnest and it was only the day before Christmas.

CHAPTER 12

Salt Lake City – December

LEE WANG WAS WORRIED. HE had just said goodbye to his best friend Carlos that morning when he received a phone call from another friend he hadn't seen or heard from since training on Chongming Island nearly 30 years earlier. His cell phone rang about an hour after Carlos had left, and Carlos was his only American friend who he thought he could trust to ask for help.

"Mao Jong, why are you calling me, and how did you get my number?" Lee Wang stated rapidly in Chinese into the phone while looking around to see if anybody was listening to him.

"Lee Wang, I live on your old street three doors down from your first house in Cupertino where you lived many years ago. I found out from your neighbor, Mo Sing, that you are in Utah. Remember, you called him a couple of years ago saying that you were on your way to a secret observatory in Utah and you wanted to know if anybody had received any mail for you from the boss?"

"Yes, I remember that call," Lee Wang replied, still confused.

"Well, Mo Sing saw your caller ID on his cell phone and wrote it down to remember. When I moved in, I asked him who he had seen from the island and he mentioned you. I asked him for your contact number and he gave it to me. I wanted to phone you, but then remembered the rules about communicating with each other and the penalty of being returned to China, so I didn't until today."

"So?" questioned Lee.

"Mo Sing and his wife and two sons are all dead, so is your old neighbor, Dong Tung and his whole family," continued Mao Jong in rapid Chinese. "They all died in a fire last night when three houses burned down. The police think the fire was too powerful to be an accident and told reporters that they suspect somebody is starting fires."

"I'm very sorry to hear this bad news about our friends," replied Lee. "But I don't understand what this has to do with me?"

"They are not the first," replied Mao Jong, Lee hearing the worry in his voice. "I have heard from others that a dozen people who live here in America and were trained in Chongming Island have died in accidents in the last month alone. Two are friends I trained with and lived in San Diego. Do you remember Ju Ma?"

"Yes."

"He also died last week in Washington, D.C. in a house fire, and it was on the news yesterday that the four dead bodies had been shot first through the head, execution style. Also another person I know was killed in Seattle nearly a week ago, again a house fire and three dead bodies with gunshots in the head. The police still don't know that they were also Chinese people, but I knew him on Chongming Island. He was my neighbor and we had communicated. Now they are looking for me. I got rid of the cell phone I had used to talk to my friend in Seattle, and yesterday morning after I had left for work my wife saw a car drive by our house slowly with four Chinese men in it. Late last night, we left through the back door with all our valuable possessions. I waited until dawn in a safe area, went to my bank, withdrew all our money, paid cash for Greyhound tickets and we are now staying in a motel in Las Vegas. Lee Wang, they know where you live and I think you could be next."

"What should I do?" He asked his friend.

"If they know where you live, they will know where you work. Get somewhere safe. Go somewhere where there is American Army or police. Stay away from your home and your work. Keep your cell phone and I will try and call you again. I'm calling from a call box so they cannot trace this call, but I know your number and they might make me give it to them if they catch me. Be careful, friend Lee, be careful."

There was a click as the caller ended the call. Lee Wang immediately called home, his face now white with worry. His wife Lin answered and he shed a sigh of relief and he quickly told his wife the story from Mao Jong.

"What should I do?" she asked him, worried. "We are both here in the house. Shall we leave?"

"Yes," he replied. "Lin, get everything we have of value that you and Ling can carry. Draw the blinds and check to see if any Chinese in vehicles are driving past the house. If you see them, use the binoculars in my study and see if you can get the model and license number. When you think it's safe, and there are no cars in the street, go out the back door and climb over the fence to the Moores' house behind us. The trees will hide you. They should not be home, but don't stop there. Be careful and get across their road to our friends, Pat and Mark, on the other side. Pat will be home, so get inside her house without being seen. Also before you go, take the checkbook out of the old car and take it with you. We will need some money. Close down the house so that it is very dark inside and stuff the beds full of pillows and blankets to look like we are sleeping in the beds. Do Ling's bed too. I'm sure that they know she is visiting."

"Do I hide there?" she asked, scared.

"Yes, wait for me. I will get a car from somewhere and come and pick you up. Now hurry and get out!" Lee ordered, putting away his phone, looking up and straight into the female face of a co-worker. She was American, so he was not worried about her.

"Are you in trouble?" she asked with a serious look on her face. "Can I help you?"

"Please, Ms. Dennis," he replied. "My wife is not well, my daughter just called me and I need to go and take her to the doctor, but my old car is not working well."

"Take my car, Lee," she insisted. "I'm leaving it here over the Christmas break since my boyfriend is picking me up later and we are going south to spend the holiday season with his parents in St. George. I won't need it for a week. Take it. Here, here are the keys. Just drop them back at my station when you are done. It's the old blue jeep parked in the back."

He thanked and bowed to her as he went to find the supervisor to tell them he had to leave and it was an emergency. Then he ran outside and saw his own car parked outside the door of the observatory. That was not a good place to leave it—he didn't want them to burn down the valuable observatory building. He chose to drive his car to the main building a hundred yards away from the observatory itself, closer and in better view from the entrance to the gated compound, just in case. Lee left for the day and drove slowly in the jeep. He was not a good driver and his eyesight was getting bad.

The jeep was old and had over 100,000 miles on the odometer and he felt inconspicuous in it. The drive was 40 minutes down the mountain the same way Carlos had driven earlier, and it wasn't long before he drove into his neighborhood, put on a pair of sunglasses to hide his face, and drove up to where he had told his wife and daughter to hide. He phoned them from his cell phone and told them to open the garage door, if there was room for him to drive inside.

The automatic door opened and as he drove in, it closed behind him as he parked the jeep away from prying eyes.

"We saw Chinese men in a car!" his wife blurted out as he got out, greeting them. "It was a black SUV, a Cadillac, and we saw most of the number."

Pat, their friend came into the garage and asked what all the fuss was about.

"I think our lives are in danger," stated Lee. "Some Chinese men, I think a Chinese gang, are trying to make trouble for Chinese-Americans and we want to get out of here without being seen, just in case."

"This is America, Lee," stated Pat sternly. "That's absurd! Things like that don't happen around here. They wouldn't dare, especially in this neighborhood. We have three sheriff families living around us."

"We need to leave for Christmas, just in case these men are bad," replied Lee. "We don't want to cause you any trouble and we will go on vacation for a week until these men go away. If something happens to our house while we are away, please give the information about the black SUV to the police. Maybe they can track them down. Also, phone us on this number if you see our house on fire or anything out of the ordinary." He bundled his family into the jeep, throwing all that the girls had carried over from the house into the back and asked Pat to open the garage door. He ordered the two girls in Chinese to lower their heads so as to not be seen, put his sunglasses on, and started reversing slowly out of the garage. He stopped and waved goodbye to Pat standing inside the garage by the door-opener, still looking very puzzled, and looked into his rear-view mirror. A black SUV passed behind them and he could see through the darkened glass that the occupants were looking in the opposite direction. He couldn't see their faces but he felt like he knew who they were. He pointed the vehicle in the opposite direction and left the housing division, driving as slowly as he always did.

His first stop was the bank to draw out the several thousand dollars he had saved there, and then drove to a gas station on the highway to figure out what to do.

On the I-85 and ten miles north of Salt Lake City, the gas station felt safe, and then he suddenly remembered that his friend Carlos was going to Hill Air Force Base and he might still be there. He knew the area and worked out that it would take him about 20 minutes to get there.

Ten minutes later, Pat called screaming on the phone that she saw flames and black smoke coming from the area of their house and what should she do? "A fire truck is coming into the housing division," she said urgently.

"Go around to our house when you think it's safe and give the SUV information to the police or firemen. Tell them that this car came screaming down the road dangerously just before you saw the fire. The SUV's California plates should make them want to check it out. I'm sure the nightly news will tell us if they got them, Pat. And don't you worry, we will be okay until we know and then we will come back. Thank you and Melly Clistmas to you and Mark." Lee Wang was not above a little humor, even in an unpleasant situation such as this.

He drove up to the main gate at Hill Air Force Base, and the guard thought that this Chinaman was lost until Lee Wang told him about his friend's old silver airplane.

"Oh! I let in a civilian earlier this morning who is friends with the commanding officer. He flies an old Mustang. I'll phone through to the main office and see what I can do," said the uniformed guard. He was on the phone for several minutes before he returned to the jeep. "The commanding officer is coming over to see you. Come in and park in those visitors' spaces over there," he ordered.

Lee felt a little safer as he drove through and the boom was lowered behind them.

It took 20 minutes before a military car approached them. A superior officer got out and the guard saluted him and motioned him in the direction of the jeep.

"Can I help you?" the General asked Lee Wang, still sitting in the jeep with the window down. “I was told that you are friends of Carlos Rodriquez. You just missed him. He flew out less than an hour ago.”

CHAPTER 13

Jiangsu Province, China – December

THE BOARDROOM WAS AGAIN in session, the same men in the same seats, and not a piece of paper in sight. This time there were no assistants in a line of chairs against the wall opposite the large windows. The room was empty except for the sixteen men sitting around the boardroom table.

The Chairman was again at the podium, this time asking questions to the others, one by one. “How is the government reacting to our latest communiqué to them last week?” he asked one man.

“They are not happy, but have heeded our warnings and said that they will have all commercial and military aircraft grounded in Chinese territory by midnight,” was the answer.

“What vibrations are we getting from our generals and armed forces about their ability to fight wars?” he asked another man.

“They are not ready. The new aircraft carrier will not be able to accept its aircraft for another month to six weeks. The army is worried that they might have purchased the electronic parts from third-party deals. The Air Force doesn’t care to talk to us as they have so few aircraft with any global attack capabilities. The Navy wants to go straight in and attack anything disabled they can find with their submarines. They could be a problem, Chairman Chunqiao."

"Do we have any control over their submarines?" the Chairman asked the same man.

"No, Comrade Chairman, we don't, except to cut off the serpent's head if they get out of control."

"Get three termination squads into Navy Headquarters," he ordered. "Activate the squads on December 30th and we will take control of the submarines earlier than planned."

"What about our current intelligence leaders controlling our glorious China, Comrade Yun?" he asked the man on his right.

"They are 45% positive on numbers, Chairman Chunqiao. We hope to have a positive majority in the government by January. They are going to stay out of our way, but I believe they will cry foul if anything goes wrong. Many of them are currently happy to wash their hands over the project, but take over if we are completely successful—combat cowards every one of them."

"Do we have them in our pocket, Comrade Yun?" he asked more seriously this time.

"Yes, as long as everything goes according to plan," was the answer.

"Comrade Chief Engineer Gung, you are our designer and in charge of the billions of electronic parts around the world," continued the Chairman. "We have had several reports recently about early malfunctions in several America nuclear power stations, three European power stations, and a Japanese power station. Why is this?"

"Chairman Chunqiao, we have done exhaustive tests on all the parts and systems we have had installed in many power stations around the world. All we can find is that the excessive energy caused by the massive outputs of power these nuclear plants are putting out is making the Strontium in our parts unstable. Still, up to now we have had less than 0.1% failure rate with all our parts in the nuclear power stations worldwide, and I feel no blame has been put on Zedong Electronics as of yet."

"I agree with you Comrade Gung, but what about other early malfunctions, especially in directional equipment? We had that problem with the American/Russian space station. The same problem was seen in several aircraft, commercial and military. What I'm getting at is the big question: what will our success rate be when we deactivate the billions of parts and systems around the world? What will our deactivation failure rate be—also 0.1%? That is a big number when we talk billions."

"We have tested every design and there is Strontium in 60% of the older parts we first manufactured. The destruction of the Strontium should give us a 90% success rate when we first transmit its destructive break-down high frequency to the electronic parts through the antennae. Then the backup electronic deactivation system in every single piece of electronic equipment or part we have ever made, plus the dozens in every complete system we have made should be our fail safe when the time comes. I'm willing to state that if we have more than 0.000001% failure rate in the small parts, which will be a failure on my side. That number means no more than 1,000 failures in every one billion parts."

"Let's add the total of 100 billion parts, of which 60% of them are bound together with other of our electrical parts in a system; that leaves a balance of 40 billion single parts operating on their own. The worst scenario is that 40,000 parts may fail. In 190 countries, this number is again divided. Our game plan was to have a 99.9% success story, Chairman Chunqiao, and we are well above our numbers. I believe only God could have done a better job than you." The Chairman smiled at the last sentence.

"Comrade Wang, a report on your dealings around the world with our past and present employees," stated the Chairman, looking at Lee Wang's old friend and initial employer, the man he had met when the older man was cleaning floors many years ago.

"Our squads have done a good job so far with only seven terminations to go—three of these in the United States. Asia has been 100% complete for a month. Australia is now 100% complete and the termination squads have gone 'underground' in Sydney. Africa is 100% complete. We only had 120 operatives in Africa, 112 returned here and the final eight were terminated in South Africa last year. Europe has four terminations to go. We have missed one termination so far in Europe, and we have lost contact with one in Italy. He worked with Fiat and Ferrari and we missed him, but we managed to terminate his Chinese girlfriend. Currently he is in France and we are getting closer. I believe it's now a matter of days."

"There are three missing in Russia. They just disappeared off the map and we have six teams searching for them in Moscow, which is the only place where they can be hiding. Two of our teams were terminated by Russian gangs and we have not retaliated yet. If we don't find them, the Russians will kill them anyway so we have nothing to fear. Canada became 100% terminated early this morning with our last operative terminated at the BlackBerry Company. I'm sending the ten Canadian squads down to the United States, to prepare for our next phase and help look for a family we missed in California. We had six families in that area and four are terminated, one is still in operation for another week and one went missing when the squad went in. He has left a trail and we have three squads on his tail. Washington and Seattle were completed yesterday, but unfortunately the news media got hold of the Chinese family deaths, and blew it up. We have a Chinese reporter, one of ours, telling the media that the crime was all Hong Kong gang-related and the Americans believe him. Our teams are on the trail of our final terminations with our best operatives, and the project will be completed a day or two before Christmas."

"I want a completed report once you are done, Comrade Wang, and I want all the 400 trained men in the 100 termination squads in America to be joined by the ten squads arriving from Canada and be prepared to attack and kill military and any civilian outposts. Ammunition, money, whatever they need."

Comrade Wang nodded.

"And make sure they transfer to old carburetor vehicles before Z-day. I think we should end up with an army of 20 squads in Los Angeles, 20 squads down on the American southern border killing Americans trying to escape south, 20 squads in New York, and at least 50 of the squads spread around elsewhere in the bigger cities. We certainly won't have any problems with smaller rural areas."

CHAPTER 14

The Fly-in over Christmas and New Year's Eve

CHRISTMAS MORNING ARRIVED in North Carolina at the Strong Farm with its usual sleepiness, the sun attempting its cold rise over the horizon at 7:44 am. It was going to be a beautiful day, not a cloud in the sky, and the temperature usual for the time of year—35 degrees. The two large aircraft sat patiently at attention next to the barn, as did the two aircraft and helicopter on the apron. The lights at either end of the runway had been replaced in case of any night emergency landings, and the two Ferret armored cars, the Saracen and the two Rat Patrol jeeps displayed a ring of ground protection around the apron. All regained their camouflage colors as the sun climbed over the trees and lit up the area.

Apart from the noise of the birds, the runway, closed hangar, and dark house were silent, as all of its many occupants—even Oliver—were still fast asleep.

David was sleeping at Joe's farm in the guest room. It had been a loud night on Christmas Eve, and the party had finally died down a couple of hours after midnight. Nobody was expecting to fly for a couple of days. The plan was just to enjoy each other's company, catch up on their lives, and enjoy the togetherness of people who loved airplanes and flying them.

Oliver was the first to make an appearance, as dogs usually do. He had a special doggy door he could use if Preston and Martie slept in, which was at least every Sunday. His brown coat shook as he exited the door. He looked at the sun, then in the vicinity around him, and then naturally towards his favorite tree. Oliver couldn't lift his leg like smaller, less weighty dogs could, but he made a half attempt anyway and missed the tree as he always did. Then he walked around in a circle to see if there were any foreign smells. He was now acquainted with all the new adults he had memorized by each of their smells. It was hard work for a dog to get used to the heavy movement between the hangar and the house and so he went further afield to try and water the new and sterile-smelling tires around the apron.

As usual, most of the tires were dry after he left, with only small marks of liquid pretty close to a couple of them. One got hit, but with so little moisture that it was dry a few minutes after the dog had departed—the radiant sun was already doing its job. Oliver slowly loped along the whole runway smelling for any other dogs or animals that might have crossed it since he last checked a day or so ago, but as usual there were very few smells from small animals. The aircraft noises kept away most of the larger animals, and half of the farm was fenced in many areas where the farmer had thought it necessary many years ago.

His patrol and duty done to his master, Oliver returned and looked for that steak bone someone had thrown him the evening before, and his next big decision was to either chew on it for a while, or find a place to bury it. He dropped down and decided that his first choice was the best place to start, and he got busy.

With the bone chewed on for an hour, and the remains now not worth burying, Oliver heard movement from the hangar. The side door opened and Sally emerged. She headed off to the two aircraft on either side of the barn and Oliver jumped up to follow her.

"Hello, boy!" she said, ruffling his ears. "You're up early. You must be on early patrol duty." She knew the 30-foot runway was far wider than she had needed in the C-130. She had had at least nine feet of asphalt on either side of her twelve foot wheel-span, but compared to the large airfields she was used to, this one was tiny—apart from the dozens of dirt landings she had done in training. She marveled, though, at the time and effort Preston had put into his airfield and never thought for one second that she was in danger coming in with an empty aircraft. She and Jennifer had fueled the aircraft for the a one-way flight into Pope and Seymour and the tanks were empty, with just enough fuel aboard for another hour's flying plus 45 minutes in reserve. "I reckon I can get her off the ground in 2,000 feet," she said to Oliver, still looking happy for the company beside her as she lowered the side steps and walked into *Jerry* to collect the Christmas presents for her friends. It was Christmas Day after all. She did a quick ground check on both aircraft, checked the tires for any brake wear or damage and returned to the hangar.

Carlos was also up and chatting up a sleepy-looking Captain Watkins by the coffee machine. Sally Powers knew she was going to marry Carlos Rodriquez one day, if she had anything to do with it, but she knew that playing hard to get and waiting for the right moment was necessary to keep him interested. Carlos smiled as she walked in and she walked up to him and kissed his cheek playfully, showing her wingwoman who was boss around here.

"Do that again, Captain Powers, and I'll have to ask you to marry me." He looked at her seriously.

"You keeping on wishing, Señor Rodriquez, and it might just happen one day," she replied, putting the wrapped gifts by the Christmas tree, which was still lit up from the night before. "Come on, Carlos, help me put all these foul-smelling glasses into the dishwasher, then we can start partying all over again."

"I'm thinking that David is quite a good-looking guy," mentioned Jennifer, picking up some of the two dozen dirty glasses sitting on every flat surface available. "I was talking to him last night for quite a while. He was in the Israeli Special Forces for over a decade before he came over to live here in the States. He is twenty years older than me, but I suppose that's not really a lot, if you don't want it to be." She sighed.

"Well, look at the one following me like a puppy dog, Jennifer," Sally added, putting some glasses down and then thumping Carlos in the side ribs with her fist. "He's not that much younger than David, but better looking, and I think our friend Carlos here has a few manners more than Oliver."

"Age means nothing when you have experience," answered Carlos, winking at her.

"Carlos, don't give me that crap," laughed Sally. "You have never really been interested in women, or known to be a famous porno-movie star, or even had that many girlfriends! That's what your friends say, anyway. I've checked up on you."

"Maybe he's scared of REAL women?" laughed Jennifer.

"Or maybe I'm being a little old-fashioned and keeping myself for the right woman," added Carlos, tactfully.

"Oh, Bull H. Crap!" interrupted Martie, walking in. "Carlos, poor Preston has been defending me from you ever since we first met. And I saw you trying to chat up poor young Jennifer last night with that bottle of red wine in your hand and all those hand movements you were doing with your other hand."

"I must admit that's true, sweet Martie," answered Carlos, trying to save face. "How can any man stay cool while you're around? And we Latinos do gesture a lot when we talk. It's the way we are made."

"Sally, Jennifer, you had better watch Carlos. I've known him to be as smooth as a blunt knife through butter and as gentlemanly as a snake in the grass can ever be," added Martie. "I could have fallen for him myself if he didn't have such big eyes for you, Sally Powers, when you're around."

"Well, if he wants to marry me, he'd better put those big eyes and any other big things away until I'm an astronaut," replied Sally, trying to be serious while filling the dishwasher. "I'm not on the market until I reach my zenith."

"I could be older than David and even Martie's grandfather by then!" exclaimed Carlos. "I could be in a wheelchair and over the hill years before that."

"News, Carlos!" added Preston, also walking in. "You and I are already over the hill for these young man-killers." Carlos laughed and nodded his agreement and got another punch in the ribs from Sally as Preston reminded the three women to stop bullying his friend.

* * *

By 11:00 that morning, Martie had two large turkeys baking in the dual ovens in the house and a large ham warming in the hangar's kitchen oven. Pumpkin pies arrived with Joe, his five boys, and David. Several dozen presents also arrived for everyone until the tree was nearly hidden by gifts. The two older men, Grandpa Roebels and Michael, arrived shortly afterwards and Martie thumped on the ceiling below Buck's room with a broom to get them up. They came down sleepily a few minutes later.

There were many presents to hand out. Martie, with the help of the girls, turned several bottles of the red wine into hot German *glüwein*, and by the time the presents had been distributed two hours later, most of the crowd was already loud and boisterous. Joe had given all his sons new hunting rifles, and they were easily visible under their Christmas wrapping.

The hangar phone rang several minutes after the last present had been opened and Martie answered it. It was Maggie in Los Angeles, three hours behind, shouting Merry Christmas over the phone so everyone could hear. Maggie had good news for Martie. Will had to work over New Year's Eve and he had given her three round-trip tickets aboard Southwest from LAX to RDU for her, Ben, and Oprah to visit them in Raleigh for two days. Martie jumped up and down with excitement, and Sally happily grabbed the phone out of her friend's hand.

"I told you he would!" shouted Sally into the phone to her friend. "I told you, I told you! He loves you so much. Don't you ever let him go!" she laughed, giving her friend a kiss over the phone and handing it back to a happy Martie.

"I have two extra single beds at home," injected Joe once the call was over. "There is enough room in Carlos' room to put another single in there and Carlos can sleep on the other down here."

"Good idea, Joe," replied Preston, slapping Carlos on the back. "Carlos, you still have a couple of nights in that new bed upstairs. It sounds like they are only coming in on the 29th or 30th. Oh, I forgot, what about your friend coming in. Where's he going to sleep?"

"No problem," laughed Carlos. "He has a bed in the back of his aircraft."

"A what in his where!?" asked Preston, again looking worried.

"Well, if it's Air Force One, Preston," laughed Sally, "Maggie and the kids can move in with the President and his wife. I'm sure they won't mind," watching Preston's face go totally white. It took him a couple of seconds to digest what Sally had said before he laughed, realizing that there was no way Air Force One could land on his short airstrip and that Sally was playing her usual jokes.

"Don't worry, Preston, my good friend," smiled Carlos. "This is a supercharged short-runway medium-size turboprop, and the joke will be on Sally when he arrives." Sally now looked at him totally puzzled and Carlos just winked at her, shrugged his shoulders innocently and gave her a triumphant grin.

The rest of the happy day was a party that could only be

enjoyed with a group of maniac flyers. There was much jousting, much drinking and eating, and commonly making a fool in front of their friends. It was a good day.

The weather was still fine on the morning after Christmas. It was a Wednesday, and with the holiday break between Christmas and New Year's Eve underway, it was time for a little flying. Martie switched on the television to hear the weather report to see if Maggie was going to have any problems getting out of California on the 29th.

"A couple of small ships collided in the English Channel on Christmas Day," stated the male newscaster. *"One of the ships changed course for no apparent reason. It is suspected that the crew must have been dozing or not at their posts. She veered off course and into the way of a second ship going in the opposite direction. This ship was a coastal oil tanker with 10,000 gallons of heating oil aboard and both went down within minutes—the second one leaving a massive oil slick several miles long and wide. Oil experts are already flying in to try to contain the oil spill."*

"An Indonesian Boeing 737 with 124 aboard crashed minutes after takeoff last night. It was just before midnight, the weather was clear and the aircraft, bound for Jakarta, flew straight into the side of a mountain. Air traffic control was not able to communicate with the pilots after takeoff, and the aircraft did not follow its usual flight pattern. Nobody survived the crash and a search is underway for the two black boxes."

"Locally, a military aircraft went down in the sea just off the San Diego coast early yesterday morning. The Navy jet was on a transfer flight to a U.S. aircraft carrier just offshore when its jet engine cut out and the plane crashed into the sea. The pilot escaped moments before using his ejection seat and was picked up by a Coast Guard cutter with only minor injuries."

"A spate of Chinese killings ended in Salt Lake City with the shooting of a gang of what the police and FBI called "Chinese

thugs." Law enforcement closed in on the group of four Chinese men after a tip-off in a Salt Lake City neighborhood. They presumably set another, the seventh house this month, ablaze. They were seen driving a black SUV north along Highway 85 and several police cars closed in. A firefight on the highway commenced, and the four men were killed. Seven innocent civilians, three policemen, and two FBI agents were also killed in the firefight, which lasted for well over an hour. The four men were well-armed with automatic weapons."

"I didn't know you had Chinese gangs in Salt Lake City?" Preston asked Carlos.

"Me neither," he replied, all watching a taped recording of the end of the gun battle from a news helicopter. There were bodies everywhere on the ground, with several crashed cars all over the highway. "That's weird; I drove on that piece of road just the other day. I take that road to get to Hill Air Force Base. That fight was about five miles south of the base."

The helicopter zoomed in on the smoking SUV and California license plates could be seen on the rear of the vehicle. "The SUV is from California," continued Carlos. "The only Chinese guy I know of in Salt Lake City is Lee, our cleaner guy who you spoke to on the radio. He certainly wouldn't be involved in gang activity. He's an old man."

"The gang of four with their California-licensed SUV is believed to also be connected to the many house fires in California in December where 17 Chinese family members lost their lives. Ten of the victims were said to have been shot in the head before their houses were set on fire to disguise these execution-style killings. The other three house fires in Washington, Seattle and Durham, North Carolina just before Christmas couldn't have been the work of the same gang, and the FBI believe that a second, or even a third gang squad could still be on the loose. An APB has been posted nationwide by the FBI, and the public are being warned against getting close to any group of Chinese

men. The four men killed in Salt Lake City worked with military-style precision, and were professionals. It seems that Chinese gang violence is on the rise. Several large attacks killed American troops in the war-zones around the world on Christmas day."

"The Pentagon has not released figures yet, but several attacks on American bases across the Middle East and South Korea looked like they were well-planned to disrupt Christmas for our troops. We will give you more news later today when the Pentagon releases more information."

"In other news, Christmas has been a normal weather affair for most of the country, except for the West coast, where rain and high winds pelted Seattle and Portland in the early morning hours of Christmas Day. The fast-moving storm is heading due north out of California and not expected to cause delays for New Year's Eve travelers, except across the northern areas of the country."

Martie switched off the television. "I just wanted to see if Maggie would be okay," she said. "The news is getting worse and worse."

"Then don't listen to it," replied Preston. "I get a better weather report from NOAA than the news anyway. Okay guys, tomorrow is our first field trip down to Charleston for lunch at a friend's restaurant. Let's get everyone in here and file flight plans."

It took several minutes, but eventually everybody arrived, including Joe, David, and four of his sons. They were all looking forward to a flight in *Lady Dandy*.

The DC-3 had very uncomfortable side seats on both sides of the aircraft. Usually they weren't needed, but they could be dropped from a vertical position against the side walls. Bob had installed a dozen on each side in case he needed to carry passengers, but being in a permanent cargo setup, they were not practical for long flights. Sleeping bags and mattresses laid out on the floor were certainly a more comfortable arrangement.

"We want to fly, don't we?" Preston asked, and everyone nodded. "I have reserved a table in a friend's Greek restaurant in Charleston, actually on a beach called the Isle of Palms slightly north of the city. We have five aircraft flying in—the three P-51 Mustangs that Martie, Carlos, and I have been waiting a long time to fly together, Sally's Pilatus with her and Jennifer, Grandpa Roebels and Michael, and Buck and Barbara flying in *Lady Dandy*. Martie, Carlos, and I are flying on flight plans over Ocracoke on the coast. Martie, Carlos, and I will continue out to sea and then drop down to below 3,000 feet and practice some formation flying, and after that we'll meet up with you guys over Charleston. Hopefully our formation flying won't be noticed by any excitable air traffic controllers. Our destination airport information is Mt. Pleasant Regional Airport, Faison Field, just north of Charleston International."

Preston gave them the airport's latitude and longitude. "Asphalt runway is 3,700 feet, longer and wider than mine. Distance from here is 240 miles direct. If flying over the Outer Banks, add on another 150 miles. To recap: the three of you are with Sally," repeated Preston, nodding in Jennifer and the older men's direction. "That leaves you and your boys, Joe, and David with Buck and Barbara. I suggest that we all fly in a non-formational group over the Outer Banks and then both Sally and Buck fly separately or together down to South Carolina. The views will be nice tomorrow. The weather is perfect and the sea is expected to be calm. You guys do what you want to do and we should be no more than 30 minutes behind you."

Preston scanned the room for any signs of questions from the beaming faces around him before continuing. "There is no tower at Mt. Pleasant and pattern altitude is 1,000 feet MSL. We are expected at the airport at exactly midday and my buddy Joe will have two vehicles to take us to his restaurant for a traditional

Greek meal. It's good. Martie and I have been down there many times—it's one of our favorite food destinations." There were nods of approval from the group.

"OK, refueling. Carlos you need to fill your tanks. Since we can only fuel one aircraft at a time, you will refuel first tomorrow morning. Then, the turboprops—Sally you fill up first with jet fuel and then you, Buck. We take off at 10:00 am on the dot, and Oliver is coming along. David, do you mind looking after him on a leash in *Lady Dandy*?" David affirmed that he would be happy to.

The next day was clear and the flying fun. The three Mustangs, together only for the second time in their history, flew low and fast to the Outer Banks, 30 miles out to sea, and practiced tactical maneuvers and tight-formation flying. The Pilatus and *Lady Dandy* were left far behind by the faster Mustangs, and flew together to the coast with the occupants enjoying the view.

Lady Dandy needed most of the runway to get airborne. With tanks half full and a small cargo of humans and one excited dog, Buck taxied her to the south side of the runway as a light 3-knot wind came in from the north. He turned her around to face the 2,970 yards of asphalt, with his rear wheel in the dirt. He was going to use every inch possible. It was his first take-off from such a small field, and he did not want to take any risks with extra people on board. Preston wanted him to go first. Buck was the slowest and everyone else could easily catch up with him. The Pilatus was already warming up on the apron. The three Mustangs had been pulled out with the tractor a couple of hours earlier and were in a line facing the warming Pilatus.

Buck and Preston had talked about the take-off the previous night, and Buck had allowed his two large turboprops to get warm before he taxied down to the runway end.

Everyone waited in their respective aircraft as *Lady Dandy's* engines began to rev up for take-off. Buck pushed the throttles to maximum, and kept his feet on the brake until they reached a crescendo. The aircraft began to shake violently and then he moved *Lady Dandy* into forward motion. With her two massive propellers biting hard into the oncoming air, she rapidly gained momentum, and by the time she passed the Pilatus still waiting on the apron, her rear wheel was rising. Preston noted that Buck still had 100 feet or so of asphalt left when the large front tires left the ground. Buck pulled her up a little steeper than normal, quickly retracted her undercarriage, left the flaps down, and rose gracefully into the air. Within seconds he was over the trees, a couple of hundred feet higher than the highest one.

Preston signaled to Martie and Carlos to start up, and the three Mustang engines coughed into life as the Pilatus moved onto the runway headed to the south end and neared the end of the runway to turn around. Sally already had her checks done and her engines warmed, and she quickly turned and began her take-off. She let the engine increase its revs as she was moving. The Pilatus was a single-engine turboprop, much less than half the size and weight of the DC-3, and the smaller aircraft left the ground several feet earlier than Buck had. Sally had the engine under full take-off power, quite light on weight as well, and she climbed quickly like a fighter pilot, turning left as her wheels retracted to follow *Lady Dandy*.

The three Mustangs taxied to the end of the runway together, lined up one behind the other and each one let go of the brakes as the one in front left the tarmac. They were gone in two minutes and the farm suddenly became quiet and peaceful with no one home, not even faithful Oliver.

Sally caught up with *Lady Dandy* within five minutes and she past her about 100 yards away on the DC-3's right side. She climbed up to altitude, circled, and waited for *Lady Dandy* and then lowered her cruising speed to 230 miles an hour as the four aboard relaxed. The three Mustangs reached the right side of *Lady Dandy* a couple of minutes later, slowed down to *Lady*

Dandy's 230 mile-an-hour maximum cruising speed, and each waggled their wings and waved at the occupants.

"Buck, you had 100 feet of asphalt left. If I removed the lights, I reckon you could get out with full weight," Preston stated over the radio.

"Roger that!" replied Buck over the unused radio frequency they had all agreed to use as a chat frequency. All the aircraft had one radio tuned to the air traffic control frequency they were all currently using, and the other for chit-chat. *"I'll try that when I need to, not before."*

"Sally you had at least 200 feet remaining—just letting you know." He received an acknowledgement from Sally, and then Buck and Barbara watched from the front as the three fighters climbed away at full power at Preston's command, disappearing into the blue sky a minute or so later. They were certainly beautiful to watch.

Lunch was excellent Greek food, with no drinking for the pilots. Only the ground crew captained by Grandpa Roebels ordered a couple of bottles of imported Greek wine. They were not under flying laws and the pilots were happy discussing sweeps and turns without needing alcoholic support. They would get theirs back at base. Oliver was spoiled, behaved admirably, and achieved a large pile of rack-of-lamb bones on the ground by the table, as well as a doggy-bag for home consumption. Martie was sure that he would have to find a new burial ground to deposit all the bones.

The food, friendship and weather made it a perfect day, and the group arrived backed at the Strong Ranch airport in a stretched out group of aircraft, again allowing *Lady Dandy* in first. She needed less of the runway than Buck had needed on her first landing, as the wind had strengthened to ten knots with strong gusts from the northwest and he put her down perfectly. They cleaned, checked and closed down the aircraft and the next party began in earnest.

A late morning was expected the next day, and Oliver was again the only one awake early trying to figure out which bones would fit in what holes. At 9:00, the phone rang. Preston got out of bed and sleepily walked to the entrance hall to answer it.

"Strong Ranch," he spoke into the phone.

"You must be Preston," said the caller on the other end of the line. "I'm Pete, and I'm planning to fly into your field just before lunch—a day early than expected. I'm currently in Huntsville, Alabama, but I'm leaving in an hour and need your runway length."

"Okay, Pete," replied Preston. "Runway length is 2,970 feet of asphalt. We are expecting clear skies, but a cold wind in from the north. I suggest a long final into Runway 25 from the southeast. Winds are expected to be 10 knots with gusts up to 15. Temperature will be around 45 degrees at midday. Do you need long and lat?"

"No, thanks, Preston. Already got that, see you later today."

Preston put the phone down, wondered who Carlos had invited, and forgot about it as he went to fill the coffee machine.

It was another hour later before the hangar gang got their coffee machine fired up. Everyone was in a sleepy daze as the machine burbled, and all were dressed mostly in simple T-shirts and denims.

Sally and Jennifer still had their hair all over the place, and Carlos, Buck, and Barbara did not look much better. Nobody had moved for their first hour, drinking coffee and chatting, when an aircraft could be heard approaching from the south. Jackets and outside shoes were slipped on to head outdoors and watch the arrival. Carlos was a little perplexed. Pete wasn't due in for another day and then he remembered hearing the phone earlier. *"He must be coming in a day early,"* he thought to himself, smiling.

They all shuffled out of the side door and onto the apron where Preston, Martie, and Oliver were already watching the incoming plane. The glare from the mid-day sun was behind the plane and nobody could tell what she was until a few seconds before touchdown.

"Oh my God!" exclaimed Sally, putting her hand to her mouth with her face going white. "It's General Allen's Blackhawk C-12! Oh my God, Jennifer!" Sally was in shock.

Carlos smiled a very wicked smile in Sally's direction.

"Will he be able to get out of here?" Preston quizzed Sally as the aircraft guided over the trees. That's a King Air B-200. Its needs more runway than I have."

"Not the C-12 Huron," she answered back still in shock and looking up at the aircraft. "The Air Force has full Blackhawk and Raisbeck upgrades on her. She is also fully equipped down to 3,200-feet landings and take-offs. Nearly as good as *Jerry*, but I could beat her any day with four turboprops instead of two."

"Well, what about 2,970 feet?" asked Preston, as the tires shot up small plumes of blue smoke right on the very end of the asphalt and plumes of dust rose behind the aircraft as the plane landed. Its front wheel came down fast, the propellers were feathered, and the brakes were applied, all within a second. Air brakes appeared under the wings, and the King Air came to a stop only several feet from the runway end, turned around, and began its taxi trip to the crowd on the apron.

"I suppose that answers your question," replied Sally, her face still white. "For take-off, the General will have to copy Buck and release brakes on full revs, and again I'm sure he's light on fuel. Jennifer, we are not dressed for the arrival of a four-star general."

She turned on Carlos. "I'm going to kill you for not giving us any advance warning! I'm going to shoot you out of the sky the next chance I have! Any dang ideas of marriage in your head better fly out of the window fast, Mr. Rodriquez!" she growled, trying to compose herself.

It was the first time that Preston had ever seen Sally's

feathers ruffled, and he knew Carlos was going to get it. He looked over at Carlos and smiled with him when he saw his friend enjoying Sally's meltdown. The smile of revenge on Carlos' face made Preston's day.

The aircraft came over to the middle of the apron. Preston used his apron batons to direct and halt the aircraft, which was painted in silver and white with Air Force insignia on its sides. She looked full of many extras on every part of her fuselage and rear wings, and her engines sounded as powerful as a lion's roar as the pilot shut them down. She was no bigger than the Pilatus, but much heavier and usually the King Airs needed more than 4,000 feet of runway. The rear side door opened, the stairs unfolded, and Preston and Carlos walked up to receive their newest guest.

"You must be Pete?" welcomed Preston, shaking the man's hand as he stepped onto the ground dressed in civilian clothes and looking nothing like a four-star general.

"Hello, Preston Strong," replied General Allen smiling. "Pete Allen's the name, flying's the game. I've heard a lot about you and your little mercenary Air Force you have hidden down here in the South, here in the hangar I presume."

He turned to the second man. "Hello, young Carlos, how are you? I had dinner with your father in Washington two nights ago and he told me to give you a belated Christmas present from him and your Uncle." He held out a small package with one hand and shook Carlos' hand with the other. "I see that our Air Force is also on display here at your fly-in, and I suppose the two young pilots got them in without a scratch?"

Pete turned back to Preston. "I couldn't resist a visit after Colonel Mondale over at Seymour Johnson told me about your perfect P-38. Your buddy Carlos here told me about your fly-in months ago, so I allowed our two young pilots to get *Tom* and *Jerry* in and then I thought 'What the heck! I might as well join in myself for New Year's Eve.' Carlos suggested that we keep the visit quiet, a surprise for our two pilots, I would assume."

"You are very welcome here," replied Preston warmly.

"Don't worry about a bed for me, Preston. I had this old girl fitted out with a bed in the back. I spend a lot of time in her and often get caught in interesting places in extended bad weather conditions. Cuba was the last place I got stuck, thanks to a tropical storm this summer. She has a toilet at the back, heat and air. I just need a 50-amp connection to power her up."

By this time Sally had regained her composure, as had Jennifer, and they came forward in their ruffled condition and stood at attention.

"At ease, ladies," the General ordered, who was also in civilian attire. "Not as crisp as the last time we met, Captain Powers, but you had just completed Hawaii tanker training. From here on, I'm a civilian, and so are you two."

Sally and Jennifer both nodded and dropped their ramrod postures.

"So, let me introduce myself," Pete extended a hand to both women. "Hello, I'm Pete and you are Sally and Jennifer, I assume?" They both nodded again. "And don't think I can't party, girls. Apart from that good-looking gentleman coming out of the house over there," he nodded at Grandpa Roebels in the distance, "I reckon I'm the oldest one here."

Preston asked Martie to do the remaining introductions while he went in and grabbed an electrical connection on a long yellow cord for the general's aircraft. He would need to tow the King Air to the side, pull the Pilatus away from the hangar, and place the new aircraft closer to the hangar side so that the cord would be long enough.

Pete enjoyed meeting everybody and he requested a guided tour of every aircraft this side of the runway.

He enjoyed *Lady Dandy* and *Baby Huey* with Buck as his tour guide while Preston sorted out his aircraft. He chatted with

Buck for several minutes in each aircraft. Then he asked Sally to show him her new toy. They spent another several minutes in her aircraft while Jennifer snuck back to her room to tidy up.

Then there was the hangar. Pete whistled when he saw the four aircraft stationed in the warmth of the building. He asked permission to sit in each and asked the owners all kinds of questions. He sat for a long time in the P-38, with Preston going through the instruments, every one original except the Garmin GPS system he had in a corner of the dashboard and out of the way.

Pete was impressed with the display. He had already met Grandpa Roebels and Michael outside, and coffee was served by Martie while Preston went out to check on his electrical work with the General's aircraft. The three older men talked for a good hour with everyone listening in, except Sally, who noticed that Jennifer was now smart and cleanly dressed and snuck away to do the same. Joe and David arrived an hour later to find a new aircraft freshly parked where the Pilatus had been, with the Pilatus now taking second row between the hangar and the runway. Preston was climbing out of the new arrival as they drove up.

"Wow!" he exclaimed as the men drove up. "That is the most sophisticated aircraft and instrument panel I have ever seen. And it has a toilet, a bed, a Lazy-Boy, and a large-screen television in the back. An RV has nothing on this baby!"

He explained about the new arrival to the Joe and David and they went inside to be introduced. Once again, Pete was excited to meet Joe and David, and quickly enjoyed a grand tour of all the land vehicles on display outside.

"May I assume you have already checked out my ride, Preston?" Pete asked, smiling at the younger pilot. Any good pilot would do so automatically, and there was nothing secret about his aircraft, as far as civilians were concerned. "The C-90 designated as Air Force One had a lot more stuff than this one. I used to fly President Johnson in it."

Pete settled into the party routine nicely. He was a martini man and had his stock aboard his ride. He brought out several bottles and the necessities necessary to make everybody martinis, and after a long liquid lunch, the guests rested and relaxed. Sally and Jennifer were now more comfortable with their superior officer, who was in line to be Chief of Staff with the change of power in Washington next year, and talked war stories with him for a couple of hours with everybody listening raptly. Many in attendance had military experience and interesting information was gathered from each of them.

Once things had been cleared away, Carlos took a nap, as did Buck and Barbara, and Martie and Preston took Oliver on a walk around the perimeter of the farm—a good two miles of trail. Most of the farm was desolate and natural bush. In the New Year, Preston wanted to borrow a large yellow Caterpillar that Joe owned and pull out more trees to make another 100 feet of runway, as well as push the undergrowth away from the existing runway to give him more room.

"I checked this out a few months ago," he said to Martie as they stood at the end of the southern tip of the asphalt runway trying to find where the general had put down his tires. There were black strips within a foot of the end of the blacktop—too small for *Lady Dandy* and the C-130s—and a second set six inches to the left of the first marks that started two feet further onto the tarmac.

"These are either Sally's from yesterday or Pete's from this morning. Anybody who can get their wheels down within two feet of the start of the tarmac is a pilot in my book. I think Sally was less worried yesterday on landing compared to her first one. There are no C-130 tire tracks, which mean that she had her C-130 wheels on the ground long before they touched the asphalt, same with Jennifer. They couldn't brake hard until the front section was on the ground, most probably 100 feet into their landing."

Preston looked over at Martie with a grin. "Sorry, I got distracted. As I was saying, if I angled a second runway another ten degrees to the west, or from 250 degrees and 110 degrees to 260 degrees and 120 the a form of a triangle with the triangle being at the southern tip here, the runway would be 150 feet over there," he stated pointing directly west. "I would be able to build a second runway, use the current one either to take off and land like we do now, and the second one, also 30 feet wide, could be increased to fit easily into that corner of the property over there. I would still be 200 yards from our perimeter and I could increase it by another 310 feet, giving me over 3,300 feet of tarred runway. Also, with the angle change, I could overlap our current one and add another 200 feet on the north side. I would be pretty close to our driveway entrance but nobody lives or even comes close to our entrance. Thirty-five hundred feet of runway would mean small jets, and since we land more from the south than the north, landing aircraft could turn onto the old runway and taxi in leaving it clear for the next guy."

"Great idea, but are we going into competition with Raleigh/Durham International, or shall we just turn it into an air museum for all aircraft?" laughed Martie. Preston was always trying to increase his airport size, but nearly had a heart attack if anyone drove onto the property. "Thirty-five hundred feet of 30-foot wide prepared runway plus a lighting system?" Martie questioned. "Hmm, what would that cost us so that Preston can decide which runway to use with his yellow crop-duster that completes 99% of the annual landings and take-offs on The Strong Farm/Ranch/Airport, or whatever you want to call it—a million dollars?" she laughed at him and smacked the back of his head with her hand. "Dirt maybe, but not 30 feet of asphalt."

"Half a million—a small amount, but I suppose you're right," answered Preston. "The old motto 'if we build it nobody will come,' I suppose would be the end result."

"We could do a couple of world cruises aboard the new *Queen Mary*, or whatever her name is, for that amount and that sounds better to me," laughed Martie.

The next morning, Preston warmed up the old truck to go and collect Maggie and the kids from RDU Airport. It was a 20-mile drive, and they were due in on the first flight in from the west coast, just after midday. They left on a new Southwest Airlines route from Burbank, straight into RDU. It had been in service only a couple of months, and lucky for the Smarts Burbank was the closest L.A. airport to Antelope Acres. A five and a half hour flight non-stop across the country, their flight had left early at 7:00 am and they were due to arrive in North Carolina at 12.30 pm. Sally and Martie begged to go along and there would be just enough room in the big Ford.

It was weird driving the old truck after flying the airplanes. It was slow heavy and felt like a tank. They drove down Preston's 300-foot driveway, once they had passed the end of the runway, over an old and dry 20-foot riverbed to a private dirt road. The large farm-style gate automatically opened and closed. The only gate-openers were in Joe's, Martie's and Preston's vehicles, in the hangar and in the house.

A couple of years earlier, Preston had mounted a camera on a high pole 20 yards inside the gate. It was the only way to see who was ringing the electric bell at the entrance to the property so far from the main house. He had laid 800 feet of wire for the project. The front perimeter of the property was also well-fenced and maintained.

They turned right onto a slightly wider dirt road, maintained primarily by Joe, and drove another 100 yards to the south before making a left-hand, 90-degree angle turn due east to connect onto a tarred feeder road and then down two more miles to Highway 64. Joe lived at the end of the dirt road, half a mile further down from Preston's entrance. The two farms were the only houses on the road and on the side of the tarred feeder road stood their mail boxes. Even the mail truck wouldn't go any further.

Preston waited until there was a hole in traffic on 64 and then gunned the track over the west-bound lanes and turned left into the east-bound lanes towards the airport. The eastern edge of Jordan Lake was only 100 yards away from the road entrance, and much of the ground south of the farms was part lake itself—a natural barrier for most of the farm's southern and western boundaries. To the east and on the other side of the feeder road was a protected forest of several thousand acres and only towards the northeast a couple of miles away were there any neighbors. They were well-hidden in their little corner, and rarely got any unscheduled visitors.

The scenery never changed on their way into Raleigh on NC64. The highway was dual-lanes through the Apex area and 15 minutes later, Preston turned onto the 540 beltline headed north and toward the airport exit. They arrived at exactly 12:30 pm, and the three Smart family members were already outside the baggage claim area waiting for them. Preston honked the horn and Martie and Sally waved at the three through the front windshield. The Smarts were carrying a backpack each and looked like they did not have any other baggage.

"Hi Maggie, Ben, and Oprah! How come you are so early?" asked Preston, jumping out and grabbing their back packs and packing them into the rear bed of the truck. "I was just going to keep going around until you showed."

"You should know, Preston," replied Maggie after being hugged by both Sally and Martie at the same time. "With the big storm going through, it was bumpy as hell for the first three hours. The pilot said that we had a vicious tailwind all the way through Arizona, New Mexico, the top half of Texas, and Oklahoma before we flew south of it and they could start drink service. We arrived 20 minutes early, had no baggage, and were out here a couple of minutes before our limo arrived. I hope you look after your flying machines better than this poor truck. It's worse than ours, and I thought ours was bad."

"The rust keeps it together," laughed Preston. "I heard that even Warren Buffet drives the exact same model. This is a real rich man's truck!"

The trip back was full of talk and chit-chat between the three women with the two kids sitting in front. The former roommates had been bumped to the rear seat by the Smart kids, as they knew that a verbal barrage of words would start between all of them. It always did when they got together.

"How's California treating you guys?" asked Preston of the twins sitting in front.

"Great, Preston," Oprah got in first. "We sold our sixth electrical generator last month to our last neighbor. Now all seven houses in our neighborhood are feeding into the power grid."

"We have a fun bunch of neighbors, Preston," added Ben. "We wanted to be here, but we all had a great Christmas with over 40 of us eating together at one house. It was a swell day, but I'm glad to be back in North Carolina."

"Your dad is really a good guy after all, giving you flights for New Year's Eve. Martie was really sad when she thought you guys wouldn't make it. I would have enjoyed finally meeting your Dad. I don't understand his fear of flying."

"Nor do we," added Oprah.

"But at least he was okay about us to coming over to see you guys," interrupted, Ben. "We miss Oliver."

"Hey, guess what?" Preston asked them, having to shout over the laughter coming from the three in the rear seat. "I hitched up one of the big diesel motors to the hangar and the house, exactly how I showed you when you visited over the summer and boy, has it got power! Martie and I turned everything on that we could and the diesel just sat there on idle and took the load without breaking a rev or a sweat!"

"Don't you still have more of the big ones?" Ben asked.

"I've got a couple more that can be turned on anytime and another couple still at Joe's farm I've been working on. It wouldn't take more than a couple of days to finish them up as well."

Within an hour and a half, they arrived back at the farm gate and Preston pushed the remote on his sun visor to open it up and let them through. The new visitors were introduced to everyone, and had to tour every single aircraft and vehicle. Ben did not want to climb out of the Saracen, but the three ladies offered to work on dinner so they could be alone in the house kitchen with a couple of bottles of wine. They had a lot of catching up to do, and it was only 4:00 pm.

They produced a nice hot meal for the 14 guests that were staying that night. The number had grown since Christmas and the large hangar room was now always busy. The Smarts had been satisfied with Carlos' old room, and he had moved his one backpack downstairs and out into the hangar. It was the evening of December 30th and nobody really wanted to go all out and party, but a steady line at the bar was obvious all night.

Martie had felt like using Bloody Marys to celebrate that evening. The three former roommates had often guzzled them in their dorm room at MIT, and they had stopped on the way home and bought the shop out of fresh free-range eggs, 20 packs of bacon, a large bag of tomatoes for breakfast, and a dozen big bottles of normal and spicy Bloody Mary mix. The hangar bar's stock of a case of vodka had hardly been touched thanks to Pete and his stash, and there were still a dozen cases of champagne of all types for New Year's Eve.

After dinner, everyone sat and chatted in the hangar room. The troops overseas were a favorite topic and Pete was all for bringing every one of them home. Some of the wars were a decade old, never winnable, and aggression against U.S. forces on all fronts had escalated drastically throughout the year. He mentioned that the increase in factions opposing U.S. troops looked like it might be coming to a climax soon. With over 2,000 deaths in the last several months alone, more than in the previous five years, something was going on.

Buck and Carlos agreed with Pete, adding in the equation of all the electronic malfunctions around the world in the last couple of months—more than in the last decade combined. Preston shared that it would take months to get all the troops back that the President promised by the end of January, and everyone agreed with him. Even Pete, who did not discuss military issues very much, said that a full pull-out of 250,000 troops, using all available Air Force and available commercial air transportation, plus the use of the majority of the US Navy in different parts of the world, would take at least three months to execute. It would take over a year to get all military, civilian, and motorized personnel back to home soil. The White House did not understand the vast maneuvers that would be necessary to pull out such large numbers, and did not seem to listen to advice from anybody.

Then the conversation turned towards the President himself. Most agreed that they liked the man. He had taken over lousy administration problems from the previous President, had no better opportunities after the last change in government, and apart from sending more and more troops out of the country, many at the White House were going deaf to the warnings by the President and most of the top brass. Congress had listened to the "let's-take-over-the-world" military personnel in charge for so many years, and did very little positive for the American people. Gas prices were up to record levels, the U.S. dollar had devalued by over 15% compared to strong Asian currencies. U.S. unemployment stood at 14%, empty and foreclosed houses stood at about 1 in 40 countrywide. The jails were filling up with homeless and hungry civilians, and the news broadcasters continued to say that we were in the healthiest economic times America as ever seen.

"Bullshit!" exclaimed Carlos and a few others.

"Maybe it's time to head to the islands somewhere," suggested Barbara. "We have our Army and Air Force. We just need a few old naval frigates and submarines to stop the unwanted, take some farmers, some good-looking men and women with us, and start our own country."

There was much agreement and laughter in reaction to her comments, but most agreed that it was certainly worth thinking about.

"It takes a lot of work and a lot of people to make a country go round," interjected Preston. "Just here on this airfield, the daily chores never stop. Martie and I work hard, and so does Joe next door, just to keep our farms intact. I'm sure it would work, but if we do go to an island, could it be a small one with fewer chores?" They all laughed at that one.

The last day of the year for billions of people all over the world started just like any other day. The sun rose and electronic apparati starting buzzing, blaring, heating, cooling, ticking, warning, and generally making as much noise as possible—especially in the United States, which had billions of every sort of electrical gadget money could buy.

On the ranch, it was the second to last day of partying, as most of the departures would take place on January 2nd. Martie, Sally, and Maggie had spent the whole previous day catching up on gossip—enough to sink a battleship, as Carlos stated that morning over coffee. The weather was beginning to turn. The big storm was hitting the northeast and North Carolina was getting the fringes of it coming across from the west-northwest and just off-center of the runway.

The wind was gusting at 15 knots, and it was the day planned for helicopter flying. *Baby Huey* had already been moved on a dolly and refueled by Buck, Preston, Carlos, and Pete earlier that morning. She had been rather thirsty from her trip down, since she did it non-stop, but 200 gallons of jet fuel later she was ready to fly. Buck's Huey, the UH-1D version, had the extended body and could take 14-15 people seated in four rows of four behind the two pilots. Buck had found some old light-weight folding tin chairs at a military auction a year or so earlier and had brought them with him for this trip.

It was going to be crowded, and the seats were not comfortable, but nobody cared as long as they got aboard. Barbara decided to stay behind, and that gave David and Joe a chance to get a seat. Grandpa Roebels was in the right seat next to Buck, and the rest just crammed in behind them. With the large cargo doors on either side pulled shut, they were already facing into the wind, and Buck started the turbo-shaft motor.

Preston had filed a flight plan out to Wright Field at Kitty Hawk on the coast, and it would be a 70-minute flight. Weather at the coast was clear but windy. Everyone was aboard. Luckily, two of the passengers were kids and that left a little more room for the adults. The three MIT girls were not allowed to sit together, so Sally, Carlos, Pete, and Ben sat in the first row, with Martie, Preston, Joe, and Oprah in the second, and Maggie, David, and Jennifer in the last row. Michael had been a passenger in Hueys often and had decided to stay in the hangar. There was something on television he wanted to watch.

Buck warmed up the engine, brought the revs up, and felt the extra weight as she used a lot more power than normal to get airborne. He let her lean forward and the rotor blades bit into the wind and climbed quickly in a west-northwest direction, directly over Joe's farm and then over the lake. It was noisy. This wasn't a commercial flight, and the real thrill was being in a loud military aircraft and flying over the rest of the world at 130 miles an hour. They climbed up to 5,000 feet, and the heater worked hard to keep them warm. Everyone had worn warm outerwear, and some were even wearing winter gloves and hats. The colors were certainly not military, and they looked like a bunch of beginner snow skiers in a cable car.

"Do we have permission to land at Wright Field?" shouted Buck to Preston.

"No," was the simple shouted reply. "But I don't think they'll mind. We are in an aircraft nearly as old, it's the middle of winter, and it's been closed for several weeks. The only parts of the field we can hurt are a couple of blades of grass and there are acres of room."

They came in low over the old and famous field, and Buck decided to put her down close to the main building where it looked like there were one or two small cabins. The wind was stronger than back at the airport, which forced him to come in slowly and put her down very gently. He let the rotors come to a halt before he allowed the side doors to open, and they all got out, walking around and stretching their legs.

The sun was still shining, but only just, and it would be an even colder trip back home. The place was empty of life and they spent the next hour inspecting the hill, the markings where Orville and Wilbur had taken their flights and felt the importance of the first place where man had actually flown in an aircraft so many years ago. For them, it was an important place to be. Even Pete Allen had never been here before and enjoyed reminiscing about the Wright Brothers and their expertise in bicycles which led them to be the first of millions of pilots to come—including them. Martie and Preston had packed some blankets, thermoses of coffee, and sandwiches, and they stopped behind one of the buildings to enjoy a picnic of sorts.

Once everybody was ready and everything packed back into *Baby Huey*, Buck warmed her up. This time, he turned the helicopter's nose directly north, as the wind had changed direction. He turned to starboard as they climbed and he took them over the beach and out to sea at 500 feet. Several people walking the beach pointed up to them as they flew by.

The Huey then flew down to within 100 feet of the waves, and the ride become exhilarating. This was what helicopter flying was all about. For 15 minutes, Buck flew south a couple of hundred yards off the outer beaches on a slither of land called Cape Hatteras, still at 100 feet until Ocracoke came into view. Ocracoke was the southern town on Cape Hatteras, and once they flew past, he turned inland, rose 100 feet higher and flew over the vast waters and marshlands of Pamlico Sound.

For 20 minutes, they flew all the way over water nearly up to the small town of Washington. A few miles out, Buck climbed up to a safer altitude of 4,000 feet, and they flew back to Apex, passing 30 miles north of Seymour Johnson. They landed at the Ranch just before dark and everyone helped move the helicopter back into place, tie it down, and check the other aircraft. Then they all rushed inside to the warmth of the large hangar. It was getting cold outside.

It was cold enough for several rounds of *glüwein*, so Martie warmed a case of red wine on the stove in a large pot in the hangar while Michael and Barbara walked in with interesting snacks they had made while the crowd was away. The New Year's Eve party had started. It was nearly 6:00 and they still had six hours of the old year to go.

Michael and Barbara had done a great job on food, and with the warm wine going down rapidly, and Cokes for the two young ones, Martie put U2 on the stereo and everybody finally got into the last party of the year.

CHAPTER 15

Jiangsu Province, China – Lunch, New Year's Day

CHAMPAGNE WAS READY IN ICE BUCKETS next to the buffet lunch table in the board room at Zedong Headquarters on the 30th floor. Three young girls would soon arrive and distribute lunch with glasses of champagne shortly after 1.00 pm. The men in the boardroom were excited. Thirty years of hard work was about to reach its conclusion. Secrecy was becoming unimportant at this delicate time, as the point of no return had already been reached and there was nothing anybody could do about it.

At precisely 12.30 pm, the room went quiet as Chairman Wang Chunqiao got up and moved to the podium. Behind him on the large wall were two digital, flattened world maps 30 feet across with a flickering live feed from three Ziyuan-2 Chinese communication satellites designed and now privately owned by Zedong Electronics.

The three satellites showed the entire world in its immediate situation. A computer situated one floor below the boardroom in the building's electronics control center mapped the three live feeds together in one long, flattened world map, and displayed two individual maps on the wall, one underneath the other, by projector.

Day and night could be easily seen on both maps—the only difference between the maps was that on the top one, all the world's city lights across the dark area of the planet glowed brightly, and on the second one below it, many thousands of small markers showed up around the world each with a small light representing an aircraft locator number. Asia and Australia were in sunlight, as was Hawaii. It was 11.30 pm in Washington D.C., but the sun was just about to set in Hawaii. There was a clear and frozen dawn in Moscow and daylight across much of Russia.

"We have reached our beginning. We have finally reached our Z-Day after 30 years of hard work," the Chairman spoke from the front of the room. "I would like the final reports from the members who have scheduled reports to offer at this time. Once the reports are done, we will have lunch, view our live screens and watch our 30 years of planning and dedicated work change the world maps behind me. As most of you know, these are live pictures of our planet—fed from the three satellites we built on behalf of the Chinese government. We took over complete operational control of the Ziyuan-2 satellites yesterday, and from this morning forward they have been renamed their original names, after our Comrade Professor Jianbing who designed them. The three Jianbing satellites are communication satellites that do not carry any of our electrical parts; instead using parts purchased from a private Russian satellite company several years ago, and will be the only usable satellites in space once Z-Day is activated in 27 minutes. We designed them to work for our glorious government under our supervision until we are ready for them to work for our own project. The government was warned in Beijing two hours before we shut them out of the control-loop since they had directional communication information still running through them."

"Our valuable Zedong Electronics aircraft—the 30 Boeing 747-400ER aircraft and five Airbus 380s we leased to the government—have been made safe and are on the ground. We also warned our government about possible aircraft losses 24 hours ago. So, it has taken us 12 hours to move the three satellites into the same orbital speed as Earth, and they are exactly 294 miles out. They will give us live pictures of Earth until we need to move them in closer for our scheduled invasions around the world over the next 12 months."

The Chairman looked around the room. "So gentlemen, in a few hours the whole world is going to shut down and go dark. It will become very cold in the northern hemisphere once the inhabitants run out of any heating reserves, which is estimated to be seven to ten days. We will also terminate military establishments in our own country, to make sure that our own government does not and cannot oppose us and try to close us down here in Nanjing and Shanghai."

"We completed Phase I of our project last year—placing 110 termination squads with 440 of our well-trained Red Guard termination squads on the east and west coasts of North America. They have special satellite telephones and will be our ears and eyes. As you all know, I have a total distaste for the United States of America and what it stands for, and we will leave the other first-world countries to self-destruct over a much longer period. We are attacking the United States first. Our plan to invade America still stands, gentlemen. With over 440 specially trained killers already in America, we will give the people three weeks to destroy themselves, and then our food ships will go in and offer the remaining few food once they accept our new, red Chinese passports. We will have ten cargo ships fully loaded and ready to enter New York and Los Angeles, five on the Atlantic side and five on the Pacific-side two weeks later. Zedong Electronics will deploy our 30 commercial jumbo jets and the five Airbus 380s to ferry in troops at the same time our new aircraft carrier and escort arrive with the cargo ships in New York Harbor. That is 20,000 troops going into three airports around New York that will have been made safe by our 440 men on the ground."

"Another 4,000 Zedong Red Guard marines will be on our support vessels, and our four modern warships which will protect our new aircraft carrier, the Shi Lang. She will have her 30 fighter jets ready to make sure that we succeed and destroy any opposition at the most important entry points into our new country—New York Harbor, Washington D.C., and then Los Angeles. We will all be aboard the Shi Lang when we gloriously enter America under the Verrazano-Narrows Bridge, which I will rename the 'Comrade Wang Chunqiao Bridge.'"

The Chairman paused while the room applauded his announcement. "Gentlemen, there are 16 large bridges in New York, and each one of you will have a bridge named in your honor once we change the name of New York City to Zedong City and Washington D.C. to Jiang Qing City a week later when our jumbo jets return with another 20,000 troops for our new capital. I will remove the statue of Lincoln from his memorial and replace it with my own, which is currently being made in Shanghai. We will have succeeded when I sit in the President's chair behind the desk of power in my Oval Office. Any questions?"

There were two.

"Comrade Chairman, what about the 90,000 estimated American troops left on their mainland, and armed American civilians turning themselves into armies? Surely a large number of American civilians will survive with many guns?"

"With no electricity, no radio communications, no satellites, and no way to control millions of hungry, angry people, I will be surprised if there is anybody left when we arrive. Any males that are left, except male farmers, are to be executed by our termination squads. The termination squads are to look for any pockets of resistance and destroy them. We, with our allies; Iran, North Korea, fighters in the middle east and Afghanistan, and fighters in Africa who are to be our future work force, have pushed their attacks in the last year to levels where the American President and his miserable government have deployed 91% of all American troops and 80% of the American National Guard to foreign lands where they can never get back to America. They will be easily attacked without all their fancy military equipment, and each American soldier will be killed. The old U.S. Armed Forces will never be a problem to anyone again. These poor, miserable soldiers with have nothing to defend themselves with, apart from their little guns and a few rounds of ammunition. In America, there will be no vehicles for moving their few troops around, except maybe a few old vehicles. They will have absolutely no fighters or bombers. They will lose 99% of their Navy—a few old ones might remain, but will not be a problem with our five stronger, modern naval warships."

The Chairman paused for effect, his room full of colleagues sitting in rapt attention. "I'm also 100% positive that every movable machine in America has one or more of our electronic parts installed. The Americans upgrade everything all the time, why not the old equipment? And even with troops or teams of civilians becoming a force against us, our termination squads are better armed and have modern and working radio communications. We have stashed away mountains of ammunition over the last five years and will be able to destroy anybody in our way. The squads' orders are to kill any adult males they find and leave the women and children for us to use as a work force to re-build our new country. America currently has 310 million people. Comrades, given the time we will allow our enemy to kill themselves, I believe that there will be less than 50 million starving, weak capitalist women and children who will join us, the leaders of the new Communist Republic of American People."

"Comrade Chairman, could you please explain why your plans are to attack the east coast first. Surely it is a long way to go, where Los Angeles, San Francisco, and Seattle are half the distance?" asked one man.

"An excellent question and one I pondered on for years. The answer, Comrade Bo, is that I believe the remains of the American military, if they happen to understand our plans, will be based in the West Coast cities for any potential attacks. I think that if they get that far and realize that another country was behind the electrical attack, they will think that either the Russian government or our own Chinese government was behind the attack, not Zedong Electronics. I'm sure many clever people will survive and analyze possible answers. I want them to, because America is vast like China. If I can get the remaining troops to one side of the country like the west coast, then the other side—New York and Washington D.C., the White House where I will reside, the Pentagon, and all the country's wealth—will all be immediately vulnerable to our occupation. There should be less than 10 million very hungry and cold people in that area."

"The military might take days to hear of our final invasion planned for exactly three weeks after we activate Z-Day, but will be powerless to walk across the continent before we have amassed our 25,000 well-armed troops in New York and then our 20,000 troops in Washington. My belief is that their military, from all around the country, will start walking east. Our termination squads are expected to leak the information to them, and they will walk away from the west coast, leaving it undefended, and we will attack Los Angeles after they have left. We will also have full control of the Panama Canal within a week. A special secret force of 1,500 specially trained Red Guards are to take control of the Canal and they are already in position. They have been transported by submarine over the last several weeks. Once we have control of the Panama Canal, we will be leaving here and our East Coast Attack Force, including all of you, will depart for our new country. That is all I have to say at this moment, time is running short. Comrade Wang, your final report please." This time the Chairman did not leave the podium.

Lee Wang's old boss stood up where he sat. "Comrade Chairman," he began. "We have completed our mission in the United States. All our operatives are now terminated. Unfortunately one of our termination squads had a gun fight with the local police force in Salt Lake City. Thankfully they were killed only after they had terminated the last operative and his family. Our four-man squad was terminated by U.S. police and our media team sent out more news about Chinese hit squads being paid by the Russian or Italian mafias We had the same problem in Las Vegas the same day. One of our California operatives had realized what was happening and tried to evade us by running with his family to Nevada. The first squad on the scene terminated him and his family in one of the hotels, but was seen by a civilian. The squad immediately left Las Vegas and headed out into the desert where a gun battle ensued. We lost eight men in the two attacks, and the American FBI and local police force lost 27. It shows the strength of our termination squads."

"We sent out the news relating to possible Italian mafia gang fights in Las Vegas, and the news went national. I think the FBI is currently looking for a group of Italians all over the United States. Their media is so easy to manipulate—seems they will do anything for a story. The two unfortunate occurrences happened too close to Christmas and our Z-Day to give us any problems, except that we are eight good men fewer in the United States." He sat down.

"Unfortunate, Comrade Wang, but we must expect problems. I agree with you about these problems being so close to Z-Day, and we are now only 20 minutes away from Z-Day, and then we will enjoy lunch and celebrate."

Two other reports were given to the room, neither of much relevance to the current situation, and the time slowly ticked by

—the minute hand of the large clock above the maps getting closer and closer to the top of the hour.

"You have all noticed the five red, armored-glass protected buttons on the board table in front of me," announced the Chairman. The 15 other men in the room nodded.

"The first four are not locked and will be operated in this room. The fifth one is locked. The first one on the window side of the room will send the electronic destruction signal through our three two-way satellites operating above the Earth, linked up to each other, and set our first action in motion to shut down the first three billion of our older electronic parts that include Strontium in every corner of the world. It will take about a minute for all of these parts to react. The Strontium is slower than our more modern electrical impulse chips that we started producing in the mid-90s."

"Then I will press the second button, which will send a termination impulse to the part's backup systems just in case the Strontium hasn't reacted to the first signal. That will only take seconds."

"The third button will terminate all our new, modern parts and manufactured units built after 1994. Their reaction time is instantaneous for all our specially-made electronics, and they will close down opposition government and military installations and weapons, including all American and Russian nuclear missiles—every single one."

"The fourth button is for our allies. We also have specially designed parts on a separate frequency in their governments, military installations, communications, and weaponry in case they decide to attack us. If we are attacked here, it will only be two types of people who have the ability to do that after the first three buttons are activated—our allies, including North Korea, Iran, Pakistan and Syria, or our own government here in China. The fifth red button will close down all of China. Exemptions to these five buttons are our own electrical power systems, factories, all the aircraft and shipping we own, our buildings, and our satellite communications. Nobody can close down Zedong Electronics... nobody!"

"If I'm killed because our current friends in the government decide to rise against us, the fifth button gives us complete world domination if we need to activate it, and it sits under a locked, protective glass shield. Only I and three of you in this room secretly have the code for it. This system is fully Wi-Fi and a special squad of twelve Red Guard marines, hand-picked by me, will guard it day and night after this meeting. It will always travel with me and will be moved to America when we move. According to the atomic digital clock underneath each map, it is precisely 310 seconds to 'go.' Any questions?"

There were none, and the men in the room sat grim-faced as they watched the numbers tick down from 300.

At precisely 1:00 pm local time, and midnight on the U.S. east coast, Chairman Wang Chunqiao opened the glass protection cup over the first button and pushed it. All eyes were glued to the two world maps on the wall behind him, and he slowly turned around to watch the wall above him. Several parts of the world went dark during the first minute after the two digital clocks had reached zero.

He then opened the second glass protective cup over the second button and pushed it. This time, changes on the top map became more apparent. The whole area of lights over the eastern coast of the United States disappeared. Hawaii, now dark, had disappeared and so did all the lights in Mexico and most of Canada. Parts of Spain and Portugal went black and then it happened—hundreds of split-second flickering lights as all assumed that back-up systems were going on and off instantaneously, and then the whole of the eastern seaboard of the United States and Western Europe went totally black. South America had gone black during the first minute. To the fascinated eyes watching the destruction of the world's entire electrical grid except in China, North Korea, and several other small areas where only a percentage of the lights disappeared—even the darkened coastlines of the continents disappeared as the lines of lights blinked out. The islands of the world disappeared before the Chairman pressed the third button.

"The lower map shows every aircraft in flight around the world. Their commercial locator beacons or transponder impulses are being kept active by our satellites even though air traffic control worldwide is already dead. Even though most of these aircraft are now dead and falling to Earth, most of these transponders are backed up by battery power and will continue to send out impulses until destroyed."

The number at the bottom of the map showed a total of 4,597 impulses worldwide. The number quickly dropped down to 4,571, then 4,538 and then 4,511 and then stayed there for several seconds.

"The first decrease, I assume, represents aircraft either landing or taking off and very close to the ground," explained the Chairman, still looking at the map behind him. Then the number began to drop quickly over the next 30 seconds to 2,049. "Aircraft at lower flight altitudes," he explained to the men around the table. He glanced at the clocks and noticed that 160 seconds had elapsed since he had pushed the first button. By this time, the smaller number 979 showed up on the bottom screen. "You will notice on our top world map that much of northern China is now blacked out, especially around Beijing. The more southern areas like Shanghai and the area around us will not change, apart from several military barracks that will black out, and every vehicle in them. I decided to cut our own country's strength with the government and military being destroyed by half. Also, apart from our allies and China, the whole world is now becoming completely dysfunctional."

"There are a group of specialists on the floor below us watching the maps and are ready to send our termination squads into areas that display a visible light in America 24 hours from now."

"I doubt there will be many, but we are ready. In the sunlit areas, the same has happened, but we cannot see it as well. We can tell our success by the number of aircraft remaining, and as you can see, flying numbers have been reduced to 63 aircraft worldwide. These we will assume are old, mostly propeller-driven aircraft older than 1982, and most of them have very little chance of landing safely in America and Europe as the ground is totally black beneath them and they have nowhere to go after their fuel expires except down. Remember, gentlemen, the aircraft sitting on the ground, except for ours and our allies, are also now pieces of junk and will rot and rust at their current locations. That includes every military aircraft, every electronic piece of weaponry, and every naval ship in the world. We have now completed our mission for Z-Day."

He paused, sighed, and was silent for a few moments. "Gentlemen, 30 years of work have paid off admirably, and we are only at the beginning. Let's eat lunch and celebrate with the best French champagne. I got a container load in for our consumption only a few days ago."

CHAPTER 16

Midnight, Eastern Time – The End of Modern Civilization

THE PARTY WAS IN FULL SWING, the music was loud with much laughter, and a television was on in the corner—the sound muted for the ball drop on "New Year's Rocking Eve" with Ryan Wavebreak.

"Hey everybody!" shouted Martie. "Five minutes to go and we can watch the ball drop in Times Square! Maggie, Will is working and your west coast festivities are still three hours away, so relax!"

Everyone laughed. "Sally, Maggie, help me open bottles of bubbly, would you? Let's get them uncorked and make sure that everybody's glasses are topped off before the ball drops."

The television screen displayed images of bands and celebrities getting pumped up for the ringing in of the New Year, with location shots from a very white downtown New York City full of fresh snow, people, and freezing temperatures. The usual television commentators could not get enough air time and worked hard to get everybody excited as the crowd seemed to be around them in Times Square.

Champagne corks began to pop as bottles were opened and glasses filled to capacity in the hangar lounge. The twins were happily dancing together—the Rolling Stones blaring from the sound system since nobody really wanted to listen to the audio from the TV. As Preston said to Martie every year, people who watched the dropping of the ball with the sound on were either drunk or sitting up in bed with curlers in their hair with nothing better to do.

At one minute to midnight, Martie started quieting everybody down and making sure that everyone had a glass of bubbly. Her grandfather was sitting in a chair, and he raised his glass to her as she looked in his direction. He had a large smile on his face and she assumed that he had finished at least a whole bottle or more by himself. She remembered the kids and grabbed two champagne glasses, filling them with a can of Coke she pulled out of the fridge and got Maggie to get them into the kids' hands. She clinked on a spare champagne glass and the room went quiet.

"Okay, friends, Romans and countrymen," she shouted in rather a tipsy voice, raising her glass. "I would like to thank you for all coming to our most successful fly-in to date. So much so that Preston is designing a new runway for larger aircraft for next year's shindig already. I think he took Sally's joke seriously and is thinking of the footage needed for Air Force One."

The rowdy crowd burst into laughter and several partiers clapped Preston on the back. "I would like you all to count down the old year with me and let's enter the New Year together, with hope and expectation that this world is going to become a better place!" Again the crowd burst into applause agreeing with Martie.

"Somebody turn the volume up on the tube!" Marti called as she held her champagne glass up high. "Here we go!" She and the rest of the crowd started counting down the numbers as they watched the ball descend on the screen in Times Square.

"Nine... eight... seven... six... five... four... three... two... one......... Happy New Year!"

Everyone started jumping up and down and shouted and started hugging and kissing each other. Nobody noticed the television screen go blank several seconds later, then fizzle with white and black colors for a few seconds and then go completely dead. Even the red light showing the television was on "Off" mode, came on for a second and then also died.

The jubilant and noisy crowd did notice a couple of minutes later when the loud music blaring out of the new music center died, and the room slowly went quiet. As they all quieted down and peered around to see who had stopped the noise, they noticed that the television was also blank and assumed somebody had turned it off.

"I think you guys jumping around has messed up the new music system," laughed Preston. "Don't worry. I have a backup. My trusty old system I've had in here for years. Martie, give me a cassette, any cassette." He reached over behind the kitchen counter and brought out his old one he had put away when Martie had showed him the new one a couple of weeks earlier.

"Did you say 'cassette'!" joked Buck. "That thing must be from the Stone Age." Again, there was laughter.

"Yeah, Buck, it's old and I think Fred Flintstone or Barney Rubble gave it to me as a gift, but I bet it still works. Maybe the sound isn't as good as my Christmas present from Martie, but I reckon that with all the Ph.D.s in Electrical Engineering in this room, somebody can look at the newer one and fix it while we enjoy this one." Music immediately blared out of the old one—this time it was Chuck Berry and a lot of twisting started immediately on the dance floor.

The noise hid the explosion of an airliner crashing into Jordan Lake three miles away.

Unconnected to the outside world the party went on for another 30 minutes, the ranch being so isolated and independent from the rest of the world. Nobody noticed anything different. Buck looked at the new sound system for a few minutes, scratched his head and put it down. It was completely dead. Nobody even thought to look at the television.

Oprah and Ben were getting bored with all the adult revelry, and decided to go and listen in to the ham radio in the house. Grandpa Roebels was still at the party, and with Preston's permission they walked out of the hangar and over to the house with Oliver. They could listen in on the radio chatter until Martie's grandfather wanted to go to bed. Ben saw several parts of the horizon lit up. He was used to the bright skies over L.A., and with this being New Year's Eve, he thought nothing of it.

They approached the quiet radio and sat down to listen. It was on the usual frequency they all used to talk to one another, but the set was totally quiet. It was humming, and the dials and tuning screen lit up as usual. Built in the late 1960s, the set was an old one but extremely powerful.

The kids waited for ten minutes and not one voice came on. They got bored, and Ben pressed the talk switch and called their house to see if their father was home, even though they knew he wouldn't be. He was at the station in Lancaster on night duty and wouldn't be home until early morning when they had arranged to speak to him at early east coast time.

There were a couple of scratches as the set picked up something. Ben thought he heard somebody calling for help. It was very faint and he called the unknown caller back. Everybody else they usually talked to was at the party, and they finally gave up on the radio when Michael helped in a singing Grandpa Roebels, winked at the kids, and swayed down the hall to put his happy father to bed.

* * *

Times Square quickly became a mess. It was only seconds after the ball had dropped when the large advertising banners lighting up the Square started flickering on and off. A large car, out of control, crashed into a group of pedestrians alongside the barriers that blocked the area off for the immense crowd of partiers. Then another car went out of control a few feet behind the first one. Suddenly, several other motor vehicles either came to a halt or seemed to spin, hitting the snow mounted on the sides of the roads, and smashing into several people on the street and onto sidewalks. One cannoned through a shop window. What had been a happy occasion moments before became a scene of intense confusion and hysteria as things seemed to go horribly wrong. Then, several seconds later, all the advertising banners went out completely, and the street lights followed suit. Shop windows went black as their lights went out. The sky was very overcast, and it started to snow again.

After several more seconds, the whole city light system went out, and apart from a few automobile headlights that were still on, the city around Times Square went very dark. Screams erupted from within the crowd of over one million people in Times Square. The Square, plus dozens of roads and side streets were crammed with party people who had just been dancing, enjoying the togetherness of the holiday scene. It was eerie as people, now virtually blind, tried to move in different directions to escape the blackness. Shop owners quickly closed their doors, scared that bad people might use the darkness to steal their tills. Others in stores sat there perplexed at what to do next. Many were from out of town, and only needed to walk to their hotels, which they assumed would have electricity, or at least back-up generators. This was America for God's sake, and New York! The power outage was surely for a short period of time.

Thousands immediately got on their cell phones to call friends and family, wanting to tell them about the excitement, but not even the lights of the thousands of iPhones, BlackBerries or hundreds of other types even glowed in the dark like they did moments before. They were all as useless as pieces of simple, molded plastic.

On the streets, it became blacker and blacker as lights from cars went off here and there. Screams increased as people fell underfoot in the masses who all wanted to scramble in different directions at the same time. A fire started in the shop the car had crashed into, and a little light came back to Times Square. Candles came on in several apartments around the area and the snow started falling harder. A bitterly cold wind began to blow down the streets, increasing the wind-chill factor.

Suddenly, the first gunshot of millions more to come in New York and around the world, was heard as a policeman tried to stop someone stealing from a shop that was ablaze. The policeman went down, the man and his gun could be seen in the light of the fire, and immediately another three policemen were on the scene, guns blazing at the man. Several bystanders who were trying to get past the fire and did not see what was going on became the victims of those bullets. They fell and the thief who had shot the first policeman disappeared into the dark shadows. More policemen arrived from the other side of the street and they all were trying to sort out the mass of bodies into orderly queues with a couple tending to the dead on the ground.

A few seconds later, the wind starting howling as a storm gathered strength and a massive stampede ensued. People went down in the thousands, trampled underfoot until their cries for help died with them. On the fringes of the massive crowd, people began dispersing onto other streets—many back to their hotel rooms. Fires were beginning to envelop the cars and buildings they had crashed into. Slowly the streets became visible again as the light and heat of the fires intensified. Fifteen minutes after the crisis started, a gas main blew just south of Times Square and a thousand people disappeared in the blast of searing heat that came with it. The massive explosion disintegrated several shop windows and weakened the whole 12-story building above them.

Only minutes later, the whole building came crashing down

onto the swollen mass of dead and injured people in the street, and killed hundreds more as it bounced against the building on the other side of the street and exploded outwards for another block in either direction—bricks and pieces of metal scything through the crowds. The gas explosion had reached out a couple of blocks and had started another dozen fires on the streets around it. The streets that had been dark and cold only moments before became hotter than hell, and the noise of the growing flames was pierced with hundreds of high-pitched screams of the people who could not escape the devastation.

Within minutes of the dropping of the ball in Times Square, hundreds of people around the Square were either dead or dying. The area had no place on the ground where a body didn't lie. It was carnage like New York had not seen since 9/11.

The rest of the city was in just as much turmoil. There were fires everywhere. Millions of people were trying to get somewhere to either escape what was happening behind them, or because they thought that somewhere else there must be a safe haven from this nightmare. Where occupants were awake in city buildings, candles lit up every window and thousands looked down into the worsening streets below them and watched as people ran here and there. The fires seemed to grow from nothing. The snow was falling heavily now and the flakes made the views from the windows more surreal. This was the United States of America. This didn't happen here in New York. Everyone did what they always did when they had a few spare feet and could take a breather—they looked at their phones and shook them, tried to text with them, or just shouted into them hoping they would get a response.

There were no fire engines, ambulances, or police cars screaming by, their sirens making that noise that comforts everyone in the middle of a crisis. Apart from human screams from every direction, and the crackling of fires in the vicinity, the snow made New York eerie and visibility was only several yards in either direction.

For many who reached their hotels, they found the doors locked and the insides darker than the streets outside. There were already people banging on the doors to be let in. The occupants of the buildings higher up could see no more than the people in the streets far below them.

The weather predictions came true 30 minutes after midnight. Newscasters had warned partiers to get somewhere warm and safe because the whole of Manhattan and most of New York and New Jersey would experience white-out conditions within an hour or two after midnight.

The three airports in the metro New York area had been exchanging inbound and outbound flight as fast as possible all evening. There were 35 flights on final approach to the three airports and another 12 only minutes into the air. These flights, in their most critical stage of flight didn't see the first 60 seconds into the New Year, as their systems died and 41 aircraft fell out of the skies, igniting entire suburbs and whole city blocks with their deadly cargos of fuel.

One experienced Southwest pilot felt his aircraft's controls go dead a minute after takeoff from La Guardia, and immediately veered around to return to the airport to land. But the area he had just taken off from was completely black, as the electrical grid closed down around the airport. The snow had not started to fall and he could still see what he thought was the Hudson.

It had been done before, and he followed his instincts to copy the pilot who had survived the emergency landing before him. Several other pilots were thinking the same thing, and there were now black shapes everywhere that were out of organized patterns trying to make emergency landings in the same spot. Two collided in mid-air, their fuel igniting immediately and lighting up much of the surrounding area for several seconds as pieces of wing and fuselage fell to the ground beneath them, starting hundreds of fires and killing hundreds of people in their homes.

The first pilot to react had a manifest of 137 people and six crew, and the light from the mid-air collision gave him an opportunity to set up his approach. Nothing worked apart from manually flying the aircraft—his landing gear was up and he had one small chance to do it.

He watched as the water flowed up to meet him, gliding the aircraft down as best he could and setting her down gently with his tail and waiting for the shock of the two engines to hit the water. He had manually done what he could to help the landing. The aircraft's wings hit the water and the whole aircraft, somehow still intact, came to a halt still floating in the flowing river with its right wing caught up on some obstacle, turning the aircraft toward the river's edge and out of the strong flow mid-river.

Within seconds, the experienced crew had the doors open and the passengers were grabbing coats and anything to keep them warm as it began to snow outside the opened doors.

The passengers scurried and slipped down the wing towards the jetty, fires in the area giving them enough light to see, and helped each other. The pilot left the fuselage last, and as he did, another aircraft flew straight into a building on the other side of the river and a warehouse erupted into flames. He could not help but watch. A second aircraft blew up on a bridge to their south and two more seemed to collide in midair, only 100 feet or so above a 30-story apartment block about a mile away. The explosion disintegrated the whole building as it erupted into flames. His co-pilot John screamed at him just in time for him to see the shock wave coming across the river from the first blast. He was the last to jump onto the jetty as their aircraft was forced against it by the blast. The wing buckled and it started turning and continuing its journey, being pulled along and out into the river's flow.

A large boat of some sort suddenly came out of nowhere and collided with the tail of the aircraft, only feet away from the end of the jetty. It was a large boat, far bigger than the tail area of the aircraft which was starting to sink in the water, and the momentum of the boat pushed it over the rear of the aircraft, snapping the tail off completely. The 737 disappeared in seconds, and the boat crashed into the next jetty further downriver, immediately buckling the whole side of the wharf.

Someone had found a door that had been broken open by what looked like a large metal piece of another aircraft, still smoldering. It was in the warehouse building in front of them and the entire group ran into it and out of the elements outside. The night was as bright as day outside, with fires in every direction. The warehouse looked safe and the snow had started to fall in earnest.

The surrounding area around JFK International Airport was hit harder than other parts of New York. The aircraft were bigger, with more international flights landing and taking off. With the wind direction from the north to northwest, large 747s were also taking off, one per minute in a northwesterly direction. Full of fuel, they were at their most dangerous and five were in the air over separate areas—two over Ozone Park and one each over East New York, Brownsville, and Brooklyn. As if part of a ballet, all five aircraft lost power at the same second, their left wings already lower because they were all banking left, and they went down fast.

The cockpit and passenger windows went dark and at 250 miles an hour, the first two hit the ground, erupting in massive fireballs that could be heard 50 miles away. They were over Ozone Park a mile apart, still very low, under full power and very heavy as fuel to their engines was suddenly cut off. These aircraft had been the last two to take off; both flying to Europe, and it took only ten seconds for their engines to die and the first aircraft to hit the ground.

The lowest aircraft was still rushing forward as it belly-landed and fell on a block of single-story houses, still traveling at 220 miles an hour. It became a speeding bomb as 64,000 gallons of jet fuel blew up all at once and white-hot fire blasted out in all directions—immediately flattening three blocks of houses around it. The moving firebomb kept on for another mile, the blast following it, and the fire reaching 1,000 feet high and wide, killing thousands of people in its path and setting fire to thousands of houses as bits of white-hot metal and other flaming parts flew in every direction. The same happened to the second and third aircraft—both a mile and two miles further out, respectively.

Whole suburbs and housing districts disintegrated. Brownsville was no more, and within seconds over half of the buildings in the area were destroyed in an explosion of jet fuel or exploding gas mains.

The fourth Jumbo Jet crashed in Brooklyn seconds later, and this one was nearly vertical as it went in—the blast so strong that it blew out windows as far as Manhattan. Hundreds of buildings exploded, first from the aircraft's energy and then from gas mains erupting along streets and into buildings for miles around the massive eruption of absolute energy. Flaming pieces of aircraft and masonry flew in all directions, setting fires and killing anything in their path.

The last aircraft went down a block from the water in Richmond, doing similar types damage in that area. Several jets coming in to JFK flattened miles of housing around Long Beach, Lawrence, Inwood, and Woodmere, with four going down within seconds.

It had only taken three to four minutes, but the ground had shaken as badly as the massive earthquake in Japan in 2010, and east of Manhattan the scene worse than bombing had inflicted on German cities during World War II. The fires grew by the second and gathered momentum faster than people could run.

They joined together and became hotter and hotter, causing more explosions and from the highest windows in New York, three separate fire storms began to glow brighter and brighter as they destroyed everything in their wake. The red glow in the night sky from these large deep fires could even be seen through the thick snow that was now falling over the city.

It was the first time in American history that not one emergency vehicle could move. They were all as dead as the aircraft hitting the ground. There was no electricity, and the gas mains became the second enemy. At the gas supply depots, attempts were made to turn off gas flow, but these electrical units malfunctioned, doing nothing to prevent more gas from going down the lines. There were backup teams of men at the massive gas storage tanks who managed to close down many feeder pipes manually. It took 15 minutes to close down dozens of pipes, but by then the worst damage had already been done.

Manhattan became silent, with hundreds of fires raging out of control. Areas around southern and eastern Manhattan had fires that were several miles wide and only water could stop their destructive paths. The wind increased in its intensity and so did the snow, which melted long before it hit the ground in many areas.

With the added problem that nothing electrical worked, there was no communication via television, radio, or phones of any sort. Nobody knew what was going on, no one could get information, and many died sitting up in bed and wondering what was going on outside. All over the United States and the world, the same was happening in urban areas. Aircraft were going down everywhere.

In daylight areas such as Australia, where it was hot and sunny, pilots tried to glide aircraft of all sorts into survivable landings.

Unfortunately, these aircraft weren't made to have zero-engine power and very few survived the turmoil in the air. Every major city in the world, except for three countries, had aircraft somewhere over them. Chicago, Los Angeles, London, Paris, Frankfurt, and several major cities worldwide now burned as brightly as New York, and there was not one fire truck available to put the fires out.

Hundreds of aircraft over the oceans, their passengers often fast asleep, just fell into the water, exploded, and disappeared.

The Capitol building in Washington D.C. had two near misses from opposite directions within seconds of each other, with a third going down less than a mile away several seconds later as the pilot tried to turn back for Reagan. A large Airbus went into the middle of the Pentagon, full of fuel, and literally blew the insides of the building to bits of rubble. The White House was also nearly hit as an aircraft flew blindly overhead less than a hundred feet over the roof. It was shot at by over 100 troops around the White House grounds, peppering the aircraft, and it went down and exploded on the National Mall, destroying several Smithsonian Museum buildings in its path.

* * *

Space was now a major problem for those who were in an unfortunate place at the wrong time. Commander John Scott, currently in control of the world's space station was looking down at Earth, holding a small glass of California bubbly that had been sent up with the last resupply for the New Year, when entire areas of the Eastern seaboard where his wife and two kids were already fast asleep, and western Europe as far as he could see, suddenly blinked and went black. He looked down, puzzled for a split second, when suddenly more than 50 alarms sounded inside the craft, telling the crew of malfunctions in every part of their living habitat.

A second later, he and his crew were also in blackness, and the cold of space instantaneously filled the inner craft, turning the warm 65-degree inside temperature to 160 degrees below zero. A totally frozen Commander Scott still looked down at a black earth, now lighting up again with new fires. He hadn't had time to move and the frozen glass suddenly shattered in his hand.

All the other hundreds of unmanned satellites and craft orbiting the Earth, as well as far off in space on missions, with Zedong Electronic parts in every part of their complicated structures, copied what the latest millions of electronic gadgets did down on earth. They shut off, never to work again.

* * *

By the time Comrade Chunqiao and his team sat down for lunch and champagne served by pretty young girls in red dresses, the western world was ablaze, cities already on the verge of destruction, and over fifty million people already dead or dying—and they were the lucky ones.

* * *

Many millions of people around the world did not live in cities. They lived in rural communities or poorer countries that did not have plane parts rain down on them from the air. Problems in these areas were more minor for the first 30 minutes and millions slept through the carnage going on in other areas. Most cities that had large commercial airports had some sort of aircraft landing or taking off and were therefore ablaze and many rural areas between those cities where aircraft flight lanes existed also heard explosions and fires erupting where aircraft went down.

It only took a few minutes for the flying bombs to finally cease, and in many areas not immediately affected, peace was supreme.

The world was so quiet that farmers woke up thinking something was wrong, and people looked outside their rural communities in the dark and daylight to see why their televisions, radios, phones, computers, and all the electrical appliances in their houses were not working.

Many Americans were already asleep, warm and cozy for one last night and totally oblivious to the destruction around them.

* * *

Raleigh-Durham International Airport had only one flight coming in and one going out. A second flight was about to take off, as with nearly 300 airports worldwide, and in most cases the pilots immediately reacted and aborted their takeoffs as the airfield around them blacked out. Many aircraft managed to complete their landings and waited on, or at, the end of the runway as the lights and their aircraft stopped working. There were no instructions for them to proceed. The out-going Raleigh flight dove into Jordan Lake a couple of miles south of Preston's farm. The incoming flight, 12 miles east of Preston's farm, also fell to earth, exploded in a wooded area, and then swept through a housing community killing dozens in its path. It became the only beacon of light as the whole area went black, apart from Preston and Joe's farms.

A couple of aircraft further out went down seconds later, the noise of their explosions hardly noticed by anybody in the Raleigh area.

* * *

The small town of New Hill ten miles away had a nuclear power station. Shearon Harris was the only power station in the immediate area, and Zedong Electronics had cleverly designed circuitry and automated shut-down programs that could be controlled from a separate microcomputer in their shut-down units, purchased by every power station in the world. Even the United States and Russian navies used them in their nuclear ships. Zedong Electronics did not want to destroy the world, just take it over, and the correct shutdown of the 400 plants worldwide, including plants in China and numerous military mobile nuclear systems was necessary.

Shearon Harris had hundreds of backup systems, as did all power stations of this type. Zedong had electronics in all the systems, and once the special microcomputer and its second and third backup microcomputers noticed severe problems in the running of any part of the power station, they activated themselves to close down the dangerous radioactive plutonium tubes into safe mode and immediately began to shut down the system for sleep. The Chinese-made fail-safe systems, powered by backup generators that still worked, would supply the cooling water to keep temperatures down for as long as it was needed for a safe and complete shutdown. The 104 nuclear power stations in North America, and all the nuclear stations around the world, closed themselves off and slowly cooled over the next several days and became dormant, waiting for their new owners—and there was nothing anybody could do about it.

* * *

Shipping was another problem, as the downed flight in the Hudson had found out. Many ships just lost power and came to a halt, relying on Mother Nature to leave them alone. The nuclear warships around the world were no different, except the submarines which lost every mechanical system on board when their nuclear power systems. Back-up system came on, but many of them were new, modern and fitted with fancy miniature parts from China. As their power units decreased power, the submarines began to dive, just as all the aircraft had done minutes earlier, and many disappeared into the depths never to be seen again, landing on deep sea floors where it was too deep to try and escape. Many were docked in naval bases, on jetties, or moored in shallow water where they were still floating, and they shut down and became expensive pieces of junk.

Commercial shipping, steaming on cruise power around the world slowed down. In busy shipping lanes, ships began to collide with other ships, or grounded themselves on land, gouging open their thin bottom plates and spewing their goods. Many were anchored, on-loading or off-loading materials, and all the mechanisms helping them stopped and would never move again. Several older ships still had engine power and carried on. Unfortunately, their automated directional systems and modern controls had newer electronics and they continued, now uncontrollable in forward movement. One old World War II destroyer was steaming into Sydney harbor for some sort of celebration and its engines were on three-quarter power and going under the bridge when her modified directional system shut down. The shutdown spun the wheel hard to starboard and the ship went straight into the Sydney Opera House, destroying that part of the harbor area and several blocks behind it as it exploded with a massive blast.

* * *

Preston and friends were slowly heading off to bed, leaving only Sally and Carlos downstairs. Sally had offered to help a pretty drunk Carlos carry his bed into the party room that now reeked of all kinds of booze. Instead, she pulled his hand to the larger bed in the hangar that was still made up, and she told Carlos to get into bed while she switched off the large lights. He did as he was told, undressed down to his undershorts as Sally turned off all the lights as well as the lights in the party room. She left a single light on so people could find their way out of the side door to get to the house.

Sally turned as she was about to turn out the light, and surveyed the black shapes of the aircraft still and silent in the large hangar. It surely was a sight to behold and a nice place for a pilot to sleep, and to start a relationship with the man she was intending to marry. She sighed, looked in the direction she had to walk back to Carlos so she wouldn't trip over anything, and went over to join her man.

Martie and Preston were also getting ready for bed. He had turned off the radio in the lounge so it would not make any noise while the guests slept, and noticed that Oliver looked a little worried, sniffing the air as if he sensed something in it. Preston switched off the lounge light and got into to bed. The only noise that could be heard was the faint grumbling of the diesel generator behind the shed. He couldn't even hear the usual noise of the refrigerator in the kitchen, but his father's old and never-missed-a-second alarm clock next to his side of the bed showed 12:55 in big red letters, and he shrugged off checking the refrigerator until morning. The old electric house's radiant heaters were keeping everybody warm and there was nothing amiss, or so he thought.

* * *

At the same time, lunch was a loud affair in the 30-floor board room in Nanjing. There was much celebration going on. If they could see what they had started, then most of them would be sickened by the carnage going on around the world. But in this large room, and with warm sunlight coming through the large windows, they were a long way from the realities of the rest of the world.

"Excuse me, Chairman Chunqiao," started one of the men looking at the large maps on the wall. "It looks like the electricity has come on around the world. There are as many lights, even brighter than before."

"Very observant, Comrade," replied the Chairman. "Several thousand aircraft, all being destroyed at the same time, display about as much power as the old electrical systems. Those, comrades, are fires—fires burning whole city blocks, fires burning whole cities, fires burning capitals all over the world with no fire engines to put them out. Gentlemen." he paused and looked over the room. "That is our army!" he shouted to the men looking at the world maps and again he raised his glass. "To the army of fire, the army of Zedong Electronics, and to the stupid capitalist Americans who thought they had the strongest army in the world. Where is their army now? In pieces all over the world! Their transport is dead and their military power will be destroyed one by one by our allies. Ours is now the stronger army. That is why we will wait to send in our army, let the fires to do their business and then die down. Soon we will go in and pick up the remains and build what remains into our country, our world, and then the whole world will be ours. Our last success will be the termination of our own government—terminated like the trash they do business with. Then we will be the next Chinese dynasty—and the first dynasty ever to rule our whole planet!"

* * *

Out of the 7.2 billion people on Earth at one hour past midnight on January 1st, Eastern Standard Time, 3.8 billion people were having problems they did not have the day before. One billion people were asleep, 1.2 billion were poor and lived in areas where nothing had changed except that the stars looked brighter, 1.15 billion lived in countries that were allies of Zedong Electronics, including parts of China, 250 million people were in desperate trouble, and in uncountable bad situations around the world, dying at a rate of over 100,000 a minute, and the balance,

250 million, were already dead, disintegrated, or within seconds of death, in many countries around the world.

The Internet was down, and no communications were possible. There was no electricity, nothing electrical worked and whole countries in the northern hemisphere began to freeze. Roads everywhere had people wandering around by the millions trying to help others, or waiting for help they expected would come. Billions of cars were still and silent everywhere in all kinds of places. Some had crashed into buildings, houses, shops, hedges, trees and many into each other. There were pieces of metal everywhere.

Every now and again there was vehicle movement on the roads and highways. Older vehicles with carburetors instead of engine-control systems still worked, but they could not get away from the crowds and broken vehicles around them and were quickly mobbed by people begging for a lift. In many cases, the occupants were thrown out and their vehicle taken over by new people, many of whom were armed. Hundreds of shots rang out as people tried to protect what belonged to them, or what they had just commandeered.

The bullets were not picky in choosing their targets—men, women and children fell prey to them on an hourly basis, or were just plain run over if they got in the way. As soon as the current occupants ran out of ammunition, others shot them and pulled them out of the vehicles to take over. Civilization, which had taken more than 2,000 years to create and modernize, disappeared within the first hour in some areas.

Life was a little better in sunlit areas. The daylight was not as scary as nighttime and people took a little longer to turn on their fellow man. Many helped others, who in turn helped others, but panicked people were always everywhere and they had different thoughts about helping people. They were more interested in helping themselves to other people's food and water, which were the first two priorities in life, after oxygen to breathe. It was only in high-density areas where already scared and lonely people were trying to wait it out until help arrived, or the lights came back on, and everything would go back to normal. It had to happen!

Apart from the 16 men in the board room on the 30 floor at Zedong Electronics, the whole world, at war with their current situation, believed that help would come. It always had before! Why not now?

* * *

Will Smart was in the station in Lancaster when the world went black. The phone he was on, at one minute past nine that evening, went dead in his hand seconds after the lights flickered, went on and off several times, and then decided to stay off. He looked at the phone in the dark and tried to place it back on the receiver. He had a powerful flashlight in his bottom right-hand drawer next to his police-issued revolver, and he grabbed both. Will was the first to switch a light on, and the several people who had been working around him looked back at him as he played the light on them. Some still had their dead telephone receivers in their hands.

"What a blackout," he remarked, waiting for the lights to turn back on. "Even the emergency exit lights are dead. Mike, have you ever seen that, the emergency lights going out as well?"

"No, Will," answered his partner. "Normally we can still see with just the emergency lights on when the overheads go out. This is really a black-out, man, it looks just as dark outside."

They heard a sudden crash and vibration through the floor as unknown to them, a car plowed into the building a floor below them. They all got up as one, now with three flashlights working, and headed for the stairs with guns in hand. Even the emergency stair lights were dead so they used their flashlights to jump down the stairs.

They arrived in a group to see that a large SUV had come through the front corner of the wooden four-story building at some speed and the policeman on desk duty was pinned against the wall with blood coming out of his mouth. The lights of the SUV were still on and showed that the policeman's eyes were already lifeless. As a team, they automatically lifted their guns and aimed at the SUV.

They didn't need to see that the two young men in the front seat were in trouble—blood everywhere and the driver's mouth trying to word something like a fish. His passenger was lifeless and bent over double, a wooden beam sticking into his chest. Two police officers rushed across to the driver's side to help the young man, who didn't look older than twenty, and the rest pulled out their police radios to summon an ambulance; the radios were all as dead as the passenger in the SUV.

Will's mind was ticking faster than it had ever worked before. He rushed outside through the hole the SUV had made. Lancaster was not as big a city as Los Angeles, but not one vehicle was moving on the streets that he could see or hear. He stood on a dark street corner with the streets going north to south and west to east. There were dozens of vehicles just sitting here and there on the roads; some had been in accidents but most of them looked like they had just come to a stop and people were walking around them. Several had their headlights still on and he could see a local transit bus to the west of him on the opposite side of the road with a line of people getting off. The driver was in his seat, his headlights and interior lights still alight, and he was trying to start it.

Suddenly, there was a loud explosion on the east side of the city, about a mile or two away and he turned to see a mushroom of flames and smoke erupt into the night sky. A second, fainter explosion happened seconds later, this time to the south of the city, and he looked in that direction and could actually see the large explosion on the hills above Palmdale, several miles away.

Then a third explosion lit up the skies again to the east, but the noise was distant and far away.

"Somebody is bombing us!" he shouted to his partner. "Get the keys to a black and white. I'll meet you at the entrance to the parking lot. Hurry!" he ordered Mike, who ran in to get keys off a long rack at the rear entrance to the police station, and then rushed out the back to a line of police cars waiting to be used.

Will ran around to the west side of the building to get to the vehicle gate when another explosion, fainter and in the direction of Los Angeles, faintly lit up the sky on the southern horizon. He stopped by the police parking entrance. Since it was on an alleyway that extended directly to the south, he could see explosions, one after the other, light up the skies over the hills and inside the built-up area of Los Angeles.

Then it occurred to him that no partner was arriving with a car, and he ran to the parking area to find Mike trying to get a black and white started.

"This is the second one I've tried," Mike shouted to Will. "It looks like they are all dead."

"How can that happen?" asked Will. "The only thing I know that stops all vehicles is a nuclear explosion. I've seen of those in movies, but none of those explosions I saw in Los Angeles were big enough for that, or we'd all be toast by now. It must be something else. Let's try my old truck."

Will's truck was much like Preston's—it was an old 1981 Ford 150, and it started on the first try. That totally confused the two detectives who just sat there with a rumbling engine and tried to figure out what was going on.

Another truck suddenly drove past the gates going east, and that prompted Will to follow it and find out why they were able to drive and nobody else could. They couldn't catch up to it due to all the cars and people milling around, but he did get a look at it in a set of headlights and saw that it was an old Chevy truck, smaller and older than his. Then it was gone.

Will decided to investigate the closest explosion and drove slowly west for several blocks, driving around dozens of stopped vehicles. Everybody seemed unhurt. The speed limit in this part of the city was 25, and apart from those two dead kids who must have been going double that, everyone seemed dazed, had worried looks on their faces and were either trying to start their cars, or had the hood up and were looking inside.

The glow in the sky got brighter and brighter as they neared the scene. Will had to stop a block away because it was too bright to drive, and they parked on the curb, locked the truck, and walked the last block, shielding their eyes. He recognized that the block after this was a park with a large pond and walkways where hundreds of people spent time walking their dogs and have picnics on the grass. The park, however, was no more.

A jet engine, or what looked like part of a jet engine, was silhouetted by the 40-foot high flames behind it. The engine was hanging in a massive tree it must have landed in and parts of the tree had been crushed nearly flat. The blackened engine was supported by the flaming tree, a couple of feet above the ground, but the rest of the aircraft, if there was a rest of the aircraft, was behind the wall of heat and flames. He looked up at the buildings above him and was shocked. These old brick buildings used to be five stories high. Three stories were missing! Will then realized that an incoming aircraft must have hit them on impact and then blown up in the park.

It was then that he noticed bricks, metal beams, and what was left of a dozen cars, and hundreds of people to his left and right and several bodies lying on the street directly in front of him. There was a sudden explosion to his left and on the north side of the park. He could see part of the street 100 yards away, and suddenly a dozen cars erupted into midair on both sides of the road as an explosion ripped the entire street open and ignited several old houses adjoining the park as the gas lines exploded.

Both he and Mike had to retreat behind the corner of the building as pieces of shrapnel screamed past where they had just been standing, breaking windows. Larger chunks started falling all around them. A body of a man in what was left of his red car landed a few feet away in the street directly in front of him, and the man was sitting in the driver's seat, with his seat belt still tight around him. He looked like he was in shock as the remains of his car bounced once on the remaining roadway, and then skidded into a large, broken display window on the corner opposite them. The shock wave hit at the same time and both Will and Mike cowered behind the corner of the building.

"I'm getting out of here," Mike shouted to Will, and they both got up and ran back in the direction of the truck when a second explosion from the far side of the park two blocks away erupted, sounding like another gas line had blown up.

Will squealed out in a U-turn and nearly drove into a couple running for cover. Then a street one block away to their north went up and they were shielded from the explosion as they crossed the junction and were behind the corner building as a massive ball of flame passed down the side street, just yards behind them.

"This city is imploding!" shouted Will. "Why isn't somebody turning off the gas?"

"Hell knows!" Mike shouted back. "I only live a few blocks from here. Please, Will, let's swing by and pick up my wife and kids. These explosions could just go on and on." Will nodded. He knew the best way to get there and still could not do more than a couple of miles an hour. There were fewer people around now, many hopefully finding shelter somewhere, and he managed to drive three blocks before he had to turn left.

Several blocks later, they pulled up outside Mike's small, dark house.

"I think it's safer to get away from here," Will said as another explosion, this time a couple of blocks away, lit up the street and he heard a thump as something landed on the roof. A dead pigeon, dripping blood, slipped down his windshield. Mike got out and ran for his front door while Will switched on wipers, squirted water over the blood, and swished the bird off the car.

The mess cleared, he looked through the cleaned windshield straight into the eyes of two young men with pistols drawn Hollywood-style—horizontal and too far above their heads to be accurate. They shouted at him to get out of the truck. One pointed his pistol—a large one, Will noticed—and the other kid shot into the air.

"Get out, you son of a bitch!" he shouted. "Get out now! We're taking your truck!" The other guy shot again, this time lower and just above the roof of the car. "Listen up, or the next one's for you!"

Will noticed that Mike had not yet come out of his house, went for his gun on the seat next to him and opened the door as two bullets hit and went through the door inches from his hand holding the door handle. He immediately rolled out of the door, shooting six bullets with his weapon in his right hand as he hit the ground and cleared the car door. Both men immediately fell where they were standing and stayed there.

"What happened?" asked Mike, coming out of the front door with his wife and two girls.

"They wanted the truck, shot at me, and I had to shoot back in self defense. Dang, Mike what the hell is going on?"

"God knows," he replied, getting the three girls into the back seat and throwing several bags into the bed of the truck. "Let's get back to the station and you can file a report about the shooting." Suddenly, another gas line went up, only a block away, and the two men ducked and climbed into the truck. Will did a U-turn to avoid the two bodies in front of him and headed away from the carnage.

When they got close to their police station, however, the whole street erupted about 300 yards away in the direction they were heading, and in the exact spot where the police station was located. Will quickly pulled the wheel to the left and into a side street as the powerful explosion ripped up the buildings in front of them. He straightened the wheel to correct, pushed on the gas, and the girls screamed as he bounced off a parked car as he fought to get behind a building. This time he wasn't quite fast enough, and the blast coming down the street caught the back corner of the truck as it sped between the buildings. The blast turned them around 180 degrees and pushed the truck into another car on the opposite side of the street before it came to a halt, facing the way they had just come.

It took Will a second to react before he ripped the side of his truck and the car it was pinned against trying to spin the truck around and head in the direction of Antelope Acres to the west.

"What time is it?" he shouted to Mike, the noise around them still deafening.

"Nine-thirty," Mike responded. "Where can we go? It's like a war zone around here!"

"I'm going to head out to my house. There's no gas around there and we should have electricity. Hopefully we can call somebody. Something has to work. I want to get on our radio to Maggie—she's still in North Carolina—and see if she and the kids are okay."

It took Will twice as long as usual to get out of Lancaster. The roads were strewn with motor vehicles. It seemed that the explosions behind them had eased up, but flames lit up the sky and it was like daylight as they drove through the streets at less than 25 miles an hour.

As it got dark again, Will looked south toward Palmdale and Los Angeles and was shocked at how bright the horizon behind the hills was—so much so that he couldn't see where the aircraft fire on their side of the hills was anymore. Every now and then, they came across a car or house on fire. They were beginning to travel through housing suburbs and leaving the larger city buildings behind. In every window he saw people peeking out at them and his truck, probably hoping that it was help arriving.

He reached the outskirts of Antelope Hills and was glad to see the houses around his still lit up with electricity. For a moment, he thought that things were coming back to normal and maybe the electricity was back on, but then he remembered the generator sales of his kids, and he knew that the only houses with power he could see were the ones with generators.

There were only a few cars in the middle of the streets here, and he drove around them slowly. Again the horizon lit up to the south—some massive explosion must have happened somewhere in L.A.

The house was quiet, as if nothing had happened, as he looked down his 100-foot driveway and pushed his gate-opener button at the entrance. Nothing happened. He looked up at the controller up on his sun visor and noticed that the usual activation light did not blink on. It was dead.

"Even my gate's electrical system isn't working," he observed to Mike sitting next to him. "I just can't understand it."

Will got out and opened the gate manually. Mike slid over on the front seat and drove the truck through the gate. Will closed and locked the gate with the large padlock he kept for that purpose when they left the ranch unattended, hopped back in the truck, and they drove to the house. The porch light was still burning, and so was the inside light he had left on. Even their dog Jamie, a black and brown Bull Mastiff/Labrador mix was there waiting for someone to come home.

"Weird, very weird," mumbled Will, his brain trying to fathom what was going on. It was 10:30, and 91 minutes ago, life was the way it had been for as long as he could remember. But in the last hour and a half, he had seen more carnage in Lancaster than his whole time on the force in downtown L.A.

"Mike, I just don't understand it. We've just gone through scenes like something out of 'The Apocalypse,' and now I get home and life looks just like when I left. There must be hundreds dead back there in Lancaster alone. And by the glow over L.A., I reckon that we are certainly glad not to be there tonight either. There must be thousands upon thousands dead over there."

"I just don't know, Will," was the reply. "It's like the world's coming to an end, just like those religious guys or the Mayans predicted. I have never seen anything like it, not even when I was over in Iraq with the military."

"Well, I think we just wait it out here tonight. I'm sure dawn will bring some answers, and I have to get on the radio to Maggie and the kids to see if they are all right." With that the five of them climbed out of the truck and went inside. Will gave the dog a quick pat. It was quiet in the house. All he could hear was the ticking of the mantelpiece clock in the living room. Everything was where he had left it earlier. He quickly walked into the kitchen and turned on the light. He was quite surprised that it worked! Then he opened the refrigerator—it was not working and the inside light didn't come on, nor was the oven working, as the LED clock was not on. Not one of the three LED clock lights were working in the kitchen he was so used to. Mike tried the television in the living room. It was dead. He then tried the stereo and the computer. Both were as dead as the television.

"What heat do you have, Will?" asked Mike, walking into the kitchen.

"Gas with electrical back-up," replied Will, checking the warm air inlets. The heat was working. He felt warm air on his hand. "It's working. I suppose the gas doesn't have a brain and nobody told it to die on us. I had the tank filled about a month ago and reckon we have enough for a couple of weeks, or even a month, depending on how cold it gets. It's ten degrees above freezing at the moment," he reported, looking at the outside thermometer reading by the kitchen door.

"Everything I've tried doesn't work," Mike continued. "My wife and kids are sitting in the living room."

"Oh! I'm sorry, Mike, let me show you to our guest room. It's a big room, and I have two cots we can put in there for your girls for tonight. Tomorrow we can organize ourselves a little better depending on what dawn brings. We are safe here tonight and Jamie will keep guard. He'll tell us if there is anybody out there. I think everybody will stay indoors tonight and I don't think there will be anybody on the streets—especially not in this area. I'm going to load our two shotguns just in case and place one by the front door and one by the back door. They each carry five rounds with one in the chamber, and both are pump action if you need them. Tell your girls not to touch them. My police weapon is also loaded and I suggest keeping yours handy as well. I'm going into the office and try to contact Maggie. It's nearly 2:00 am in North Carolina and hopefully somebody's listening to their radio."

Will helped Mike and his family get settled in the spare bedroom. "You and your family go to bed and get some sleep," Will ordered after they were finished. "You can all use the bathroom in the hall. I have my own in our bedroom."

For an hour, Will tried to get someone on the radio, but to no avail. It was as quiet as the streets outside. He was worried, but knew that Maggie and the kids were as safe as he was. Preston also lived rural and the streets around his place were most probably the same as around his house, if they were going through the same situation.

Will checked the outside temperature. It had gone down a degree and it was now close to freezing outside. Ben put on a jacket he found hanging by the front door and went outside with the shotgun in hand and with Jamie eager for some attention. Together they walked down to the gate to the entrance of the driveway. It was surreal as he left the lights of the house and walked into the semi-darkness. Los Angeles was lit up like a roman candle. So was Lancaster, although not so bright. To the northwest there was a dim glow where Bakersfield was, and everywhere he looked the horizon was brighter than usual.

It was also a strange kind of quiet, as if the world was waiting for something to happen. A grumble of noise came up faintly from the south and he stood, leaning on the steel gate and listening. He stood there for several minutes—the scenes from the last hour or two going through his mind, especially of the two kids he had shot. They hadn't looked scared when they approached him. They had looked excited as if they were playing a game and actually had smirks on their faces, like they were having fun trying to get his truck away from him. Will shook his head and looked down the street in both directions. It was empty of vehicles, nothing looked amiss, and he walked back to the house and went to bed.

* * *

In over 10,000 cities and large towns worldwide there was chaos and death. In the same number of towns and smaller villages worldwide, many did not realize that civilization as they knew it was coming to an end. They were either asleep or wondering what was going causing their power outages. Many millions in poorer countries, who didn't see much civilization, continued their daily lives, oblivious to the reality that there was now no difference between them and the rich. From this point forward, money was close to being worthless. All the luxuries in life were of no value. There was only so much food on the planet, and within days the rest of the planet would be as hungry as they were.

CHAPTER 17

Z-Day 1 – Dawn

FOR MANY, THE COMING and going of sunlight wasn't as important as what was going on around them. Of the millions of people who had been in Times Square several long hours earlier, a large majority were dead. In between the buildings and the dozens of crackling fires that flickered in what used to be Times Square, there were piles of dead bodies, now covered with an inch-thick layer of blown snow. Cars were turned on their sides, on their roofs, on top of other vehicles, and even buses stuck out of blackened buildings, most of them now covered in snow. There was no movement, except for a faint cry for help from here and there. In every nook and cranny in every building, people were cowering and trying to keep warm.

The wind had died down an hour before dawn and the sun rose, but hardly anything could be seen through the thick smoke that still hung everywhere. Whole buildings were still burning, sometimes burning as high as several stories above the street. The city was darker than a park in a forest fire and the people who had survived did not know what to do, except find warmth. Their bodies, still dressed in warm clothing, were losing valuable body heat and the fires still burning on the street looked inviting.

It was the piles of bodies everywhere that kept them where they were, too scared to be the first to move.

The sight from the buildings in upper Manhattan was not much better. The smoke had dissipated somewhat through the early hours of the morning, but still hung in a dense cloud below the skyline. Many who had taken sleeping pills, or somehow had slept through the destruction the night before, couldn't believe their eyes as they opened their blinds to see why their apartments were so dark and chilly. Many were not yet cold, but the majority's heating systems had gone out with the electrical failures. There was no lighting and the only way to get light was to open the blinds and curtains.

Manhattan's skyline looked different to those who had survived the night. There still were large buildings everywhere above the smoke, which many thought was clouds, but one or two of the skyscrapers looked different. People quickly realized that flames were coming out of several of them on many different levels.

Further out of the center of Manhattan, nobody could see very much. It was surreal, apart from the crackling of flames from every direction. Nobody was moving and no vehicles could be heard in the streets anywhere. The thousands of high-rise occupants checked lights and heaters. They all tried to complain to someone over their cell phones, laptops, or intercoms, but the whole city was dead—electronically dead. They tried their neighbors, who they barely knew, and doors were not opened and most were told to go away.

On the East side, miles of blackened areas, once peaceful houses and buildings continued to blaze. Where there were wooden structures, one caught fire after another and masses of people were being chased by flames this way and that. In areas with more brick buildings, a little normality could be seen, but there was no street that hadn't been damaged or had cars and rubble strewn all over the asphalt and sidewalks. A whole building was still on fire here and there, and once again people in every corner were trying to get to safety by banging on hundreds of closed doors, or shouting up at windows in buildings, begging for anybody to take them in.

Whole neighborhoods were no more. Half of Brooklyn was a blackened mess of smoking ruins, many buildings still blazing hundreds of feet into the air. In every direction, there were dead bodies strewn like confetti and many injured people begging for help. There was no help, however, and no one knew if it would ever come.

Gunshots could be heard every now and again. People were beginning to loot the dead bodies, feeling in their pockets for anything valuable. Everything and anything was taken, especially any fancy new cell phones. Many still seemed to think that they still had value.

In less damaged areas, people looked outside their windows and many had guns in their hands, looking for anybody who might want to cause them trouble. In the less-damaged suburbs, hundreds of people were walking around aimlessly, looking for people they knew. A couple of men were molesting a girl—she was pushed up against a wall, screaming her head off, and people just shuffled by, oblivious to the attack going on.

Corner stores were becoming dangerous areas as the masses became hungry. Many families had enough food stored in their still cold refrigerators and pantries to last a few days, but many had nothing, and shots began to ring out across New York as shop owners began defending themselves against people with hoods over their heads who were quickly forming into groups or gangs.

Several of the warehouses on the Hudson River were still ablaze, the flames reaching as high as 100 feet in the air. The 143 survivors of the only aircraft in the New York area were huddled and reasonably warm in a massive walk-in refrigerator they had found in the unheated warehouse. For the first couple of hours, they had broken the doors down of several offices and sat in the blackness, using the warmth trapped in them until it got too cold to stay. A half-empty bottle of bourbon was found in one of the office desk drawers, and several of the passengers decided that consumption of its contents was necessary.

The 45-degree temperature refrigerator was found by the co-pilot John while he inspected the large warehouse for a warmer place than the offices. It was 5:00 am when he informed the captain what he had found and ushered his group of 40 people with him in one of the offices down the flight of stairs and into the large refrigerator.

The captain, once he had checked the area for safety, sat back behind the desk in a soft leather chair in the most luxurious corner office in the warehouse, and put his feet up on the desk. Two of his flight attendants were stretched out on couches and were comfortable, watching him. Captain Mallory went through the desk drawers, found an old bottle of extremely good quality single-malt scotch and pulled out three of the four glasses, pouring three large tots and giving one each to the two girls. He savored the beverage, one of his favorites, and placed the only hundred-dollar bill in his wallet back in the drawer as a replacement cost. At 5:00 in the morning, with the office getting cold, he decided to get up and look around again to check out what John and his group had found.

Under normal circumstances, the warehouse would have been well-secured and should have been. There were security cameras everywhere. Many people had stood in front of them for the first hour, dancing and waving and trying to get noticed so that help would come and find them. They certainly did not know what was going on anymore than anyone else, but were determined to stay in the warehouse after several had gone to the large doors and small steel-caged windows around the building to look outside. They saw and heard flames, smoke, and saw snow falling sideways, and dozens of explosions. There was a red glow in every direction, and they felt safe with the cold Hudson just a few yards away, a water sanctuary if the building caught fire.

Inside the warehouse, and for the ones interested in looking around, a couple of powerful flashlights had been found in a security office. All the monitors were centralized in this office, but they were all dormant and every switch was tried to see if they could turn on something, with no luck. The three food dispensers in the small cafeteria had already been broken open, the captain noticed on his second inspection, and the spoils must have been taken back for the hungry to eat.

He checked the door through which they had initially entered the building. Their entrance had been a thick wooden door, forced open and its lock broken by a large and heavy piece of falling debris, which he noticed later was a sliced-up end piece of a winglet from a Boeing 747—far bigger than the aircraft he had ditched successfully earlier. He could see part of the last couple letters and the colors of Lufthansa once he and several others had pulled it away from the split door. It was still very warm to the touch. He and the co-pilot had closed the door once they were all inside. One of the passengers had found a forklift and a pallet of boxes. Because it was a gas-operated forklift, the passenger had gotten it to work and positioned it by the door so nobody could open it from outside. The good guys coming to rescue them would have sirens blaring, they figured.

Captain Mallory's flashlight was a powerful one, and it lit up large areas of the cavernous space. He found the refrigerator door and noticed that the temperature inside was a little warmer than outside. He told his co-pilot to stay put—he was only doing a security check since his passengers were still his concern.

Then he started seriously looking around. There were hundreds of wooden cases on several steel packing shelves in the middle of the warehouse. Underneath the second-floor offices were several luxury motor vehicles neatly parked in a row, which looked like they were in bondage, or had just come off or were going on a ship. He was beginning to realize that they might be in a customs warehouse and that this was good for security, but bad when the office personnel came in and found their whiskey stolen. He tried each vehicle which had keys in the ignition, but they were all lifeless. He assumed that their batteries had been taken out for shipping purposes.

Then he found a section of military vehicles in the far corner under the offices. Again, there were several trucks and Humvees in a neat row. He tried several of them and they were also dead. It was as if nothing worked. He gave up searching for transportation and went back to the office. The two flight attendants had found a couple of blankets and were fast asleep, huddled up on one of the couches head to foot to keep warm.

He dozed off for a couple of hours and woke up at dawn to the sound of gunfire outside his office window. Captain Mallory carefully moved the blinds, noticed the thick steel bars on the window, and was shocked at how bad the smoke and air was outside. He couldn't see much, but the gunfire was pretty rapid. A few seconds later, he watched as a dozen uniformed security police came running down the road past the warehouse, their pistols drawn and firing behind them as they ran. Then, an old 1960s Chevy truck came into view with several non-uniformed men in the cab and standing in the back, firing at the security guards with shotguns and hunting rifles. The captain saw two men go down and the truck drove straight over the fallen bodies, one who was trying to get up as it drove over him and out of view following the rest. The captain just stared at the two still bodies lying on the ground.

"What's happening out there, Captain Mallory?" asked Pam, one of his flight attendants, now awake and watching him with big eyes.

"I can't believe it," responded the pilot in shock. "It's like a Hollywood gangster movie out here. I saw a dozen armed security guards being chased by a truckload of what looked like thugs and they killed two of the guards, right there in front of our building. Look, their bodies are still down there."

A few seconds later more gunfire could be heard, and then an explosion. The captain, still looking out of the window, saw a couple of the thugs he had seen in the truck seconds earlier come running back. This time they were being chased and they were firing behind them. One got hit and fell; the other just left him and ran out of view. Then several of the same police officers came into view. They looked tired and dirty with black marks all over their uniforms. Only one was wearing a hat, but suddenly Captain Mallory felt good. The police were there, everything was going to be ok! We are going to be saved!

The good feeling only lasted for a second or two.

What happened next he couldn't believe and made him want to be sick. The six police officers ran up to the man on the ground who was now injured. He was not badly injured. His shotgun was lying several yards behind him where he had dropped it and he lay on the ground on his back, unarmed, and put his hands in the air. One of the policemen picked up the shotgun, checked that it was loaded, walked up to the surrendering man on the ground and literally blew the poor man's head off. The rest in police uniform just watched and then they all turned and then carried on running after the other one who was already out of sight.

Captain Mallory's face went white. What he had seen was not right. He had just witnessed a policeman commit murder and several of his colleagues just looked on and did nothing. What was going on out there? Then he realized that there was much more going on than he had realized and that he, his crew, and his passengers were in more danger than he had anticipated. It was time to find something to protect his crew and passengers, just in case. He suddenly didn't know who the dangerous people were, and they would have to leave the warehouse at some point.

As he was thinking this, several more shots rang out and now he could hear them in different directions with different types of weapons, and he wished he had taken the cockpit revolver with him when he had left the plane.

It was time to look around the warehouse again.

* * *

Washington looked no different from New York and a thousand other cities around the world. Fires were devastating large areas of the city, and rich and poor people alike had the same problems. Whole suburbs were still burning, or were smoldering ruins where the fires had run out of fuel or had moved on to richer pastures. Parts of the nation's Capital were on fire. The fires from blown gas mains had kept the entire area aglow for hours as they burned with a white hot heat.

By dawn it was still extremely hot, with fires starting up and dying down, hundreds of buildings crumbling into burnt ashes, and whole streets becoming unrecognizable. People had long forgotten what fire could do to buildings without the presence of fire departments. The Pentagon was still standing, but half of the building was a smoldering mass, as were many of the main blocks in and around the city.

The White House was still in one piece, with the large expanses of open ground around it dark and quiet. The large building was as dark as the rest of the city blocks which were not on fire. Several flashlights belonging to security personnel could be seen on the grounds and candles were in many of the windows.

Hundreds of military figures huddled around as the sun came up, and even through the smoke, which was being cleared by a gentle easterly wind, new sandbagged machine gun and mortar positions could be seen all over the gardens.

Inside the White House, the halls around the Oval Office

were protected by several soldiers and police with weapons ready—the President and a couple of his staff were working hard trying to find lines of communications that worked so they could get information on who had attacked the United States of America.

"What do you mean we don't have one line of radio, satellite, or even a pair of bongo drums for communication? I thought we had the best in the world?" he shouted at two men in military uniform, one a Major and one a Colonel—the two most ranking officers at the White House that night.

"Everything is down, sir," replied the Colonel. "Satellites, microwave towers, computers, radios, even my BlackBerry doesn't work, Mr. President."

"Even the coffee machine is down, sir," added the Major to try and emphasize the seriousness of the situation. "The kitchen is trying to rustle up some food for you and the First Lady, sir, but they can only cook on one gas oven right now."

"I can't understand, where are all the troops we have in the close vicinity around the White House, and we have seen no reinforcements since midnight?" questioned the Colonel looking worried. He was not used to being in the Oval Office itself, since he was only in charge of last night's security for the White House and a mere minion in the system. "Andrews should have sent in more troops by now. I've heard word that the Pentagon took direct hits, but we haven't verified the information, Mr. President."

"Then why don't you get a Humvee and drive out to take a look?" asked the President sarcastically.

"Nothing works, sir," replied the Colonel. "Not one vehicle on the White House grounds—civilian or military—works, Mr. President. There is not one electrical machine in the White House, or outside the White House, that works, sir. We've tried for hours. We've had everybody who knows anything about electronics working since midnight. We can't even get your coffee machine to work."

"Is there no traffic on the streets? Flag down a car or bus or something. There must be something that is moving out there," the President added, now getting angry.

"We saw an old car light up the street and pass a couple of hours ago, but it disappeared before any of our troops could commandeer it. There's one thing one of the cooks told us about an hour ago and we are looking into it, sir. Something about President Kennedy putting in a back-up electrical system in the 1960s—The Bay of Pigs time—in case something like this happened and he had to hunker down here. We found an old safe room, prepared for a long stay. It hadn't been opened for years, but has a vast array of canned foodstuff. We have a team carefully going through all the known parts of the basement areas looking for something that might have been walled up or closed off. Until then, sir, it's tea and BBQ until we get the electricity back on."

"How many troops do we have here currently, Colonel?"

"One hundred and forty Marines, 25 police officers and 20 members of the Secret Service. For civilians, we have you and your family, your mother-in-law, six cooks, three service personnel, three cleaners and a couple others. New Year's Eve is known to be the quietest time at the White House. Even you and your wife were meant to be out celebrating, sir."

"I don't know if my wife's migraine was good news or not," he replied. "I suppose we could be stuck in a worse place than here."

"The Secret Service would have had your back, sir, even though your vehicle is as dead as the rest."

* * *

The source of the American President's current problems, Comrade Chunqiao, was still in the boardroom. Lunch had been a long and grand affair. For three hours they had eaten, drank, and talked among themselves discussing the cleverness of their leader, who was now the leader of the whole world, as well as the latest news he had given them—his secret plan to destroy their own government. Nobody spoke badly about the plan. Nobody knew who to trust, and if negative words reached back to the Chairman, their fate could be the same as their current government leaders.

It was just after 8:00 that evening, and the sixteen men were drinking *shaojiu*, the local Chinese liquor warmed up expertly by the girls in red, just as Lee Wang had done years earlier. Many looked at the screens as the light and dark areas rotated with the Earth's movement and one thing was always there. As soon as the sun set in new parts of the world, the lights of large bright fires could be seen. There weren't many in Africa. Several large lights could be seen in Cape Town and areas of Johannesburg, Cairo, Nairobi and Kinshasa where aircraft must have gone down. The rest of that continent was dark.

Many parts of Asia looked untouched and were still lit up, but Singapore, Kuala Lumpur, and Hong Kong had fires burning as large as New York. New York was about to see dawn on the east coast. Much of Japan and South Korea had the same-sized fires burning. China was darker in certain areas and normal in others. Beijing was a total black-out, but Nanjing where they were and Shanghai looked normal. Russia had been dark everywhere, but its major cities had fires burning, and the same with Australia and New Zealand.

The map on the bottom was totally devoid of movement. The number of working aircraft transponders was zero. There was not one aircraft in the air anywhere in the world.

At precisely 8:00, the Chairman approached the podium with a smile on his face. The room went quiet, the girls in red left the room, and the men sat down in their comfortable, leather board room chairs.

"It is done," exclaimed the smiling Chairman to his audience. Many were not as sober as when they had arrived 12 hours earlier, but the Chairman himself was in much the same condition. "Our first phase of the timeline is complete, Comrades, and by the lights on our top world map, our success is as I planned. We have run many scenarios on our computers over the last couple of years and will never know for certain what we have achieved, as we have no ears and eyes out there except our three satellites. The first scenario after the pushing of the first button was for a timeline of between seven to twelve hours. At this time, we are about to see dawn appear on the American east coast. It has been daylight in Western Europe for five of those seven hours, and the scenario I felt would be most accurate would be the following information, based on the world's current temperatures. First, the United States of America would be worst hit. Purely on weather conditions, the numbers of aircraft in the air, and the cities destroyed, the American population, by my best scenario, should have decreased by 35 million people."

"The reduction in Canada is far less, but both American and Canadian death toll numbers will increase in the next 12 hours with people beginning to freeze to death. Within another couple of days, another 50 million Americans and 15 million Canadians will die. That is a potential total of 100 million people terminated in North America alone. South America is of little concern and that includes Mexico. We have 50 of our termination squads moving along the America/Mexico border ready to terminate anybody moving south. In Europe, 30% of the population of the most northern countries will be dead from fire or from exposure. That is another 100 million people."

"My favorite scenario shows that 200 million people in Russia and another 150 million Asians in areas with below freezing temperatures will die from exposure within the next 24 hours. In Africa, we expect our smallest losses at only 25 million dead, and in Australia and New Zealand, another 5 million deaths due to city fires. My goal was to rid this world of 500 million people within forty-eight hours of me pushing the first button, and the current winter conditions in the northern hemisphere are nearly perfect for achieving this. That is Phase I; Phase II's timeline is one week, or 168 hours from the beginning. In this scenario, we have nothing to do but see if we can get correct estimations of fatalities back from our termination squads using their satellite radios. In this phase, I expect another one billion people worldwide to begin killing each other over protection, hunger, warmth, and water. With the millions of weapons owned by the people in the United States alone, they should do a fantastic job of killing themselves for us."

"The hated Americans should decrease their own population by another 100 million in this timeframe. All the sick in hospitals and the millions of aged people around the world will die in this phase—people who are of no use to us as a workforce. The United States will fare better than Canada in this second phase, due to the southern areas being warmer. In this phase, I expect that 35% of the population of Canada will freeze to death. The U.S. and European populations should be down to 60% by the conclusion of this phase and we will begin to activate all our termination squads to kill every remaining male over ten years old. They will take over every military installation, which should be virtually powerless to resist, and turn them into concentration camps for the women and children under ten. Our squads are equipped with ground-to-ground missiles and these, with mortars, should give them the upper hand against any remaining soldiers stationed at their bases. We will do the same with the Pentagon and the White House."

"I have ordered that the American President must be kept alive; we could use him to stop any upsurges of power against our squads if they are having trouble. I believe that the American people will listen to him on military radios, of which I'm sure there are many old ones from the Vietnam or Korean War eras in museums and in and around bases across the country. We expect some sort of fight from the remaining American people, but not from any large groups once we have killed the remaining soldiers. The American soldiers will not be spared. Any questions about and up to the end of Phase II, gentlemen?"

One man put his hand up.

"Comrade Chairman, what about our squads needing ground-to-air missiles against possible aircraft attacks?" the man asked. There was silence, and the Chairman shook his head.

"Comrade Gung, are you blind and stupid?" the Chairman asked sarcastically. "How many aircraft do you see flying to protect the world? How many aircraft are in the sky at this moment?"

"Zero, Comrade Chairman," replied the man, now fearful for the first time.

"And how many aircraft will we see on our screens tomorrow, Comrade Gung?" asked the Chairman, looking at the man with pity.

"Zero, Comrade Chairman," replied the scared man, his face now white.

"I'm sure there are several aircraft left around the world, but any aircraft still flyable are old, small propeller-driven aircraft, have no guns, and cannot hurt our squads. We will not need any ground-to-air missiles. If we see a transponder, our squads will search it out and destroy the pilot and his plane. We have absolutely no worries of any attack from the air ever again. And Comrade, I find your question belittling and mocking considering my 30 years of planning."

The ashamed man shrank down into his chair and tried to make himself small and inconspicuous.

* * *

Dawn at the Strong farm was relatively normal. Oliver was out earlier than usual, sniffing the air. There was something wrong in the human world he knew so little about and he was worried—worried enough to omit a bark at the new female human and the little humans coming out of the side door of the hangar. His bark was more of a warning than anything else, but he thought it necessary. The kids ran up to him and stroked his head, back, and tail and he forgot about the problems that weren't really his concern.

Maggie was up early, as well. It was just before 7:00 am. She was in a hurry to get to the radio in the house, feeling pretty lousy, and had woken the kids up to speak to their father. There was a very slight smell of smoke in the air, but used to living rural, she dismissed it as normal.

They walked into the darkened house and turned on the radio set Preston had switched off when he had gone to bed. It took a couple of minutes to warm up, but it soon glowed and its two dials showed movement. Maggie went into the kitchen to put on the coffee machine. She filled the machine with ground coffee and water and switched it on. It didn't work. She looked around the kitchen and saw that the LED lights on the stove, the microwave, and the coffee machine itself weren't lit up. She opened the refrigerator and found it to be dark inside and cool but not cold. It wasn't like Martie to miss things like this, she thought, as she tried the kitchen light switch. It worked, and this made her even more puzzled. Why would there be electricity, but every appliance in the house not working? The radio and the lights were! She went back into the lounge and tried the television and computer on Preston's desk. They were as dead as the systems in the kitchen. Then she walked to Preston's bedroom door and quietly knocked.

"Preston, Martie, wake up. Something's wrong. You need to come and see the kitchen, nothing works. There's a problem," she stated firmly, but quietly so as not to wake the others.

It took a minute, but both came through the door, both putting on dressing gowns as they looked just as bad as Maggie felt—their eyes still sleepy and half closed.

"What's the matter, Maggie?" asked Preston. "What time is it, anyway? My LED alarm clock by the bed isn't working. I don't even know what time it is. Don't you know its New Year's Day?"

Maggie said nothing as she grabbed Preston's hand and dragged him to the kitchen. "Ben, make sure the volume is up on the radio. I want to speak to Dad as soon as the set warms up." She showed the two sleepyheads every electrical instrument that didn't work in the kitchen. Preston automatically tried the light switch and realized that the main kitchen light was already on.

"That's funny," was all he said before Will Smart's voice could be heard in the lounge calling them urgently on the radio.

"Hi, Dad, Ben here," they heard Ben say.

"Are you okay, Ben?" asked Will. *"Get your mother immediately!"* he shouted on the radio as Maggie got to the radio and Ben relinquished his seat.

"I'm here, Will," she pressed the talk button. "So are Ben, Oprah, Preston, and Martie. "What's the matter? You sound worried."

For the next 20 minutes, Will told the now white-faced listeners about what had happened the night before. He told them about the aircraft explosions, the gas explosions, having to shoot the two teens, and then odd detail that nothing in the house worked when he and Mike got there. He had tried all night to get them on the radio. Preston apologized about turning it off. Maggie told him that some things weren't working where they were, either, and that she had smelled smoke in the morning air. There was silence on the radio as each group thought about what had happened. Preston was first to speak.

"Will, what do you think has happened? I want you to think about it very seriously while we get everybody up and we can get together here in the lounge and discuss the situation. We have an Air Force general with us who certainly would like to know what's going on. If you can give us 15 minutes, we will all be here," he asked, giving Martie and Maggie hand signals to go get everybody else up. "Is that ok with you?"

"That's fine with me. Mike's up, he's my partner and he's trying to make us coffee on the BBQ on the porch outside. Remember, it's still night here," was the reply.

It took several minutes, but slowly everyone came into the house. Martie was surprised to find the large bed in the hangar occupied by both Carlos and Sally, who both looked much the worse for wear—Sally's long red hair was all down in her face. Martie smiled at her friend. She had known that the two of them would eventually get it together. She woke everyone in the hangar and then met Preston outside. He had awakened Pete in his aircraft and Pete, also with dressing gown, was walking back to the house in step with Preston.

By the time they returned, Martie had woken up Michael and her grandfather, and there was a growing collection of interesting dressing gowns waiting for them to arrive.

Barbara and Jennifer were the last to arrive, and Martie was carrying a large pot of water to the grill on the porch to make hot water. Some guests looked at her as if she was crazy.

"Quiet everyone," Preston cleared his throat. "We've been on the radio with Will Smart, Maggie's husband in Los Angeles. He has told us an incredible story about his area literally blowing up last night. We thought he was pulling a prank at first, but he mentioned that none of the appliances or electrical devices in his home are working. We've discovered that same phenomenon here since we woke up this morning, So, I'm warning you, that even though I'm struggling to believe what Will has just told us, think we all need to hear his story and then we can go from there. Will, do you hear me?"

"Roger, Preston. I hear you clearly."

"Will, let me introduce you to everybody. Folks, on the radio is Will Smart, an LAPD detective which many of you have met, Maggie's husband. On this side, Will, we have Grandpa Roebels and Michael, Martie's grandfather and father. We have Pete Allen, Sally, and her friend Jennifer, who are all Air Force. Sally, you know Will. Buck and Barbara are here. You know Buck well and Barbara is his lady friend. Then there is Carlos, whom you have met, and then Martie and I. Maggie is here, and so are your two kids. What I want you to do is to tell us what happened to you last night and then hopefully answer my original question, which was 'what do you think is going on,' ok?"

Will acknowledged and told the same story for the second time. This time, he decided to omit the killing of the two teenagers, since it was not their problem. The audience listened in shock, their mouths open.

"Will, Pete Allen here," said the General. "What do you think happened? Preston said that you live close to Edwards Air Force Base, is that correct?"

"May I talk straight?" Will asked.

"Absolutely," Preston radioed back.

"I have thought about the situation for a couple of hours now while trying to reach you guys on the radio. My thoughts are these. Nothing works. Cars don't work. No electronic devise in this house works. I did not see one police car, fire engine, and ambulance last night, so they can't be operational. My partner Mike tried a dozen police cars last night and all were useless. Not one vehicle has passed by our house since midnight, yet my truck works, and I saw a second old truck in town driving, so something works out there. But why do they work and why others don't, I don't know. I suggest the first thing you try is to see what works and what doesn't work at your place, Preston."

"As far as the explosions we saw and heard, I saw a burning jet engine in a tree in our park, so I'm assuming a commercial aircraft was to blame for our park blowing up. I've never seen an aircraft crash before, but this looked like one. Then I saw

dozens of explosions over the hills in downtown L.A. and an explosion in the hills by Palmdale, a town to our south. That looked like another aircraft going down. So if these explosions were all aircraft, my theory is that every aircraft in the sky acted like my coffee machine. How long would it take for every aircraft flying around here to hit the ground?"

"About five minutes from the highest altitudes," replied General Allen, with all the other pilots nodding in agreement.

"Well, that's about how long it took from start to finish," replied Will. *"Several came down pretty quickly over L.A., but then the explosions seemed to happen all around us. Even Bakersfield was lit up like a candle last night and I heard another explosion off to our east, which seemed to be the last one. To answer your question, Preston, I believe that every electrical thing in California or at least in the L.A. area has stopped working. Why it is the same for you, I don't know yet, but I believe that every airplane flying in L.A. airspace crashed last night, all five or so minutes after midnight."*

"Thanks, Detective Smart," said General Allen. "I'll get on my radio and check out the nearest Air Force base and see if they can give us more information. I'll let you know if they give me any information that can help you."

With that, the General got up and walked outside to his aircraft communication center, hoping that someone could give him more information about what was happening.

The remaining guests all asked Will questions for another ten minutes, trying to find out more, but he had already told them everything he knew and what he thought. Then the General, now dressed in his uniform, walked back in and sat down. Preston put his finger on the talk button and silence reigned.

"My aircraft is dead. Every single part of it is totally dead. I can't even fire up the engines. Not a single switch on the front dash works. It has battery backup and battery backup for that backup. There is no way my complete aircraft can be turned off, ever. Even my dash clock doesn't work, or my coffee maker. My 30-year old electric razor is the only thing that works in that whole damn piece of junk out there. I plugged it in the one of your hangar sockets, Preston."

"If that happened to every aircraft flying around the United States, or even the world, then they would all fall to Earth within the five minutes that Will described," replied Preston. "That means all our aircraft are now nothing more than scrap metal out there. Will, let's all meet back here in 15 minutes. We are going out to see what works and what doesn't work, and we'll come back and let you know. You said your truck works, but your police cruiser didn't? That's where I'm starting." Preston left the radio and went out the front door still in his dressing gown, toggling the light switch for the lounge as reached it. It worked. The whole group suddenly heard an engine coming up the driveway, and Preston saw Joe's jeep coming around the corner with him and David in the front seat. It pulled up with a cloud of dust next to the front door and they all rushed out of the house totally shocked.

"Something's weird," Joe told Preston before Preston could open his mouth. "Nothing works at my house. The kitchen's dead, the lights work because of the generator, but apart from all our vehicles we've already tried, everything else is dead. Even your gate didn't open. David and I had to manually force it open to get in here."

"We know," replied Preston. "We heard from Maggie's husband in L.A. and you won't believe what he told us. Joe, David, come with me. We need to find out what works around here." The two got out of the truck and followed Preston to his old Ford. The rest were all headed in different directions to the aircraft parked around the vicinity. Preston got in the truck, and as usual it started the first time. He sat there thinking and started putting two and two together.

"Everything that's old still works," he stated to David and

Joe, who were standing by the open driver's door. "Joe, you tried everything mobile at your house. What vehicles don't work?"

"None," replied Joe. "But then everything I own is old. Even the trucks are all 1970 models." Preston heard *Lady Dandy's* engine start up and that really caused his brow to line. "Old engines work, but why?" he mused. "That thing got carburetors in it?" Joe pointed over to the DC-3. Preston nodded and suddenly knew what Joe was thinking.

"If the carburetors are the reason the Ford and the DC-3 both work then that's why the general's plane doesn't work," added Joe. "Its engines must be electrically controlled. It's not the engines that don't work," stated Joe, seeing the light. "It's the electrical controls."

Preston turned off the engine, got out, closed the driver's door, and walked towards the aircraft with Joe in tow. He heard and noticed Baby Huey's twin rotors starting to turn. "1960s equipment works," observed Preston. Then he stood still as the Pilatus' one engine started turning. "1970s equipment works," he added. "You're right Joe, it's not the engines in the aircraft, it's the modern electronics that surround the running of the engines." That means every aircraft in the hangar will work, but my crop sprayer was built in the 1980s. Let see if my theory is correct." Preston tried to open the hangar doors, but the button did nothing. "All this stuff comes from the late 1990s and doesn't work—same with the gate opener."

By this time, he had reached his crop sprayer, which was still parked outside and out of the way. He climbed in, and turned on several switches, and the engine turned normally as he pressed the starter. The only thing dead on his dash was its new GPS system.

"Everything works, Joe, except my new Garmin GPS. Once again, this old bird's got carburetors." Pete Allen came up to the other men and watched. "Carburetors work, engines without carburetors don't work. What's the difference?" And then it hit him. "Yes! The electrical components in the engines and engine-management systems—engines work, but anything electronic and GPS systems don't work," Preston said to the two other men. "Here's something funny. I have the usual two radios in here. One is working and one isn't. The old one—the original one that was installed in this aircraft in 1982—works. The other one quit on me a couple of years ago and I installed a new one. It's a Bendix King and is about three years old. I installed it from King Aviation myself and it is as dead as your whole aircraft, Pete."

"That figures," replied Pete. "My King Air is the most modern you can have—the Air Force doesn't care what it costs—but the Pilatus started the first time. Old electronics seem to work; otherwise the Pilatus would be as dead as mine. Let's go over and see what's working on Sally's bird. That could tell us more," he suggested.

Preston got out and they walked up to the Pilatus. Both engines were running and Preston gave Sally the sign to kill all engines by moving his right hand flat across his throat. It wasn't usual procedure to switch off engines before letting them warm up, but Sally responded. As the engines came to a stop, she opened the rear door to let them in. That wasn't necessary, however, as Preston immediately asked her what was working.

"Engines are fine as you just saw. Radios are original and they both switched on. Radar is dead, and both GPSs and all the more modern directional equipment other than the standard stuff is dead. All original instrument still works, Preston—altitude, compass, radios," she answered.

"I assume that your electrical ignition switches, starter switches, and fuel pumps are all original—what, 1970s?" asked Preston. Sally nodded. "So anything that is modern or post-1980s equipment, or added as modifications doesn't work. It must have something to do with electronic breakdowns or sabotage," stated Preston. "Let's get the hangar open and check out the aircraft inside."

"Sally, take Jennifer and start up those babies you came in on," ordered the general. "I want to see if anything U.S. Air Force is operational. Those two nearly original C-130s might be the only operational aircraft the Air Force has right now. Preston," continued the General. "Your radio in the lounge works and you can talk to some guy near Edwards Air Force base, which is 3,000 plus miles away, but I can't talk to the Pilatus from my aircraft over my radio, which is a matter of 20 yards away. Why?"

"Good question, Pete," responded Preston. "My ham radio is 40 years old, original, and doesn't have any upgrades. The set Will Smart is talking to us on is the same model. I used to have two, but I gave my additional unit to young Ben for his 10th birthday. Also, my nearest antenna is on my forest ranger fire tower over there, and the height is 59 feet. That antenna connects me to my second antenna 24 miles away atop a cell phone tower. I installed it at a height of 250 feet and included a solar-panel backup and battery. There is no way that my system can ever go down, unless a battery fails. It doesn't take much power to receive and re-transmit. I assume that the cell phone towers are down, but the dozen or so antennae I installed across the U.S. are still operating. It seems that what is down is the whole electricity grid." Preston stopped and watched for Pete's response. Seeing nothing but rapt attention, Preston continued. "Will has a generator at his house, and so do his neighbors. I have a generator, and so does Joe. We all have power and all the antennae atop the towers that relay our messages are on solar backup. Buck has the same set as me, and so does Carlos in Salt Lake City. I installed a couple of antennae specifically to talk to Buck in New York and nearly a dozen across the country to California. The setup took me six months of work. Does that answer your question?" The General nodded.

"So, apart from an area around Will's house and this airfield, we don't have a clue what's going on around the country?" Pete asked. Preston nodded.

"Then it's time we did some flying around here and find out," suggested Pete. As he said it, the massive engines of both the C-130s turned over and were quiet again, the girls obviously not wanting to fully start them up. "At least we have two aircraft. I need to speak to Detective Smart and see if he can do me a favor," announced the General, walking back towards the house.

Pete got back on the radio to California again while Preston and the rest wrestled with the large hangar doors to try to open them. Once they were in, they checked the instruments in the four aircraft and turned them over once without starting them. They all worked.

"David wants to go back to his place and see what's up," stated Joe to Preston. "We will take the jeep and check out the roads."

"You'd better take some protection," suggested Preston. "A couple of those hunting rifles you gave your sons and a shotgun might be a good idea. We don't know what's out there and it's a pretty good chance that the cops won't pull you over for carrying loaded weapons if their cruisers don't work." Joe nodded.

"We'll be careful. I'll take a couple of my boys, arm us to the teeth, and report back in a couple of hours," Joe replied, and he and David drove off.

Preston suddenly wanted to check something out. He ran over to his fuel station and tried to turn on the pumps. All five electric pump motors that brought the fuel from the underground tanks to the surface were new and thus they were all dead.

"Motors," he thought aloud. "I need old motors, or even one old motor, and then hitch them up to one of the tanks to pump. I know the smaller generator has enough power to pump the fuel up, and we will need to manually move it and connect it from one tank to the other when we need to pump the different fuels. Buck will know how to make this modification."

He went and found Buck, who relished the idea of being the first one in America to beat the system imposed on them. It took Buck only a minute before he reported back to Preston.

"You did what?" Preston responded. "You jumped my system?"

"It was simple," laughed Buck. "If the electronics are not working, it doesn't mean the motor isn't. The pump was ready to pump, but need an electronic impulse to turn on. I just by-passed the electrics, the same way anybody would steal a car. I by-passed the electrical brains of your system."

"Genius," replied Preston, slapping Buck on the back. "We must remember that, because I assume that there are more problems like these out there. If the electrical brains of simple mechanical motors of all types are dead, then we can by-pass them by jumping them."

"Correct, unless the electronic brains actually run the whole system, like a vehicle, or an aircraft with a computerized fuel-management system," answered Buck. "That is why your old truck works, but all vehicles since around 1985 won't work because they are not natural mechanically-run engines anymore. Their engines run on computerized controls, and if those are kaput, then the vehicle can never be repaired."

"Unbelievable," replied Preston. "My old Ford is now faster and worth more money than every new Ferrari or Lamborghini worldwide—if this is a worldwide problem. But, the million dollar question is, how did whomever or whatever manage to destroy, or make inactive, every electronic part in the United States at the same time—we must assume around midnight Eastern time last night? The LED timer that I use for the exact amount of time my sprays are on to tell me how much I'm using in the crop sprayer was still lit up. It doesn't turn off. It was still lit, but the time was showing 12:03 am last night."

"That is the question nobody can answer," Buck replied. "My only thought is that it was a flare-up from the sun that fried everything. But that shouldn't work around the world at the same time, and at midnight East Coast time, we were on the opposite side of the planet from the sun. A sun flare should have fried electronics in Australia, but not here, or not so perfectly that all five of your fuel pumps don't work. I want to take one of them apart and try to figure out what caused the outage."

"I suggest you do it now," replied Preston. "I'm going to see what the general wants to do. I'm sure he's pretty worried." Preston left

Buck at the fuel tank control system and went in search of Pete Allen. He found him in the house with Maggie, talking to Will Smart.

"Will, what I want you to do for me," Preston heard Pete say into the microphone as he walked in, "is to drive to Edwards, which is what—eight to ten miles from you?"

"Thirty-four miles," said Maggie to Pete.

"Sorry, Will, Maggie says 34 miles. I want you get to Edwards and tell the gate that you are working on my orders and that you need to see Colonel Makowich immediately. I want a report on what's operational at the base. If he has no communications, then tell him to go back with you to your house. They must have some sort of vehicle working..."

"The older the better," interrupted Preston.

"Hold on, Will," stated the general. Preston showed him how to leave the microphone on so that Will could hear both of them and continued. "The problem Buck and I found was engine-management systems. Any engine operated by a computerized, or any other type of electronic system, is dead—kaput. My truck and your truck work the old way without any electronic aids, right Will?"

"Yes, my truck has a massive carburetor I have to get tuned every so often," replied Will.

"Will, Pete here. I want you to order the colonel to bring everything he can out of mothballs—jeeps, radios like this one, even check the oldest aircraft and helicopters he has, because Buck and I reckon that anything older than around 1985 and unmodified with newer electronics will work. That means that our entire Air Force has been terminated by whatever attacked us?" Pete looked at Preston, his face going completely white.

"We might have the new U.S. Air Force right here," stated Preston seriously. "Plus whatever you guys can bring out of museums and mothballs."

"Very little," the general replied. "I must get down to Seymour Johnson and Pope Field immediately. Will, go to Edwards and bring the colonel back to this radio, or at least set up a relay station with military radios so that we can converse, or take the radio to him. If the colonel wants more proof, tell him that his wife's name is Mary and that he has three sons—William, Jonathan, and Little Sam who is six. Tell him that my incoming code for my aircraft is 'Allen Key.' That will get you in. Let's meet back here in three hours at 11:00 hours on the dot. Also tell the colonel to give you something better than police pistols, and take your police badges for identification. The base's security is going to be pretty edgy, and Will, tell him everything you heard Preston explain a minute ago."

Will had nothing better to do, plus it would give him a reason to venture out into the area and see what was up. He told the general that he would take his partner Mike as a bodyguard and that they would both travel armed. The general reminded him to hand in the guns at the gate to avoid any security problems.

General Allen thanked Maggie and left the room, asking Preston to follow him. He was now all business, and walked up to Sally and Jennifer, now in pilot overalls and prepping the two C-130s for flight.

"Captain Powers, I am going with you to Seymour Johnson. Captain Watkins, I want you to go to Pope Field and get a 'Sitrep'

(Situation Report) from the base commander. I need to know what can fly and whether he has communications. How much fuel do you both have?"

"One hour plus reserves," they both said together.

"Preston, how much jet fuel do you have here in case they cannot refuel and need to return?"

"Forty-six hundred gallons," Preston answered.

"Not much," was the response. "Captain Watkins, you have enough to get from Fort Bragg back to Seymour Johnson. I want a full Sitrep. You have 90 minutes to get into Pope, get my Sitrep and then get over to Seymour Johnson. If you can refuel there, get it fuelled up since you will be going straight on to Andrews. Also, get a copilot and engineer aboard—anybody you know or anybody you can commandeer. Tell the base commander that speed is of the essence—I told you so. Organize an emergency field operations tent, a field hospital tent, at least two field accommodation tents and any working radios. I also want some fire power. Get the Camp Lejeune commander on the radio, if you can get into communications. I want a full report on what he has in his armories that works, and any vehicles he can supply. Now get going. Our aircraft radios should work between our two aircraft on the ground, and if they do and you have any questions, I'll have someone here manning the radio. Now get *Tom* out of here."

"Yes, Sir," she saluted and ran to the C-130.

"Preston, I want you and Carlos to get into the air. I don't care what you fly, but I would like a report on the surrounding area around Raleigh-Durham and a situation report on RDU International Airport. I'm looking for fuel, safety, and if need be what we can commandeer in terms of other aircraft. What we learn from the condition of Raleigh-Durham International could be much the same as any other commercial airport. If we have no fuel, we are in trouble. I assume we need Buck to go along and hotwire the gas tanks, or whatever he has to do to get fuel out of something."

"I would recommend the Huey," Carlos said to Buck as Jennifer started up her first engine and the group ran back to the hangar to be able to talk. The General ordered Sally to get the other C-130 warmed up and ready for takeoff.

"She should get her off in about 2,500 feet. She is very light, so it might even be 2,200 feet," stated the General, still wanting to talk, but also wanting to view the takeoff. There was no wind, and the windsock was completely still. Jennifer turned left and the C-130 cruised down to the northern end where there was a bigger area to turn around, left the asphalt, and created a small dust storm as she turned right on the end of the asphalt. She sat there for a minute warming her four massive engines as Sally's first engine turned over.

Jennifer pushed her four throttles much of the way forward and Preston's lights blew over and the bushes and trees starting waving in the high wind behind the aircraft as she released the brakes and the large aircraft lunged forward. She quickly pushed her throttles to full power as she started moving, and the old aircraft leapt forward like a racehorse out of the starting gates. She passed the hangar, with everyone holding their ears, and sprayed dust and dirt as she moved faster and faster. Her front wheel came off the ground, and she became airborne with about 500 feet of runway to spare, rising quickly and pulling up her wheels and turning slightly towards Fort Bragg—30 miles to the south—as she rose over the trees at the end of the clearing.

"I reckon she took 2,300 feet," said General Allen. "I think they can get in and out of here with full fuel and about a 50% load weight. Coming in heavy will be a problem more than getting out. They are strong old birds and will do whatever we want them to do."

"How many aircraft do you think the Air Force still has flying that are older than 1985?" asked Carlos.

"Not many," replied the General. "a couple of old fighters, zero bombers, maybe a couple of old helicopters, several fuel tankers—but they will be useless with all their modern instrumentation—and maybe a another dozen of these older C-130s in much the same condition as these two birds, completely decommissioned and all their ultra-modern electronics removed. *Tom* and *Jerry* are as original as when they were purchased, apart from their extra armaments and added fuel drop-tanks, which haven't been removed yet, thank God. There is an old F-4 Phantom at Hill, and I know of two more that are ready to fly if you guys are correct about the electronic side of flying. Is your Huey refueled, Buck?"

"No, but she has enough for about 40 minutes flying time, plus reserves. That'll be enough to do a 20-minute sweep of the area and 20 minutes to return here from RDU. We can refuel when we get back."

General Allen suggested that Buck, Preston, and Carlos go in the Huey, and take some sort of protection. Preston had a shotgun and a hunting rifle in the house and headed off to get them while Buck went out to start *Baby Huey*.

By this time, Sally was waiting for the general on the runway in front of the apron. He ran over to the open side door, and Sally closed the door behind him. She took off the same way Jennifer had done five minutes earlier.

Ten minutes later, *Baby Huey* rose into the air with the three men aboard and Carlos acting as co-pilot. Preston had volunteered to take the job as side-gunner. He tried to sit on the side with the door open but it was too cold, so he closed the door a couple of minutes after take-off.

The girls left with Michael and Grandpa Roebels having a cold breakfast and deep in discussion, discussing the electrical problems facing them. They were the real experts in the field of aviation electronics, older and more experienced than the younger men around them.

Everybody reckoned that they were pretty safe on the ranch—after all, they had Oliver as a guard dog and Joe would have re-locked the front gate when he left earlier.

It was weird at first, to see no moving vehicles on the streets. Baby Huey and her crew flew low at first trying to get Air Traffic Control on the radio. There were no voices on the radios apart from theirs. Preston asked Buck to set the second radio to the farm's frequency, and Martie returned a call saying that the reception was perfect and that she and her father would be monitoring the radio.

They were civilians and didn't know the frequency the Air Force would be using if they had anything working at all, and Carlos was sure that the general was communicating between his two aircraft on some other frequency. *Baby Huey* had a small storm radar called a storm scope and a Garmin GPS, but both were dead. All the other instruments worked, though.

They looked out of the windows on both sides to the ground below. Preston was sitting on the right side and when he saw objects glittering in the lake water to their south, he told Buck to bring her around to inspect. They swept around and found the broken pieces of a downed aircraft. There were thousands of small pieces floating in the still water, including several bodies and part of a tail that had Southwest colors visible on the largest piece.

"She must have gone in hard by the size of those small pieces," observed Buck as they swept over the water a second time looking for any survivors and then headed in the direction of Raleigh. They were quiet for several minutes flying over Apex, Cary, and then Morrisville near the airport. Not one vehicle moved. There were thousands everywhere, many burnt out or still on fire. Then the radio tuned into the farm's frequency lit up.

"Flying helicopter, this is Joe and David. Is that you, Buck?

We can't see you but we can hear your rotors. You sound about three miles to the west and north of us."

"Hi, Joe," stated Buck. "I have Preston and Carlos with me. Direct us in and we'll come overhead. Are you guys all right? Is there enough room to land? Over."

"Will do, but don't try to land. This place has trees everywhere and the only open place is the two-lane road in front. We heard a bit of gunfire a few minutes ago in two different directions and I don't think it's safe for you to land. We are okay, but come over and case our surroundings anyway. We have a ton of stuff we are packing into the truck and we will need to return again to clear all the stuff we could use. I won't say more in case someone is listening in."

It only took a minute as Joe guided them in close to David's home and they circled a couple of times and found nothing out of the ordinary. They said goodbye and headed toward downtown Raleigh. Here, the buildings were taller and many were occupied. As they got overhead at 2,000 feet, people started waving at them from the taller buildings. One even had a helicopter landing pad on top and people quickly gathered and waved them down.

"We can't stop," explained Buck. "We don't have enough fuel and I'm sure those people have supplies for a few days." The other two agreed and they flew on to RDU airport.

They could see a large fire on the other side of the airport and decided to fly over there before coming in to land. Buck repeatedly tried to get Air Traffic Control on several different frequencies, but the radio stayed silent.

As they flew over the fire, which was actually several dozen houses in flames in a housing subdivision, they saw the tell-tale signs of an aircraft crash—a line of blackened houses in the direct path of one of the airport's runways. The flames were still high in some areas with other areas already blackened and smoldering. There were no fire engines or police cars or any other vehicles apart from stationary ones that could be seen everywhere. It was time to land, as their fuel gauges were close to the reserve markings. There was still no wind, so the smoke from the fires hovered and the several windsocks around the airport drooped towards the ground. They came in to land away from the commercial terminals on the apron where several destroyed and some still burning private aircraft were located.

Preston and Carlos surveyed the scene, while Buck decided to land close to some smaller fuel tanks by one of the hangars close to the smaller and private aircraft terminal. It was surreal. There were several aircraft, mostly Southwest and Delta specimens, sitting with their "walkway" doors pressed against them—looking as if they were loading or unloading passengers. There was even a Southwest supply van standing in the middle of the tarmac, deserted. A fuel truck was sitting next to a smaller twin-engine Delta jet, and looked like it was being refueled. Again the whole apron area seemed deserted.

The private aircraft terminal looked worse. A small aircraft, probably a jet based on the amount of damage caused too many of the Cessna single-engine aircraft that must have gone out of control at takeoff, had left the runway and ploughed into several stationary aircraft. Preston looked at the runway and saw two more commercial aircraft just sitting on the runway in unusual places, as if they had just been left there. They were all complete, except one, it looked like it had landed with its wheels up and gouges could be seen on the runway behind it. Preston reckoned that the small jet must have been taking off when its systems went down, went out of control, flew somewhat, and then rolled into the group of parked aircraft. It had missed the terminal by feet and a smoldering pile of blackened remains lay a dozen yards or so on the grass past the terminal. Out of the 20 or so aircraft on the apron, there were piles of smoldering aircraft and several aircraft still untouched.

Buck landed the Huey and they looked around and nobody

came out to greet them. He had touched down a few yards away from the gas tanks, one housing jet fuel and the other normal aviation gasoline.

"I'm sure I'm going to have to hotwire them to get them working," he suggested to Preston. "The gauges won't show how much we put in, and your gauges on the farm won't either, but full tanks are full tanks. Do you think we are safe?" he asked.

"I haven't seen movement anywhere, but I want to go over and look at those three gas trucks over there. Carlos, I think you should stand guard, just in case." Carlos nodded.

It took Buck several minutes, but Preston heard a motorized pump start up and turned to see Carlos helping Buck get a line to the Huey's gas tanks Preston got in each truck. They were tractor-trailer gas trucks with a company logo on them, and they were dead to the world. The keys were in the ignition, but the trucks were stationary dinosaurs.

He went around to the trailers where the fuel controls were. The first was a pretty old trailer, and the dials came to life when he operated the on-off switch. The three gauges showed full tanks and the notation "Jet Fuel" was underneath each gauge and showed 2,000 gallons each. The other two trailers were similar, and one was bigger, showing 3,000 gallons on its three gauges. It was full of aviation fuel, not jet fuel. He switched on the master switch of the last tanker to start the pumps, but apart from the gauges showing the tanks were full, the motors were as dead as the truck's engine.

He spent several minutes looking carefully around the underside of the belly of the tanks and saw manual wheels that could be opened to at least dispense the insides with gravity. "The system to clean the tanks," he said aloud, "but I'm sure Buck could hotwire these pumps as well."

Preston looked around, but there was still no movement. "Where is everybody?" he shouted to Carlos coming towards him.

"I would assume they've gone home to be with their families. There couldn't have been any more flights after the remains we saw coming in, and the last one out I presume was the one we saw in the lake. Most of the aircraft over there," Carlos said, pointing to the commercial terminal, "look like they were overnight flights ready or being readied for early morning takeoffs. Let's go and look around."

"Okay. *Baby Huey* is nearly full," Preston replied. "Buck is going to take off and place her away from the terminal in case we have company."

Carlos fell into step with Preston as they headed toward the smaller terminal. "I had a quick look in the windows," said Carlos as they walked. "The building is completely locked, the gates are padlocked, and someone would have to climb over the fence to get onto the airport grounds. I think the whole airport is on lock-down since security would have come over to us by now to see who we are. I've never seen an airport so full of stuff, but so empty of people. Let's see if the commercial terminal is open."

They did, and walked up the stairs by a Southwest Airlines 737 sitting at a gate. The door opened and they walked up the passenger walkway connection to the security door that led into the terminal building itself. It was closed, but because there was no reason to have security on the outside, it opened. Carlos realized that if it shut they would not be able to get back out, so he asked Preston to hold the door while he went to get a chair from the lobby. He rammed it into the doorway so that the door couldn't close, and then, with their exit open, they went on an inspection tour.

There were papers, food bags, cleaning bins, and vacuum cleaners everywhere. The terminal was completely empty of people and it looked to both Preston and Carlos as if there had been a semi-orderly clearing of the building before it had been closed and locked down by security. The bar area was clean, the bar stools neatly stacked on the bar and the whole area locked down with a steel mesh. They could see bottles of alcohol still on the shelves. The newspaper shop was locked down, but yesterday's newspapers and hundreds of books still lined the shelves. The lobby areas were clear, and apart from the windows letting in light, the place was dark and void of life.

"We had better get moving," suggested Preston to Carlos. "I want to be back by 11:00 and we only have an hour left." Carlos agreed, and they moved back to the door from which they had entered and down the passenger aisle. Carlos tried the door to the aircraft on their way by. It wasn't locked, so he walked into the plane. The aircraft had been cleaned inside and, as he had suggested to Preston, was ready for flight the next morning.

"Such a pity, such a beautiful airplane," Carlos stated to Preston.

"I've always wanted to own one of these. Like John Travolta, who can go anywhere around the world in his. The private version is totally intercontinental with the extra-large fuel tanks. Let's see what works on the flight deck?"

It was as dead as the General's fancy Air Force plane, and Preston felt sad seeing such a piece of beauty totally helpless. They left the aircraft and walked down to the ground to discover that Buck had moved *Baby Huey* closer to them.

"I saw a small truck and what looked like an old Toyota Camry, or whatever they used to call them in the 70s, drive past the airport terminal on the road side," explained Buck. "I couldn't see more, but I thought I'd get over here in case you were in trouble. I checked out the Southwest supply truck. It's as dead as a doornail and so is the fuel truck over there by the Delta jet. But it's still full of fuel and I could hotwire the fuel pumps if we needed more fuel."

"I checked out the ones by the terminal and we could do the same to them," added Preston. "That's about 20,000 gallons of both jet and aviation fuel in these four trailers. If we need them, Joe's got two old semi-tractors that still work and we could come over and connect them up. The connection attachments are manual labor anyway."

"The Southwest truck is full of stuff. Since we are empty, I reckon we should full the Huey up with what's in there before somebody else decides to help themselves."

"Do you know how much crap I've got?" laughed Preston, thinking about his stash of stuff already in the hangar.

"I'm sure," replied Carlos. "But we could be in this for the long haul and I'm sure that if we need to help other people we will most probably need every bit of food we can get our hands on. Think, guys, every freezer in every supermarket is not working anymore. Every refrigerator and freezer in every house, apartment block, or office building isn't working. How long before people run out of food and become hungry? I reckon it'll be less than a week before this place, and every other place where food can be found, will be a mass of people grabbing anything they can find—even the bottles from the bar we saw back there. I reckon we have a week to arm ourselves and protect what we have at your farm. I think we have to stock up as much as we can. Thank God we have Pete Allen and the Air Force bases to back us up."

Carlos then turned to Buck. "Hey, I want to use my share in *Baby Huey* here and head up to Washington to get my father and his uncle. I reckon we are the lucky ones so far and the larger cities are already in chaos."

"Sure," answered Buck. "We can fly her up together once we've had our 11:00 meeting. I'm sure we can get the General's permission to hotwire the fuel tanks at Andrews."

"Let's load this baby," interjected Preston. "We can always repay it if the world gets back to normal."

They had an hour to get back, so they worked fast. The re-supply truck had everything from cleaning utensils to boxes of miniature alcohol bottles and soft drinks. There were over a hundred cases of supplies and they took everything that could be of—even the clean towels and the pile of cabin blankets.

Now sweating, they closed the door and Buck lifted the heavier Huey off and headed out of the airfield. As they left, they could see an old truck and a blue car leaving the airport area. "I bet they're casing the joint and we scared them off," said Carlos.

The farm became busy for a few minutes as everybody got back at once. Preston could see Joe opening the gate to the airfield and Joe circled his arm around his head to tell Buck to go around—presumably to see if they had been followed. There was no movement or any other vehicles the three men in the Huey could see, but they did hear the two C-130s patch into Preston's airport frequency and ask for landing instructions. Carlos undid his seat straps, climbed out of the right seat, and gave Preston the headphones.

"You are now Air Traffic Control, literally," smiled Carlos to Preston as they passed in the narrow space.

"Preston to Sally and Jennifer," Preston spoke into the mic. "I recommend using first names instead of aircraft descriptions in the future. A precaution, nothing more, nobody needs to know who we are. Wind is zero. What's the temperature down there, Ground Control?"

"Martie here. Outside temperature is 45 degrees, zero wind."

"Roger, Preston, Martie—a good idea about identification," responded Pete Allen's voice. *"We should use as little information as possible in flight. We are on long finals incoming from the south."*

"Roger that," replied Preston. "We have you visual and you are cleared for landing. We will land after you. Over."

It was amazing to see the C-130s land. The first pilot touched down where the lights should have been. Preston assumed that Martie had moved them earlier. The large aircraft turned on the runway, returned, and stopped on the side of the apron next to the refueling point before the second one came in on final approach. It landed the same way and parked on the apron as close to the hangar door as possible

Buck then brought *Baby Huey* in and landed her on the dirt next to the hangar to get her unloaded. Martie came running up and stopped short when she saw what was inside. More cases of candy, this time with 'Southwest' written all over the boxes. Maggie came running up and a line was formed by the growing group.

"Bottles of miniatures of gin, rum, and whiskey?" she asked of Preston as the boxes passed her. "We need this stuff?"

"Better than dying of thirst," Preston replied, smiling sweetly at her. "The truck was sitting by itself on the tarmac and there were weird-looking vehicles driving around trying to figure out who we were. It was Carlos' idea."

"There must be a million little bags of peanuts," Martie sighed looking at the sky above her.

"I would like *Tom* refueled first," asked the General, as he came up to see what was going on.

"Sorry, General," replied Preston, smiling. "We'll only be another few minutes. Carlos wants to get up to Washington to get his father and uncle and he and Buck are taking off ASAP. Buck, go and hotwire Tank #-3 while we empty your Huey for you. That's the jet fuel the General needs." Buck nodded and went over to the refueling area.

"Understandable," General Allen replied, and turned to whistle in the direction of the closest C-130. A dozen Air Force troops came out running to help with the unloading. A minute later, Buck and Carlos were preparing for take-off as the last boxes were carried into the growing pile in the hangar. Martie ran into the house and returned with two Tupperware containers and a small cooler.

"Lunch for you two since you are heading out. We packed sandwiches, a bag of potato chips, cookies, and an apple for each of you—also a six-pack of cold Cokes." Carlos and Buck, already in the seats, thanked Martie as Preston reminded them about first names. General Allen gave Buck two automatic carbines and told the Huey pilots that he would be landing at Andrews a few minutes after them once he refueled the C-130.

Baby Huey took off a minute later, and Preston walked over to see Jennifer waving out of the small open pilot's window. "Fill her up lad, unleaded, and 2,000 gallons. Hurry up!" she shouted down at him and Preston presented her with one finger of his right hand.

"How do we fill her up?" asked Preston as the General caught up with him.

"We have openings on top of the wings for gravity filling. It looks like your gas line should reach our guys who are climbing up there right now. We can't fill her fuselage tanks because they need pressurized filling, but Captain Watkins can drain the fuel we put into the wing tanks into the fuselage tanks. I want just enough to get to Andrews and back. That's two hours of flight so about 1,800 gallons would be safe."

"Our meters don't work, General. Can Captain Watkins tell when she has enough?"

"Easily. Fill the left wing tank. That should hold a thousand gallons," responded the General. "Captain Watkins can route the fuel into the fuselage tanks, fill the same wing tank again, and then she can route the second amount into the other fuselage tank. That will keep our center-of-gravity balanced and get us there and back. Now let's go in for some lunch and I can fill you in while they refuel."

Maggie and Martie were out giving Jennifer and Sally lunch boxes, so Preston led the way into the house. Joe and David were already there eating with Michael, Barbara, Grandpa Roebels and the kids, and Preston noticed that Joe's truck was full of military gear.

“Lunch, everybody,” stated Preston. “Thanks guys for waiting for us workers out there.”

“Orders from General Martie who overrides you, Captain Strong,” joked Joe, his mouth full of food.

“I have 20 minutes to eat and then we will have our 11:00 meeting at 11:30,” stated General Allen with a smile. “Discipline has gone to pot.” Sally, Maggie, and Martie came in and joined in the group.

“Well, since we’re all here, I guess we can get started. I’ll share my news while I’m waiting for Detective Smart to come back online,” stated General Allen. “Joe, David, you can report after I do, and then we’ll hear from Preston. Hopefully by then we can hear from California. I’m sure he’s running late.”

The general sat down while Martie worked on serving the two men some lunch. “Seymour Johnson is down, and so are Pope Field and the whole of Fort Bragg. I think they have two old jeeps between them that did garbage duty or something. At the moment, we have the only two flying Air Force aircraft. Pope has a couple more C-130s that will take a few days to get flying again. Both bases have zero communications, but are on high alert. There are a couple of radios that we can have operational in a day or two, but not long-range like yours, Preston. Neither base has any electricity at all. There are several old generators and we have engineers working on them right now, but they will take a week or more to service and get active. Preston you told me the other night that you have a few big diesel generators to spare? I need them. How many can I have?”

“I have two that will work immediately and we have the forklift that can get them into the belly of a C-130,” replied Preston. “There are two more that will take a day or so of work to put together. Actually, if I give them to you, your diesel engineers could get them up and running within hours and your Air Force electrician could feed their electrical needs straight into the diesel engines within a day or so. It is simple electrical engineering."

"Good!" exclaimed the general. "We will load the two perfect ones once we have fueled up. I want to take one to Andrews and then I'm flying over to Hill in Salt Lake City, fuel permitting. Whatever you want in return is yours, Preston. I'm worried about the President. I believe he must be trapped in the White House if Andrews is closed down, and I want to see who's running this country. It could be us for all I know. Now Joe, David, let us have your news, please. What did you see out there?"

"A lousy world is beginning to stir out there," started Joe. "We saw two old vehicles running around, one with a bunch of teenage kids with guns. As soon as they saw we also had guns, they drove away like a bat out of hell. They were just looking for trouble. We saw three dead people. Two had been run over—I don't know if by accident or intentionally—and one old man had had his head shot off. Other than that, we saw masses of dead vehicles of all sorts out there, and a group of people ripping through a supermarket and taking food and stuff to their houses on dozens of lawn tractors. One guy was even patrolling his yard with his lawn tractor and he had a shotgun at the ready. He just gave us a nasty look when we drove past. I'd hate to see him if those kids in the car find him. There'll be a gun battle for sure."

"It's going to get pretty ugly out there in about a week, or even less I reckon," added David. "I need to go back and load up about a ton of ammo for my Ferrets. I'm glad we'll have armored vehicles and I believe we are going to need them. Joe and I are going to his house and set up the forward and rear-standing machine guns on both the jeeps. I'm going to get my Ferrets loaded and we'll be ready to ride shotgun for you guys in less than about four hours, with Joe's sons' help. I believe we need to arm ourselves, and quickly."

"Preston?" asked General Allen. Preston told them about the

situation at the airport and the four gas trailers totaling 20,000 gallons that could be commandeered. Joe cut in, adding that he could get two of them today with some help, and then work on getting the other two the next day. Preston suggested that he, Michael, Joe, and David should be enough.

It was then that Will Smart called them from California. They were eager to hear some good news, but there was none. Will said 'Hi' to Maggie and the kids and got on with his news.

"The roads are nearly impassable with dead cars everywhere. It took Mike and me 90 minutes to get to the main gate at you-know where. The boss of the place told me not to say anything over the radio. The guards told me to scram, until I told them what you had told me to tell them, General, then they escorted me in my truck to the colonel's office, since they had nothing working in the whole place. The colonel was sort of relaxed when I gave him your call sign and told him that you were in North Carolina and, as far as we all thought, reckoned that this problem was countrywide and could even be worldwide. He told me to give you the message that all birds are down and that includes all the blackbirds, whatever that means."

"I can't say over the microphone, Detective, but I will fill you in when I can. Carry on."

"There is nothing moving at that place—no cars, trucks, no planes, no helicopters, no electricity, no nothing except guns and soldiers on foot. The old man has old radios that will take a few days to power up their old batteries, but none of them will reach you on the East Coast. I told him that you are mobile and he asked you to come and visit. Other than that, it's fine around here. There is a sort of quiet that could break at any moment, but we haven't heard any gunfire yet. Our supplies will last us a couple of weeks, because for some dumb reason our old freezer is still working and I found our old refrigerator in the

shed is still working. The old stuff RULES here, man!" Will ended.

"What do you want us to do?' asked Maggie.

"Hell, Mags," he replied *"I reckon you are safest over there. Let's see what tomorrow brings and if it gets bad over here, I'll head back to the base with Mike, his wife, and his two girls. We were offered a place to stay since we're friends of the General and all that."* Everybody in North Carolina laughed.

"Will, I will be coming over there soon," added the general "Let's keep a steady connection because we will lose you if you move, unless you can take the radio with you. Preston, can Detective Smart move his radio?"

"Sure," interrupted young Ben. "The way we've got it set up is that as long as it's within 90-120 miles of the closest antenna on the cell phone tower, or in direct sight, it will work. And the closest cell-phone tower is about 50 miles east of Edwards, which is even better."

"Will," Preston said, getting back on the radio. "You can move anytime you think it's necessary and it will be better for everyone concerned because we will all have communications. Do you understand what I mean?"

"10/4. Understood loud and clear. I just pick this baby up and transport it, right?"

"Yes, as long as the antenna connection is separated from the set, it should be easy to carry. If not, you can always to get the electricians on base to help you, I'm sure they will be more than willing."

General Allen thanked Will and left with Preston to load the generators outside. The fuelling was complete and it took them half an hour with the forklift, including tying the heavy engines down inside the aircraft, to get them all loaded in. Preston was becoming amazed at what these C-130s could carry. The engines weighed a ton each and Jennifer told him that the aircraft wouldn't even notice the weight.

They watched as Jennifer and General Allen took off, to the north this time, and the aircraft didn't use a foot more runway than the last time. Preston shook his head in wonder, but there was more to be done. It was time to help unload Sally's C-130 and here he got a shock. The soldiers and all the remaining civilians started working to carry tents and supplies out of the rear door of the large aircraft. They asked Preston where they should set them up, and he suggested each side of the old barn. It was time to keep all the working aircraft on this side of the runway and move the General's dead King Air to the other side out of the way. Michael had already moved the Pilatus off the apron and it stood facing the runway on the other side of the fuel tanks.

"You guys got families?" asked Preston as he went up to help.

"Yes sir," was the reply from the man who seemed in charge. "I'm First Sergeant Perry, sir. The married men living off base are allowed to go home on a day's leave to see their families. The married men on base are on guard duty and have nothing better to do since our families are already on base, sir. Where do we put these machine guns?"

"Machine guns?" asked Preston.

"Yes sir! We were ordered to bring a couple of them. Actually, we have six of them plus 12,000 rounds of .50-caliber ammo. The General said that we should set one or two up on your guard tower to face your entrance. The guys back at base are searching for a couple of old 500-pound bombs for your Mustangs and we might even have some rockets for your P-38, if you're lucky. Tech Sergeants Smith and Matheson over there, sir, are experts on armaments and the rocket hitches we brought along, and they are itching to work on your aircraft, sir. We also have a dozen rolls of barbed wire and were ordered to place them around the gate at your entrance along the frontal boundary, and we will bring in more if needed on our next trip."

Preston noticed that a couple of the soldiers were far older than he was. These weren't kids, he realized. The General had brought men who knew their trades.

"The gate and tower is your concern, and you know what to do. Just don't shoot anybody coming in. The ammo dump is in the old barn over there. Use the fork lift. You'll be surprised what we already have in there. They," he motioned to the tech sergeants, "don't touch my aircraft without my permission, understand?"

"Yes, sir," was the reply.

"Are you guys going back today?" asked Preston.

"No sir. We are here on guard duty under your command until the General tells us otherwise. We have our own field tent, food, and everything we need and we will be on guard duty in shifts of four, every four hours until further orders, sir. I plan to have two men constantly up in the tower and two walking the perimeter around the entrance area at all times. I just need to know where we can place our four porta-potties, sir."

CHAPTER 18

Z-Day 1

IT WAS MID-DAY IN Minneapolis, and several other cities in the north. Temperatures had risen slightly to -10 degrees and it was far warmer than it had been several hours ago. Parts of Canada were still in the -20s and the two major problems facing people still alive were a warm place to stay and food to feed their human bodies to create inner warmth.

Even though most of the northerners were used to extreme cold weather, they did not live in it for long periods of time. Some were lucky and had their heater systems working—mostly gas or very old building furnaces that were fed fuel oil or could be heated with wood or coal. For many in new and modern buildings, it was worse—the more modern the building, the worse it was. For the ones who were outside, they congregated by the fires burning since midnight. Others started new fires, sometimes lighting up wooden structures like single-car wooden garages, or their own garden tool sheds.

Many tried to stay in bed, the only place to keep the body warmth in, all thinking that this was temporary and the authorities would get the electricity back on soon. Parties were starting as fast as others were dying. People who had heat allowed others to share their heat if they brought food or gas for the grill, the more food and drink the merrier. Shops were beginning to be broken into. Many were protected by their owners, but the supermarkets were devoid of people and they were prime targets.

On the first day, and with no police around to curb shoplifting, all supermarkets were still pretty much secure. Here and there, the first brave people had broken a window and were sneaking around trying not to be seen and helping themselves to all they could carry—fresh produce, milk, eggs, the unfrozen meat in the deli, bakery items, and of course beer, wine and all bottles of alcohol. Many were still disciplined by their upbringing and tried to pay for the food at the unattended cash registers by leaving money. Then they bartered food from their escapades to get into the houses that still had heat if theirs didn't.

Where there was fire, people began to gather and meet new friends, to try and help the elderly, and to be good citizens, while others were contemplating how to become rich, stay alive, and protect themselves from others who thought the same way. These people needed transportation, men, and guns.

Still, for thousands of people in the smaller, less crowded cities, many were learning quickly how to stay alive. Everyone was sure that somebody would turn on the power at some point. For others in worse areas, there were many dead or dying—frozen corpses in bed, outside in their vehicles, in hospitals that were becoming devoid of help, in old age homes, and in prisons and other places where people weren't free to move and their controllers had disappeared to look after their own families. These unfortunates were next, the cold quickly seeping into their veins. With each subsequent cold, dark night, the death toll climbed, taking its victims from those groups of people who were the oldest and weakest.

Times Square was now deserted, apart from the bodies of the thousands of people who hadn't made it out. Several fires were starting to die down, while others continued to find new fuel.

Here around the fires, people could be found trying to keep warm. The underground areas were full of hopefuls who were just waiting for the electricity to come on. At least there was no wind chill, and the temperature was the same as the earth around them—a warmer 40 to 50 degrees. The Metro was a place where many of the visitors had found refuge. The platforms were filled to overflowing. Most of the crowds kept warm by huddling together while they waited for the next train that would never come. In some stations, the trains were stationary in the station and even more people had fitted themselves into the enclosed areas. Many were sleeping or sitting on the seats, eating whatever they had found or stolen, smoking, drinking, or just trying to stay out of each other's way.

Tall buildings were still secure, nobody wanting to climb up the long staircases, or down them. Here, wind chill was a factor. The buildings were slowly losing their heat and the constant cold winds were gradually stealing the warmth through the many windows, balcony doors, cracks, and holes. The death rate had slowed for the first time that day by mid-day. For millions of people in the upper northern areas around the world, who were safe from crime and the streets, it was a day of waiting—their faith constant that the power would come on. They had food and drink, although many only had cold sustenance and their questions were: *"Where are the police, fire engines, and ambulances?"* and *"When is that asshole in charge of all this going to turn on the power!"*

* * *

The warehouse on the Hudson was quiet. Captain Mallory was the only one awake, and had started taking notice of the hundreds of packed cases around them. There must be food in them somewhere. Then he remembered the refrigerator many of the passengers and crew were staying warm in and he thought it was a good place to start. He opened the door to find many still asleep, curled up close to each other keeping warm.

He flashed the torch around for the first time towards the rear of the fridge and saw boxes of food items tucked away in the dark recesses. Cheeses that looked like they had come from Europe with the description on the cases seemed to be in many of the boxes. There were other cases with Chinese, Russian, French and German writing on them. And it looked like there was enough to last all 143 of them quite a while.

He walked to the back, over sleeping bodies, and took a smaller box off one of the shelves. Then he noticed a second door on the rear wall. It looked like, and he assumed that it was, a freezer door. He was right and in it his flashlight identified cases of frozen meat. The captain closed the door quickly as the cold air rushed out and prompted several complaints from the bodies on the ground.

"I've got the cheese," he reported to his co-pilot John, half asleep on a chair by the door. "I'm off to find something to go with it."

It was time to seriously look around, but he wanted to locate the rest of the passengers, who were in a couple of other areas in the warehouse. He returned to where he had found the luxury vehicles and as he thought, others had found them as well based on the mist on the inside of the windows.

By now, sunlight was streaming through the east windows and he noticed another door leading into an area behind the back wall. This door had steel bars over the windows and he tried the door and looked through the window. It looked like a museum—a vehicle museum—or at least a storage area for old vehicles. He could see what looked like a 50-year old fire engine, an old 1950s Studebaker police car, a couple of old SWAT team police-blue vehicles that were definitely from the 1960s, and then what looked like a couple of old white ambulances. The large area looked like a movie set, or at least storage facilities for movie equipment, since there were also steel lifts, cameras, and other film-making equipment.

Then he saw what he thought was more important—a couple of fancy home gas grills standing in a corner, already set up to feed the workers or something as they stood under a old steel kitchen hood where a more permanent cooking area must have been. He could see holes on the opposite wall where plugs or equipment had been removed. This part of the high-ceilinged room looked like some sort of old restaurant. The front area was wood-paneled and on the walls hung old black and white pictures.

The door was firm and locked as he tried it for the second time. His co-pilot and a couple of the flight attendants found him still trying the door.

"There are cooking facilities in there," the captain explained to the new arrivals. "Where there are gas grills, there is a way to cook food. John, I want you to back the forklift up to the main door to the outside and let me slide out. None of the inner doors work or will open. They are all heavily secured, we have no keys and no way to open them from the inside; hopefully I will have more chance from the outside. I want to go around the outer building and see if I can get into this room behind the door. I think it's time somebody looked around it and it might as well be me."

John nodded and he walked back to the forklift. He got in, started it up, and looked at the controls for a few seconds trying to figure out the workings of the machine—it certainly wasn't a 737. He figured it out and slowly let out the brake, the forklift moving backwards slowly and the door opening.

"Three loud slow thumps on the door followed by three quick ones will be me wanting to come back in," ordered Captain Mallory, and he squeezed through the narrow gap. John moved the machine into forward gear and closed the door tight behind the captain and sat there waiting.

The outside air smelled horrible—a smoky mist hung in the air with a slight breeze moving it across his nostrils. He knelt and looked around carefully. Nothing, apart from the water, was moving. The wharf was mostly destroyed by a couple of boats that were half sunk or stuck into the banks on both sides of the river. The other side was a couple of hundred yards away and a massive fire was still in full swing burning up a warehouse much like the one they were in. It was a few hundred yards further down river, and what he could see on his side wasn't much, but it was time for him to move. There was debris flowing past in a non-stop tide as he slowly moved along the wall of the warehouse upriver, his eyes noticing every bit of movement. He looked up and couldn't see the sky at all from what looked and smelled like Los Angeles smog.

He got to the first door and tried it. This side of the building had no windows on the river side. It was where the kitchen might have been and the door was most probably the rear entrance at one time. It was steel, locked, and felt like a safe in a bank vault.

"There was no going in this way," he thought to himself, and ran for the corner of the building. There was about a 50-foot space between warehouses and the next warehouse showed signs of damage where parts of an aircraft had gone through the roof and upper wall. He could tell because part of a rear wing was sticking out of the wall next to a flight of blackened stairs. The building was wooden rather than brick, and part of the wall was black and half-disintegrated as well as the roof above it.

"Its most probably the same wing that crashed into our warehouse door." He ran across to look inside, and apart from a few smoldering fires, the warehouse was virtually empty, apart from several bodies lying here and there like rag dolls, and a group of offices that were on the far side where the whole side wall had disappeared and was still burning quietly.

He ran back to his warehouse and to the front corner facing

the street. The road was double-lane in both directions and empty apart from the three bodies lying there—killed hours earlier. There was no door on the side and he knelt, listening for noise, and looked in every direction before moving slowly forward. It was deathly quiet apart from the crackling of fires coming from all directions. A part of another building somewhere else fell down and there was a roar of movement as a wall or roof fell in then the crackling and cracking continued. He reached another door at the front of the building. This time it was a garage door, freshly installed compared to the sight inside the room. It was a heavy door, would open upwards and there were two massive steel locks holding it down. The top of the locks were as thick as his little figure, and the steel security around the locks was the same strength.

"It would take a welding torch to get through those," he thought and moved on to the next door. This was an entrance door to the offices. He had noticed a narrow parking area in front of the building and between the main road and the building itself. Again, the door was steel, had a sign reading "U.S. Customs" on it, and was as sturdy as the one on the wharf side. A combination box was on the door, the same as all these doors had on the inside, and the captain realized that electricity would be needed to open the doors—something they were lacking right now. He then ran to an iron fence around the large vehicle-entrance door on the front of the warehouse. The fence separated the entrance from both sides and had a locked sliding gate located directly on the road with a small security booth next to it. Here, the door was bigger—big enough to allow a tall delivery truck in. On this door was a sign that stated what would happen to anybody entering these premises illegally in big letters. A set of non-working traffic lights were in front of the gate and security booth, and the captain had to go around the fence and onto the road where the three dead bodies lay to get around.

He noticed a pistol tucked in one of the dead men's belts and he ran up to the body, pulled out the pistol, checked both men for life, found a small clip of ammunition in one of the leather jacket pockets, and ran back around the fence to the other side. Again, the warehouse on the fourth side was totally secure, and he arrived back at the entrance to give the coded taps on the door and re-enter the building.

"This place is as secure as a prison. We are in a U.S. Customs bonded warehouse," he told the group waiting for him by the door. "There are three bodies outside the front door, so don't think about taking a walk. There are fires and dead bodies in every direction and no electricity anywhere. We are as safe as can be for today. John here can show everyone the refrigerator where several people slept last night. There is food in there—cold, but better than nothing—and hopefully you all have a gourmet palette. I'm going to get into the room next door. There are a lot of old vehicles. I'm sure they are useless, but I want to check out the appliances. Some of you try and get a sort of food table organized for everyone, and I'll work on the gas grills and see if we can grill up some warm food."

After he showed the group the way to the refrigerator unit, John helped the captain case the entire wall outside the vehicle room. There seemed to be no way in, until they came across a heat and air vent hanging underneath the office space. The air vent was an addition and a metal, round air tube going through the wall into the other room. It was just wide enough to allow a human body through, and they had to find a crowbar to break a medium-sized padlock keeping the exit vent closed. Once open, Captain Mallory was able to climb into the tube. He was helped by several men and first he gingerly tested it to see if it would hold his weight. It held, so taking his flashlight, he slowly inched his way towards a second vent 20 or so yards in front of him and directly over the other room.

The vent door on the other side was also locked but with a

padlock this time inside the vent to stop anybody from the other side getting inside the tube. It was rusty and old and the captain shouted down the tube for the crowbar to break it open. It was difficult since he had only a little room to work in, but after drawing blood on one of his fingers by cutting it on a sharp metal splinter on the inside of the tube and cursing a few colorful words, he managed to snap the lock. The steel vent was rusty and hadn't been opened for a long time, but he used his weight and slowly the vent opened downwards letting him slide, butt first into the second room. He managed to unfold his body and hung from the vent before dropping the last couple of feet to the floor below.

He stood up, wiped the dust off his trousers, and looked around. It was pretty dark, the only light coming from barred rectangular windows about 20 feet up and only a foot or so wide. They stretched around the three outer walls and gave him enough light to see the whole room. It was the size and height of a couple of basketball courts and there was an actual movable basketball pole and net in one corner. There were only five vehicles in total—it was large mirrored walls on the opposite side that had made it look like there were more vehicles in the room, and only one ambulance.

"The ambulance must have been used for several things in its lifetime," he thought to himself. The room now really looked like a film storage room for equipment. There were camera stands, a dozen movie cameras on a shelf along the wall, microphones, and grips. Chairs were neatly stacked in one corner and he looked towards the other wall by the old kitchen area where there was an obvious workshop where repairs were done. There was also a large six-foot chest freezer and stand-up refrigerator behind a partition, with two restaurant-style bathrooms in two enclosed areas to the rear.

The gas grills had been used recently because there was a smell of food hovering around them, and he opened the refrigerator to find it stocked with full cans of still-cold beer and soft drinks, pounds of butter and a couple of gallons of milk. There was the odd chocolate bar, the same type of Swiss cheese he had taken out of the fridge on the other side of the warehouse, and what looked like someone's uneaten sandwiches in a plastic container. In the little freezer were three bottles of Russian Vodka, still semi-iced—two were full but one had been nearly emptied.

He looked toward the door into the main warehouse and gave the thumbs up to the three or so faces staring at him through the small jail-sized window. He decided to try the freezer next and was happy to see the still-frozen packets of hamburger and hot dog rolls, hamburger patties, hot dogs, sausages and several more cases of deli meats, frozen bottles of orange juice and more bottles of the same vodka. There were also three cases of Omaha steaks wrapped in bacon—enough for lunch for the whole crowd with 48 steaks to a case.

Above the chest freezer was another shelf stocked with several large commercial cans of baked beans, corn, a few five-pound cans of skinned tomatoes, and smaller cans of other greens. There was also an open case of chocolate chip cookie packages.

He returned to the gas grills, opened them both, opened the gas knobs on the small bottles underneath, and found a box of matches on a shelf. The smell of gas hit his nostrils as he lit both of them. He switched them off and went over to the door to the warehouse. There were no locks on his side and no way to open it. It was thin steel and secure.

The captain then searched the workshop area and found a welding-cutting torch and gas bottle and hauled it back to the door. The torch lit on the first try with a match and the captain played around with it until he got the bluest flame, then proceeded to try and cut a hole in the door by the lock. He was sure that it wasn't on the best heat, but the door heated up and a small hole appeared after a few minutes. It took him about 30 minutes before finally, with the room full of smoke, the heated metal around the lock fell apart and the hot door opened in towards him.

He felt good, a little worried about how he was going to explain and probably have to pay for all this damage, but happy enough to shake his co-pilot's hand on the other side. He looked through the door and found many eyes watching his progress and several others standing by a set table with an odd assortment of food on the table.

"What have you guys found to eat so far?" he was curious.

"Cheese and caviar!" was the not so enthusiastic answer with 'eews' coming from a couple of the kids in the group.

"No cheeseburgers, I'm afraid, but I found steak, hamburgers, and hot dogs for lunch." Several cheers went up from the crowd. He then asked his flight attendants to help supervise the cooking. He didn't want to pay for the whole warehouse, just the portion he had destroyed. He was hoping that the airline would foot the bill for the food.

The crew got busy while he inspected the vehicles. They were in good condition and had obviously been recently wiped down and polished as there was only a very thin layer of dust on them. The two bigger vehicles were real-looking SWAT Team trucks with the letters SWAT on each side, as well as the NYPD insignia on the driver and passenger doors. In the rear of the trucks were seats along the walls for about two dozen adults at the most. A small, thin, barred window stretched along the top on both sides. In the cab was enough room for another two or three adults, and the cab roof had a sliding glass sunroof. A radio caught his eye and he switched it on. It was an old 1970s CB-style radio that the police must have used back in the early days and he realized that these were not models but real 40 year-old trucks that the NYPD had once used as SWAT trucks. The radio was silent as he played with the dial and a crackle was the only thing he heard. He sat there for at least 20 minutes and played with the radio.

He couldn't find any life out there in radio land, and gave up. The tank was half full of gas and he switched on the ignition and the engine turned over without starting. It worked! The second truck was exactly the same, maybe a few years older, a little more scratched and beat up inside, but everything including the starter motor worked.

The police car was next. His father had driven the same Studebaker when he was a kid. The keys were in the ignition and the dash lit up as he turned the key. It also had a simple radio, older than the ones in the truck, and it turned on as he turned the dial. The gas tank was full.

The old ambulance with a large red cross on each side was an old white Chevy, built in the 1960s, and was completely empty. In the back were a few folding chairs and a couple of click-boards used to start filming. The engine turned over, just like the others, and it had half a tank of gas. Last was the fire engine, also around the same era. It was a beautiful 1960 Howe fire truck in perfect condition with side pipes and everything. There were three rows of three seats, enough for nine adults, and again he switched on the ignition and everything lit up on the dash. The gas tank was nearly full, the water tank showed a 12,000 gallon maximum and the current level stood at just under a quarter. It had a slightly more modern radio than the old 1950s Studebaker.

Captain Mallory did the math. If, or when, they had to move, he could cut the outside locks, open the doors, and if everybody squashed in together, and another dozen or so on the back of the fire engine, they could just about take everybody. Did everybody want to go somewhere? That was the next question he wanted answered.

By the time he got back to the cooking, the second round of burgers were on the grill with many already eating their first real food in 24 hours. He was handed a burger and sat down on a nearby drum to wolf it down hungrily. He hadn't realized how hungry he was until he had the burger in his hands.

As he was sitting there, it suddenly occurred to him that there were two 44-gallon red drums of fuel. He was sitting on one and John was sitting on the other. He dinged the side of the drum and it sounded half full. The co-pilot saw and copied, dinging the can he was on. It sounded full.

"Thinking of getting out of Dodge?" John asked. He had watched his boss the whole time, knowing that anybody who could land an aircraft and save his life once, and then find him a burger this good, was certainly worth following into the gates of hell, if he asked him to.

"After what I saw this morning—people being killed on the street outside, the whole area around us looking like a war zone —I think we might need to get out of Dodge at some point," Captain Mallory replied.

"Where would we go?" asked his co-pilot, munching on his burger.

"Well, if the electricity comes back on, which I'm still thinking is a possibility, then we are all saved and I'm in big trouble for breaking into a government facility and stealing food. If it doesn't come on, say by tonight, it's going to get colder and colder in here. We have enough cheese for a couple of days, and these burgers and hot dogs will last us until breakfast tomorrow morning. If nothing has changed by breakfast, and we hear gunfire outside tonight, then I think it is time to leave for greener, and in my mind, less snowy pastures tomorrow. I would set a course for due South."

"Sounds like a plan," replied John. "I prefer Florida at this time of year anyway. Do you think a daylight escape from whatever is out there, is safer than under darkness—say tomorrow night?"

"Well, we will be in official vehicles and I'm thinking any unsavory types might think the cavalry is coming and leave us alone long enough for us to get on I-95 south. All the vehicle radios work and we can fill up the tanks before we leave, since there is a hand pump in the workshop. We can take the rest of this fuel with us and make Washington or even down to Virginia before we have to stop. It's hopefully much warmer down there, and I will be more than happy to explain myself to a police or Army check point. There must be something going on that is bigger than this city's total destruction."

As he said that, they heard a large rumble followed by an earthshaking explosion in the direction of Manhattan, and several people rushed upstairs to the high windows on the second floor. Several came back down to report several minutes later that there was smoke and dust everywhere in the center of the city and it looked the same as on September 11th, 2001. Nobody said much for a while after that. Lunch was over, jugs of defrosting orange juice were passed around, and the captain asked the flight attendants to get all the people together. It was meeting time.

"We seem to be several people short," he noted, scanning the crowd in front of him. "Someone has already left?"

"Some guy said he had had enough of you breaking up the place," said a teenage boy. "He said he was going to get help and find the police. He was pretty pissed off and had a big mouth. He ate three of the burgers and then he rounded up a bunch of people, mostly men, and said that they were going out to search for help. They left about three minutes ago. The door is still open where they reversed the forklift." The co-pilot immediately got up to close the heavy door and asked the chief flight attendant to count the remaining people.

"Ninety-seven passengers and five crew," Pam Wallace, a pretty blonde, told them several minutes later. The co-pilot returned, reported that he had looked around outside and saw the missing group of passengers walking towards Manhattan where the dust and dirt was everywhere in the air. There were at least 40 of them.

Suddenly, they heard gunfire coming from the outside the building. It was several shots, and from different guns—a couple sounded like shotguns and at least two from a high-powered rifle. It was enough to silence the group.

"It's dangerous out there," said the captain. "I saw a man shot by police officers last night, execution style, and that made me worried. New York cops just don't do that. Most of the other guys I saw out of the windows are not the type of guest you want your daughter to bring home for dinner. By the sound of that explosion just now, I reckon that was a decent-sized building going down. Most probably an aircraft and then the resulting fire were the cause of its demise. My co-pilot and I saw at least a dozen aircraft crash last night while I was getting our aircraft down in the river. We were very lucky with our landing and I don't know about you guys, but I feel that I'm already on borrowed time."

Heads nodded in agreement as the remaining crowd listened intently. "My gut feeling is that the things we have seen and heard are not just limited to this city, but are more widespread. We all have family somewhere—maybe here in New York, maybe in other places—but they are not going to find us here. I think we need to go and find help ourselves, or we could very possibly freeze to death once the food is gone. With the vehicles we found today, we can drive to the I-95 corridor and make our way south to hopefully find help. Once we leave here, we are not coming back. I would prefer to be out of a city with no electricity than in one—in greener pastures, if you know what I mean. Maybe there is help just outside the city. Maybe we are in a war zone, but we won't know until we move. I would like to leave tomorrow morning directly after breakfast, if the electricity doesn't come on by then. Each of you will need to make a decision—either to stay here and wait for help, or get in one of these vehicles and leave with the rest of us tomorrow morning. Each of you must make a decision that you can live with. Of course, we will take the extra gas and as much food as we can carry, and I'm going to inspect every one of these crates in the warehouse to see what's in them before we leave. Any comments, now is the time?"

"What do you think are our chances of being rescued if we stay here?" was the first question.

"50/50," was the reply. "And every day could be better or worse here in the city as the gangs with weapons begin to rule if the Army and police don't get control," the captain answered.

"What chance do we have if we go with you?" asked a young girl.

"50/50," was the same reply. "I prefer the country over the city. There's more chance to find food, less chance of violence, friendlier people, and possible warmer temperatures. I think that we have enough fuel for at least 400 miles, maybe more, if we turn this place upside down and look everywhere."

There was a lot of mumbling as people looked at each other. Most of the passengers were single people, with several couples and three families with children. There was a young girl—the young girl who had asked the question—who was special cargo, or under 16 and under the protection of a flight attendant.

It was time to check boxes.

* * *

Parts of Washington were slowly burning. Whole streets were alight with fire and others had none. There were more wooden buildings in the older and poorer parts of town—houses and three- to four-story buildings closer together and a slight wind from the East, five-ten miles per hour, had picked up. The city was going to get some rain later that night, and the moisture in the air was starting to feel obvious. It was being fueled by warmer air being pulled in from the coast, and the temperature was several degrees above freezing.

A section of the Pentagon was now nothing more than stone rubble and blackened embers. The visible fire was out, but the building still glowed from the inside as fires many levels below the street still burned. Georgetown was a mess. Many streets were also blackened. Fires were slowly being fed by the wind and embers were blowing toward new food to feast on.

There were masses of people on the streets in Washington in comparison to New York, where it was colder and everyone was either in buildings or underground. Many carried guns for protection, many were keeping their eyes on the fires, and many were turning over bodies in the streets looking for valuables. Confrontations were beginning to happen. There were groups of people beginning to get angry at the lack of electricity and warmth, angry about their depleting food resources, and angry about people robbing valuables from their poor dead neighbors.

On one street, there were two teenagers with pistols aiming them at anybody who looked at them. They did their best to look mean and were trying to hold up their trousers at the same time. The third was kicking bodies and turning them over with his feet and then bending over to check pockets or pull the clothing off.

Half a dozen men walked out into the street from two houses 50 feet from the three boys, who immediately trained their pistols in the group's direction. One swore at the men and told them where to go, that this was their domain. The third one ripped the jacket and skirt off the body he was searching on the ground and growled at the men mockingly like a dog baring its teeth, smiling and telling his accomplices to kill the approaching old men. Two men in front of the group kept walking towards the boys, and a second later they moved aside to let the next two men through.

They had shotguns, and used them, as the smiles on the boys' faces disappeared in a split second. The two younger bodyguards holding pistols literally flew into the air, splattering the middle boy with blood as a round of buckshot hit them both square in the bellies.

The third turned to run as the second line of men allowed the third pair through. The last looter flew higher than the first two, as two shotgun shells hit his head, back and legs all at the same time. There wasn't much of him left as he collapsed on the ground and lay still.

"Let's hang these bodies up at either end of our street and write a warning to anybody who wants to enter here," shouted one of the men who had led the group in. "And I think we should carry all the other dead bodies to the end of the street and hope somebody comes to pick them up. It really pissed me off to see Tom's daughter being pulled apart like that. We need some dignity in this neighborhood, and I think we should get our friends on other streets around us to set up neighborhood watches and protection details."

* * *

The President was frustrated. There was nothing he could do. They had the gas in the kitchen going and a hot meal was being provided to everybody. He ate with the staff. The food was good and plentiful. His bodyguards ate after the rest had eaten, and they were unsmiling and fidgety. The President told them that he had had enough stress for one day and that they were getting on everybody's nerves.

There was nothing anybody could do but wait. News came from the basement that an old electrical generator had been found behind a bricked up wall, and two electricians were trying to get it working. It was an old gasoline-run generator, of all the things stored in the basement of the White House, and the panels and switches looked like they worked. They needed to rewire it from the generator panel to the one of the main electrical boxes to feed power into the system. They would need gas, and the President had ordered his Secret Service men to go and find some containers and fill them up from any stationery vehicles. When they refused he had blown his top.

"Who is the President of this country?" he asked them, furious. They nodded to him. "Who gives you orders?" he asked. They replied, "The Director of the Secret Service."

"And who gives him his orders?" They shrugged and a couple murmured that only the President could. "So, who is the President of the United States at the moment?" Again, they nodded towards him. "Good!" the President replied. "Since your boss is nowhere to be found, I am officially taking over. I'm now your direct supervisor. Is that clear? Now leave me alone and go do what I asked you to do. If you don't, I'm going to order those soldiers over there to shoot you, and they WILL listen to my orders, capich?"

They all nodded, looked at each other, looked at the several armed soldiers looking at them, and smiled, deciding that it was in their best interests to do as their new boss told them. That was when they heard an incoming helicopter approaching from the direction of Andrews AFB.

"Thank God!" exclaimed the President. "At least something works in this country."

Everyone was surprised to see what they considered an ancient Huey approaching them. The Secret Service immediately pulled their guns, and the President angrily told them to go and do as he had ordered—his hands on his hips. He asked a couple of soldiers to form a barrier between him and the landing site, and they walked out to the lawn as the helicopter approached. It didn't come in on the same line the usual helicopters used, but it was a sight for sore eyes, nevertheless. It was a foot or so from touchdown when the side door opened and an Air Force general jumped out. The pilot lifted back up, turned, and leaned the helicopter forward to leave in the same direction it had arrived.

"General Pete Allen, Mr. President. I'm second in command of the Air Force. You may remember me. You were considering me for possible promotion with the retirement of General Miles in March."

"Have we met, General?" the President asked.

"We have been introduced by the Chief of Staff and by my good naval friend, Vice Admiral Martin Rogers. We met at Andrews about a year ago. I'm in charge of Andrews and every U.S. Air Force base around the world."

"That's right," the President remembered. "You were standing at the door when I entered Air Force One for the first time."

"Correct, Mr. President. One of my jobs is to check your aircraft before your first ride to make sure everything is in order. I used to fly President Johnson around Texas in the old days. I have come to brief you on what we know so far. It's not much, and we have no answers but, at I can at least fill a few holes."

Buck and Carlos left the White House in the Huey, amused to see every weapon in the area trained on them.

"Thank god I didn't need to fart back there," laughed Buck. "We would be full of lead, I think. Where's this embassy you want to check out? The general said to be back in two hours."

For the two hours that Buck and Carlos were gone, General Allen sat with the President in the Oval Office. He couldn't answer many of the President's questions, but he did bring him up-to-date.

"So, you are telling me that either some type of electrical storm from the sun, or an attack from another country, has brought the United States to a complete electrical halt—that every electrical piece of machinery here in the United States, as well as maybe the whole world, is now defunct and useless?"

"Yes, Mr. President. We have heard the same story in California through the only system that I know is operational—a private ham radio link that we are hoping will be only the first of many between the West Coast and the East Coast. A third ham radio, belonging to the pilot who flew me in, is in New York and he is on his way to see if his home in Long Island is secure. If it is, he will pick up his radio and then hand it over to the Andrews Air Force Base Commander when he returns to pick me up. That will at least give us a triangle of communications. I believe that we will have several short-range military radios working soon, which will patch you into Andrews if you decide to stay here at the White House. The only other place I suggest you set up headquarters would be Andrews, but of course it will not be as comfortable."

"And you say this helicopter that brought you in is the only one in operation?" continued the President. "Does that mean that the Air Force doesn't have a single fighter or bomber in the sky to protect America?"

"Apart from two old C-130 transporters, we could have another dozen propeller aircraft operational within a few weeks. We are going to have to get aircraft out of museums and fly them, and some could take weeks to make ready."

"We have a farm in North Carolina that I'm going to turn into a Civilian Air Force Base. It is a collection of World War II aircraft—three P-51 Mustangs, one P-38 Lightning and the Huey. We also have a DC-3 and the two 1956 models of the C-130. These World War II fighters can be armed with 500-pound bombs and old Sidewinder and Falcon heat-seeking missiles left over from the Vietnam era. Why we still have several dozen of these old missiles in storage at Nellis AFB in Las Vegas and Edwards AFB in California, I don't know, but I have ordered the base commanders at Edwards, Seymour Johnson and Pope Field at Fort Bragg to search their old stock piles as well. I'm heading over to Hill Air Force Base in Salt Lake City and Nellis AFB in Vegas tomorrow. The first report from the base commander at Fort Bragg is very bad. Our fire power in the Army is currently just men and rifles. Absolutely nothing that could be considered mobile works, apart from old jeeps, trucks, and howitzers. Mr.

President, I'm going to stay overnight at the Naval Air Station in Maryland to see what they have for fire power and then I'm going down to Naval Station in Norfolk to see Martin Rogers. I want to set up a defense of some sorts to repel any possible immediate attacks. If the whole world is in the same situation, and this destruction was the cause by Mother Nature, or the sun, then we should be safe from attack. If it was caused by another country, it should only take them a short time to get into range to attack us."

"What about our satellite system? Surely something must still be working?" asked the President.

"We have absolutely no communications—satellite included. If this problem is only here in the United States or North America, then our troops and aircraft carriers are on their way home right now. If the problem is worldwide, then our naval ships could be floating steel hulls, our aircraft scrap-metal, and our troops cannon-fodder for whoever has electrical power out there. We will not know that answer until someone, or something comes over the horizon—either our own troops coming home or an attack force from the only country that can attack us, which is Russia."

The President was silent for a few minutes, thinking hard and about to ask the million dollar question. It was difficult to get his head around the enormity of the situation.

"So, General, my coffee machine doesn't give me coffee in the kitchen because we have no electricity, correct?" The General nodded. "Yours and everybody else's on the entire continent don't either, except where private generators are running, and these generators are old truck engines. Your complete Air Force is as good as my coffee machine, not due to a lack of electricity, but because they have no electronics working. You believe every flying aircraft in the United States crashed last night when every electrical component in them died." The General nodded again.

"You said that half of D.C., including the Pentagon and whole districts around us, are on fire."

"Correct," the General replied.

"You flew over Richmond, Virginia and Raleigh, North Carolina, and both cities looked the same as Washington. There are no vehicles moving in the whole country, military or private, but the big question is: 'What have they got to do with the electrical grid?'"

"Electrical-management systems were built into all motor vehicles starting around 1983 with Japanese vehicles. Vehicles older than 1980 still work, it is the electronic management systems, or the vehicles' onboard engine computers that died, and today's engines cannot run without input from onboard computers," replied the General.

"So, all of our engines—cars, trucks, jets—still work, but their computers are down?" the President asked.

"Yes, Sir."

"Our satellite systems are down because of electrical malfunctions. Our televisions, radios, the Internet, my BlackBerry, everybody's communication devises are down because of electrical breakdowns. Then who made all these parts?" the President asked.

"Probably China..." the General replied, suddenly realizing that there was a pretty good chance that it was not a sun flare or an act of God that took out the whole electrical grid.

"But China doesn't have the capability of attacking mainland United States," the President observed.

"They could be working with the Russians," suggested General Allen. "And if they are, we are done for. Our whole county's fire power is thousands of miles away. If they get back in time, then we have a chance. If this catastrophe is worldwide, apart from Russia and China, I believe they will destroy our troops over there and then walk in here and take over. There is no way we can stop the Russians from coming in and I assume that

NATO, Europe, Australia, and the rest of the world are in the same boat as we are."

The President thought for a few minutes. "But if China is behind this, why have they done it? Do we have anything to fire back at them? Anything older than 1980?" the President asked.

"Electrical parts have been made in China since God knows when. They were cheap, they worked, and even I'm shocked but they had the potential to control the world with chips, fuses, and God knows what—little things that cost less than a dollar. Your Blackberry, Mr. President, was made in China. So were all Apple products—iPhones, and iMacs and so on. If they weren't made in China, then they contain parts that were made in China. Engine-management systems for automobiles were made in Japan, Europe, the United States, South Korea, and other countries. If they weren't made in China, then we can probably assume that fuses, chips, bulbs, and anything that costs less than a dollar has killed all the vehicles running around earth, even if they weren't made in China."

General Allen paused for a moment as he continued to think through his growing theory. "Any piece of machinery that was made in America and other countries, which do not have electrical computers or controls, or shall I say some sort of electrical-management system, will still be operational. Even my Air Force aircraft is scrap metal, just like your Air Force One, but the old Huey is totally original, apart from its new radar and GPS system, and it flies. The radar and GPS are totally dead."

"So what are our options?" the President questioned.

"I think our only option is to assume that either every electrical gadget in the world has been affected, which means that Russia might be in the same shape we are," General Allen replied. "China and its allies might be in control, which would include Iran, North Korea, and maybe Russia. They could have been delivered parts that still work once everything else is shut down. If there was somebody, or a government behind this, then they could have doled out parts as they saw fit."

"So our country's defense is basically useless, unless our overseas troops return. And if somebody wants us, then they certainly won't let our forces return," replied the President. The General nodded.

"And, all these parts or things that don't work anymore, won't ever work anymore?" the President sounded weary.

"I'm not sure, but I doubt it," the General answered. "My biggest worry now is the nuclear power stations. They could rip this country and the rest of the world apart and the radiation from over 400 power plants worldwide would certainly kill even the guys who want to take us over. I think my first task is to visit one immediately and see if they are shutting down. If they are, then we will survive as a nation until an attack comes. All I can do, Mr. President, is to put up whatever defense we can muster between now and then. We have no eyes and no ears, but I believe we have some time to get ready."

"What about the cold and the people in the frozen parts of the country? What about the cities? Are these people going to be looked after by their local police forces? Can farmers even feed us all?" the President continued, now looking very worried.

"After what I saw flying over Washington and Richmond, I hate to fly over New York and Los Angeles," the General replied. "With all the aircraft going down at the same time last night, all full of fuel and the size of Air Force One, the 9/11 disaster would be miniscule in comparison. There must be millions of Americans already dead, or now dying from the cold. We were slated to get a big snowstorm last night, too! I imagine that once urban food supplies run out, people are going to start killing each other over a piece of bread or a can of Coke. The massive problem is that not many police, fire, or other emergency vehicles work, so I doubt that many people can be helped. I don't think there is much help for the majority of people living in northern North

America, or northern Europe for that matter, until somebody turns on the lights!"

"Whoever did this did a kick-ass job," replied the President, his face ashen. They both heard the helicopter returning. "Joe," shouted the President to his main Secret Service agent standing outside the closed Oval Office door. The man entered. "Please be very polite and ask the two gentlemen in the helicopter to visit with me in the Oval Office."

General Allen heard the rotors cease turning and they waited for the Buck and Carlos to enter. Both General Allen and the President were deep in thought when the door opened and the agent returned.

"There were seven in the chopper, Mr. President. Three are guarding the Huey, refusing to come in, and there are four men here to see you, as you asked."

"Bring them in, Joe," ordered the President, and was quite surprised to recognize one of those who entered.

* * *

When Carlos and Buck left the White House in the Huey, Carlos guided Buck in the direction of the Colombian Embassy. It was a little difficult, as it all looked so different from the air and the clouds of smoke didn't help. People waved at them from rooftops as they flew low overhead.

"There it is!" shouted Carlos to Buck "The building used to be the Russian Embassy many years ago and they still have a helicopter landing pad on the grounds. It's small but you can get her in." Buck could see the cross on the asphalt. There were already men with guns on the landing pad looking up at them. The windsock above the three-story building showed a light breeze from the South so he came in to land from the North.

"I hope they don't shoot us," replied Buck. "I'll try not to fart for awhile."

"They won't," replied Carlos with a grin. "They are just as much in the dark as anybody else." They landed lightly with automatic weapons pointed at them, and Carlos waved to his great uncle who stood looking down at them from a second story balcony. Orders were shouted and the troops backed off.

The rotors ceased and Carlos got out. Buck said he needed a bathroom break, and he closed *Baby Huey* down and locked up. Carlos' father came out to greet them, and they waited for Buck before walking back to the dark building.

"We have an hour, Dad," Carlos told his father. "This is my friend, Buck, and that's the Huey I told you about. I've come to get you and Uncle Philippe out of here."

"Apart from here in Washington, is the rest of the world working?" his father asked. "We have nothing working here at the Embassy. Even the radios are down."

"I know Dad, it's the same all over the United States, maybe even the whole world, and people are dying everywhere. We just left General Allen with the President at the White House. He's briefing the President on what we know. After we pick him back up, we are headed to Norfolk to visit Vice Admiral Rogers on the way back to North Carolina. But first, Buck and I have got to hit the bathroom—we've been flying for hours!" They entered the building to find gas lamps and heaters working overtime.

Uncle Philippe was briefed, as was Carlos' father. They sat in silence while Carlos told them what had happened based on what Will Smart had reported from California. Carlos invited the Ambassador to join them in North Carolina. The older man gave orders for his overnight bag to be packed, and for Manuel and a couple of bodyguards to do the same.

"How many can you fit into that Huey?" asked the Ambassador. "I flew in several around Colombia, and I think I sat with around a dozen troops."

"Ours is the extended version, Mr. Ambassador," explained Buck. "If necessary we can squeeze 14 into her and two crew, but comfortably around nine. I don't know if we will be taking the President anywhere, so I think I can probably only take seven or eight from here."

"We have a platoon of 30 men here and ten staff, so they will have to stay until I can help them. They'll be all right—we have several gas heaters on. The Embassy is quite warm, and if we close down unnecessary areas, they will have food and warmth for at least two weeks or more here. Do they have gas at the White House? Knowing the staff there, I bet they don't, so I will take a couple of heaters and several gas bottles for the President—a gift from the Colombian Embassy. I want to see the lay of the land, so Manuel and our three bodyguards should come with. We can pack a week's supply of gear and a few automatic weapons for protection."

"I don't think coming in armed to the teeth will do us any good at the White House," grinned Carlos. "We were nearly blown out of the sky on our last visit."

"We will hide them under cloaks and winter clothing," replied Manuel's father, leaving the room to pack.

"So, you think this problem is a big deal?" the Ambassador asked Carlos, while they were waiting for the others to return.

"Preston Strong, Martie Roebels, Maggie Smart, Buck and I all have various advanced degrees in engineering, mostly in electrical engineering, and I specialize in communications. We chatted on the way up. Uncle Philippe, the whole country is down. The whole world could be down. Nothing in our industry works. Buck just hotwired the fuel depot at Andrews Air Force Base to get gas. The whole base has only one or two mobile back-up generators from the 1970s. Everything newer—and boy they have back-up on back-up on back-up—is all dead."

"We had to top the Huey's tanks with a 5,000-watt old Army-issue camouflaged generator that Buck was able to start, and use it to hotwire and start the motors of a truck's fuel pumps. There no way that we could start up the truck or its pumps until we used the generator to get it going. The tanker has seven thousand gallons in it. We used 100 of that and the rest is going into the C-130 the General is using to fly up to Andrews. Once that truck is empty, they might have one or two more hanging around, or they can drain the tanks of all the dead aircraft sitting around. Air Force One is always fully fuelled, and that will last them a while, but they are going to need a miracle to get the fuel out of the underground and big storage tanks. That needs big power to get the fuel moving. The electrical engineers at Andrews are working on that now."

The others arrived. Buck was introduced to Manuela, Mannie, and Dani—the three guards accompanying them. The Ambassador gave orders to defend the walls of the Embassy at all costs, and said he would return within the week.

* * *

"Mr. Ambassador, I never thought the Colombian government would be a part of my rescue," the American President stated, shaking hands with the four who entered.

"Unfortunately, it looks like we are in this together and I'm here to help. This is my nephew, Chief Aide Manuel Rodriquez. You have met him before, and this is his son Carlos—the co-pilot of our transportation. Last is Buck McKinnon, a fellow American of yours and the co-owner and pilot of the helicopter. General Allen, good to see you again."

The General came up and shook hands with his old friends and held the Ambassador's hand with both hands warmly.

"May I quickly intervene?" Carlos asked. "Mr. President, Ambassador, General, we have about three hours of daylight left. I don't think flying at night is a wise choice with the only safe airfield with runway lights we know of being located in North Carolina, three hours to our south."

"Well said, Carlos," stated the General. "Buck, we need to be out of here in 15 minutes.

"You have no heat here, Mr. President?" asked the Ambassador.

"Not yet,"

"Buck, Carlos, please go and fetch the gas heaters and gas lamps we brought from the Embassy. It will help until the electricians get something working here." The President thanked the Ambassador and invited them to sit down.

They discussed the situation until one of the heaters and gas lamps was brought into the Oval Office. Then, General Allen got down to a quick situation report.

"At the moment, gentlemen, I'm temporary Chief of Staff under the Commander in Chief, who is going to stay here at the White House as long as he can. I'm going to get fresh troops in here tomorrow. The distance is about 11 miles. I know we have one old jeep and by tomorrow maybe a troop carrier and truck or two, but we are coming in with the best fire power we can muster. I think the best defense around the White House would be old ground-to-air missiles. I'm bringing in a company of 100 men with field tents and gas heaters, if we can find them. We have tons of rations at Andrews, so food is not a problem—only heat and electricity."

"I'm going to get a ride with you guys back to Andrews and then fly into Virginia to see Vice Admiral Rogers in Norfolk and see what the Navy can muster for a defensive perimeter. Buck, Carlos—you fly down to North Carolina, stay the night, and then find out what you can. I need you to visit that nuclear power station in Newel, or New Hill, I think it's called, just down the road from Preston's place. Get in there and get me a report. I want to know ASAP if there are problems, or if the whole system is shutting down by itself automatically. Here's what the President and I have discussed..." and he told the room what they had theorized about in the last couple of hours. "Carlos, we have no eyes to protect us. Remember you told me about a satellite—what was it called?"

"Navistar P was its data output," Carlos replied.

"The Navistar program, I'm sure you know, Mr. President, is the entire world's GPS system that we put up in the 1970s. Carlos here has been doing research in the mountains above Salt Lake City, in the observatory NASA and the Air Force use to track the space programs as well as do space communications research. A couple of weeks ago, he found a project we had lost several years ago. It was a secret project—a complete Navistar satellite built as a prototype to send photo data instead of location data for our flying aircraft—a giant 'eye in the sky,' if you wish. It is the only one we have left up there. It's older than 1980, and it could still be made operational. The other early satellites have been replaced, are out of commission, or burned in re-entry, or as Navistar P did when we lost her, went off course, closed down her transmissions and lost contact."

"That was way back in 1981, and since then the program has been deemed a failure. We really packed this one full of solar gear to power itself up from the radiant heat of the sun and send back digital photographs to Earth. Remember, this was back in the 70s and all more modern spacecraft are much more powerful than this old girl. Navistar P was the only one of its type. She was designed for research and one of the first ever solar and super-powered units of its day. We might be able to power her up. Given a generator, we might even be able to get the Salt Lake City Observatory up and running, which might give us very basic eyes to see."

"Get it done, Pete," ordered the President. "Carlos, once I have a radio, we should be able to communicate. As soon as that happens, I want a report from you on a daily basis."

"Hold on," suggested Buck.

Pete Allen knew exactly what was going on in Buck's head and spoke the words for him. "It's two hours flying time from

Andrews to your house. You pick up your radio and with five minutes to pack your essentials, you can get back to Andrews before dark. You are flying in daylight, so fill your tanks to the last drop. You will also need to take 50 gallons in 5-gallon canisters with you. Fill the tank with them when you land and that will get you back to Andrews with just enough fuel. Great idea, Buck! By midnight, Andrews Air Force Base will be able to communicate with North Carolina."

Buck smiled at everybody. It was exactly what he had been thinking.

"Mr. Ambassador, Manuel," continued the General, "you guys will stay with me at Andrews tonight. Buck, you get *Baby Huey* lit up, take us back to Andrews so you can top off your tanks, and then you and Carlos head north. The weather looks clear, so you should be able to pick up your radio and stuff and get back to Andrews. I'll leave the light on for you."

"Mr. President," Buck began, "it's going to be a long flight. May I use your Oval Office bathroom?"

The President laughed for the first time that day.

They took off ten minutes later, the Ambassador staying with the President, and Manuel going back to Andrews. They touched down close to the truck where they had filled up hours earlier and the General and Manuel got out. Orders were shouted, and men arrived with ten steel gas containers. A fresh Carlos took over the left seat for the flight up to Buck's house, with the three bodyguards as protection. Buck had been flying all day and needed a break. They were quickly refueled, every drop possible squeezed into the Huey's tanks, and then Carlos took off to the north.

The ground below was bleak and still, and the clouds were low, but Buck knew the layout of the land. Without the helicopter's GPS, flying was more difficult, but all pilots had trained without it. Buck had asked for flight maps at Andrews, and with Carlos flying and Buck navigating, they followed the coast all the way up. The weather grew colder outside and twice they flew over snowstorms several miles across.

An hour or so later, they flew in close to New York at 13,000 feet and the devastation over large areas could be seen. They all sat in silence as they saw miles and miles of blackened smoldering ruins—so bad that smoke was becoming a problem for Carlos to see, even at their high altitude. Most of the blackened areas ended at rivers and waterways. Many large fires were still burning everywhere and Manhattan looked very different. Smoke covered everything. Only a few dark grey buildings were recognizable above the smoke, a couple on fire and spewing out more smoke. Carlos turned slightly eastwards at Buck's instruction and they lost altitude fast, getting closer to the area in which Buck lived.

"The road outside my house is not wide enough to land, Carlos, and there's electrical wires everywhere. My area looks like it's not on fire," he observed, looking forward into the smoky air a couple of miles in front of them. It was starting to get dark as the sun was setting early behind the high layer of smoke to the west. "I think we will have more daylight once we get closer. There's my street. My road crosses another at an intersection one house away from mine. There! You can put her down on the cross streets. There are no cars in the intersection. Carlos, shut her down quickly. I'll take Dani to help me, Manuela can keep guard and Mannie can help you refuel. Don't let anybody close guys. If anybody shoots at us, you shoot back, fast and hard." The guards nodded.

Carlos put her down close to two stationary cars that looked like they had tangled in the intersection and then cannoned into a building, leaving the complete square of intersection clear. He did as Buck had asked, shutting her down quickly as everybody cleared out in different directions. Buck and Dani ran for a beige-colored house, and Carlos watched as Buck unlocked the front door and they went in. Carlos got out and showed Mannie how to open the containers, and one by one, they poured the 50 gallons of fuel into the main tank as fast as they could—it took less than 15 minutes.

By that time, several people were already running up to the helicopter and Manuela fired warning shots to keep everyone away. They were not the rescue squad everyone was expecting, and Carlos knew they couldn't help the dozens of people in any way.

Carlos ordered Mannie to pile the empty canisters away from the rotors; they were not taking them back since they had just enough to get back without the extra weight. He jumped back into the seat to begin his take-off checks, noticing that the fuel tanks registered just over half full. It was going to be close, but they had 50 gallons less weight on the way back. He looked across his instruments, and surveyed the outside at the same time. There was a dead body on the ground past Buck's house on his left several houses away. It looked like another car accident and the car had hit a telephone pole. The intersection accident directly in front of him had two broken and badly damaged cars sticking out of a corner store, one a sedan in the window and one, a Dodge Caravan sticking out of the store's corner doorway.

A swinging sign above the store said Marcy's Designs, and he suddenly saw movement in the back of the Dodge Caravan. A face had appeared and then quickly disappeared. There was a body—it looked like the body of a young woman—lying on the ground beside the car on the driver's side. The passenger side was in the darkness of the store and he couldn't see anyone else. He checked the compass reading. He was facing west and he realized that the light was fading fast. Carlos checked his instruments again and looked outside for a second time, the rotor beginning its first turn. There it was again, a face starting at him from the back of the Dodge, a little face with what looked like a teddy bear. A couple of people were attempting to get closer to the helicopter, and further down the street to his left, Manuela fired several more warning shots.

He caught Manuela glancing around and then at him. He caught her attention with his free hand, pointed to his eyes with two of his fingers and pointed in the direction of the Dodge. Manuela signaled back, looked around 360 degrees, and made a run for the corner of the store. Carlos again checked his instruments, noticed Mannie glance quickly in the direction of Buck's house, and saw the two men exiting. Buck had the radio and mass of wires in his arms, and Dani had a bundle of items that looked like bags. He immediately looked back to Manuela and heard Mannie fire off several more rounds. Manuela was reaching into the back of the Dodge and when she came back out, she had a little girl holding a puppy and a teddy bear in her arms.

Everyone arrived back at both open side-doors at exactly the same moment. Mannie fired off a long burst and Carlos got a pat on the back from someone, heard both doors slide shut at the same time. He increased the engine revs and the spinning rotors lifted the Huey vertically into the air. He had to go straight up to get out of the way of the street wires, and once clear of the building level; he leaned the helicopter towards the sea a hundred yards in front and went straight out over the water. Staying low, he turned the Huey southwards, thinking that this would be the safest move in the increasing twilight around them. He got on a direct course to Andrews, then climbed rapidly and relaxed slightly. He heard whimpering in the back.

"Who was that face in the car?" he shouted to Manuela.

"A little girl," Manuela replied, "with her little dog and her teddy bear. Your eyes are good, Carlos. Her name is Beth. She's five and very scared and cold and tired. I think her mother was lying by the car and there was a dead man inside. She was nearly passed out with cold and she's hungry."

"Dani, get the food I got out of my refrigerator," suggested

Buck, climbing back into the right front seat. "Not the bag I put Smokey in—Smokey is in blue Nike bag. The black one has clothing and the smaller brown one has the food and drink I grabbed out of the fridge. Give her and the puppy something to eat. Smokey is my cat, Carlos, and I don't think a puppy lover at the moment. Dani, open the bag a little and let the poor cat breathe."

There was silence as the little girl and her puppy ate whatever was given to them—the little girl had some cheese and an apple, and the puppy gulped down the rest of the brick of cheese.

As they climbed, they stayed in the sunlight with the ground below just visible with the setting sun and they knew they had about 20 minutes of daylight left. Going south would give them extra speed with an expected tailwind.

The weather cleared as they left New York behind them, and the rain clouds moved out to sea. It looked like a clear flight into Andrews Air Force base, two hours away. An hour later, the only light around them was the instrument panels in front and the switches above the pilot's heads. They were very faint, turned down by Buck so he could see outside. They could still tell the difference between the water and land, 12,000 feet below them, as a big full moon was raising its head over the horizon. They were doing well, and both tanks were still slightly over a quarter full.

"What reserve fuel does she have? How much extra fuel do we have, Buck?" Carlos asked. Buck was reading the old flight manual.

"The General was spot on. We are cruising at 115 MPH. Fuel range with full tanks is 325 miles at optimum altitude, 12,000 feet. We have been flying very light, so we must have saved at least a gallon or ten. Total fuel is 200 gallons plus 30 minutes reserve, which should mean another 40 gallons. Our flight in was 223 miles, estimated. Our flight back at least ten minutes shorter. That's 446 miles round trip. Buck was on his calculator."

"Buck, it's simpler than that," stated Carlos. "The tanks were a slither above half when I took off from your house. Half fuel plus a slither, plus 30 minutes reserve, range is 325, half of that is 160 plus the slither, I'd say an extra 25 miles plus reserve—half of 115 miles an hour hoping we have no headwind. Boy!" exclaimed Carlos.

"Either Pete knew what he was talking about, or we won't be handing him his radio. It's going to be damn close."

"Ok, 185 plus 60 is 245 miles and our distance needed is 223, say 225. Now those tanks were filled to the brim, so I reckon we will have around 20 miles of reserve fuel by the time we get to Andrews," added Buck, smiling at Carlos.

Forty minutes later, and as Buck changed the fuel controls onto their reserve marks, the radio squawked and made everybody jump with fright. It was certainly not something they were expecting. The radio had been silent ever since they had left Andrews.

"Pete to Buck, do you hear me? Over."

"Read you loud and clear, Pete. We weren't expecting that," replied Buck in the right seat. "Carlos is in the left seat and I'm taking a rest—we have just switched to reserves."

"Roger. We have a large mountain of old wooden pallets collected on the apron in front of hangar holding the boss's old ride, the 747, and we will pour gasoline onto the pile. You should be able to see it. I assume most of the country is dark beneath you, over?"

"Roger, Pete. We have seen a couple of very faint lights up here, but you're right it's black down there," stated Buck. "I'd say you should hear us in about ten minutes. We will reduce altitude to 8,000 feet and you should hear us pretty soon. You might as well light the fire. It's cold as hell up here and we should look for it in case we're off course. Over."

"Roger that," replied the General from the flight deck of the C-130's radio he was using on the apron. He shouted over to the

men for the gas to be poured and the fire lit. It went up with an almighty whoosh, as everyone ran for cover.

"We have visual, Pete," observed Buck, as Carlos brought the helicopter around several degrees. The fire was slightly to his right. They were about 30 miles out and the new faint spot of light could just be seen on the horizon. Carlos increased the forward speed to the maximum, 135 miles an hour, and aimed the Huey at the new light on the horizon. They decreased altitude quickly and came over the large fire at 600 feet, about 15 minutes later.

"Wind 10 miles an hour from the north, no gusts," Carlos heard Jennifer tell him on the radio, and he whipped *Baby Huey* around in a tight, angled turn and came in steeply from the south—about 100 yards from the fire. All the buildings could be seen in the light of the flames, as well as the C-130 a hundred yards or so to the north and the white fuel truck next to it.

"Jennifer, get us some rations. We are hungry. We are fueling up and heading south ASAP," explained Carlos as he touched the helicopter down.

"Roger," she replied.

They handed the radio equipment to several engineers who were standing by. Buck told them what to do and how to get it up and running. He explained that there should be one of Preston's transmitting towers pretty close by for them to pick up on, and he explained the radio's current frequency settings and told them to call the Huey when they had it up and running which shouldn't be more than 20 minutes. They could then test it while they were flying between Andrews and North Carolina.

The Huey was still quiet in the back, and he let everybody stay aboard—fuelling regulations were out the window for now.

An hour later, and half way to Preston's farm, Pete came on the air. The radio was working. Preston was listening in and heard Pete as well, and for the second time today there was a new long-distance communication link in the United States of

America. Preston asked them how they were doing. Buck, who was flying again, shared that they were an hour out and tired. Preston reminded Buck to click twice on the radio intercom and he would turn the runway lights on. It had been a long day for *Baby Huey*.

* * *

It was only ten minutes after Buck and Carlos, when Preston heard Pete's voice at the same time Will Smart came on line from the California radio. He also sounded tired when he spoke, but now he was being heard on multiple sets.

"Preston, Preston, Will Smart here. Do you copy?" Will's voice woke a sleepy Carlos and Buck up from their sleepy autopilot flying. Radio life was getting back to normal, thank God, and the channel was getting busy.

"Preston here, read you clear, Will. Maggie sends her love and the kids as well. Joe gave them a new engine to work on—an old lawn mower engine—and they are all in the hangar with Maggie pulling it to pieces."

"Preston, I need to speak to that Pete guy. I am at the new location with Mike and family. We moved the radio over earlier and a couple of the guys have set it up and it's now working. You are hearing me, aren't you, Preston?"

"So is the Pete guy, young man," the General piped in from Andrews. *"Thank you, Will, and your partner Mike for your help... Al, are you there? And on this baby, we go by first names in case we are being monitored."*

"Hi, Pete, this is Al. It's good to talk to you again. Where are you?"

"I'm where the boss keeps the big baby, Alpha Foxtrot One. Al, I just want to see who is with us on this call. Preston, I know you are there. Buck, Carlos, are you guys listening in? Jennifer, are you in range?"

"We're both listening, Pete, and about 50 minutes from Preston," Buck answered. A very scratchy Jennifer came on the radio, much fainter than the others and said she could just barely hear through the static.

"Carlos, Jennifer is going to your old hunting grounds, where I want you to fly your fixed wing in tomorrow. Understand and confirm please, Carlos,"

"You want me to fly in to where I flew out of last week in my faster ride than our current baby, correct?" Carlos asked for confirmation.

"You got it, brother. Try and find a ride to your old place of work, take some electrical power with you, and search for our call sign 'P' for Pa-Pa—the object in the sky we discussed earlier. I will be there later tomorrow. Preston, tell Sally I want her up here bright-eyed and bushy-tailed tomorrow by 0800. Buck, I want you to check out that powerful mama we talked about and fill Preston in when you get there. Preston, you need Joe and David to get you more fuel from the airport ASAP. Sally is going to run you dry tomorrow and I'm working on something you might like. Sorry, Al, that this all sounds like gibbery-gook, but it's the only way for now. Preston and others, Al and I are leaving you for an hour, we are going on another frequency in case we are being monitored and I will fill you guys in when I see you tomorrow. Good hunting. Al, go to the third emergency frequency on your list for radio procedures on today's date. Goodnight everybody, and thank you."

"What was that last part all about?" asked Martie, sitting next to Preston with a glass of wine. Barbara was also there sitting on the couch with Sally, Michael, and Grand Pa-Pa. Joe and David had left an hour earlier tired and were going to bed. They already had two of the airport's jet-fuel tankers by the side of the farm's fuel depot. Preston had worked on the electrical connections and managed to hotwire the systems and the tankers. The one still behind Joe's old rig was empty since Sally already had full tanks of gas. The guards were outside or bunking in the hangar, and doing what they were supposed to do.

"I'm sure Buck will let us know when he arrives," Preston replied. "I didn't understand what he was talking about either, but it looks like we have a full day's work tomorrow and it seems that Buck must have gone up to New York to pick up his radio and then returned to Andrews. *Baby Huey* must have been breathing fumes—that trip was totally out of her range, but it looks like they must have gotten some gas up there."

* * *

The earlier ride into town had certainly been interesting. On David's first trip, he had returned with a dozen old backpacks with Israeli army radios. Preston and his team of engineers—Maggie, Ben and Oprah—had powered up the batteries, and now the guards outside each had a radio with one next to Preston's ham radio. It was connected to the electrical system and would be on 24/7.

It took another hour, but Preston, Joe, and David, with the help of Joe's five sons and the two experienced tech sergeants from Seymour Johnson fitted the four machine guns Preston had given Joe to his jeeps. Now he had two machine guns per jeep with belted ammunition feeding into the guns. They were ready to fire, the front gun pointing forward and the rear gun on a steel pole three-feet high that could swivel 360 degrees.

The boys had drawn straws to see who would "man" the rear guns. The two armored Ferrets had also been loaded with boxes of ammo and their machine guns ready to fire. The Saracen was not ready, but would be by the time they got back.

The Air Force guards and the convoy would be in constant radio communication, and the maximum range of the old radios was around 50 miles. Before the convoy left for RDU, everybody was tuned to the same frequency, and they agreed on a second back-up frequency in the event that the first one was compromised.

They left the Saracen and the armored cars parked in a neat row, their forward and fully armed guns pointing down the driveway, and everybody piled into the two jeeps. Each "Rat Patrol" jeep, now named "Rat One" and "Rat Two" for radio purposes, needed a crew of three. There would be a driver, with one gunner on the forward machine gun and the third crewmember manning the rear gun. Martie wanted to go along and was given the driver position in the rear jeep. Their places set, Joe and Preston drove the two tractor trailers out of what now looked like a military compound, with Joe's eldest boy driving the first jeep with Martie bringing up the rear.

It took them a while to get to the main intersection along the US64 dual-lane road since Joe used his truck here and there to move cars and other vehicles out of the way and permanently clear the road so that the convoys would have a clear path on their next trip. They went down 64 without seeing anyone, turned left onto the 540 belt-line. Preston had noticed from the air that the highway looked less polluted with dead vehicles.

They were halfway down 540 and about to cross I-40 when they saw movement up ahead. Two small trucks—an old green Dodge and a small Ford—had several armed men around them and it looked like they were checking inside the cars. They were pulling bodies out of them and searching them for whatever they could find.

The looters saw the convoy approaching, still half a mile away and fired several shots in the convoy's direction. Several of the blasts sounded like shotguns, and Joe's eldest son Jack and David behind the machine guns laughed aloud because they knew that a shotgun was totally useless at this range. David cocked the front machine gun, ready for use, and Jack did the same with the rear gun, swinging it around to point forward.

The looters must have seen only the two tractor trailers and not the jeeps because a couple of men jumped into the back of one of the trucks—the green Dodge. The wheels spun and the little green truck came rushing towards them with several guns blazing wildly from above the cab.

A round came close, and Joe hooted from behind. The two machine guns began firing back, their much louder and more powerful noise shutting out any noise from the front. The bullets began hitting the green Dodge, now only a couple of hundred yards away. The engine exploded, as did the cab window, and the truck skidded, bounced, and then rolled fast and furiously, spewing car parts and bodies everywhere. It hit the guard rail, flipped over, and disappeared from sight over an embankment. David immediately trained his hot, smoking gun on the second truck. It was already turning around and heading away, with several people shooting in their direction. Again rounds went straight into the rear of the Ford. It burst into flames on the bridge over I-40, also hit the guardrail hard and bounced over, disappearing with several still aboard.

Despite the three still bodies on the side of the road where the green Dodge had disappeared, and two more where the Ford had gone over, the convoy carried on as if nothing had happened.

"I hate looters," David said to the two boys. "Anybody who loots except for food to live will steal from their grandmothers. I've seen it far too often in other parts of the world. The noise of our automatic weapons will tell others that they are not alone in their new concrete jungle."

They turned off 540 and went south towards the airport. On the airport road, there were more and more cars, naturally helpless and in the way. Joe had told Preston that on their first trip, he and David had freaked out when they saw cars at dead traffic lights. Cars were stopped in lines just as anybody would on a red light, but the lights were dead, the cars were empty, and still sat in rows waiting for the 'dead' lights to turn back on.

Finally, they turned onto the airport feeder road and suddenly heard tires screeching as a car came out of the airport. An old, red Mustang convertible with a couple of teenagers in it sped by on the other side of the island and out of the airport. No shots were fired and the car sped off.

As expected, the only large sliding gate into the terminal was locked with a massive padlock the size of David's fist. He had brought a cutting torch with him in Joe's tractor-trailer and he walked back to get it. The airport looked just like it had earlier that morning. Joe got out, helped David with the torch, and within minutes, the broken lock dropped onto the tarmac surface. David slid the gate open.

Preston pulled in behind Joe, David got back in the jeep and allowed Martie to drive through, and then he turned it around and faced the jeep toward the exit and ready for action. Preston and Joe got out and Joe and his boys went to work.

The changing of the tractors on the trailers full of fuel was the hard part. First, Joe and two of his sons raised the trailers off the dead tractors, moved the gear of the tractors into neutral, attached the steel chain they had brought with them, and pulled the tractors out of the way. Then they reversed their working tractors underneath the attachments, lowered the trailers, and connected them together. The hard work took ten minutes each.

Preston heard an aircraft engine start up. He looked over to see Martie waving at him from an old Cessna 210, untouched on the apron in front of the private terminal. He had seen it earlier. The 210 had a cargo door, not often seen on aircraft of its size, and he ran over to see what Martie was doing.

"Preston, this baby can get off roads and bicycle paths if necessary. She's a turbo Centurion II turned into a little cargo aircraft with a cruise speed of 220 miles an hour. She can reach Washington in an hour, and somebody has modified her to carry freight. With the turbo and one pilot, I reckon she'll easily get off the ground with 1,200 pounds of cargo. She could come in handy and give me and Maggie something to do. We could ferry in ammo from Seymour Johnson or something."

"I agree," replied Preston, and he ran back to Joe and the boys.

He told them to continue without him and Martie. The convoy left the airport and Preston latched the new padlock to the inside of the gate for the next visit, hopefully from the air. *"Someone could fly in and open the gate. It would also be harder to pick the lock if the lock is on the inside,"* he thought to himself.

He looked around. They had about two hours of daylight left, and it was time to think like Martie. She had a good idea, and these aircraft were useless standing here and sure to be vandalized pretty soon. He searched for another aircraft.

"Where did you find the keys, Martie?" he asked as she shut down the engine.

"Where everybody puts their spare key, above the left front seat's sun visor," she said, excited.

"Let's do a full ground check. Then you can start her up again and taxi me over to the FedEx building. I've got an idea," Preston instructed Martie. They spend several minutes checking the Cessna from the outside before jumping in and making their way over to the far side of the airport.

While she taxied, he checked the instruments and turned the radios on to see if they worked, and set them to their local frequency.

The radios were both old Bendix King models and Joe's voice came back when they called him to tell him they were already halfway home and everything was quiet. There was a new Garmin GPS in the dash which was useless, but the rest of the dials worked perfectly. He turned on the storm scope—a simple type of small radar screen that showed electrical storms—and he was surprised that it actually worked. It must have been an original early 1980s model.

They reached the FedEx terminal and three large jets faced the terminal in front of them. On one side, Preston found what he was looking for. It was a Cessna Caravan Cargomaster—a single turboprop the size of Sally's Pilatus and used by FedEx for rural pickups around the country.

There were five standing there and he tried the first three. They were quite new and were totally dead. The fourth one looked much older, but the keys were not in the ignition. He checked above the sun visor and found what Martie told him he would find.

He turned the key and all the dials twitched. It worked! The fuel gauge showed it was a quarter full and he looked around her. She was old and scratched but in good condition. She also had the extra fuel tanks he knew a few of the older ones had, as winglets. They weren't big, held maybe 25 gallons each, but he had read years ago that this aircraft had a range of 1,400 miles. These Cargomasters were used to hop from town to town picking up parcels from the smaller FedEx depots, and ran all day at over 200 miles an hour on one tank of fuel.

It took several turns of the propeller, but she finally fired up. He let her warm up and got out to try the fifth Caravan. She was one of the newer ones, and would never fly again. Preston had just had a hunch that the older model would be there, and he had been correct. He got back in and let her warm up for another few minutes and then he remembered all the bottles in the bar.

Martie got the 210 out of his way as he taxied the larger Cargomaster to the commercial terminal door he had walked in earlier, shut the aircraft down as close to the door as he could, and walked inside.

The inside of the terminal looked the same as it had looked earlier, except this time a mouse scurried away from him. He opened the steel gate to the locked bar area with a piece of broken pipe from outside the gate and went to the back exit of the bar, unlocked the outside door and saw what he had seen from the outside—a steel cage holding several 100-pound tanks of gas used for cooking. His next problem was to stop the round tanks from moving while in flight and he noticed several full cases of alcohol. Shrugging his shoulders, he picked up the first gas tank.

He found a luggage trolley, loaded three full gas tanks and trundled back to the door. It was hard work, but he got the first three bottles into the aircraft. By now he was sweating hard and he went back and got the other three. This time, Martie helped him and it was quicker.

"They are going to roll if you are not careful," she cautioned, looking at him inquisitively.

"I've already thought of that," he smiled. "I think we are going to need extra cooking facilities pretty soon. I'm positive our numbers are going to grow and these bottles will be the first to go. It's a pity that I'm going to have to use cases of booze to make them stable," he smirked, and Martie gave him one of her looks.

He went back with the trolley and placed half a dozen cases of alcohol on it and carried them down the outside stairs of the walk-on to the Cargomaster. Martie looked around in the other shops and returned as he got the last six boxes onto the trolley and returned to the ramp. She helped him, and a total of twelve boxes were placed around the bottles to secure them in flight.

"Booze for the troops," he laughed, and she rolled her eyes. He left the trolley by the door in case he might need it the next day when they picked up the next two fuel trailers, and they both climbed in and started up their aircraft. Martie had far fewer checks to do, and she didn't even stop at the Eastern end of the runway. She went immediately into her take-off roll and rose a few hundred yards down the asphalt. Preston took another few minutes to complete his take-off checks, looked at the load behind him and took off, the Caravan hardly noticing the weight in her cargo hold.

It was a ten-minute flight, and Martie was already down, her aircraft parked by the old shed on the opposite side of the runway and Maggie was running up to see the new acquisition as Preston came in on finals from the southeast. He also landed close to the old shed, which was filling up fast with ammo and now with alcohol. Preston asked the soldiers to help him unload and then asked them to gather all the men—it was time for their daily meeting.

"Today seems to have gone well," Preston started, the sun going down and the windows darkening as he held the meeting in the house lounge. Everybody was squashed into the large room. Twenty people filled it up quickly.

Barbara came out of the kitchen and put up her hand to interrupt. "I have potatoes and veggies ready to be steamed for dinner. We thawed two dozen large steaks and I need a volunteer or two to start grilling them outside once Preston is done with the meeting." Two of the off-duty soldiers immediately offered.

"We need to figure out what our plan of action is," continued Preston, "so we'll have a meeting every day from now on at the airport here. To re-cap what has happened in the country so far and try and figure out what the hell is happening, I'm going to state what I think. All electricity went off at around midnight last night. I know it seems like weeks ago, but not even 24 hours have passed since the beginning of whatever this is. All the aircraft in the air at the time—we heard from California and have seen them here—went down, killing I don't know how many people, most probably thousands. Every single motor vehicle that was not from the early 80s or before is dead, scrap metal. Even the General's aircraft is scrap metal until somebody flips the switch and turns everything on again. Can that happen? Maybe, but not for the thousands of aircraft that crashed last night. They can't be turned on again, and with so many people already dead, this is the real thing, guys—whatever it is. It is not just a little power outage. Any thoughts so far?"

Grandpa Roebels put his hand up. "If it was a sun flare," he started slowly, "which I doubt since more stuff would be kaput, even your fancy old aircraft dials out there would be dead. So, if somebody has turned off all the country's electricity, then I don't believe that the electricity is meant to be turned on again. Also, all the car batteries will only last a week or two in this cold winter weather before they need electricity to power them back up. If it was a country or an army who wanted to attack America, why would they want to turn the electricity back on and let all our troops return? If it is the work of a country wanting to attack us, then I believe everything is kaput until they want it turned on again."

"My thoughts, exactly," replied Preston. "I believe we must now act as if the world has changed forever. It's already getting mean out there. The real problems will begin when the gas runs out in most of the houses around here, and when the pantry becomes empty. We were shot at once today and people were killed. There are dead people lying in their cars. Most of the cars are empty, but we saw looters on the highway and they were ready to shoot to kill. They were young kids who I assume think this catastrophe is nothing more than a big computer game and are ready to kill the moment they walk out of the door with their father's rifle or pistol. Weapons in this country are in nearly every household and it is going to get worse, even by tomorrow. Good people are going to need help. Do any of you soldiers know what food stores you have at your Air Force base?"

"General Allen might be better at answering that, sir," said one. "At Seymour Johnson, many of the soldiers' families were already housed on base. I heard that they were going out of the gates in squads and rounding up the family members of all the airmen, here or overseas. That should fill up the empty housing on base and I think Pope Field and Fort Bragg will be doing the same. We supply the overseas troops from Pope and Seymour on a daily basis with C-17s. There are two large warehouses where millions of tons of supplies are kept. Hal, here, is one of the loaders for one of the warehouses. Hal, tell them what's in there."

"We have everything to run a war, sir," described the second soldier. "The hangar is about 20 times the size of yours, and we have two of them constantly full to the brim. When I left earlier today, both were full and on lock-down. We have had to resupply so much stuff by air lately that we have had to keep them full. We've had more than a dozen C-17 Globemasters going out from Seymour Johnson every day. Just the freezer for the frozen food is bigger than your hangar. We also have tents, hospital equipment, whole mobile base camps, and emergency equipment for disasters. I've been over to Pope's supply warehouses. They have much the same. There are several Abrams tanks there awaiting delivery and a complete armory full of everything you could wish for in a war. If that ever blows up, the landscape is toast for miles."

"So, I'd better speak to the General since my concern is what do we do with starving civilians when the time comes? We have already run out of sleeping room here. I'm thinking about clearing the hangar of aircraft, getting a bulldozer from Joe—you still have that old thing you helped me clear the trees for the runway, don't you, Joe?" Joe nodded. "I need to increase the clearing on the other side of the airstrip for protection as well as a parking place, and start putting people into the hangar to sleep. Tents won't work since the floor is concrete and you can't put in tent pegs, but we can hang lines and make rooms and get military beds in."

"Preston, before you get carried away and save the world, do you know how many people are out there?" asked Joe.

"I understand what you mean, Joe. Somebody started all this

for a reason and either we are going to get attacked, or everybody is just going to be left to die. The country will shut down. People up north must already be freezing to death. My question is what do we do when people come knocking on our barbed-wire gate for food and shelter?" The room was quiet.

"Give them each a packet of Southwest Airlines peanuts," suggested Martie. "We have 300 million packets!" The room shared some nervous laughter. "No, I agree with Preston. We must think of the future. It will take about a week for the people out there to get cold and hungry. Another week after that, there will be ten times more hungry people. Let's say it takes a second week to clear out the supermarket shelves and shoot each other fighting over the last Twinkies. Then our troubles will really start. The military troubles will also start because bases will be overrun with people fighting and begging and killing to get in. We will be forgotten, or not, but with aircraft flying in and out every day, somebody is going to follow those aircraft to us and we had better be ready. What happens if there are people already watching us with radar?"

"Radar is down," shared her father. "The only way they can track us is now from space. Only Russia and China can do that on a grand scale."

"They can't track our aircraft," responded Martie. "They are too small."

"Maybe they can, maybe they can't, but if I was a foreign power and wanted to invade another country, I would want to track their armies, ships, and aircraft."

"How would they do that?" asked Preston. "There is no way to track an F-16 fighter or a C-130 or a C-17 from space, unless they are tracking the heat omissions, or the metal of the aircraft. How else could they know where every aircraft is?"

"Easy," added Grandpa Roebels. "The same way air traffic controllers monitor the skies. I might be old, but I saw the birth of civilian and military aircraft transponders years ago and was behind the design of several military versions with Michael in San Diego. Remember, we sold our company to Raytheon, and our products were just added to their sales inventory."

What Martie's grandfather said hit Preston hard, and he stood there and thought about aircraft transponders for a couple of minutes.

"So our enemy, if there is one, already knows we are here in Apex, North Carolina. Our flight transponders are sending beeps into space, being caught by their satellites, and they have already seen the several aircraft arriving and departing. When they attack they'll come here first because we have the only aircraft flying around. And they already know that the country's commercial aircraft, the whole U.S. Air Force, the Army, and most of U.S. Navy around the world are not using transponders anymore and are totally useless to defend anything."

"I think you have hit the nail on its head," replied the old man. "Military transponders can be turned on and off at will. Civilian transponders in all the old aircraft you have out there also have a transponder on-off switch. All the newer civilian aircraft were automatic. They are all dead now so it doesn't matter. But if you do not switch on your transponder, like you all do in your pre-flight or warm-up checks, then you have hidden yourself from anybody tracking the transponders, unless they have heat, infra-red, or metal radar-detection capabilities in their satellites up there."

"I think from right now, pilots, we will stop using our transponders. I don't think anybody is going to turn the power on soon and I don't think we will be attacked tomorrow, but I think we must barbwire this base as much as we can and be prepared for an enemy attack within the next couple of days." Everybody agreed.

"What about arming your aircraft, sir?" the first sergeant asked. "Our two tech sergeants here are the best in the business. Both men have been arming everything coming into Seymour

Johnson since 1978—over 35 years. Tech Sergeant Matheson is retiring this year. He's 55 and looks his age," the sergeant joked.

"What can you do to our three P-51s and the P-38?" Preston asked the tech sergeant.

"Everything you want, sir. I took a sneak peak at the P-38 earlier. It was originally set up with rocket pylons and the electronics are still in place inside the wings, just deactivated by law. It will take me a couple of hours and there's room for two air-to-ground rockets on each wing. Any newer rockets than the older versions are most probably as dead as the motor vehicles out there on the roads. I mounted a couple of air-to-ground rockets on a P-51 a couple of decades ago, and I think two of yours have rocket setups already in the wings. I'll have to go back to the armory repair shops and see what they have in storage."

The tech sergeant looked around at the rest of the group, who were all listening intently. "We'll arm all the machine guns for you, give them all a clean and get them ready. Remember, sir, your center of gravity will change in flight because the added ammunition weight in the P-38 is forward of the cockpit."

"You have my permission," replied Preston. "Start on the P-38. Do you have air-to-ground rockets here?"

"No, sir, but I'll bring what we have at Seymour Johnson on tomorrow's flight. Just get me General Allen's permission and I can relay that to Colonel Mondale," was the reply.

"I'll fly them in for you, Preston," added Sally.

"Are there any questions?" Preston asked, and there were none. "Today's meeting is adjourned. We are still waiting for Buck and Carlos in *Baby Huey*. Keep some food hot for them, Chef Barbara, and let's all eat dinner."

Buck and Carlos flew in three hours later, both exhausted, and everyone went out to help them. They had passengers, and Preston knew that this would be the first of many new visitors in the near future.

Carlos got out of the right seat and shook Preston's hand and then Sally ran up and jumped into his arms, much to the surprise of many standing around. Both Martie and Maggie both smiled, however, knowing much more than their male companions. Two stern South American men got out of the rear, leaving a young woman sitting on the helicopter's floor holding a sleeping girl, her long blonde hair falling out of the blanket she was wrapped in. Martie immediately went over take the little girl, and Maggie lifted a sleeping puppy, which was also covered in a blanket. Manuela slowly unfolded her stiff body and stood up to exit the aircraft.

Carlos did the introductions. These three were his father's bodyguards. His father had stayed with General Allen at Andrews while he and Buck and the bodyguard had gone to New York, where he had seen the little girl in the remains of a vehicle. Manuela had gone to get her out, but they believed both her parents were dead in the accident and they couldn't just leave her.

Martie carried the child, and both Maggie and Barbara helped a still stiff Manuela into the house to warm up.

"Let's close your bird down, Buck," Preston ordered as he was handed a bag with a growling cat in it.

"I hope Oliver likes cats. That's Smokey," laughed Buck. "Poor *Baby Huey* and Smokey have had a busy day."

"We can refuel the Huey tomorrow," continued Preston, holding the cat away from him and noticing Oliver's sudden interest in the bag. "Let's go into the lounge. We have hot coffee and a few steaks, and I'm sure a couple cans of beans can be added to the mix."

Everybody who had exited the helicopter was tired, thirsty, and hungry. A case of beer was brought in from the cold porch and dinner was served by Maggie and Barbara.

Martie, still holding the young girl, sat in one of the chairs until the little girl awoke from all the noise. She looked up into

Martie's face, not recognizing the person holding her, and her big blue eyes searched Martie's face.

"My mommy is dead, isn't she?" the little girl asked, and Carlos came over to answer her questions.

"Was your mommy in the car with you?" he asked gently.

"She was lying on the road all day and wouldn't get up. She's dead, isn't she?"

"I'm afraid so," replied Carlos, sadly. "Who was the other person in the car with you?"

"That was my uncle Michael. I shook him for a long time but he had blood coming out of his head. Is he dead too?" Carlos nodded at her. "Is my puppy dead?" she asked, and her face lit up as the dog and her teddy bear were handed to her. "Spot and Teddy kept me warm. It was very cold in the car."

"Where is your daddy?" Martie asked.

"He's in the Army. I haven't seen him in a long time. Mommy said that he was coming back soon. I guess God needed my Mom with him, right?" She looked up at Martie. "Will you look after me until my Dad comes to get me?"

"Of course," replied Martie. "I'll be your Mommy for awhile, until your Dad finds you or we find you a person to take your mommy's place, okay? What is your name?"

"Bethany Jones, but everybody calls me Little Beth. You look just like my Mommy."

Martie was hooked. Preston knew that he now had real competition. Since the child was not hungry or thirsty, Martie put her to sleep in their bed.

By this time, Oliver had gotten acquainted with Spot the puppy, and the cat Smokey had already disappeared somewhere in the house. It was necessary for Oliver to show the happy little canine furball the area, such as where to pee and which bones not to steal, and they left through his doggy door in the kitchen, much to a hiding Smokey's relief.

After the meal, and with a bottle of whiskey and vodka open

on the coffee table, Buck and Carlos brought them all up to date. Buck explained that the general wanted the nuclear power station inspected early the next morning. He told them about the possible Chinese or Russian threat, and that if the nuclear power stations were shutting down in safe mode that meant that no one was going to fry, but it also meant that an attack from somebody was a definite possibility. Carlos joked that Buck had nearly hotwired the whole of Andrews AFB, and that he should hotwire Air Force One next for Preston. Everyone laughed, the alcohol having a calming effect on the people in the room. Everybody was there, including the eight off-duty soldiers. Preston had told them that they were part of the need for information and needed to be briefed.

Buck was quite proud to say that he had met the Colombian Ambassador and the U.S. President all in one day and that he and Carlos had actually sat in the Oval Office and used the same bathroom President Clinton had spent a lot of time in. Again, everyone laughed. Carlos added that he honestly thought that he had landed *Baby Huey* on gas fumes alone. Tech Sergeant Matheson said that there was nobody on this earth who knew more about flying, aircraft, and how to make them ready for war than General Pete Allen. He had worked with him for 20 years.

Preston then asked Carlos about the 'P' thing in the sky and Carlos told them about the Navistar P he had found by mistake just before Christmas.

"I'm getting a manual on it at Hill when I get there tomorrow," continued Carlos. "Pete wants me to get up the mountain, take some power with me, and try to wake it up and get it active. If we can do that, he reckons that her cameras could give us a picture of the United States from space, if we can position her correctly."

"We have a recently transformed riding lawnmower, thanks to the Smart family," stated Preston. "Its engine can either propel the mower or be switched into generator mode."

"It can't do both at the same time," added Ben and Oprah together. "We assembled it this afternoon and a couple of the soldiers helped us."

"How can I get it to Salt Lake? I'm supposed to fly there in the P-51," replied Carlos.

"FedEx," replied Preston.

"FedEx!?" Carlos reacted, looking at his friend. "What have you been smoking while we've been away?"

"A FedEx Cessna Caravan Cargomaster," replied Preston. "Hold on. Her range is too short. Okay, *Lady Dandy* has the range and can take your lawnmower generator to Hill for you."

"Preston, I was wondering why we had a FedEx Caravan and a Cessna 210 visiting us here at the airport?" Buck asked.

"It is on loan. Short hops, mail, food and booze delivery, supplies, dancing girls! You know, Buck, that sort of stuff—in and out."

"Cut the crap, Preston," replied Carlos.

"Ok, I want to check with a few farmers around here and see what they can offer in fresh food for people who are going to get hungry pretty soon," continued Preston, in a more serious tone. "We have supplies here at the airport for all of us for about two months, maybe three. Other people don't, and they are going to run out much quicker than we are. I'm just thinking beyond tomorrow and we won't have the airport in Raleigh much longer. Somebody will be in there soon and I'm sure will vandalize the place. We are going in tomorrow to get as much food and fuel as we can and then I'm sure we will have to go further afield for supplies. Carlos, about that satellite, we chatted this afternoon and came up with some ideas. If a country is going to attack us..."

"China IS going to attack us," replied Carlos.

"Why China?" asked Preston.

"Who made all the parts that don't work?" was the reply.

"China!" was the response from the room.

"But they don't have the military ability to attack us," Preston argued.

"They don't need to if we all kill ourselves," Carlos replied. "General Allen thinks that if it were Russia, they would have just nuked a few of our nuclear power stations and several of our cities once we were electronically disarmed. They haven't, so he believes that they are in the same boat as we are. Europe, Australia, and every country in the world other than..."

"China," interrupted Preston. "Sounds logical. They are the only country that would be able to disarm every electronic device, or parts of every new device in the world, because they built them all—everything!"

"Correct," replied Carlos.

"So we should expect an attack right here by Chinese troops?"

"Why right here?" asked Carlos, now puzzled. Preston told them about the transponder discussion and it hit Carlos and Buck like a ton of bricks. "Of course!" exclaimed Carlos. "How many military aircraft can still fly—maybe a couple of dozen worldwide? How many civilian aircraft can still fly worldwide? Dozens of old private civilian aircraft like ours. It could be their next step to attack any opposition before they take over the country. I must tell Pete about that tomorrow. That means that their satellites have told them our location, but they must invade the United States first."

"Not necessarily," added Sally, deep in thought. "Remember just before Christmas, there were all those attacks on Chinese families in California and Washington? Maybe all of you didn't hear it, but dozens of people were being killed—their houses set on fire and murdered by what the media called Chinese drug gangs from Hong Kong. Carlos, there was even an attack in Salt Lake City. Some Chinese family was killed in their house and a neighbor was quick enough to call the police. There was a shoot-out just south of Hill Air Force Base. It was all over the national news. Didn't you hear about it?"

Carlos shook his head that he hadn't.

"Lee Wang!" exclaimed Carlos. "His is the only Chinese family I know of in Salt Lake. I'll ask around for him tomorrow if I see anybody I know."

"We now fly without transponders starting tomorrow morning. Sally, make sure you tell General Allen. If these Chinese gangs are working for the same people, then we are in trouble because they know exactly where we are. I bet this was the busiest airport in North America all day today, and we must have shown up on their screens like a nightlight," concluded Preston. "We have fresh guards tonight. The Chinese can't act that quickly and there is only one road in. We might want to get a spotter plane up high tomorrow. I saw a couple of nice, undamaged Cessna 172s at the airport. They are slow enough for spotters and their radios should be working." Preston got up and stretched. "Let's all get some sleep and be up early to send Sally off at 7:00 a.m. First Sergeant, we need several more camp beds and blankets in the hangar and a couple in here. Guys, it looks like I have two blondes in my bed, so Oliver, Spot, Smokey and I are camping in the lounge until further notice."

* * *

The boardroom was dark and empty. Only the lit-up screen on the wall with the two world maps was any indication that electricity was on in this part of the world. On the top map, many of the fires had disappeared in the darker, nighttime areas. It was 6:00 am on Z-Day Two, and it was far too early for the 16 seats to be full of bodies.

There were larger patches of black over the darkening areas of Europe and the U.S. Eastern seaboard. On the bottom map, and easier to see on the dark part of the map, were just three beeps—three transponders working in the whole world, their positions showing. Transponder Three showed an aircraft close to Washington D.C. and moving south.

The large room below the boardroom was a totally different room. The ceiling was normal height and the room full of a dozen working computers showing all sorts of readouts. One of the screens was showing the same beeping transponder and a recording was being made of the flight by the person behind the screen.

A couple of hours later, the board table began to fill up. Green tea was served by the usual girls with small snacks for anyone who was hungry. At precisely 9:00 am, a side door opened and the Chairman walked in. The room quieted.

Greetings were given and the Chairman looked refreshed and in a good mood. He was followed in by the person who had been sitting behind the television monitor, watching all the world for aircraft, who put a piece of paper down on the podium, bowed to the group and left. His shift was over for the day. The Chairman studied the list for several minutes and then looked at Comrade Wang.

"Comrade Wang, do you have a report of the whereabouts of all our termination squads?"

"Yes, Comrade Chairman," he replied.

"Flight 1: What do we have in Auckland, New Zealand?"

"Three squads on the North Island," Comrade Wang replied.

"There were two aircraft that took off from Auckland's airport, flew south to Wellington, and then returned to Auckland. That, I believe, is where they are probably based. Both aircraft flew together. Average speed was 155 miles an hour. They must be light aircraft. Communicate with the three squads. Order them to destroy every light aircraft at that airport in Auckland, and stay in the area for further orders.

"Flight 2: Perth, Australia, Comrade Wang?"

"One squad, Comrade Chairman," was the answer.

"One aircraft from an airfield 20 miles east north-east of Perth. The aircraft traveled around the area and returned to the airfield. Flight time was one hour; flight speed was 95 miles an hour, again a light aircraft or helicopter. Seek it out and destroy it."

"Flight 3: Birmingham, England, Comrade Wang?"

"We have four squads around London and one in Manchester, Comrade Chairman."

"One aircraft from an airfield ten miles south of central Birmingham flew over Manchester and London. It seems to be a bigger aircraft, speed of 240 miles an hour, could be an older twin-engine aircraft. Tell the squad in Manchester to destroy it."

"Flights out of North Carolina—multiple. What do we have in that area, Comrade Wang?"

"We had one squad in Durham before Christmas but I returned them to New York. We have ten squads in New York City, five in the Boston area, three more in Chicago, and two in Orlando, Florida, Comrade Chairman."

"We had two aircraft out of an airfield 20 miles west of Raleigh—both were large, flying south for a short distance. We assume they were headed to two military bases just south of this unknown airfield, speed 270 miles an hour. Both then flew back to their original location and one flew up to what we think is Andrews Air Force Base at 295 miles an hour. At the same time, a smaller aircraft, possibly a light aircraft, flew up to the same base, at 130 miles an hour. It then flew to the White House, and I think the Capitol building, flew back to the base and then north to Long Island outside of New York City at 140 miles an hour. It flew back to Washington, and then returned to its original location. These must be military aircraft as there are still aircraft taking off and landing at this field. There are several other short flights with one currently going across the country—where to we don't know yet. Tell the ten New York squads to go to the Long Island coordinates where this aircraft went. You can get the coordinates from the officer on duty downstairs. Destroy whatever is there. Make sure they travel in a convoy and kill any men they see. I'm sure it is a week too early to attack an American military base yet, or the White House, where our men will be outnumbered. I don't want them to notice our faces, so tell the New York squads to look like western train robbers—cover their faces with cloth. Then order them to go south and search out this North Carolina airfield and destroy everything that is there. They have 48 hours to do so. Tell them to travel by day and start south tomorrow morning, East coast time. Their vehicle lights could be seen if they travel at night."

"Yes, Comrade Chairman."

"Go, Comrade Wang. You are excused. All opposition must be quickly dealt with."

To Be Continued in...

INVASION USA II
The Battle for New York

INVASION USA III
The Battle for Survival

INVASION USA IV
The Battle for Houston
– The Aftermath

Please visit our website,
http://www.TIWADE.com
to become a friend of the INVASION USA Series,
get updates on new releases, read interesting blogs
and connect with the author.

BOOKS BY THE AUTHOR

The Book of Tolan Series (Adult Reading):

Banking, Beer & Robert the Bruce
Hardcover and eNovel.

Easy Come Easy Go
Hardcover and eNovel.

It Could Happen
eNovel.

INVASION Series (General Reading):

INVASION USA I: The End of Modern Civilization
eNovel – July 2011,
Trade Paperback Edition – August 2012.

INVASION USA II: The Battle for New York
eNovel – March 2012,
Trade Paperback Edition – August 2012.

INVASION USA III: The Battle for Survival
eNovel – June 2012,
Trade Paperback Edition – August 2012.

INVASION USA IV: The Battle for Houston … The Aftermath
eNovel – August 2012,
Trade Paperback Edition – August 2012.

INVASION EUROPE: The Battle for Western Europe
eNovel – April 2013.

INVASION ASIA: The Battle for China
eNovel – June 2013.

INVASION USA: The New America
eNovel – August 2013.
(Final Novel in this seven novel series)

About the Author

T I WADE was born in Bromley, Kent, England in 1954.

His father, a banker was promoted with his International Bank to Africa and the young family moved to Africa in 1956.

The author grew up in Southern Rhodesia (now Zimbabwe) and his life there is humorously described in his novel; EASY COME EASY GO, Volume II of the Book of Tolan Series. Once he had completed his mandatory military commitments, at 21 he left Africa to mature in Europe.

He enjoyed Europe and lived in three countries; England, Germany and Portugal for 15 years before returning to Africa; Cape Town in 1989.

Here the author owned and ran a restaurant, a coffee manufacturing and retail business, flew a Cessna 210 around desolate southern Africa and finally got married in 1992.

Due to the upheavals of the political turmoil in South Africa, the Wade family of three moved to the United States in 1996. Park City, Utah was where his writing career began.

To date T I Wade has written seven novels.

The Author, his wife and two teenage children currently live 20 miles south of Raleigh, North Carolina.

8124695R00231

Printed in Great Britain
by Amazon.co.uk, Ltd.,
Marston Gate.